Praise for *The Unraveling of Wentwater*

"Lakin (*The Wolf of Tebron*) mixes classic fairy tale elements (witches, spinning thread from nettles, water spirits) with wisdom elements from the Bible in a highly imaginative amalgam that examines the making of meaning and the making of mercy. Lakin's clever revival of the power of fairy tales as she continues The Gates of Heaven fantasy series makes one miss them as a vehicle for instructing the young."

—*Publisher's Weekly*

"Once I picked it up, I couldn't put it down. For one thing, I'm a sucker for good writing, and wow, can C. S. Lakin write! I'm in awe of people who can take us to imaginary worlds that don't exist and make them feel real. She does this in this book and brings a very creepy but magical fable to life. It's a story of superstitions and the reality within. If you're looking for a little escapism in your busy world, I highly recommend this one!

—**Kristin Billerbeck**, author of *A Billion Reasons Why*

"Take the fable of Snow White, disguised almost beyond recognition, add a huge portion of love for language and the power of words, throw in a collection of sometimes haunting tie-ins to previous books in the series, and you have the components that make up this very unusual story . . . The writing is gorgeous as always, a true pleasure to read. Her best tale yet."

—**Grace Bridges**, publisher, Splashdown Books

"The Gates of Heaven is the series th⸻ ⸻⸻d⸻d and converted me to the fantasy genre. And this b⸻ predecessors. Lakin moves the story tale and explores the contrast betwee pitting village against town—and ⸻

come up short. It is also a love story, and the story of what one is willing to sacrifice to save loved ones. It's a ripping good story."

—**Glynn Young**, Faith, Fiction, Friends

"*The Unraveling of Wentwater* is a first-class fairy tale that deals with the power of words, and the never-ending struggle to find balance between justice and mercy and knowledge and faith. Combined with romance, betrayal, revenge, and redemption, it is sure to please all fans of this series."

—**Jonathon Svendsen**, NarniaFans.com

"C. S. Lakin has written another wonderful book. Focusing this tale on words and their importance, she unravels the two extremes of Wentwater. Then, revealing the necessity of both logic and superstition, intellect and emotions, she weaves together two communities that need each other with the greatest word of all. . . . I can't wait to read this book again. I highly recommend *The Unraveling of Wentwater* to anyone who enjoys an extremely well-written fantasy.

—**La Tawnia Kintz Reviews**

"Ready for another entrancing story from The Gates of Heaven series by C. S. Lakin? *The Unraveling of Wentwater* doesn't disappoint. Enter into a world where superstition, miscommunication, prophecy, love, envy, hope and truth all clash their voices into a cacophony striking the heart of their land. . . . Set aside a whole afternoon or evening, because once you start reading you may not be able to stop."

—**Marcy Weydemuller**, Mythic Impact

Praise for *The Land of Darkness*

"Sprung from apocalyptic vision, this adult fairy tale, which is the third in the Gates of Heaven series, brings freshness and vibrancy, based on strong ethical principles, to the realm of the imaginary. . . ."

—Lois Henderson, Bookpleasures.com

"Another incredible book in The Gates of Heaven Series. C. S. Lakin has done it again—written a masterful tale that is a page turner from start to finish. . . . The suspense and intrigue is enough to keep the reader on the edge of their seat."

—Beverly Frisby, Beverly's Bookshelf

"C. S. Lakin's deftly written book *The Land of Darkness* yet again unfailingly impresses me with its colorful language and subtle, yet effective allegorical language. . . . . This tale is still very fresh, and it has its own beating heart of deep meaning underlying its fairy-tale skin. . . . She is one of my favorite writers at the moment, whose books evoke some of the same charm as many of Madeleine L'Engle's books."

—A Bibliophile's Reverie

Praise for *The Map Across Time*

"The novel is fast-paced and tightly plotted, which means that the reader will quickly be drawn into the complex twists and turns of the story and, in fairy tale tradition, led toward a surprising yet satisfying conclusion."

—*Publisher's Weekly*

"*The Map across Time* is a fairy tale in the classic sense of the term. As J. R. R. Tolkien pointed out, fairy stories serve to draw the reader into a mythical world that conveys the joy of the gospel. Lakin's tale meets this noble task head-on. Not many Christian novels manage to blend great storytelling and scriptural truth—but here is a book that does!"

—**Bryan Litfin**, author of *The Sword and The Gift*

Praise for *The Wolf of Tebron*

"Much richer and deeper than traditional tales from fairy-land . . . what Lakin does so well with her fairy tale is to provide images which remind us of what God has done for us."

—**Mark Sommer,** Examiner.com

". . . Lakin's work is stylistically beautiful. The exotic locales are vivid, from dark north to burning desert to misty jungle. I found myself looking forward to each leg of Joran's journey just so I could experience another part of her story world."

—**Rachel Starr Thomson**, Little Dozen Press

"This book is filled with beautiful literary allegory and symbolism. I enjoyed the fairy tale world C. S. Lakin created for her characters to navigate. I love how the story unfolded in the end and look forward to more in The Gates of Heaven series."

—**Jill Williamson**, author of *To Darkness Fled*

"Lakin has masterful control of the writing craft, developing her characters and drawing the reader to see the world through their eyes."

—**Phyllis Wheeler**, The Christian Fantasy Review

THE UNRAVELING OF WENTWATER

A FAIRY TALE BY
C. S. LAKIN

LIVING
INK
BOOKS
Writing Worth Reading

The Unraveling of Wentwater
Volume 4 in The Gates of Heaven® series

Copyright © 2011 by C. S. Lakin
Published by Living Ink Books, an imprint of
AMG Publishers, Inc.
6815 Shallowford Rd.
Chattanooga, Tennessee 37421

This is a work of fiction. Names, characters, places, and incidents either are the product of the author's imagination or are used fictitiously. Any resemblance to actual persons, either living or dead, events, or locales, is entirely coincidental.

Print Edition	ISBN 13: 978-0-89957-892-7
EPUB Edition	ISBN 13: 978-1-61715-319-8
Mobi Edition	ISBN 13: 978-1-61715-320-4
E-PDF Edition	ISBN 13: 978-1-61715-321-1

First Printing—June 2012

THE GATES OF HEAVEN is a registered trademark of AMG Publishers.

Cover designed by Chris Garborg at Garborg Design, Savage, Minnesota, and Megan Erin Miller.

Cover Illustration by Gary Lippincott
(http://www.garylippincott.com/).

Interior design and typesetting by Reider Publishing Services, West Hollywood, California.

Edited and proofread by Christy Graeber and Rick Steele.

C. S. Lakin welcomes comments, ideas, and impressions at her Websites:
www.cslakin.com and **www.gatesofheavenseries.com**.

All Scripture quoted in the discussion section in the back of this book, unless otherwise indicated, is taken from the New Revised Standard Version Bible, copyright 1989, Division of Christian Education of the National Council of the Churches of Christ in the United States of America. Used by permission. All rights reserved.

Scripture marked NKJV is taken from the New King James Version. Copyright © 1982 by Thomas Nelson, Inc. Used by permission. All rights reserved.

Please note that Scripture verses quoted by characters in the novel are paraphrased as the author deemed appropriate for the story.

Printed in the United States of America
17 16 15 14 13 12 –V– 7 6 5 4 3 2 1

To Megan and Michael
May music and love entwine your hearts together forever
July 21, 2012

**Books Available in
The Gates of Heaven® Series**

The Wolf of Tebron
The Map Across Time
The Land of Darkness
The Unraveling of Wentwater

PROLOGUE

IRIS STEPPED out onto the creaking stoop of her cottage as a chill breeze wafted down the mountains and bit her cheeks. She sniffed the heavy air of a lingering winter. "Snow? This late?" The thought sent a shudder through her bones. She called back to the house. "Justyn! Make haste. The sun is coming up. Rouse your brother."

She humphed and bent over to lace up her boots, grunting as the waistband of her smock dug into her bulging stomach. Out of the corner of her eye she spied a feather—burnt red, streaked with amber—lying on the dirt. "Oh my . . ." She straightened and clomped down the steps to her front yard with a furtive glance to see if any neighbors were astir, praying no one was watching from behind curtained windows. She swept up the feather and stuffed it into her apron just as she heard the door open behind her.

"Iris, the porridge. What in tarnation are you fuddling about in the yard for?"

Sweat trickled down the sides of her face as she hurried back to Fen. She hid her trembling hands in her pockets. "Nothing. Just erasing the chicken tracks is all."

"Well, you can do that on your way out. There's time." Fen nodded to the kitchen in reminder. As Iris rushed to the stove to rescue the pot of porridge from the heat of the crackling fire, Justyn shuffled to the table, rubbing sleep from his eyes.

"Where's Fromer?" She scooped a dollop of pasty oats into Justyn's wooden bowl as Fen lifted his coat from the hook by the door. She eyed her husband. "What? No breakfast this morn?"

"Had a biscuit. Can't let them lie around too long. It's Tuesday."

"Oh, I forgot." If she crumbled up the remaining biscuits and fed them to the chickens before noon, that would do. With this strange weather, no sense taking chances.

"Fromer," she yelled. "Come to the table. We can't be late to the baby naming. It's bad luck."

"Everything's bad luck," Justyn muttered, spooning steaming oats into his mouth.

"What's that, lad?" Fen asked, stuffing big arms into his coat sleeves.

Iris threw up her hands. "Heavens, child. Don't say such words. Here," she said, handing him a small bowl of salt. "Toss a pinch over your shoulder. Your left shoulder." Her stern voice made Justyn sit straighter. Her eyes bored into his until he slumped and, with a sigh, took a pinch of salt and did as she directed.

"You're just askin' for trouble, lad." Fen threw open the door and the aberrant wind blew in, fluttering the tablecloth and sending another shiver up Iris's spine. He scanned the horizon stretching beyond the village's rooftops. "I don't recall snow coming this late in the spring. Something's amiss."

"What do you think it portends?" Iris asked, her voice quavering. She did not like the way this day was starting out—not at all.

"Did you lock all the hens up last night?" he asked, his stern glance lingering on her face.

"Of course."

She gripped the edge of the table and waited. Fromer stumbled in and plunked down in his seat, his hair askew like a plowed-over field of wheat, still in his nightshirt. Fen pursed his lips and swung his carry bag over one shoulder.

"I'm off then, to the shop. Have three sets of boots to finish by the end of the day. And a delivery of leather coming in first thing. Don't forget the straw."

Iris nodded; words failed her. The straw! She had almost forgotten that too. Her forgetfulness would be their undoing if she wasn't careful. The door slammed shut behind Fen. She made a mental list as she scraped the last portion of porridge into her younger son's bowl. Seven sheaves of straw, tied in twine. Brings good tidings and fast recovery for the mother. A potato with no eyes—to keep the mother's milk from turning sour. Let the chickens out of the coop; first erase any of yesterday's scratchings. But—that feather! Where had that come from?

No time to ponder the implications. She led Fromer into the washroom, tidied his hair, and helped him dress. Justyn's scowl appeared in the mirror as she looked up from tying the neck string on Fromer's tunic.

"What?" she asked.

"Why do we have to go to some stupid baby naming? Can't the mother just name the baby without the whole village there?"

"Of course not. And if we don't show up, you're the one who will suffer. You're the firstborn. You wouldn't want an accident to befall you, would you, Justyn?"

"But we've already been to two of these this month. I'm missing school."

"And so's the rest of your class. It's only for a short time. And then off you'll go. So stop your whining and pull on your boots. And help your brother with his."

Iris fretted as she hung up her apron and gathered her things. As she put on her heavy woolen coat, she noticed a loose button. "Oh dear, oh dear," she mumbled under her breath. She fingered the button and gave it a little tug. "Should hold, and there's no time to restitch it." She thought longer, mulling over the consequences of losing a button along the road. She dared not take the chance. A lost button would make the hens stop laying eggs for a week.

Without a second thought, she stripped off the coat and rummaged through the trunk by her bed. Only last week she had put away their winter things. But now—perhaps she'd have to pull them all out again. And what did this erratic weather portend for the crops and gardens? A late frost would kill the early buds and ruin the first harvest. Had one of her neighbors done something unthinkable? What about old Lady Denton? Her mind was so addled, no doubt she was to blame. Probably broke a bootlace or planted seed on a new moon. The possibilities were beyond count—and worrisome.

As she uncovered a thick gray shawl from the mounds of clothes, she heard a noise outside. The sound froze her heart. She rushed to the window and threw open the shutters. To her horror, the rooster stood on the ramp to the henhouse, his head craned back, exposing his ruby throat.

"No, don't, please—"

But the rooster paid her no mind. He opened his beak and crowed loudly—for all her neighbors to hear. Iris's gaze darted from the rooster to the horizon, where sunlight dripped over the rooftops of the cottages like warm honey. Iris clutched her heart and felt a tug on her dress. Fromer looked up at her, worry in his eyes.

"Mum, are you sick?"

Justyn pulled Fromer away from her, taking his hand and leading him out the bedroom. "It's just the dumb rooster."

Iris's jaw slacked. She spoke in a whisper, as if afraid someone would hear. "When a rooster crows after the sun comes up, it means, it means . . ."

She shook the thought from her head. In the kitchen pantry, she tossed potatoes until she found one free of prying eyes; it was small but would do. With the bundle of straw in one hand, and Fromer's little hand in the other, she marched down the steps of her cottage—resolute and confident. A baby naming was a blessed event, she reminded herself. All the women of the village would attend to give the child gifts and well-wishing. The ceremony was the oldest tradition in Wentwater, dating back before the Great Flood. The eldest woman of the village bore the responsibility for the name, and the name given portended the babe's future.

She chuckled thinking back to Fromer's naming. How old Gladys, with only a few teeth remaining, had announced the name, hovering over the cradle and waving her sheaf of straw. "Fromer," she had called out, eliciting a roomful of puzzled expressions and quiet murmurings. What kind of a name was Fromer? But no one dared question the name or what it meant. Only hours later, after Fen walked the old woman back to her cottage, was the mystery clarified. Gladys had meant to say "farmer"—indicating that Iris's son would find his gift in tending flocks and raising crops. But the words had become tangled in Gladys's mouth, from old age and lack of teeth. And with her poor hearing, she hadn't realized the word had come out wrong. A silly misunderstanding. But, once spoken, the name was cast. So, Fromer it was, and would stay.

Iris gave the yard a once-over, and when certain all the hen scratchings were swiped away by the soles of her boots, she let the chickens out of the coop. Justyn dipped the cup into the feed sack and scattered seed over the ground, which sent the birds cackling in a flurry over the food. If only Fen had tarried longer this morning; he knew how to read the patterns in the feed. She caught a glimpse of the rooster as he rounded the corner of the house, and the sight sent a stab of pain to her gut.

"Hurry, lads," she said, rushing out the gate and down the lane. As they passed the row of cottages, Iris looked up at the cliffs in the distance. Torrents of water poured down the sluices in the dark green rock, thick and swollen from snowmelt. Lake Wentwater shimmered at the base of the mountains as the sun rose over the village and cast its pastel light upon the wind-ruffled surface. Fields of new grass spattered with creamy buttercups and purple lupine wrapped the lake and fragranced the air. But the beauty of the countryside failed to still the frantic beating of Iris's heart. A few fat flakes of snow landed on her eyelashes and set her to muttering again.

"Mum, slow down," Fromer said, tugging on her hand.

She looked down at her son, took in his bright blue eyes and sweet face. "Sorry, Fro. We're almost there."

Justyn shuffled his feet, lagging back a few steps. Iris studied him in a glance. His brooding manner and the set of his mouth were just like Fen's. The lad was growing more like his father each day—thick brows and dark straight hair, serious and intense. Wanted to study books more than play with his mates. And so difficult.

But Fromer . . . Her heart warmed at his adoring eyes and trusting heart. He'd be a good lad, this one. Grow up to be a farmer, tend a flock, live a good quiet life, marry, raise a family. But would Justyn be all that had been foretold of him? Iris thought of the noble roles outlined in Justyn's future: a leader, a fair and just voice for the people, a righter of wrongs. But none of these qualities seemed to suit his temperament. Yet, there was no fighting fate. He would become the man he had been named seven years ago. Time would tell how her older son would bend to his destiny. Bend or break, as they say. Hopefully, Justyn would soften in time. Not be so serious and . . . doubting. Doubting was dangerous.

A crowd had already gathered on the large porch outside her neighbor's cottage. Dineen's firstborn was a girl, and Iris had heard the labor had gone without a hitch. Long, but with the lass born before the moonset, and that was a good omen. Iris didn't know this woman or her husband other than by sight. Fen had made boots for the man, and Iris sometimes saw the wife at market and heard she planned to open a bakery. But they were quiet and fairly new to Wentwater. Iris wondered what had brought them all the way from Sherbourne to their village, but it wasn't her business to ask. Sherbourne was a sprawling city—or so she'd heard. Who in their right mind would want to live in such a place, knocking shoulders with neighbors and having to push through crowds to get to market? Wentwater afforded all a peaceful, undisturbed life—so long as everyone abided by the traditions.

She had to admit—most of the rituals and practices followed no clear logic. But who was she to question the wisdom handed down from one generation to another? Time-tested and true, they were. She'd seen what happened when someone overstepped or failed to respond with the proper remedy. Disaster struck—that's what came of such behavior. And every once in a while, a fool would recklessly ignore tradition, resulting in banishment. Perhaps outsiders would think such a punishment harsh, but there was no getting around it. Their village would suffer the consequences— just as in the days of the Great Flood, when all was swept away, leaving little more than a handful of ruined cottages and barns. The few survivors'd had to rebuild the village from the pieces of broken timber and downed trees, having suffered the loss of family, friends, and all their possessions. All because someone ignored the traditions. Or so the story went. The old ones who rebuilt Went-water had long passed away, but their warnings still rang out afresh in the hearts of the villagers. One and all knew better than to step heedlessly where angels feared to tread.

A drumbeat signaled the commencement of the ceremony. Iris wiggled through the crowd, greeting her neighbors, leaving the boys to stand with the other children on the porch. Dineen's husband, coaxed outside by flapping hands, positioned his hat on his head and made for the center of the village without a glance back. Iris watched him walk down the rutted lane until he turned the corner a block before her husband's cobbler shop. Only women remained inside the cottage, crammed to the corners, spilling into the farther rooms. Iris added her bundle of straw to the growing mound on the table. The scent of straw and wildflowers blended with the sweet and smoky aroma of the beeswax tapers burning on the sideboard.

Iris recognized Arlynna, the current matriarch of the village, standing beside Dineen. Her gray hair was twisted in a bun atop her head and pinned with irises. She signaled the women to silence and began her oration. Iris half-listened as she looked at the tiny baby buried under blankets in a finely crafted wood cradle, the mother standing by with adoration in her eyes. How many times had Iris heard the words to the ceremony recited in stuffy, crowded rooms such as this one? For nearly thirty years she had witnessed the naming of every baby born in Wentwater—although those born in the Heights, far above the lakes and waterfalls, didn't count.

Iris huffed. Those descended from the noble eight families—or so they called themselves—rarely showed their faces in the village. And Iris herself had never ventured up to their strange houses, perched high in the crags and carved into rock. Why would she? Rumors warned that those living up there disdained the traditions, ignored the rituals and ceremonies. Surely, doom awaited those with such reckless disregard of tradition. And associating with such naive folk would only bring trouble. No, it was a good thing the Heights were a grueling day's climb up the mountain, a disagreeable place of moaning wind, and freezing ice and sleet most of the year. Let the nobles live in their lofty crags—as long as they kept their noses out of the affairs of the villagers.

As Arlynna droned on, wax dripped down the tapers. As tradition dictated, the three eldest of the village approached the infant. Sharla, the fishmonger's wife, bent over the first of the three candles and walked around the sideboard, studying the way the wax slid in rivulets down the taper.

"She is given the gift of beauty, a simple but striking beauty. Hair as white as snow, as graced by the unexpected wind from the north. Eyes dark as coal, and just as warm, as the embers on the hearth testify." She took her position at the left side of the display, her hands clasped behind her back.

Next, Nettie, the beekeeper's widow, examined the second candle, and when satisfied, smiled at the baby in the cradle. "She is given the gift of voice. Songs will emerge from her heart that will soothe and inspire. A nightingale that turns dark night to dawn, singing—"

Nettie gasped as a blast of cold wind threw open the door, snuffing out the flickering candles as if a divine hand had pinched the wicks between two fingers. Iris spun around, as did all the women, with an audible cry of fear. Never before, at any ceremony, had naming candles been extinguished. They were to burn to their trays, to signify a long, full life. Now, what could this mean, other than a terrible fate? Oh, she knew this would prove to be a fateful day.

She strained to see through the open doorway, where roiling black clouds invaded the skies, gathering in an angry roar. Terror bit at her heart and a whimper escaped her lips. The crush of bodies blocking the entry parted in a murmur, sounding like water rushing over rocks.

Arlynna raised her voice over the din. "Who has disturbed the ceremony? There will be a price to pay for this outrageous travesty—"

Iris clutched at her heart at the recognition of the tired, gravely voice. Such a voice could belong to no other. She wanted to throw her hands over her ears but feared drawing any attention to herself.

"Well, a baby naming! Such a sight as to bring tears to the eyes."

A smothering hush fell over the women, as if the marsh witch's simple words bewitched them. Iris knew it was fear that clenched tight her throat. Ursell—ages ago banished from Wentwater and said to live in an abandoned castle half sunken in the muddy marshes. No one had seen her in years. Why this day, of all days, had the witch decided to make an appearance?

The marsh witch turned in a slow circle, studying faces with her one natural eye, while her glass eye remained unfocused and haunting. "Ah, are you so surprised to see me? Surely, I was meant to be invited."

Arlynna dropped her clenched fists to her sides and gathered breath. "Ursell, tradition calls for all women to attend the baby naming. Had we known you were . . . still in Wentwater . . . why, of course, you are welcome."

Ursell smiled with her mouth, but her glass eye glared cold and vindictive. "Of course . . ."

A chill inched into Iris's bones, making them brittle and stiff. She wiggled fingers and toes to force out the tingling. The quiet in the room grew thick, a coating of uncertainty and trepidation that nearly made her swoon. Stories drifted into her mind, tales of woe surrounding this witch that her own mum had woven under her breath. Iris had sometimes thought her a fabrication, this stranger from the forbidden marshes. A glass eye that could see beyond and between. Beyond this land and between kingdoms. Beyond appearances and between truth and lies. Hands that stitched misery and suspicion into the fabric of the village, turning neighbor against neighbor, turning kind hearts into bitter ones. Iris recalled some rumor claiming Ursell's magic had even wrought the flood, although how could that be? Could this witch truly be hundreds of years old? The thought crept up Iris's neck and grew into a stranglehold around her throat. She choked and clutched at invisible hands, trying to loosen her breath.

Ursell turned from Arlynna and locked her glassy gaze on Iris. She tipped her head to one side and studied her, the way Iris often studied the signs in the skies.

Iris sucked in breath that found little entrance into her throat. "Please . . ." she begged, afraid to look into the witch's eye, praying for mercy, for relief. Her heart hammered in her chest the way Fen pounded nails into leather. Had the witch somehow read her thoughts?

With a slight raise of an eyebrow, Ursell released her. Iris grabbed at her throat and sucked in air, then backed away, pushing through the fear-stricken crowd of women. With effort, she fumbled to the back wall and willed herself invisible behind a coatrack, wobbly knees giving way.

"Let's see what we have here . . ." Ursell uttered in a singsong voice that grated once more on Iris's ears. Iris dared lift her chin and peek past her neighbors, then stifled a cry as she caught a glimpse of the witch's gnarled hand reaching into the cradle. The roomful of women gasped as one. Iris craned her head and saw horror on Dineen's face. Oh, this could only herald something terrible, something wicked. Why oh why had that rooster crowed after dawn? And the feather! Iris's head spun in self-recrimination. The feather was still in her pocket! Surely, Ursell's appearance wasn't her fault—was it?

Iris tried to wrench her gaze away, but she could no more turn her head than utter a cry when the marsh witch pulled back the downy soft wool blanket and exposed the baby's tiny body. Perhaps it was Iris's imagination, but the smoke from the extinguished candles seemed to whorl around the witch, wrapping the cradle in gloom and obscurity, a pall of darkness filled with unease and mischief. Ursell leaned in close to the babe as Dineen clutched at the collar around her throat. Even from where Iris skulked, she could see the mother gulp and her hand, partway lifted, tremble as if longing to snatch her child and whisk it to safety.

In a sudden movement that startled all, Ursell spun to face Dineen and pointed a finger at her, only inches from her face. "This child will be the undoing of Wentwater. Before she turns eighteen, the village will unravel and all will be lost." She searched the room, peering over heads, until her eyes lit upon a spinning wheel in the corner. "I see the thread of life tangling, her fingers spinning the spindle, stitching with thread, thumbs bleeding as she sits at the wheel, undoing, undoing . . ."

She cast a sideways glance at Arlynna, whose voice had fled the room. "You must send the mother away. And the babe . . ."

Ursell reached down and, with something akin to tenderness, stroked the child's forehead. Iris grabbed the doorjamb to keep from fainting. She strained to hear the witch's words, which came out barely above a whisper.

". . . must be put to death. Before Wentwater comes to naught."

Ursell's words dropped like stones into a deep waterless well, rebounding off the walls of the room and draining hope from the hearts of all in attendance. As the witch pushed through the mob of women in the direction of the front door and disappeared from Iris's view, chaos erupted. Voices were unleashed and gave vent to fear and hysteria. Arlynna overrode the voices around her and summoned attention.

"There is little time. We must act quickly!" With her eyes, she signaled to the two older women who had blessed the babe. They grasped Dineen's arms, one on each side, as she protested and wriggled to get away. Cries rose up in a chant to Iris's ears, although her own voice still wandered lost in the stifling room. A whirlwind of irrepressible fury howled through the hallway.

"Banish her! Banish her!"

Iris watched as more women latched on to Dineen, as another scooped up the babe from the cradle, as Dineen flailed for her child, her agonizing screams melting Iris's heart. But Iris knew there was nothing to be done, no way to stem this tide that must rush in and sweep away such a curse. If the babe was indeed destined to bring destruction to Wentwater, who were they to ignore such a warning? Iris didn't allow herself to think of the pain and terror the new mother must be feeling. Never in her own life had she witnessed such portentous omens. Had Ursell seen the future in her glass eye—or was it her malevolence and bitterness at her own banishment that had drawn her from her marsh and set her feet toward the village? Iris would never know. And she gave herself no time to ponder such inscrutable thoughts.

A voice yelled. "Burn that spinning wheel!" Another cried, "Burn down the cottage, burn everything!"

Like an errant wave, the crowd of women rose and lifted the mother and swept out the cottage, tumbling down the front steps as the gathering of children, toddlers to teens, parted to make way for the chanting and raving women. The mob, led by Arlynna, dragged Dineen down the center of the lane as snow fell thick and steady and dark clouds obscured the sunlight. The cottage emptied behind Iris, disgorging its remaining contents, and as she skittered off toward the far neighbor's yard, where the children stood huddled in the growing drifts of snow, she smelled smoke and turned.

Flames licked windowsills and shimmied up to the thatched roof, which ignited in a whoosh of bright fire and a loud explosion. Sparks and ash carried on the wind as the flames whipped and devoured the house like some fearsome beast tearing at its prey.

Pockets of heat drifted and warmed Iris's chilled cheeks. She lifted her numb hands toward the heat and watched in silence, pulling Fromer and Justyn close, her heart pounding hard against her sons' small bodies. Had they left the babe to suffer in the flames? She didn't dare let her imagination tread that path. As quickly as her sorrow swelled, she squelched it. She could not allow herself to feel for this poor woman. No doubt Dineen and her husband had done something terrible, something secretive and forbidden, to merit this tragedy. And now, whatever they had done—the whole village would pay for it.

"Why, Mum?" Justyn asked. "Why'd they burn her house? And chase her out of town?"

Iris looked into Justyn's eyes and saw a cold flare of anger, mirroring the fire gobbling up the house before her.

"It's too complicated to explain, luv. It just had to be, is all."

Justyn grunted and turned away. Iris sighed.

She could only hope that banishing the parents and destroying the poor babe would prevent the foretold destruction. But a murmur in Iris's heart denied her reasoning. Such a pronouncement could not so easily be swept under a rug. She wanted to believe that by following Ursell's directive the town was now safe. But was it? Her hand drifted to her pocket, where her fingers touched upon the feather. She shuddered. What small thread of hope still held, snapped.

With a sigh, and heavy with consternation, Iris took her sons' hands in her own and led them out the yard and into the lane leading toward Justyn's schoolhouse.

She hoped she would not have to wait long for the teacher to arrive and class to start. She had to get home and crumble up those biscuits before noon. It was Tuesday, after all.

• PART ONE •

"A famous thinker once said, 'When ideas fail, words come in very handy.' This brings to mind another proverb penned along the same lines: 'A man thinks that by mouthing hard words he understands hard things.' It is to our shame, and not our credit, that when pressed with such a conundrum as the unraveling of Wentwater, those in a position of respect and influence fell back on the abundance of words, circumlocution at its worst, to give the appearance of control and superiority. Haven't many great thinkers in history made pejorative remarks on the foolishness of pride? We, who dismissed the workings of magic as mere folly, failing to acknowledge mystery's place in the world, became the fools. I'm reminded of a verse in the Great Book: 'God chose what is foolish in the world to shame the wise, and he chose the weak to shame the strong.' Perhaps this painful experience and shaking of our world will give us pause the next time we are quick to explain away what is mystic with an abundance of verbiage. Some things, I have come to realize, must be taken in faith, when the evidence of their veracity, however seemingly illogical, outweighs the case against them."

From Volume II of *The Annals of Wentwater,* Section IV: "A Discourse on the Clash of Culture amid the Unraveling of Wentwater"

—*Professor Antius, regent and historian
of the Antiquities Board*

ONE

"WHAT AILS YOU, old fellow?"

Antius stroked his owl's silver feathers as the bird hung a listless head, sidestepping along the perch to move away from him. "It's Ambel, isn't it?"

Antius cursed under his breath as wind moaned through the small opening in the transom window. That reckless son of his should have been back to the Heights ages ago. Rushed off in the dead of winter on that insane quest. "Pah!" he spat out and secured the window latch. The fluttering curtains settled down, and Antius straightened the scattered papers on his desk. Engaging Antimony's unblinking yellow eyes, Antius scolded himself for letting that fool-hardy boy leave. A firebird! What in blazes put that notion in the lad's head? Hadn't he raised his son to be able to discern between truth and fairy tales?

He spoke to the owl in a lecturing tone. "Twenty years of schooling, advancing from first to third level in just ten years! Blue robes, top levels, highest exam scores. And just before taking his orals for purple level, he throws his wits to the wayside! Curse those two." Meaning the two boys from the village, from the backwater of Wentwater—those with the silly superstitions and loony rituals to ward off bad luck. He had tried to pry Ambel away from the influence of those uneducated, ignorant villagers, but his son wouldn't listen. Instead, Ambel believed their outrageous tales that a magical firebird, bright as the noonday sun in the flatlands, was traipsing around the world, just begging to be captured.

"Pah!" Antius spat again, then stuffed another log into the ponderous iron stove, soaking up the warmth rising into his face. "You make your own luck. How could Ambel forget his training? 'Happy are those who find wisdom, and those who get understanding. For her income is better than silver, and her revenue better than gold. Long life is in her right hand, and in her left hand are riches and honor.' The fool lad knows that true wealth lies in gaining wisdom, knowledge, understanding. *Not* in chasing after a chimera!"

Antius threw open the curtains to the pale morning sun glimmering through his large picture window. The rugged mountain peaks glinted in their severity. *Pah, I've overslept again!* Every bone creaked in protest as Antius stretched and unlatched the door to assess the weather for the day. Not that he expected any different from yesterday. Mindlessly, he ran fingers through his long tangled beard, whiter than Antimony's feathers. They were quite a matched pair—the two of them, adorned in white and silver, although Antius's years far outnumbered his owl's.

A cold, wet breeze spattered his face as he stood at the entrance to his small abode chiseled out of rock, the top of his head nearly tickling the lintel over the doorway. The onrush of spring snowmelt reverberated in the air as a dull roar, a constant backdrop to life in the Heights. He reached for his mug of hot tea and grunted thinking about the villagers down below. How they would no doubt study the tea leaves in his mug, and the clouds churning up above, to determine how they should spend their day. The fools never did a thing without bowing to some ridiculous ritual, for fear of bringing on punishment. As if some god watched from the heavens at the ready, lightning bolts in one hand and a reward in the other. How on earth could they live that way, day in and day out? It boggled his mind.

Antius secured his dressing robe around him and stepped down his carved stone steps, careful of his footing as ice crunched under his soft boots. Down below, in the valley around the lake, spring had arrived in color and warmth and fragrance. Signs of the shift in season drifted up the mountains like mist off the falls, which annually stirred up a restless distraction in his students. Every spring he had to work hard to reel in their attention, which flapped like fish for freedom against efforts to tug it along. Admittedly, part of him longed to walk the lake and luxuriate under a sun that actually gave off heat and warmed old bones, but he had exams to prepare for. He had lost count of the number of years that had passed since he allowed himself that small pleasure.

His fifth-level students—eight of them this year—were ready to graduate. He had pushed them hard, but these all showed such promise. And in a few days their grueling orals and writtens would take up a week's time, with Antius proctoring the exams. He rejoiced when his students made top level and earned the right to put on the black robes at ceremony; it took six intense years to prepare them for this moment. Having nurtured them in their studies from third level, he felt a special affection for each of them. And this ceremony was especially heartening—because of Justyn.

Students heralded from as far away as Sherbourne and even some from the south, from Ethryn. The regents of the Antiquities Board didn't accept just anyone into the university. Although they took students from as young as six, the battery of tests disqualified over 90 percent of the applicants. And rarely did a child from the village—as was Justyn—pass the first round. In all his years, only three villagers had made black. Most dropped out, caving in to the pressure of their families, parents who had no appreciation for the value of such an esteemed education—and on scholarship, no less!

No villagers would deign to pay hard-earned money to send their children to be properly educated. Superstition ingrained in those students took years of hard work to extricate, but for some, that faulty thinking hung on stubbornly, resistant to reason and empirical proof. But his prized pupil was an exception.

Antius squatted and pulled at a few stray weeds. His sequestered and sheltered garden lay in dormant beauty, spread out before him in a carefully designed array of shrubs, perennials, stonework, and pathways. Leafless miniature maples and coin trees stretched out spindly arms as if begging the sun for warmth. They would bud after summer solstice, with their leaves a burst of red and green, only to shrivel up by October. Too short a season—much like his own body that had aged and withered before he expected it to. Loneliness seeped into his heart, along with memories of his wife, gone these twenty years. And now, with his son run off . . .

Antius pushed the rush of sadness aside and attacked the earth. He liked puttering around in his garden, rearranging the stones on the low wall, deadheading blooms at the end of the short summer season with his finely sharpened clippers. His rock garden was a work in progress, an ever-changing palette of color. Now, tiny lupines and hyacinths and irises were beginning to put forth blooms. Chains of alpine blossoms flowed over the rocks like a waterfall, his own little waterfall among so many up in the Heights. His home, tucked away in a crevice of sorts in the highest of the five peaks, linked to other homes via these granite pathways. Paths that wound around crags and dipped under archways where swollen torrents of water flew off the sides of the mountain into the air, only to tumble down hundreds of yards below into more pools, emptying finally into Lake Wentwater. Wet, everything was wet, spray a constant component of the air, with rainbows dancing and rippling against the sky. Rainbows caught in the waterfalls . . .

"Antius, you'll hurt your back again, squatting like that!"

Antius looked up to see Teralyn coming through the far arch-way, her gardening bucket in one hand and a rake in the other. Mist lay trapped in her hair like a net of pearls. She wore the thick wool sweater he'd given her for her seventeenth birthday last month, a bit large, but it clearly kept her warm. A smile lifted his drooping cheeks. "Just pulling a few weeds, my dear, that's all."

Teralyn set down her tools and gave him a sour smile. "Would you put me out of a job? You know this is my favorite garden to work in. Oh, look! The muscari have all popped up their heads and they're shaking off the dirt like little moles emerging from winter's sleep!"

Antius chuckled. "Words always tumble from your mouth in rich imagery. Speaking of—how's that book of poetry coming along?"

Teralyn reached for his elbow and helped him to stand. Her eyes lingered on his face, and his heart warmed at her affection. Teralyn was the daughter he'd never had. A grunt escaped his throat. A whole lot smarter, too, than that wayward son of his.

"I've put most of them to music already. But I've broken another string on my lap harp and I'm on my last spare. Would you get some more for me?"

"Of course, my dear. You can get them yourself, though, at the conservatory. Just ask—"

"I know." Teralyn dug a trowel out of her bucket and pulled her long hair back out of her face. A breeze kicked up and a few stray strands whipped at her pink cheeks as she wound the mass into a rope and pinned it to her head with a silver clip. "But then the direc-tor would pressure me to play in the quintet, and I just don't want to anymore." She sighed and shook her head. "I get so tired of playing such long, tedious pieces." She held up her hand before Antius could launch into one of his speeches about traditional musical styles. "I know—it's important to study and play the classics. You've drilled that into me since I was five, when I had my first theory lesson. But, I want to let my music ramble and have a life of its own. Written music sometimes is a confining cage that lets a bird stretch its wings but not fly. How can I let the music in my heart soar if it remains imprisoned in a sheet of parchment, behind bars of ink?" She began digging around the bulbs, softening the hard, crusty earth battered down by the constant pounding of rain.

Antius laughed. "Well said. And I understand. Perhaps . . ."

Teralyn stopped her digging and gave Antius a curious look. "Perhaps what?"

"You might benefit from attending the spring festival. Have you ever been?"

Teralyn's eyes lit up. "The festival? You mean, down in the village? You're not serious, are you?"

Antius nodded. "Bards and minstrels from lands far and near come to the festival. You'll hear music you've never heard before. Maybe it will inspire your playing. It's wise to enrich your education with the arts of other cultures and—"

"My parents will never allow it. You know how they are."

Antius saw the longing spark in her eyes. "But perhaps they will let you go if I provide an escort for you. And I know just the fellow. He's one of my brightest, most serious students—Justyn. Do you know him?"

Teralyn shook her head.

"I'm not surprised. He buries himself in books twelve hours a day. But he's a villager—"

"A villager!"

"Yes, and so knows the town and the ways down there. He could take you to the various venues, introduce you to some of the musicians. He'll keep you safe. And you could take your lap harp. Maybe play with some of the performers. Oh, you'll love it—a colorful, lively weeklong celebration."

She pointed the rusty trowel at him. "You've been?"

"I often went—when my knees cooperated. That was my principal field of study as historian—tracing the paths of diversity and cultural nuances of Wentwater, which included art, music, folklore, and the colorful and sundry origins of such. Much of my observations have been recorded in the annals of Wentwater's history in the main library. Perhaps you might benefit from reading from the great number of treatises I wrote on the subjects of—"

"Antius, I'm sure I would get more out of the music played at the festival by *listening* to the musicians than by reading about it. Books and books! Everyone in the Heights devours books as if they were delectable pastries! You know, you can spend so much time buried in books and accumulating your precious knowledge that you forget to live life." Her look was meant to chastise, but laughter danced behind her eyes.

"Live life? And what about you? You're of age. Why don't I ever see you out with a beau? Surely there are many handsome lads up in the Heights willing to steal your heart. Maybe Justyn will interest you. The girls all seem to find him winsome enough. They flock around him at meals and in the courtyards. Perhaps—"

Teralyn's cheeks flushed. "You and your *perhaps*. Perhaps, my dear, sweet Antius, you should mind your own business."

"Hmmph." Antius walked up his steps and stopped. Teralyn had always been a shy one, and too much of a recluse, in his opinion. Even growing up, she'd be off playing by herself, reciting rhymes and silly poems she'd make up on the spot, and playing with imaginary friends. Despite his prodding, she rarely sought out companionship with others her age.

"Oh. Would you see to Antimony? He's still feeling poorly and off his food. The only thing that seems to cheer him is your singing. Would you indulge him with a song before lunch?"

"Still mooning over Ambel? Poor thing. I think he remembers how I sang to him when he was a hatchling. When I used to work in the hatchery, remember?" Teralyn chuckled. "Let me finish with this flower bed. And if you brew me some tea and scrounge your pantry for a pastry, I'll sing for your owl. A musician deserves her wage."

"That she does. So . . . you'll go? To the festival? It starts next week. Justyn will be done with his exams by then and surely ready to go down the mountain to visit his family. He usually stays the entire week in the village. But I'm sure he can secure lodging for you at one of the inns. I have a favorite—a small, unadorned facility, but their bogberry tarts at tea are not to be missed."

"Bogberries? You're making my mouth water! Well, as long as you can convince my parents that I'll be safe and won't get corrupted somehow by the villagers' ways, then yes, I'd love to go!"

"Consider it arranged. I'll inform Justyn this afternoon at class. And now . . . I'll go brew your tea."

Teralyn stopped Antius with a gentle touch on his arm. "And, Antius, thank you. You always seem to know just what I need." She smiled and turned to resume her work in the flower bed, humming a sweet tune that flitted around his ears like a moth dancing with flame. Geese chuckled overhead, on their way to Lake Wentwater, joining in with her song. Everything around him thrummed with spring.

Antius sighed and opened his door to a billow of heat that splashed warmth on his face but did little to thaw his guilt. Disturbing memories of Teralyn's past niggled his conscience. A face beckoned, one that had been visiting his dreams of late. A woman robed in sea grass and silt—a creature fashioned of water that left wet footprints on dry slate. Soaked skin, slick like feathers, mud-brown hair flowing like silk around her waist. Eyes a fathomless green, the color of the moss hugging the spiring cliffs of his home.

He struggled for the thousandth time with wanting to blurt out the truth. He was the servant of truth. His life's devotion revolved around uncovering and revealing long-sought-after facts. But what good would such revelation serve?

Antius not only preached but lived by the saying "Knowledge is Power"—the motto carved over each of the four schools' archways in every known written language in the world. But knowledge also held the potential to cause pain, and the last thing he wanted to do was cause his sweet Teralyn pain.

So, he would wait. In less than a year, Teralyn would turn eighteen. He had already waited seventeen years. What would a few more months matter?

TWO

ERALYN SAT on the bench in the foyer and laced up her boots as she watched the wind snarl and snap at the still-bare tree branches out in the garden. How invigorating it would be to leave this place where winter rarely gave up her grasp of the Heights without a fight! How her eyes longed to light on color—and not just on meager splashes of crimson and orange and cerulean displayed in the Heights' struggling gardens, but meadows burgeoning with sunlit flowers, and stalls of bright, ripe fruit stacked in display. Her eyes were thirsty for color.

A knock at the door made her jump. "Mother, would you answer that?" Teralyn tied the knot on her right boot and stood. She needed to do something with her hair or the wind would wreak havoc with it.

"Oh, that must be your gentleman friend! He's early," Kileen called out as she brushed past Teralyn in a poised and efficient manner. She gave a look that made Teralyn's cheeks heat up.

"Mother," she whispered loudly enough for only the two of them to hear, "he's not my friend; I've never met him."

Kileen waved her off and opened the door with a flourish. "Ah, you must be Justyn. Please come in. Teralyn has been anxiously awaiting your arrival."

Teralyn cringed and forced herself to turn around and face her escort. As her mother showed him in, he dropped the hood of his cloak and removed his gloves, addressing her as "my lady." Teralyn allowed her eyes to meet his only briefly, then dropped her gaze as he took her hand and gave it a slight squeeze. He stood just a bit taller, but his manner, so confident and graceful, gave him the appearance of an imposing man.

"I'm pleased to meet you, Teralyn."

Teralyn backed up a step. "And I you. I still—I'll just be a moment."

She spun around and headed to her room to finish her preparations. No doubt her mother would entertain Justyn in the meantime. As she brushed her hair back and fixed it in a tight braid, she heard the tea kettle whistle and her mother place cups on the tea service. No doubt Justyn was being plied with biscuits and questions, although Teralyn knew which would be more in abundance. Her parents were academicians, researchers. It was in their nature and their discipline to question everything. And everyone—often to the point of embarrassment. Teralyn was used to her mother's methodical questioning, but it often ruffled guests who were not comfortable with a barrage of personal inquiries that seemed neverending.

But Justyn seemed quite relaxed and engaged when Teralyn stepped into the parlor and set her pack next to the table. Perhaps his grueling studies inured him to such discomfort under questioning. She allowed herself a moment to look over her escort while he attended to her mother's garrulous conversing. He was indeed handsome, in a ruddy sort of way. She guessed his years somewhere in the midtwenties. Thick russet hair, deep brooding eyes, a student's physique—with slightly stooping shoulders from perusing heavy tomes in the libraries, and a softness about him from the lack of hard physical work. Even his hands were a bit delicate, with nicely trimmed nails and scrubbed clean, she noticed, as he lifted his teacup to his mouth. Justyn turned slightly and caught her staring at him. He smiled and again she felt her cheeks rush with heat.

"Oh, Tera dear, your gentleman friend is quite charming!" Kileen began to pour her a cup of tea, but Teralyn held up her hand.

"Thank you, Mother, but I think we should be on our way. I don't want to arrive in the village past dark."

Kileen set down the teapot. "Of course. Not in this weather."

Justyn finished off his tea and handed Kileen his cup. She gave Teralyn a wink as Justyn reached for his cloak. "I'll be sure to inform your father that you're in quite good hands. Now," she said, "be sure to send word to us that you've arrived safely. And if for some reason you'll be staying somewhere other than the Cygnet, we need to know."

"Yes, Mother."

Justyn held out his hand to her mother. "You have no cause for concern, my lady—"

"Oh, please, just call me Kileen. Formalities are unnecessary here, outside the university's walls."

Justyn nodded politely. "Thank you, but I find addressing my betters by first name most uncomfortable. If you'll indulge me?"

"Oh, no matter! Here." She picked up Teralyn's pack and handed it to her. "Be on your way, then. And Justyn—"

"Yes, my lady?" Justyn stopped at the threshold of the door and secured his woolen hood over his head.

"Teralyn's not been down to the village since she was a child. With all the festivities, it may be a little much for her. It can be easy to get jostled about and become lost. And warn her of the riffraff and pickpockets. She's a bit too trusting—"

"Mother, please!" Teralyn buttoned her heavy coat and swung her pack onto her back. She went to her mother and gave her a perfunctory kiss on the cheek. "I'll be fine. I know to be careful."

"Well. Off with you both, then, and have a wonderful time. I must get on to school. My assistants will be wondering what's delayed me."

They said their good-byes and Justyn opened the door. Wind tumbled into the house and Teralyn set her face to it, burrowing deeply into her coat collar. She tried to speak, but her words were swallowed by the bluster of the day. Justyn led them in silence down the granite pathway toward the archway that spanned from Teralyn's mountain home to the adjoining peak. All five mountains were so joined, with massive archways carved out of the deep-green slate. Artists-in-residence at the school had scrolled elegant designs and gouged bas-relief landscapes that lined the smoothed walls of the pass. Granite, although not easily found, proved the best material for the pathways, with its rough unfinished surface providing traction on the constantly wet and slick walkways. Teralyn's boots slipped neatly into the shallow valleys in the stone, impressions made by thousands of footsteps that had traversed these paths, having ground water and grit in a slow erosion over the decades.

These paths, made of pieces cut and fitted in intricate geometric designs, wended through the three levels of the Heights, leading to the many buildings that made up the four schools of Wisdom, Knowledge, Understanding, and Discernment. The school of Knowledge boasted the largest classrooms and libraries, some of which sat perched on the ledges to her left, whereas the other three schools pertained to more specialized fields, which included tangential studies such as ethics, morals, and methods of debating.

Teralyn's parents researched in the school of Understanding and headed the university's debate program. Many long, tedious hours Teralyn had spent in the auditorium listening to teams argue on philosophical topics, often not understanding a word. Those debates, to her, seemed to be all about bantering and tossing words around, like some odd sort of game, and the conditions for winning were lost on her. How could words be such a commodity—to be weighed and measured and strung together such that they trumped other words? Her parents admired high-minded concepts, abstract explanations defining existence and meaning and purpose. But hard as she tried, Teralyn had never been able to see the use for such a view of the world. You experienced the world by *living* in it, not by discussing and dissecting it. And words—powerful and precious—needed careful handling and respect.

"There," Justyn said as they turned the wide corner into the narrower part of the passageway and the wind abated. Spray-soaked rock stretched up hundreds of feet on both sides as Teralyn fell in behind Justyn, without room to walk side by side. "That's so much better. My ears were beginning to burn, even covered as they were." He threw back his hood and shook his head. "I think I've had water in my ears since the day I first arrived in the Heights."

Teralyn smiled politely and looked ahead, bypassing students in their colored robes that signified their present academic level. Other paths fed into theirs, and by the time they arrived at the large courtyard fronting the auditorium and glass-enclosed amphitheatre, they had to thread their way through the throng to get to the oval—the entrance to the university accessed by the only road coming up from the lowlands. The oval sat in a stunning setting, almost a valley—if you could call it that so high up in the mountains—and featured a beautiful cobblestone road with a fountain in the middle of the circular drive.

Antius had once told Teralyn the story of the fountain and the artist who created it. An arch of beautiful but strange fish leapt in the air as spouts of water sprayed in all directions. The fish were made of some scintillating metal that never rusted and seemed to give off its own inner light—not silver but some other ore that had been mined down in the valley before the Great Flood, in the area now covered by Lake Wentwater. An ore that had never been discovered anywhere else in the land. The artist had acquired the metal from some abandoned farm just below the dam, and the discovery had garnered much interest among the resident geologists.

Justyn stopped at the fountain and turned to Teralyn. "You don't speak much, do you?"

Teralyn stammered as Justyn studied her face a little too inquisitively for her taste. "I speak if I have something to say."

"Well, surely you must have questions. Unless old Antius has told you everything you want to know about the village and the festival." He fell in step beside her as they took to the side of the road that began the long, winding descent down the mountain. "I hear you play the lap harp. Is that what's poking out of your pack?"

Teralyn nodded. "I've been studying at the conservatory since I was small. I know this instrument isn't highly thought of, but I enjoy its simplicity. And portability."

"I don't think I've ever heard it performed. Maybe you'll grace me with a piece before we part ways?"

"All right." Teralyn grew quiet. She wasn't used to performing her own music in front of an audience. Even playing for Antius made her uncomfortable, as if her notes were being analyzed for lyrical styles and influences. On a few occasions, when she had been rehearsing with ensembles and began experimenting with chords and arpeggios, she received puzzled looks and even sensed disdain and criticism. Her instructors and peers would laugh and behave as if her "noodling"—as they called it—were attempts at levity. She longed to let her instruments sing their own stories, as if imprisoned within wood and string were songs that ached to be let out. Why didn't anyone else feel the way she did about music? Antius seemed to understand, but only in theory. He encouraged her forays into composition, but even he remarked in a correcting tone when she veered out of the acceptable constructs of classical tradition.

Teralyn realized Justyn was staring at her, perhaps expecting her to say more. "Antius tells me you're from the village. That you're visiting your family for the week."

Justyn snorted in such an indecorous manner that Teralyn startled. "I do it out of obligation. If not, my mother gives me an earful. I make my appearances dutifully, but I loathe leaving the Heights."

"Why?"

"Because I try to forget the life I left behind. Don't you know anything about the village? The people are ridden with superstition, and their lives are spent in foolish observance of rituals and fraught with worry over breaking time-honored traditions. They never question why. Never seek understanding or knowledge. It's . . . detestable."

Teralyn wondered at the sudden ire in Justyn's voice but dared not question further. "What about your family? What do your parents do? Do you have brothers and sisters?"

Justyn sighed and didn't bother to hide the disgust in his voice. "My father is a shoe cobbler, and my mother weaves and knits."

"What is that? Knitting?"

Justyn slowed his pace along the road now rutted and dotted with puddles. "Don't you know? It's a way to fashion scarves and hats using two long needles. That sweater you're wearing—that was knitted, no doubt."

Teralyn glanced down at her soft wool sweater showing under the open coat buttons. She had never thought about the process of making a sweater and found it curious she had never seen anyone doing this knitting. Her mother made nothing; she rarely even cooked. All her work was with her mind. Clothing and furniture were things people purchased, hauled up to the Heights by horse-drawn cart. Although Teralyn supposed they could be considered artistic pieces as well. She knew the university boasted artisans who excelled in woodcraft and sculpture, but did they make practical things such as chairs and shoes?

"And I'm sure you'll run into my younger brother at the festival." Once more Teralyn heard irritation in Justyn's tone. "He's a farmer. Has a herd of goats. That's where Mum—I mean, my mother—gets her wool from. And he grows apples in an orchard. Something he's quite proud of." Justyn humphed and grew quiet. Then he added, "Oh, but he plays the fiddle, which he loves more than his goats—if that were possible. I have no taste for his playing—a lot of frantic screeching and bowing and notes bleating like the animals in his pasture. He calls it music, although, I'll admit, a fair share of the villagers love the sound. He gets them up on their feet and dancing—in a disorderly, riotous fashion. You'll see. There'll be a lot of that going on at the festival. You just have to tolerate the exuberance and noise, and keep your distance from those who've had a bit too much ale. I do my best to avoid it."

"So, will you be attending the festival at all?"

"Not if I can help it. I just passed my exams, have you heard? Made black. Look." He held up his hand for her to see. "Do you know how much sweat and hard work went into earning this graduation ring? Do you know how many people ever receive one?" He gloated with pride. "But now I begin my post-exam internship in linguistics. And that means a lot of preparation. I've brought my texts with me to study."

"Doesn't sound like much fun."

Justyn stopped at a turnout on the road. They had just come down a few hundred feet and already the day was warming. The wind had all but dissipated. He stripped off his cloak and Teralyn took off her coat. A hint of warmth caressed her face, and she lifted her chin to the sky, soaking it in.

"I can't concern myself with fun, Teralyn."

The way he said her name made her breath catch. It had a soft, almost pleading, edge to it, and she closed her eyes to avoid his.

"My studies are my life. I plan to make professor by age thirty—that's only six years from now. I have it all worked out. I can reach all my goals right on schedule so long as I'm diligent and apply myself. I've gotten this far—farther than most anyone from Wentwater—and I aim to be the first regent on the Antiquities Board from the village. I have no time to waste on frivolities."

Teralyn lowered her head and glanced at Justyn, who now stared out at the view—a blanket of thick fog separating them from the village way below. Clouds drifted overhead at a fast clip, frothing and reforming like steam erupting from a kettle.

"You seem to put a lot of pressure upon yourself, to achieve these things in such a short time."

"It's a matter of principle. The regents need to see that just because I'm a villager, it doesn't mean I'm hindered or incapable in any way. And the villagers ought to see there is an alternative to their way of life. That you don't have to be a slave to superstition. I've tried to talk sense into them, but so few listen. They are so stubborn, so set in their ways. Thick-headed, the lot of them. Fromer included."

"Fromer? What's that?"

"My brother, the dreamer. The simpleton. He has no ambition whatsoever. It was foretold he would be a farmer, and why, that's just fine with him. As if some old biddies can really foretell your future, and then you just have to comply, no fuss, no personal say. It's ignorance—and stupidity. I don't see how any of the villagers get through each day with all their worrying and fretting. My mother is a case in point. If you meet her, you'll understand. And my father—he just goes along with it all, as if he hasn't a thought of his own in his daft head."

Justyn fell quiet, as if he regretted his emotional outburst. With a softer tone, he turned to Teralyn and said, "I have to work hard to earn respect in the Heights. Acquiring knowledge is everything. If I'm to amount to anything, I have to excel, surpass my peers, exceed the expectations of my instructors—"

"But why?" Teralyn asked, surprised at the conviction in her voice. "You can't weigh your self-worth by the accumulation of words—as if the mere quantity of words has some value. You don't need to 'amount' to anything. Each person is intrinsically valuable. We each have our talents and good qualities. We each have the potential for love, for kindness, for contributing to the happiness of others. Aren't those things far more important that acquiring massive amounts of useless information?"

"What are you talking about? You live in the Heights. Your parents are researchers. You've been surrounded your entire life by those pursuing wisdom and knowledge. You know the sayings; you've heard the directive of the university: 'to learn about wisdom and instruction, for understanding words of insight, for gaining instruction in wise dealing, righteousness, justice, and equity. To teach shrewdness to the simple, knowledge and prudence to the young. Let the discerning acquire skill to understand the words of the wise and their riddles. Wisdom is the principle thing; therefore, get wisdom. Give instruction to the wise and they will become wiser still.' We have no intrinsic value! We are *nothing* without wisdom. Without knowledge, we may as well be chickens strutting about without our heads, meandering this way and that, direction-less and unproductive."

Teralyn clamped her mouth shut and continued down the road. She had heard similar passion voiced by other students at the university. More like obsession, she corrected herself. What was the point of striving so hard for some future day, for some title or letters after your name, if it meant sacrificing your joy along the way? Was the prize at the end of the journey really worth the cost?

"What?" Justyn asked, grasping her arm a little forcefully. "Your eyes mock me. Tell me what you're thinking."

Teralyn pulled out of his grasp and glared at him. "I do not mock you at all. I just wonder about your unhappiness."

"Unhappiness? What unhappiness? Haven't you heard a word I've said? Doesn't it bother you one bit to see people wasting their lives the way the villagers do? To see how they live in fearful ignorance, and banish those who break their ludicrous rules? But, then, how could you? You've never really *seen* how they live, how they think. Well, this week you will. And then you'll understand the mire I've had to extricate myself from." He grumbled under his breath and picked up his pace. Teralyn hurried to keep up.

By late afternoon, Teralyn's feet ached in her boots, hot and sweaty, as the fog broke up and the sun simmered the air around them. Teralyn luxuriated in the warmth, feeling her bones thaw and tingle from months of languishing in the cold. This sensation alone made her resolve to come down to the lowlands more often.

Justyn had barely spoken to her as they descended the mountain, but as they neared the entrance to the vale surrounding Lake Wentwater, where droves of people in colorful garb milled in and out the village gates, he gestured around him and said, "Here is the village, and tonight's the first eve of the festival. I'll take you straightaway to the inn, as I promised your mother. Once I get you settled there, you can explore the festivities. There'll be music events at all the inns and taverns, and on the outside stages—along with theatre productions, juggling, and various charlatans keen on parting you from your purse. Just don't venture down any darkened streets or alleys. And if you carry coin, keep your purse well hidden. And try not to look so innocent and wide-eyed. They'll mark you and take advantage of you. Really, you'd do best if you stayed at your inn and watched the festival from your window."

Teralyn wondered at Justyn's derogatory tone. All about her, villagers exuded joy. People played on instruments she'd never heard before, reveling in the rhythms they tapped out on drums and banged on everyday items like pots and pans using sticks and small brushes. Dancers spun around her in bright costume, scarves flowing and hair whipping to the beat of tambourines and hand bells. Delicious aromas of cooking meats rose from the open fires and cast-iron pots; scents of lavender and hyacinth drifted from the flower stalls; and freshly baked breads steamed on the racks stacked alongside the entrance to the village. Teralyn's stomach grumbled in hunger. She longed to stop and sample the fares of the vendors—everything looked delicious. But Justyn hurried her along, and Teralyn noted that he didn't even give the merriment a glance as the evening sky streaked pink with the setting sun. Single-minded, with one purpose, aimed at reaching his goal.

Teralyn shook her head in wonderment. If Justyn wanted to live his life like that, his eyes so pinned on the future that he couldn't even see the world unfolding around him, well, that was his choice. But as for her, she intended to immerse herself in all the festival had to offer. And as soon as she rid herself of her grumpy chaperone and filled her belly with a hot, satisfying meal, that was exactly what she intended to do.

THREE

TERALYN DRIED her face with the dainty towel hanging beside the washbasin. She smoothed out her linen tunic and layered skirt as she scrutinized herself in the mirror that stood in the corner of her cozy room. Not often did she get to wear such lightweight, frilly clothes that flew into the air as she spun in a circle—the sight brought a smile to her face. The floorboards under her feet vibrated with a steady light thump, beating a rhythm in time with the music filtering in from outside. She could barely contain her excitement and danced a little jig as she ran her brush through her hair and tied it back with a ribbon.

Justyn had hurried off after getting her settled in her room at the Cygnet. He couldn't stay and eat with her, saying his parents were expecting him for dinner. Well, that was fine with her. She knew he would have put a damper on her spirits had he stayed. But he promised to return in the morning and show her around the village before he turned his attention to his studies. Antius expected no less, he'd said, and so she relented. And perhaps a "tour" of the lowlands and the village would prove interesting.

Throughout all these years growing up in the Heights, Teralyn had looked down into the tiny vale dotted with steams and small lakes just beyond majestic Lake Wentwater and wondered about life among the villagers. How could a society of people, living in such close proximity to the Heights, have such a different worldview? Two cultures, so radically different and so uneasily mixed—like oil and water. Villagers grew the food and made the wares that those in the Heights bought and consumed, yet what did those residing in the Heights offer to the dwellers down in the lowlands other than their coin?

Teralyn had been taught her history. She knew the university had been established ages ago, after the Great Flood had nearly destroyed Wentwater, a flood caused—or so it was said—by the foolish acts of superstitious people living under an ignorant and stubborn land-owner. Back then, before the eight noble families established their dwellings in the Heights, factions separated—those who clung stubbornly to superstition and those who touted knowledge as the only remedy to the chaos and destruction wreaked by the flood. Teralyn was unsure just *how* the flood had managed to wipe out most of Wentwater, but shortly afterward, engineers, geologists, and others learned in the sciences designed and constructed a dam with controlled waterways that even now contained and regulated the heavy flows of water pouring down the falls from the Heights. And after the dam had been built, those who could not stand to live in the village a day longer climbed up the mountains and carved a life out of rock. Leaving superstition and contention behind them, they devoted themselves with fervor to acquiring knowledge. Sequestered behind walls of water and driven both inside and inward by inclement weather, their determination led to the eventual establishment of the university and the Board of Regents.

Lake Wentwater, once a small lagoon, now stretched out across the region like a glistening sea, dwarfing the village in its magnitude. That was one thing she very much wanted to do—walk the shores of the lake. So perhaps she could convince her "tour guide" to take her there in the morning.

As Teralyn stepped out of her room and walked down the hallway, she was approached by the congenial innkeeper, a hunched and wizened old man with a cheery disposition who took her arm and led her to one of the dozen tables in a small dining room. A few other patrons eating their supper smiled and nodded in greeting to her as she sat and reached for the loaf of warm brown bread resting on a small cutting board. Before long, her host hurried to her table with a steaming meat and vegetable pie, which Teralyn had to resist devouring in a few quick bites. She declined the ale offered and asked for water instead. She'd tasted ale on occasion, but drinking spirits was frowned upon in the Heights, and her parents kept none in the house. Despite her curiosity, she knew the ale would hinder her judgment, and she wanted her wits about her as she explored the festival. Even though Justyn's warnings seemed overly patronizing, she would take care to stay out of trouble.

The moment she had long awaited greeted her as she threw open the front door and was swept up in the throng of people flowing like rivers through the lanes. In the press of the crowd, she squeezed by couples and children, carts and peddlers, those on horseback and others loitering about the entrances to taverns. Banners coiling like colorful flames performed their own dance on the breeze above the heads of the festival-goers. Music, coming from all directions, crashed in a loud cacophony of abrasive beats and chords, sounding like an orchestra tuning its instruments with an edge of hysteria.

Teralyn paused at a corner, sifting through the sounds and smells and colors of the night as strings of lamps flickered light over the scene spread out around her. Peddlers' wagons illuminated by overhead lanterns lined the street, and sellers haggled over prices with their customers as they sold jewelry, hats, perfumes, carved wooden boxes, and statues of animals. Teralyn had never heard such noise in her life. The boisterous laughing; the spontaneous singing and bellowing (of some clearly drunk); the gaiety and exuberance of children rushing down the lanes, waving wands of ribbons and glitter; and the piercing clear notes of pipes and flutes and strings ringing in the air set Teralyn's mind awhirl.

On each corner, crowds milled about fires burning in metal tubs, waving their hands over the flames to chase away the chill. A rich aroma of hot chestnuts wafted by as a man shook a metal rack of the savory nuts hanging over one fire pit. Teralyn noted the people wore many layers—bundled in coats and shawls. Yet, to her, the evening was as warm as the warmest summer's night in the Heights. She hadn't even bothered to take her scarf and felt no need of it. Feeling invigorated and so glad to be out of wind and rain, she skipped down the street, threading through the lanes until she came to a town square where four musicians stood upon a wooden stage, playing a sprightly jig.

From the back of the dancing and cheering crowd, Teralyn could barely see over the tops of heads. The music was unlike any she'd ever heard before. Her feet tapped of their own accord, and without realizing, she had begun clapping along with those around her as she eased forward, squeezing between bodies smelling of sweat and ale and smoke. As she drew close enough to the stage to make out the performers, her jaw dropped at the sight. Lanterns hanging about the stage splashed light on the musicians as they attacked their instruments with passionate abandon. A crowd sat on the apron of the stage, whooping and waving their mugs of ale, while couples swung each other around onstage behind the musicians, frolicking dangerously close to the edge and nearly careening into the players. She watched in fascination as the dancers spun their partners in quick maneuvers that looked practiced, the men fairly tossing their women into the air and twirling them around, only to catch them in the nick of time.

Teralyn turned her attention to the musicians. One held a large skin-covered drum between his knees and beat on it with two soft mallets. His hands moved so fast, they were a blur of fingers.

Another plucked strings on a strange upright instrument of wood. It looked similar to a cello, with a sound hole and frets, but only three strings stretched across its length, which the bearded man snapped in syncopation with the drummer. A woman with short-cropped hair as black as a raven's strummed a guitar of sorts, but not in any fashion Teralyn had seen before. Her fingers formed and reformed chords in quick succession with her left hand, while her right hand fluttered like a hummingbird's wings as she strummed all the strings at once, a brisk movement of her wrist eliciting loud spatters of sound. But what melded the music all together was the fiddle.

Teralyn had known that some performed the violin in such a manner, but she'd never heard one played with such ebullience before. Instead of adopting the stiff, stodgy posture she had seen in classical performances, this young man with a wild mop of wheat-straw hair rocked and swayed as he held his bow—a bow that danced across the fiddle's strings as if it played with a will of its own. Teralyn couldn't take her eyes off the bow. It mesmerized her with its skipping and prancing over the strings, creating whimsical melodies that seemed to poke at her heart, as if prodding her to awaken from an ageless slumber. Although the melody was simple and repetitive, the sweet timbre and richness of the instrument coupled with the performer's enthusiastic intensity made the music soar, touching her soul in a strange, invigorating way.

She stood in awe, letting the music fill and carry her, holding her breath as the bow sped up and, in a last frantic whirring of motion and with fingers flying all over the frets, the musician played a long, wild arpeggio to the highest range of the smallest string and let the note ring out on the air as he gave a final yell of delight.

The ensemble ended with a dramatic flair on that note, with the drummer slapping a last beat hard on his drum, and the other two musicians strumming in finality on their instruments. Without a second's hesitation, the crowd burst into deafening applause amid whistles and shouts of "another, another!" Teralyn's heart pounded so hard in her chest she thought it would burst, so exhilarated was she by the demonstration of such gaiety. She joined in with her own cheers and claps, feeling her spirit soar as never before. *This,* she mused, *is what real music should be about!* She felt as if she had been aching her whole life to hear such music, having hoped that somewhere in the world true music could be found, music that connected to her heart and made her feel so alive! To think that it had been here, down below in the village, all this time.

Joy—that's what she felt, and what she read on the faces of the players. She wondered at this joy that seemed contagious, the music itself a carrier and perpetrator of this wonderful sensation. How many performances had she herself played and attended at the conservatory? Hundreds, no doubt. Yet, despite enjoying the beautifully arranged and perfectly performed pieces, she had never been so moved. And, she gathered, no one else had either. Polite applause, even an occasional "bravo" uttered in appreciation for expertise exhibited only showed respect for the art and the training of the artist but little more. The response to music in the Heights was intellectual. It was frowned upon to show unbridled emotion. Restraint and sobriety reflected the training of wisdom. Wisdom dictated that one demonstrate self-control and a mastery over emotion and skill.

Teralyn shook her head in wonder. Those in the Heights understood music inside-out. They dissected compositions, analyzing form and cataloging styles to fit in the different defined eras. They could tout the science behind wavelengths and oscillation and harmonics. But did they ever really *hear* the music? Let it seep past their minds and into their hearts? It didn't take wisdom to see that music was a gift from heaven, designed to impart great joy, a joy those in the Heights seemed to know little about. Even their approach to faith was focused on memorizing chapter and verse, demonstrating their mnemonic abilities in being able to recite long, difficult passages of Scripture without flaw. How many of those, so proud of their minds, lived what they quoted? Teralyn recalled a verse her mind often drifted to: "Knowledge puffs up, but love builds up." What a true observation!

In their fanaticism for wisdom, those in the Heights paid a steep price, Teralyn concluded. They sacrificed the heart of music by taking it apart and putting it back together again. You could understand what a peach was by weighing it, measuring its circumference, describing its size, color, and flavor in comparison to other fruits. But the only true way to understand a peach would be by sinking your teeth into one and tasting it. She looked at the musicians, smiles wide on their faces, as they retuned their instruments and tapped out the rhythm of the next piece. They, in their own innate wisdom, knew music from sinking their teeth into it and tasting, not from dissecting it with their minds. She thought of another saying, unsure of where she had heard it: *Where words fail, music speaks.* The music engulfing her this evening didn't just speak, it practically shouted from the rooftops!

Teralyn stood and reveled in the music long into the night, until her toes were numb in her boots and she could barely stand without leaning into those pressed around her. Eventually, the crowds thinned and the night air cooled enough to give her a slight chill. A full moon drifted over the rooftops, illuminating the stage in a brilliance that dozens of shining lamps couldn't match. Her eyelids drooped as the group played one last song, noticeably slower, more of a ballad that released a glitter of notes drifting up toward the stars.

Teralyn closed her eyes and rocked on her feet, drinking in the sweet melody of the fiddle as it sang to her heart. Tears pooled up and splashed on her cheeks before she was even aware that she cried. Something the bow drew from the strings found resonance in her soul, setting off a strange harmonic. She felt awash with sorrow, with a sense of loneliness and loss, as if the fiddle was a key that had opened a hidden lock in her heart, exposing sensitive secrets that she was unaware she carried. She wiped her face and opened her eyes in bewilderment.

The young man who played the fiddle was staring at her, moonlight swimming in his eyes. Not in a rude way, but as if his gaze had followed the path the music had taken deep into her soul, and he had wandered in and found himself trapped there.

Teralyn's breath caught in her throat. She felt as if this man, who stood unmoving as his companions packed up instruments and gathered belongings, had discovered a way into her heart unbidden. How could this be? A flush of heat rose to her cheeks; she felt naked and exposed. She dropped her eyes and backed up, tripping over feet and empty mugs as she wended her way through the departing crowd, putting distance between her and the stage. She dared not look back.

All the way through the winding streets, as she let the other festival attendees sweep her along in an animated surge toward the outskirts of the village where the Cygnet was situated, she sought to shake off the strange unsettling feeling that lingered. Tonight a whole new world had opened up to her. She felt like someone blind who had been given the gift of sight. The music of the evening echoed through her head, tingling her skin as if it had saturated every pore in her body. She buzzed with life.

But the fiddler's gaze had sunk even deeper. His playing loosed something tightly moored. As full as her heart felt, she also sensed something emptying, not unlike a swollen river spilling into a sea. She arrived exhausted at the front stoop of the inn, wanting nothing more than to throw herself onto her bed and fall into a hard sleep. But calling her more urgently than her need for rest was her need to understand this strange sorrow that ached in her heart—a need that bloomed with such vehemence it pained her.

The fiddler had done something to her. Of this she was certain. But what? Had his playing cast some strange spell over her? Or was her imagination running wild?

As she tiptoed down the hall to her room and readied for bed, she tried to push her thoughts from her head so she could get some much-needed sleep. She turned the knob on the oil lamp by her bed, extinguishing the flame, but the moon's bright glare filtered through the window, spreading light across the floor but shedding none on her inner dilemma. The final serene melody the fiddler had played wafted through her head, lulling her into slumber. She finally relaxed enough to close her eyes and drift off, the notes tugging her toward some unfamiliar, beckoning shore.

FOUR

JUSTYN SIDESTEPPED the street sweeper pushing a wide
bristle broom along the dirty cobbles fronting the shops.
Dawn splashed a clear, crisp light along the lane, brighten-
ing the shop windows as he maneuvered around piles of trash and
men unloading carts full of food and wares for the street vendors
who were beginning to wake and brew tea. Morning doves cooed
in the eaves as he passed, greeting the new day. He had managed
to excuse himself from his family's home without having to bear an
insufferably bland and meager breakfast. He hoped Teralyn hadn't
eaten yet; he knew just the place to take her to start their day. With
his mother's predictable warnings and protestations following him
out the house and through the yard, Justyn hurried through the
village, relishing the draping quiet—undoubtedly a result of the
stupor of the partygoers who'd stayed out too late and imbibed too
much ale.

Teralyn's day-old remarks still simmered in his thoughts. It was
apparent she was smart and well-educated. How could she dismiss his goals out of hand like that? Antius had told him that she
worked as a gardener in the Heights—implying she held no ambition whatsoever to acquire a higher education and pursue an academic field. Why not even botany, if she loved digging in the dirt
so much? But Antius had only shrugged. Obviously, he held some
peculiar affection for her.

Justyn wondered why he'd never seen her before, in all the years he had resided in the Heights. Even though his dormitory was off the oval and her home was on second level, surely they would have encountered one another at various university affairs and functions. Or did Teralyn keep to herself? If he'd attended more musical performances maybe he would have seen her there—how could anyone miss her stunning long white hair, so unusual in its lack of color. And her face—smooth as alabaster with eyes dark as coal. He had to admit, she was lovely—in an innocent sort of way. But uncouth and ill-mannered, he reminded himself. How dare she criticize his chosen path? He was the envy of every student on his level—scored the highest marks on his exams, had a masterful grasp of languages, and could memorize practically anything with just a glance. The facts and statistics he could rattle off when asked! And she had the nerve to tell him his accumulation of knowledge meant nothing. Well, if she wanted to dig in the dirt for the rest of her life, that was her choice. He had nobler plans. And he didn't need approval from someone whose eyes remained fixed on the ground instead of on the distant stars.

He realized he was grumbling aloud; heads turned his way as he trod across the cobbles to the front steps of the inn. He shook off his mood and pasted on a smile. He meant to stay in Antius's good graces, and if that involved showing his professor's gardener around town a bit, he would comply. Besides, he relished any excuse to flee his parents' stifling home, where their cheerful, vacuous conversations grated on his nerves. He had to admit, trekking about in the warm spring weather might prove the best remedy for clearing his head. Then he could get back to his studies at noon meal while his family went to the festival to sell their wares. A quiet house—all his, until suppertime.

Justyn wiped his feet on the mat and entered the inn. Patrons sat at tables, sipping tea and eating toast and porridge. He searched the room for Teralyn but she wasn't there. Just as he approached the innkeeper, who was engaged in lively conversation with two old ladies in festive garb, to inquire of her room, he caught a flash of white from the corner of his eye. He turned and looked down the long hallway. There she was, walking toward him.

Morning light streamed through the picture window as Teralyn approached, illuminating her face and hair. Streaks of light caught in the folds of her blouse, between her fingers, flowing like liquid gold over her skin. Justyn's breath hitched. She was dressed in a soft white long-sleeved blouse and pale green skirt cinched by a leather belt around her waist, and Teralyn's singular beauty struck him hard. He knew plenty of beautiful women in the Heights, and he never lacked a date for a concert or lecture. In fact, he didn't doubt he could have any woman he chose among his peers for a wife—they all fawned over him, laughed at his attempts at humor, and teased him by ruffling his hair and winking across a classroom. But he had neither time nor interest in pursuing romance at this stage in his life. Someday, he would consider settling down—once he had his professorship and regency in hand. And he would marry a woman his equal; he would tolerate no less. But as Teralyn came up to him and nodded a greeting, his eyes lit on her impossibly full red lips, lips he felt a sudden urge to kiss.

He reined in his wayward thoughts and chastised himself for thinking such things. Coming down to the village was proving to be a distraction. Spending time cavorting when he should have his nose in his books was undoubtedly a mistake. He was much inclined to make a hasty excuse, but could not back out of his obligation. He sucked in a breath and composed himself, yet, as Teralyn's eyes met his, he found he could not avert his gaze. Her very eyes shone with some inner glow as radiant as her hair, as if she had snagged the sun's light itself and trapped it behind her dark irises.

"Well," he said, forcing the words past the obstruction in his throat. "You seem rested. Did you venture out and find some local music to enjoy?"

"I did . . . and it was wonderful. I never expected to find such passion for music here in the village. And talent! Why, the musicians played on such simple instruments, but it was as though they breathed one another's spirit—"

"Have you eaten yet? I hope not because I have a special place to take you—"

Teralyn closed her mouth and frowned. "Eaten? Why, not yet. They serve breakfast here, though . . ."

Justyn gently took her arm and led her out the front door. His fingers felt hot against her sleeve, as if he could feel her skin through the yielding fabric. He quickly let go upon entering the street. "I know a better place. They make something called waffles . . . with fresh bogberries and whipped cream—"

Teralyn laughed, and the flash of her neck in the morning light made his own throat constrict. "Did Antius tell you of my love for bogberries? I don't know what a waffle is, but anything with bogberries on top must be heavenly!"

Justyn stared straight ahead and felt his neck perspire even though a cool breeze caressed his face. "It's just a few blocks, before the marketplace."

"I passed through here last night, but oh! The streets are so empty at this hour. No doubt everyone is still asleep."

"Then there'll be little wait for a table. And I thought perhaps we'd take a hike along the lake. There's a beautiful pathway, and by now much of the meadow should be in bloom. I thought that since you enjoy gardening, you'd appreciate the arboretum."

"A walk sounds perfect. I love this warmth, and the air—it smells so thick and fresh. Oh, I'm so happy today." Teralyn began to skip in place, and then, to his horror, pulled on his jacket cuff. "Come, let's skip to breakfast!"

"What, no, I can't do that—" Justyn pulled back to extricate his cuff from her grasp, but she clung tightly.

"Aw, why not? Loosen up a little. Don't you know how to have any fun at all, or are you always so proper and stuffy?" She let go of his cuff and threw her head back in amusement. Justyn stopped in the road and watched as she danced to some inner music, humming a tune that tickled the air around him. He glanced around to see if others were about, but the road was empty of all but a cat sitting on a windowsill. His face heated up, but he couldn't tell if he was embarrassed for her or annoyed.

"You're making a spectacle of yourself, Teralyn."

She wiggled her head at him and smiled without a care. "So? Maybe I'll just perform—for that cat over there." She ran over to the cottage and curtseyed to the cat, then lifted its front paws and pretended to dance with it. Justyn couldn't help himself. He blurted out a laugh—she looked so silly, dancing with a cat balanced along a narrow window ledge.

"See," she said, pointing a finger at him. "I knew there was a laugh somewhere inside you. It just needed some prodding to get out."

"Fine," he said, more than a little irritated that he'd lost his composure. He smoothed out his jacket and ran a hand through his hair, making sure it still lay flat against his head. "We're here." He held the heavy wood door open for Teralyn, who gave him an exaggerated bow then waltzed inside.

As they drank tea and waited for their breakfast, Teralyn went on and on about the music she'd heard last night. She described the instruments and performers. But when she spoke of the fiddler and the tunes he had played, Justyn nodded and interrupted her.

"That was Fromer, my brother."

Teralyn's eyes brightened. "It was?" She grew quiet and Justyn wondered at her silence. "Will he be playing again tonight, do you think?"

"The performers move from stage to stage throughout the village over the festival week. But I'm sure you can find him again, if you've a mind to."

"I would very much like to hear more. I danced and danced! Their music is so . . . happy. That's what is missing from the music in the Heights. Even lively pieces and jigs lack spirit. Like a lifeless body with no breath. Do you know what I mean, Justyn?"

He shook his head. "I'm afraid I really don't have a feel for music. I enjoy listening to various instruments and styles, but—"

"But have you ever just had to leap to your feet and dance?"

Justyn held up his hands. "Oh, no. I don't dance, couldn't . . ."

Teralyn humphed. "Well, maybe you should come with me tonight. I would dare you to remain still while your brother plays the fiddle."

"Oh, I've heard him play, plenty enough." Justyn knew his words came out a little sour, for Teralyn pursed her lips together. "Years of screeching scales and all that. It's not for me, all right? Let's change the subject."

Teralyn let out a sigh, but Justyn was saved from coming up with a new topic, for at that moment their server arrived with two plates of waffles topped with mounds of thick cream and sprinkled liberally with deep-purple bogberries.

Justyn glanced at Teralyn's wide-eyed expression. She shook her head in disbelief, then tucked in without a word. He couldn't help but smile at her childlike excitement as she made little noises of appreciation and licked her lips.

"You've got . . . there!" She touched his cheek with her napkin, and Justyn felt his heart flutter. He pulled back and fussed. "Just some cream on your face," she said.

He muttered a thank you and set his attention on eating his breakfast. When they finished, Justyn insisted on paying, then led Teralyn through the village and out the south gate, where the cobbles turned to dirt road and entered an expansive meadow awash with new grass and flurries of wildflowers.

"Oh!" Teralyn rushed down the road and squatted to look closer. "Look—there are fire lilies . . . and anemones and angelica too! We can't grow these up in the Heights, except in the greenhouses. Oh, to be able to dig them up and grow them in pots. What color they'd add to my home." She jumped up and spun around in the grass. "It's as though heaven rained seed across the world to paint the vale!"

She stopped abruptly, then cocked her head. "Do you hear that?" Justyn listened. A nudge of discomfort made him look around. "I don't hear anything. Just insects buzzing. And the falls coming down from the Heights." He pointed and Teralyn turned to her right. Off in the distance, the mountains rose into cloud cover, and from the meadow the waterfalls looked like shimmering strands of hair falling down the rock face. The water barely soughed loudly enough to be heard.

"Someone singing. A woman." Teralyn grew still and an intensity clouded her face.

"I hear nothing," Justyn said. "Why don't we—"

"Wait!" She held up a hand. Justyn watched her face turn from puzzlement to agitation.

"What is it, Teralyn? I don't—"

Without a word, she continued down the path to the lake. Justyn followed but kept silent. He strained to hear, but the meadow lay under the quiet of morning, with an occasional bird calling to its mate. A few shreds of clouds drifted above, tossing shadows across the road as he and Teralyn trekked up a small rise that rimmed Lake Wentwater, still out of sight from where they approached.

The uncomfortable feeling Justyn had felt moments earlier now grew to trepidation. He willed his heart to slow its furious pounding as anxiety clawed at his gut. Something was amiss and he sensed danger—but how, and why? In such a peaceful place as this? He never was one for strange intuitions, but at that instant, every nerve in his body screamed at him to run—and to grab Teralyn and keep her from disappearing over the hillock.

He hurried to catch up, feeling sweat streak down his cheeks. Yet, when he joined her atop the hill, with the lake spreading out before them in tranquil calm, he saw nothing. A breeze riffled the grass around them and tickled Teralyn's skirt. Her back was to him, and she seemed to be listening. A quiet hush fell over the land, muffling all sound. The only thing Justyn heard was his heart thumping against his chest. Yet, the air seemed charged, as if the world was holding its breath.

Out of nowhere, a memory punctured his vision. Of an aberrant snowstorm—at this same time of year. Of flakes falling on his eyelashes as a fire raged and consumed a cottage in front of him. He wiggled his fingers and felt them gripping Fromer's hand, so small in his grasp. He squeezed his eyes shut, hearing the loud, angry voices of women carried on the air, bellowing through the village, until the din faded and dissipated, leaving nothing but ash turning the snow black and melting in dark puddles on the road. And the sound of a babe crying . . .

His eyes opened with a start. Teralyn was gone!

He scanned the hillside and finally spotted her down by the lake, far down, running toward the water. He called to her, but she didn't seem to hear. His legs took off running, and when he caught up with her, relief washed over him. What had he expected? Something terrible, he realized. *But, how silly*, he told himself. There was nothing threatening about the lake, or the day. No storm clouds roiled on the horizon. No danger assaulted them. Yet . . .

Teralyn sat on her knees at the water's edge, skimming the water with her hand. Glistening drops fell from her fingers like pearls. She seemed mesmerized, staring into the lake's depths, as if she saw something.

"Teralyn . . ."

She turned at the sound of her name as if he'd shaken her awake or snapped her out of a spell. He snorted. *A spell!* That was something his mother would believe. How she'd gone on about the marsh witch and some spell she'd cast over the village—

Justyn sucked in a breath. He had caught a glance of that old woman, shriveled and unbathed, that day she entered the house for the baby naming. That was years ago, nearly two decades. Why had that memory returned, and with such forcefulness? Before he could ponder the answer, he saw Teralyn's face. It was wet with tears.

His heart pained at her expression. She seemed suddenly weak and vulnerable. He longed to hold her, to wrap his arms around her and protect her. And yet, this urge seemed to come from somewhere else, from something outside him, from . . . the lake.

He stumbled backward and found his voice after some searching. "Are you all right?" She allowed him to help her stand. A chill shot up his spine. He had to force his fingers to unfurl from her arm and release her. He wanted only to hold her, and the need consumed him such that he groaned.

"Yes. I-I don't know what came over me. I heard singing, such a compelling voice, as if calling to me. And . . . it wrenched my heart . . ." She shook her head as if she had water in her ears. "But, there is nothing. Nothing here. I must have imagined it . . ."

Justyn nodded, backing away, hoping distance might dispel the discomfort he felt. "Let's just head back to the village. Maybe we've partaken of enough nature for one day. And a strong cup of tea might do us both good."

"Yes," she said, her voice empty of emotion.

Justyn exhaled and looked once more at the lake that stretched out to the horizon and lapped against unseen shores. The strange presentiment faded, as a dream vanishes upon awakening. He touched Teralyn's shoulder, to lead her away from the bank and back toward the road, then withdrew his hand. Her blouse was wet. Not just damp, but soaked. Teralyn seemed not to notice.

He looked her over—nothing appeared odd. Her clothes lilted and swayed in the breeze as she walked. Justyn followed her as she waded through grass and flowers, creating a wake behind her, stirring up sweet fragrance from the crushed flowers that drifted around his face, intoxicating him.

Whatever had just occurred lingered unresolved in the air between them as they followed the road back to the gate, unspeaking. Maybe his emotional instability was due to a lack of sleep and too much intense studying these last weeks. Preparing for his orals and writtens had taken everything out of him. He knew he'd been teetering on the edge of exhaustion. And that often led one to faulty and distorted thinking. Perhaps that could account for the strange anxiety that had overtaken him by the lake. No matter. He'd take a long nap this afternoon, put off his studies until tomorrow. Surely his mind was just overwrought from too much stress—that must be it.

He relaxed, settled in his heart, and looked at Teralyn as she stepped onto the cobbled street just past the gate in front of him. A chill shimmied up his spine when his eyes dropped to the ground.

Under the warm, dry morning sun, her dry boots left sopping wet footsteps trailing after her.

FIVE

TERALYN STROLLED the lane thick with peddler carts
and shoppers. Upon entering the village gate, Justyn had
hurried off—to his studies, he claimed. But there was no
mistaking the disturbed look on his face. Maybe she had spoiled
his morning. She hadn't meant to. She *had* heard someone singing. And she had seen something under the mirror of water, an
illusive shape, perhaps only a fish or some denizen of the deep.
Water called to water, and something drew her, stirred her blood
as a wind might disturb the placid surface of a lake. She stopped
walking and gazed back toward the south end of the village, listening once more. Nothing.

Pushing such thoughts from her mind, she fingered the soft
shawls and hats a heavyset woman displayed on her wooden table
as other customers jostled around her, sorting through the piles.
The wool was luxurious, melting beneath her touch, and light and
airy, softer than Antimony's feathers or even goose down.

"What is this wool, ma'am?" She lifted a long scarf the color of
wine; it nearly floated in her hands. The merchant raised her eyes
from the gloves she was stacking and stared at her over bifocals.

"'Tis angora, from goats. Not the meat kind, mind you. But a
breed from the Logan Valley, lass. You shear 'em as you do sheep.
Lightweight, but even warmer than sheep's wool, it is. And easy
to wash and quick to dry. That piece there—only two silvers.

Make a fine gift for yourself—or the boy you fancy, right?" The woman lifted her eyebrows expecting an answer, but Teralyn pulled out another longer scarf—a cheery blue with strands of copper intertwined.

"Ah, that's a good choice, lass. More manly. For your beau?"

"I'm thinking for an older gentleman I know. He is always a bit cold and this—why, he'd love this, I'm sure."

"You're not from the village, are you?" the woman asked, pulling out a cap with the same colors and design. "This goes with it. A pair. Three silvers for the both. Or—if you'll take the two scarves, I'll make it an even five. What do you say?"

Teralyn smiled. She could buy scarves for her parents too. An amber one for her father and the burgundy for her mother. She knew they would love them.

"I'll pass on the hat, but I'll take three scarves." She reached for a golden one. "Are these knitted then?"

"The hats be. But the scarves are done on the loom."

"A loom?"

"Heavens, lass. Just where *do* you hail from? Don't they have looms?"

"I live in the Heights—"

"Ah, that 'splains it. Not much spinning and weaving done up there, I'm told. But I sell to many in the Heights. Got to keep warm in those chill winds and all that sleet and rain. How do you stand for all that weather up there?"

"We manage." Teralyn wanted to ask more questions, but other customers were holding out their choices in one hand and coin in the other. She reached into the pouch she kept tucked in her tunic pocket and withdrew her silvers. The vendor deftly wrapped the three scarves in brown wrapping and tied it with a string.

"Here you go, lass. But be thinking about them hats. Keeps the ears warm with those little flaps. Just the thing."

Teralyn nodded and thanked the woman. With her bundle tucked under one arm, she perused the various displays of handmade pots and jewelry and clothing, letting her eyes take in all the marvelous wares nearly tumbling into the streets. It was almost midday, and more people filled the lanes, animated and searching for something special to buy or munching on pastries. A tickle of a flute drifted on the air, someone playing afar off. Already the air was redolent of meats cooking over spitfires and fried breads spattering in oil. The aromas came from farther down the lane, where all the food vendors worked busily at their fires, stirring and tossing and flipping and dipping. Teralyn couldn't resist buying a long puffed cake in the shape of a stick, covered in powdered sugar. Even with a rich waffle sitting in her stomach, she made room for her doughy treat.

After two hours of walking and browsing, she arrived at the inn eager to pull off her boots and cool her feet. She washed up in her room thinking she might take a nap before heading out for another long night of music and dancing. But her eyes glanced over to her lap harp propped up against the wall near her bed and her pulse quickened. Without a moment's hesitation, she pulled off her boots and put on her casual slippers, then grabbed her harp and hurried through the village.

The melody the fiddler had played late last night threaded through her mind, and she found herself humming it as she rushed toward a different gate—one that opened out on the north side of the village, facing open moors and rolling hills in the distance. Teralyn caught her breath and slowed, following an old cart road that wended into the hills. Sheep grazed among the willows, and a small creek, wide and slow moving, bisected the meadow. With the bustle of the village behind her, the quieter sounds of the afternoon filled her ears—insects buzzing and birds chattering, sheep bells jingling and an occasional baa. The pastoral setting and the languorous humidity of the day soothed her, this melding of meadow and spring composing a song of their own. Teralyn listened with open mind and heart as she took her harp out of its case and sat on a carpet of grass, resting the instrument on her knees.

She strummed the strings, freeing her fingers to form new chords previously untried. The notes rose into the air and spread out like thick honey as she closed her eyes and let her voice run loose. At first she let the melody unravel without words. Soft syllables carried the tune into the meadow, over the bubbling creek, joining water as it trickled over rocks and skipped down ravines. Syllables changed to words, unstrung and random as they lit on the willow leaves and sank into the rich loam around her. Soon, words gathered into phrases, and Teralyn imagined them weaving together like her scarves, threads of voice, harp, meadow, birdcall, breeze, all creating something of beauty that enwrapped the world around her, as thick and comforting as any shawl.

In this remote place, Teralyn could let her voice out of its cage. She envisioned the notes of music as fireflies lighting up a summer night. She was a painter at a canvas, painting the world anew with sound and concept. Images swelled through her mind as she heard her voice tell tales that bubbled up from somewhere deep, as if she had tapped into a vein of gold under slumbering earth, an undiscovered place of stored tales embedded in rock and longing to be released. Her heart soared as she sang, and the tinkle of bells joined in. She laughed and opened her eyes, picturing her fireflies winging around her head with little bells around their necks.

Instead, she found herself staring into the eyes of a young man with a crook in hand, surrounded by a flock of curious goats— goats with soft curly hair. Sunlight shimmered through his hair, as if he had been shaped by light.

Recognition came tumbling over her. First the wool, then the shepherd—who was none other than the fiddler from last night's performance—who happened to be Justyn's brother . . .

"Fromer!" Shaken from her reverie by his sudden appearance, she nearly dropped her harp.

He cocked his head, eyes wide with surprise. Luminous green eyes that mirrored the new grass. Eyes that had journeyed deep past hers, unbidden, in the lantern light last night.

Teralyn looked at his goats, avoiding his gaze, not wishing to be waylaid again. Yet, she was struck at the beauty of his face and stature. So unlike Justyn—with long unruly hair kissed by endless days in the sun. Skin bronzed but smooth and muscled. And his garb—a simple peasant's tunic and pants, and leather sandals. He held out a hand to her as she got to her feet. Those fingers! How they had moved like lightning over the strings, and made the bow dance, urging fervent music from his fiddle.

"You know my name." He narrowed his eyes and smiled. "Ah, you must be the lady Justyn spoke of. Come down from the Heights to attend the festival. And my brother must have told you about me. Me and my 'screeching' fiddle." He laughed good-naturedly, without a hint of malice. Teralyn wondered at these two siblings, so very different in look and manner.

"Yes, I'm Teralyn. And your playing . . . well, it was nothing I'd ever heard before in my life!"

His smile lit up his face—a beautiful, unforced smile that brought a grin to her own face. "I trust that was a compliment, my lady . . ."

Heat rushed to her cheeks. "Please, just call me Tera. My name is utterly too long and stuffy . . ."

"No it's not—it's lovely. It rolls off one's tongue. Terr*rralllllllyyyyn* . . ." He sang out her name in a sweet tone that made her tingle.

"Well, with your embellishment, you could probably make the ugliest name in the world sound like a delicious dessert."

They both laughed.

"And these goats—they are yours?" she asked. "You play fiddle by night and shepherd by day?"

"Something like that. I wish I could play fiddle every night. It's not often when I can perform with my friends in such a setting, and before such a crowd. But a man can't make much of a living as a fiddler in Wentwater. There's an occasion or two at an inn, and sometimes a wedding in the summer. A fiddler grabs what chances he gets."

"And your goats. Do they like your 'screeching'?"

Fromer bowed to his wooly audience. "A very demanding crowd," he said in all seriousness. "Hard to please. Rarely a shout of 'encore' or 'bravo, chap!' Nary a hint of applause. But . . . I can sometimes get their little hooves a'dancing. Especially if I poke them with my bow from time to time."

"Surely, you don't—"

He shook his head and chuckled. Even his laughter pealed like a melody. Teralyn reached over and stroked one of the goats. "Why, they *are* so soft. Not that I've ever petted a goat before. I just bought some scarves in the marketplace. This same wool, I gather."

"That's my mum selling those. From these very goats."

"Ah. I should wonder about the colors. They have such beautiful coats—browns and tan and beige. But she dyes the wool, I imagine."

"Sometimes. I prefer the natural colors. And dyeing stains everything. When I help her with the pots of dark colors, my hands stay purple for weeks." He laughed again. "It would be easier, I think, to just take a goat and dip it in the vat, then let the color sit on its back in the sun. A lot less trouble than stirring and prodding wool for hours over a hot fire."

Teralyn laughed. "Well, that would be a funny sight—pink and blue and purple goats traipsing about the countryside!"

"No doubt. Would send my neighbors rushing to their cottages, closing their doors in fear. Some harbinger of disaster, they'd think." Fromer pointed at her harp. "That's a finely crafted instrument."

"Yes. A solstice gift from a friend, an old instructor up in the Heights—your brother's mentor, I believe. It was made by a master craftsman."

"The scrollwork is unique. May I see it, play it?"

She marveled at his polite request and the way he handled her harp as she handed to him. As if it were made of blown glass. He carefully studied the inlaid wood, then turned it over and ran his finger along the seams. "I don't think I've seen better. I should introduce you to my friend Narice. She crafts harps similar to these. With sixteen strings though, not twenty-four. A bit smaller size too, and made of a local ash that's lighter and less resonant, I think, than this yew wood."

"You seem to know a lot about the lap harp." Teralyn watched as he sat and strummed some simple chords.

He raised his head to look at her. "It's my favorite instrument. But I don't have a knack for it. Fiddle's what calls me. And she's a jealous one, demanding my attention. Doesn't want to share me with anyone else."

Teralyn noticed his eyes dancing. They seemed so alive with life, with joy. Did his music infuse him with joy, or was it the other way around? "Oh, and what does she say when she catches you eyeing another woman?"

"I stuff her back in her case. So she won't have to watch."

"I see." Teralyn took a deep breath and let it out. She felt surprised at how easily she spoke to him. Usually when a young man chatted with her, her words garbled in her mouth and she felt terribly self-conscious. But something about Fromer set her at ease. Perhaps it was the fact that he seemed so easy about himself and life. As though he hadn't a care in the world.

His fingers began picking out a melody, plucking the strings in a three-four rhythm. The tune sounded familiar but it wasn't until he hummed along that Teralyn realized he was echoing the song she'd just improvised moments earlier as she sat in the grass. She hadn't even realized she'd composed such a pretty line of notes until Fromer sang it back at her, with most of the same words. Hearing her words and music come from his fingers and throaty voice took her breath away. As if he had drunk in her spirit and then merged it with his, concocting some phantasm with a life of its own. The sensation filled her with awe—something she had never experienced in all her years playing music.

A shiver traveled down her spine and her jaw dropped as he played. She watched him, it seemed as if for hours, but she knew only a scant few minutes passed. While he played, his eyes closed and he wandered afar—she could sense it. And just as he had followed the music into her soul last eve, she chased after him as the notes danced across the meadow. She let her eyes close and the notes became butterflies released into the air, scattering on the wind and calling her to follow. And then her song became his song, with the melodies entangling and meshing into one, finally settling down to one last chord and one last resonating pluck of string that hung in the air like a heavy, unspoken thought between them.

Teralyn opened her eyes the same moment as did Fromer. Her heart beat wildly in her chest. The very air seemed to be listening, expectant. What enchantment was this, to be able to bring music to life, to mold and shape it as though it were clay in his hands?

Could he touch any instrument and work this magic? Her heart yearned for this gift. If only she could play so powerfully.

Fromer stood and handed back her harp. He studied her face in silence, and as he did, she could hold back no longer and let herself drown in his gaze, meeting his eyes and allowing them into her heart, baring her soul that seemed to cry out to him. She could no more resist than she could stop the sun from arcing across the sky. They seemed trapped in the timeless space between a breath drawn and a breath released.

"Teralyn . . ." Her name was a prayer on his lips. Just that one word coming from his mouth soothed her cares and filled her with comfort. "Your music . . . it's sublime. When I heard you from over the hill . . ." He gestured with his hand to the copse of trees in the distance. "I thought an angel had come down from heaven to visit me. And . . . then I saw you."

He gently took the harp out of her hand and set it on the grass almost lovingly. "And I was right. She had come. You came . . . Teralyn."

She marveled at the expression on his face—one of awe and reverence and humility. As if he were honored to be in her presence. Not worshipful, but adoring. And no one, no man, had ever looked at her like this, nor had she ever wanted one to. Until now.

Fromer ran his fingers through her hair, warm fingers that made her blood rush. And with the gentleness of a butterfly, his lips glanced across hers, and, drawn as if to nectar by his urging, she kissed him, her blood coursing in her veins to a rhythm not her own, not his, but theirs.

SIX

W ELL, LOOK who's graced us this late in the day. Thought you'd have your nose buried in books until we wrapped up and came home. Your eyes tired of studying?"

Justyn shrugged. "Just needed to get out of the house. How have your sales been?" He came behind the table and stood next to his mother to get out of the flow of foot traffic. A steady wind ruffled the items on the table and Justyn pulled his jacket collar up.

"Better'n last year. With spring a little cooler this year, folks be wanting some extra warm things." Iris stopped fussing with her display and studied him. "You remember to lock the chickens up, and check for feathers?"

Justyn sighed. "Yes, I did, Mother. Although, for heaven's sake, why—"

Iris grabbed Justyn's arm in a tight clench. "I'll hear none of that talk," she said in a low, controlled whisper, her eyes darting around at her customers. "Not here, not ever."

"That yer boy, Iris?"

Justyn turned toward the woman across the way, standing at a cart loaded with pottery. He recognized her—his mother's neighbor, a nosy biddy who often came over to gab. Justyn frowned. How his mother loved to gossip. He was sure she often spoke of him to all her neighbors in the marketplace. But why should he care what they thought of him?

"The elder. Justyn."

She waved over at him, and he smiled politely.

"Oooh, haven't seen ye, lad, in ages. So handsome and proper now. Here to help yer ol' mum sell her wares?"

"Just down for break. Classes start back up after the festival."

"Hmphh!" She waggled her hand at him. "Still up at that university in the Heights? Filling yer fool head with useless bits that won't serve you. Iris, can't ye knock some sense into that boy? Wasn't he named to be a leader and righter of wrongs?" She chortled loudly, and Justyn tried not to cringe. Those walking down the lane turned heads, but he managed to keep his composure.

"He feels it's his calling. To be a teacher."

"Teach what?" she yelled while wrapping up some plates in paper. "Can't ye see yer mum works her fingers to the bone, making all those shawls and hats and gloves? And yer dah, pounding nails into boots and crafting such fine shoes. Shouldn't ye be helpin' him, the elder son, taking up the trade? P'raphs ye getting too big fer yer britches, lad . . ."

Iris shook her head and called back. "There's no talking sense to this one. Always had his head in the clouds and dreamin' big. Can't be helped. I've tried, heaven knows."

The two women spoke of him as if he wasn't standing right there between them. Justyn felt invisible. Rather than make a sound—which would only invite more barbs—he quietly slipped away behind his mother's back as she volleyed remarks back and forth across the lane. Justyn noticed other neighbors had stopped to join in, resembling in no small part his mother's flock of chickens—the way they pecked and cackled and flurried their feathers in a huff. He forced down familiar feelings of shame and hurt that bubbled up from his childhood years, feelings that he knew were illogical and unwarranted. Yet, despite all his efforts to rid his heart of such condemnation, the barrage of criticism battered at him the way the waves on Lake Wentwater pounded the shore in a March gale.

Throughout his childhood years, his parents had nagged him about his destiny. All because some old, senile woman had determined his path. How in the world could she know what vocation he should pursue? Decisions needed to be made with knowledge and understanding. You assessed your skills, balanced them with your interests. Chose a vocation based on logic and practicality. Your purpose in life couldn't be determined by how many drips of wax flowed down a candle!

Justyn felt his indignation rise as he tromped through the lanes, pressing his way around the crowds, not really thinking where he was going. He had supposed he'd be dutiful and help his mother out, but he couldn't seem to take more than a few minutes in her presence. Invariably, without delay, the grumblings would start. By now, at twenty-four, he was expected to be making a living, earning his keep and contributing to his family's needs. The first-born was meant to take over, to allow the father to ease back on work. But his father loved his work and took pride in it, and no doubt preferred spending as much time outside his home as possible. He'd wither away, if left to rock in a chair and listen to his wife go on about this and that, had Justyn taken over the business. But Justyn knew his father was disappointed as well. Often he would show Justyn how to attach soles to boots or use stamps and punches on the leather, his face beaming, eyes hopeful. Yet Justyn had repeatedly shown his lack of interest and boredom, asking if he could go home and read. And his father would just shake his head and mumble as Justyn ran out the door as if he couldn't get away fast enough.

Justyn gritted his teeth and pushed though the thickening crowd. His parents made no effort to hide their preference for Fromer—the loyal son who never voiced a complaint. Went about his happy way and did all that was asked of him. "Fromer, tend the goats. Fromer, shear them and bring me wool today—that's a good lad. Fromer, pick all the apples and bottle up cider so I can sell it at the fall harvest." The commands would be uttered and off Fromer would go.

Justyn grumbled under his breath. Fromer! He represented everything Justyn detested about his family and the ways of the village. People like his brother just perpetuated the endless cycle of ignorance and stupidity. Mindless, directionless, like waves blown hither and thither in the wind, following the whims of tradition, without question. The only way for a society to function properly was with a set of time-proven laws and rules that kept order and punished wrongdoing. Each travesty should merit the appropriate punishment—no more, no less. There was no room for sentimentality or weakness. And certainly no room for consulting the clouds or a handful of scattered grain or wax dripping down a candle. How many hours did his mother spend each day looking to inanimate objects to give her a sign, to tell her how to act? If only the villagers would look to the Heights and see how orderly things ran. No hysteria, no fear. Just proper rules and proper behavior. Everything in its place and everyone in his place.

The maddening cycle would never be broken until someone stood up and demanded a change. Justyn would do it himself—he would! But how? Village life was a tightly woven tapestry. It would take a tremendous unraveling—in the minds and the hearts of the villagers—to break down their view of life and reform it. Yet it needed doing. Or undoing. All their beliefs needed to unravel to the point where they didn't know what they believed. Perhaps, like a scarf or shawl, it would take just one hard tug on a thread to start the process. But what could that thread be? No doubt, it would need to be some monumental event. *Like the flood—that had swept away the former village.* But, Justyn mused in irritation, not even a cataclysm of that magnitude had succeeded in washing away their stupidity. Which reminded him of an ancient saying in *The Book of Kingly Sayings* from the kingdom of Sherbourne: "Crush a fool in a mortar with a pestle along with crushed grain, yet his folly will not depart from him."

Without realizing it, Justyn found himself at the door to the Cygnet. He hadn't meant to seek Teralyn out, but as he stood there, he realized images of her had been wading through his thoughts, coming into focus the way a boat came to shore out of the mist. Thinking of Teralyn muddled his mind; he needed to sort his feelings about her. She had dared him to attend the evening's festivities with him, implying he was way too stuffy and studious. Well, he knew how to have a good time, and he would show her he wasn't all that stuffy.

Her dark eyes and soft lips came to mind, and he felt his heart race. The sensation of her skin lingered on his fingertips, from when he had touched her arm. It burned in his memory, painfully sweet. He reminded himself that she was beneath him, not his type, lacked manners, and didn't aspire to his standards of excellence. He reminded himself he was not at all interested in romance or becoming entangled in any relationship that would draw his attention away from his studies. Yet . . .

He found himself breathing so shallowly that he had to suck in a breath to clear his dizzy head. A small ache started up in his heart, spurred by a need to see her—to see her at that very moment. Was she there, inside her room, getting ready to go out? Putting on a soft skirt and silky blouse, brushing out her thick rope of hair the color of moon?

Justyn pushed open the door to the inn—only to find Teralyn standing with her hand raised, reaching for the door latch. He felt the blood rush in his ears as he met her eyes—a glow of joy on her face so radiant, her inner light outmatched the moon and stars combined. And then he glanced past her to the man standing a step behind, with a hand resting on her shoulder.

Fromer!

Justyn's feet faltered as he struggled to speak. "Ah, fancy meeting you both here. I see . . . you've met my brother." Justyn's voice rattled in his throat and his palms grew sweaty. But neither Fromer nor Teralyn seemed to notice. In fact . . . with one glance Justyn realized neither really saw him standing there. Fromer came alongside her and they looked at each other. Disgust welled up in Justyn's gut as he studied the way the two held each other's gaze.

"Well . . ." he blurted out. "I, uh, had hoped to go hear the performers tonight—"

"Oh, yes, do come, Justyn!" Teralyn said, wrenching her attention from Fromer and bouncing on the balls of her feet. "Fromer's asked me to play—and I should like to have you hear us, although we've only practiced two of the tunes. And I'm not sure I'll play them well enough." Only then did Justyn noticed the lap harp sticking out of the pack slung across her shoulder. Fromer stroked her hair. "You'll play magnificently—I have no doubt."

Justyn's eyes locked on to his brother's hand, resting where it shouldn't. Disgust turned to anger, and before he could regret his words, he said, "How could you, Teralyn? Fromer is . . . a nothing. A goat herder—with a head full of obstreperous music." He gulped air as he spoke with jagged breath. "You deserve better."

Before the shock could fall from her face, Justyn spun around and stormed out the front door. Heat flared on his cheeks as he shut tight his mouth and fought a wave of embarrassment and shame. Why had he said that? Now Teralyn would think him an idiot—and jealous, something he most certainly was not! He only cared for her best interests. And Fromer would only corrupt her thinking, infect her with the ways of the village, and pull her down to a level of ignorance. Justyn had heard Antius rant over his son, Ambel—how associating with villagers had destroyed the boy's morals and values. What pain such actions had caused his teacher. And now—what would Antius feel upon learning Teralyn was cavorting with villagers? His teacher would blame *him* for letting Teralyn be so influenced, and then what would happen? Antius might withdraw support for his post-graduate work. Might even stop being the kindly benefactor and mentor he had been these last six years.

The thought sent a stab of pain to his gut. Antius—the only real father he had, a man he respected and nearly worshipped. The thought of his reproach was too much to bear.

Justyn's mind whirled with the repercussions of this impending calamity. Something had to be done—but what? Under all his anger and fear, his heart ached, but he smothered it with determination. He would have to talk sense into Teralyn. Somehow, before the end of the festival and their return to the Heights, he must find a way to convince her to leave behind the lure of village life, a life that promised a freedom and thrill but held hidden dangers. Well, he would expose those dangers and make her see. Surely, once she distanced herself from the festival and from his manipulative brother, she would come to her senses.

He hoped to God he was right.

SEVEN

FOUR DIZZYING nights of performances—Teralyn's head was awhirl. Had she ever had a happier week in her life? The hours of music had drenched her soul; melodies played in her head throughout the day, only to erupt from her voice as she sang and her hands as they picked and strummed her lap harp. Even now, as the festival wound down and peddlers began to pack up their wares and haul their carts behind horses and mules eager to head home, notes from the songs they'd played lilted in bits and pieces around her ears.

She heard music everywhere now—in the repetitious squeak of the cart wheels, the rhythmic sweeping of the brooms as men cleaned the cobbles, the horses' hooves as they clopped along the lane in syncopation. Everything around her composed a symphony of life. Why had she never noticed this before?

From the small hillock upon which she stood in the waning afternoon light, waiting for Fromer, she glanced up at the dozens of breathtaking waterfalls tumbling down from the Heights, pounding the rocks as water gushed over ledges and bounded and leapt like stags down steep terrain. If she closed her eyes and listened hard, she could hear their music as well, drifting on spray and breeze, singing only to her. As much as she longed to stay in the lowlands with Fromer and never leave his side, the falls were calling her home—with a music she recognized as the song of her very soul. She had spent nearly every moment of her life enveloped in those canopies of water, their constant roar a comforting lullaby at night and a refreshing reveille announcing the break of day. Their pounding matched the pounding of her heart—synchronous and steady. Never an interruption in their pulsing, never an aberrant beat to cause alarm. The song of Wentwater Heights was the throb of blood in her veins.

Her eyes lit upon Fromer coming over the rise from his threshing floor, his arms bulging with linen sacks. He carried the overflow in his arms as gently as one would a baby. And what of this man walking toward her, the setting sun sparking his hair with evening's fire? He, too, pulsed in her a signature rhythm all his own. Just the sight of him quickened the beat, set off drums and bells and tapping feet. She knew now that it wasn't his fiddle that was enchanted, that drew fervor from him as a hot compress drew blood to the surface of skin and affected all those around him. The fiddle was merely wood and twined metal, bowed by horses' tail hairs. There was nothing mysterious about the composition of the simple instrument Fromer held in his hand when he played. Rather, the mystery lay in Fromer himself. He was a paradox— a simple man with an uncomplicated life, yet his passion ran so wide, Teralyn could not see across such a span to the other side. The deeper she delved into his soul, the more lost she became. The way it would feel if she could fall off the very world itself into the net of stars, falling and falling and never coming to the boundary of heaven.

"What is all this?" she asked as he drew close.

"Wool. Mum sold nearly everything she'd made at the festival and needs to replenish stock in the shop." He huffed, a bit breathless, and the flush on his cheeks lit up his face. Would she ever stop staring at his beautiful features?

"What?" he asked, giving her a curious smile.

"Nothing. Just drinking you in. My eyes are always so thirsty to drink you in, as if I've been marching for ages across a hot desert and you are the oasis on the horizon, wavering and beckoning to me."

Fromer dropped his load to the grass, then leaned into her and kissed her. Warmth spread from her mouth to her toes. "You," he said, "are a weaver of words. A keeper and protector of language. You spread words in the air like . . . warm butter over bread. I could eat your words."

Teralyn laughed. "I don't think they will fill your stomach!"

"Then I will eat them forever and never become full. When you put words to my melodies, it's as though they had always been there, hovering over my fiddle, waiting to attach themselves, word to note, as a key fits in a lock. You complete me, Teralyn, in every way." He entangled his fingers in the loose hair piled over her shoulders. "I don't know how I ever played a single note without your voice to inspire me."

"And what if I were to lose my voice? What then?"

"Your words would still find a way into my heart. There is a kind of speech more potent than the spoken word. The touch of your hand sings volumes to me, in a language that needs no translating or elaboration."

He bent down and picked up his bundles. "And if we tarry too long, I will hear enough sour words to fill both ears for a week. Mum is particular about supper times."

"Are you sure you should be bringing me to your house? Won't it upset Justyn?" Teralyn recalled Justyn's face, partly hidden in the crowd and hard to make out in the dim light of the hanging lanterns. He had come each night of the festival, loitering at the venues where they performed, hiding in shadow, buried under his hood. She had sensed him there—his presence in the crowd a magnet that pulled at her concentration, summoning her somehow. He exuded waves of emotion but they were impossible to decipher. She'd never meant to anger him, yet somehow she had. And tomorrow he would accompany her back up to the Heights and return her to her home. She hoped whatever upset him could be resolved quickly, but something told her Justyn would not be mollified so easily.

"Fromer, why does he hate you so? And loathe this life here in the village? How is it possible for two brothers to be so different?"

Fromer began walking down the hill toward the cart road, and Teralyn fell in to step alongside him. The balmy, still air hung heavy. "He doesn't hate me, Teralyn. I think he hates himself, in some inexplicable way. He's never fit in here, in the village. I thought once he left for the Heights and pursued his ambitions, he would find peace. But he is ever striving, never satisfied. As if he has an insatiable hunger that never lets him be. He feeds that hunger with a feast of information, piling facts upon facts, stuffing himself with knowledge and memorizing languages he will never utter." Fromer shook his head and Teralyn saw only pity in his face. "He reminds me of a starving man coming upon a banquet, devouring everything in sight yet tasting nothing."

He stopped and turned to study her face in the gathering twilight. "You search for words as if they are treasures, each word a gem to be cherished, to string with other words to make a beautiful necklace of thought. But Justyn—he has words thrust upon him in great numbers, but they pile up in a shapeless heap and hold no intrinsic value. I don't understand the minds of some in the university. I don't understand the pursuit of knowledge for its own sake. It makes no sense to me."

Teralyn thought of her parents and how they would spend long hours—long years—following the trail of some miniscule crumb of information. A fragment of an ancient text that needed to be deciphered, obscure writing on a clay shard to place the date of its shaping. And when the answers came, how excited they would become—as if some earth-shaking information had been revealed. Teralyn never understood their enthusiasm for such discovery. It always seemed that their sense of achievement, bringing their expertise to bear on the challenge of the task, was what mattered. That, and garnering the accolades of their peers and the privilege of publishing their findings in the university journal, giving them a sense of immortality through the knowledge that their names would go down in the annals of Wentwater for future posterity to look upon with awe and reverence.

"You seem bothered," Fromer said. "I hope I didn't say anything to offend you."

"Oh, no. You didn't. I was just thinking about my parents. How like Justyn they are. But they are happy in their work and their life. Maybe they've achieved what they strove for in their earlier years. Maybe once Justyn attains his dreams, he will find peace."

"I do hope so, for his sake. But I fear his restless spirit runs deep. There is something unquenchable about him. He doesn't know how to enjoy life, and for that reason, despite all his learning, I wonder if he's learned anything at all."

Fromer grew quiet, and Teralyn matched the pacing of his boot steps. As they entered the village, the change in ambiance surprised her. The gaiety and energy had drained away, as if the very life of the village had seeped into the earth to slumber. The streets once clogged with festival attendees and merchants now resembled lonely lanes with hardly a sole treading the cobbles. The cottages were warm shelters, windows illuminated by lamplight within, and Teralyn could hear spatters of laughter and talking as they passed one row after another, finally arriving at a trellised gate leading into a simple dirt yard as the last light of evening faded.

Teralyn waited as Fromer unlatched the gate and led her up to the wooden stoop by the front door. He whispered to her. "My mum's quite strict about her traditions. Just do as she says and you'll be fine."

Teralyn opened her mouth to speak, questions forming on her tongue, but the door swung open and she found herself face-to-face with the woman she had bought her scarves from. Teralyn knew her name was Iris but was unsure of the proper way to address her. Fromer spared her by speaking.

"Mum, this is Teralyn. Ter, this is my mum, but just call her Iris. Mum, you might recall—she bought some scarves from you the other day at market."

Teralyn's neck shivered as Iris looked her over with a scrunched face and jutting chin. After a moment she said, "Well, come on in! No sense letting in the bugs, now. Fromer's been gabbing on about you. We have mutton and spring potatoes, and your favorite corncakes, Fro. Made them special for you." She tousled Fromer's hair, and he gave Teralyn a smile.

"You're the best, Mum." Fromer gestured Teralyn in through the door and followed her inside. He stooped to remove his boots and indicated with his eyes for her to do the same. After they shoved their boots under the bench, Teralyn started to follow Fromer into the large living room, but Iris stopped her with her hand.

"Now, lass, Fromer's told me you're from the Heights and don't know our ways. We do things a bit different down here, but we have our reasons, and our ways have served us just fine over the years. So, heed my instructions . . ."

Teralyn heard a cough from across the room. She turned her head and saw Justyn standing in a hallway just off the living room, a smirk on his face. He seemed amused and his expression flustered her. At least he wasn't scowling. She doubted he would make unpleasant remarks while in his parents' home—at least she hoped he wouldn't.

"Now," Iris continued. "You must turn a full circle as you stand by the door. Then, face the door and do this with your hands." Iris brushed her hands from her skirt as if shooing away a dog. "That way your shadow will stay outside, in case it's picked up something untoward. Something that would haunt your dreams. Now, be about it quickly, before the shadow has time to settle in."

Teralyn turned a circle and gestured as she commanded. She looked to Iris to see if she had performed correctly.

Iris smiled in approval. "There! You only need to do it the first time you enter a home. After that, the shadow knows it's not welcome." With a brisk clap of her hands, she yelled out, her loud voice startling Teralyn. "Fen! Supper's on." She chucked Teralyn under the chin. "Why, you're quite a beauty, with those dark brooding eyes. No wonder Fro's taken a liking to you."

Teralyn felt her cheeks flush and muttered thanks. She looked to Fromer, who seemed to beam with pride. Out of the corner of her eye, she noticed Justyn had retreated into the dark hallway, his face hidden in shadow. Fromer still held the ponderous bags of wool in his arms.

"Mum, where do you want these—in the back room or the pantry?"

"Ah, what a fine lad you are! Pantry's fine. I'll get them to soak after we sup. Justyn, help me with the fixings."

"How might I help?" Fromer asked.

A stocky man with a slight limp came from the back room—Teralyn guessed he was Fen. He took her hands in his. "Ah, the lass is here. What lovely hair you have. So white! Iris—have you ever seen such a sight?"

Iris stopped suddenly with a basket of bread balanced in her hand. She narrowed her eyes, and Teralyn sensed Iris's mood shift, the way a breeze could kick up and change course. Justyn moved in silence, setting down bowls of steaming vegetables and a platter of meat on the rough-hewn table. He seemed intent on his mother and wouldn't look at Teralyn.

"Why, I hadn't noticed in this dim light. Yes, a peculiar color, it is. But lovely, quite lovely," she mumbled under her breath.

After a word of thanks from Fen, they set about eating with a lighter humor. Teralyn watched Fromer and copied his manners—which amounted to few. His family reached across the table for whatever they wanted and spoke while they chewed. Fen related some story about a man who had picked up the wrong boots from his shop and brought them back complaining they didn't fit. All the while, another customer wandered about in his stocking feet wondering where his boots had gone to while he'd been trying on new ones. They all erupted in laughter as Teralyn politely chewed her food and smiled—all except Justyn, who kept a serious face as he ate his food with deliberation. He said nothing all through the meal and avoided her eyes.

Before long, the platters and bowls emptied. Iris pushed back her chair, and without a word, Fen ambled into the living room and plopped down in an overstuffed chair.

"Well, I'll leave you two to clear the table and wash up," Iris said. "Can't have a dish left in the sink, you know—will give you a fitful sleep." She winked at Teralyn, who nodded on cue.

After Iris left the room, Justyn brought dishes to the sink, where a tall bucket of water sat nearby on the floor. Iris called toward the kitchen as she stood at the front door, slipping on boots. "I'm off to put the chickens up and check for feathers. Fen, you still planning on choppin' wood tonight? It's a full moon." She cocked her head at Teralyn. "Wood burns hotter if chopped on a full moon. Bright moonlight, bright fire, as they say."

Fen grunted as he filled his pipe by the large hearth. Teralyn wasn't sure if that was a yes or no.

What a different family life Fromer had! At her house, a cook prepared their meals and served them on fine porcelain dishes with a full service of silverware and crystal glasses. No one spoke as they ate; only after the dishes had been cleared would her father ask how her day had gone, and then she'd be expected to rattle off her accomplishments in a list for their approval. After the meal, they'd each retire to their various rooms—usually her mother and father to their study, to read or discuss projects, and Teralyn to her bedroom to play her harp or compose music.

Fromer scrubbed plates and gave them to Teralyn to dip in the large tub. Justyn took them in silence from her, and after drying them, stacked them in the cupboards. She sensed a strained tension between Justyn and the other members of his family and thought how Fromer had said he'd never fit in. Just as she thought of something to say to him, to ease the tension between them, he placed the last plate on the shelf and left the room. Fromer looked at her and shrugged.

"Don't be upset," he said to her in a quiet tone. "He's always like this when he visits. If he's not arguing with Mum. It's often a war of wills around here, but Mum always wins." His smile lifted the concern from her heart, and she leaned over and kissed his cheek.

"I saw that!" Iris bellowed as she stomped in from the yard, her laugh causing her belly to shake up and down. Teralyn felt heat rush to her cheeks and stepped away from Fromer. "Why don't you two lovebirds come help me with the wool?" Iris asked in a teasing tone. "And Fen," she called over, "best you be at that firewood.

Fen grunted and set his pipe down in a bowl, then trudged dutifully to the front door.

Fromer signaled Teralyn to follow them into the pantry, where three giant barrels stood filled to the top with some acrid-smelling liquid. She helped Fromer open the bags and pulled out armloads of soft wool. He and Iris pulled at the piles and separated the lumps. When satisfied, she dumped an avalanche of wool into the vats for soaking, then poked the soggy masses with a huge wooden paddle until they were saturated through.

"This'll get the lanolin out, the oily coating that keeps the goats dry in the rain. But it makes it resistant to dyeing, so has to soak for most of a week in this solution, it does."

She put round wooden lids over the tubs and turned to Teralyn. "You've never done this before, have you?"

Teralyn stammered under Iris's gaze. "I know nothing about wool and weaving and knitting. Fromer's told me a bit about it."

"Heavens, lass! Don't they teach you anything practical up in those rock houses? What about stitching? You know your stitching, don't you?" When Teralyn shook her head, Iris's face turned pink with agitation. "Never stitched? What do you do when you lose a button—when your hem comes undone?"

Teralyn shrugged and felt as small as a worm under her stare. "We send out our things when they need to be repaired. I . . . I never thought to ask how they are done . . ."

Iris grabbed Teralyn's arm and nearly dragged her into the living room. She reached into a basket propped against a large stuffed chair and pulled out a piece of fabric. She held it close for Teralyn to see. The fabric was stretched tightly and held in place by a wooden ring, and an inked sketch partly stitched in thread displayed a pastoral scene of sheep on a hillside. The stitches were so tiny, Teralyn could barely make out one from another.

"This is beautiful," Teralyn said. "Did you design this?"

Iris beamed as she picked up a spool of thread and a tiny silver stick. "I stitch scenes of Wentwater, make them into pillow coverings—such as this one here." She picked up a large round pillow adorned with threads in rich colors of indigo and burgundy, depicting apple blossoms on a branch. Teralyn was fascinated by the variety of stitches used to make up such a complex pattern of color and shading.

"Now I see where Fromer gets his artistic talent from! But just how do you get the thread to fill inside your design?"

Iris tossed the pillow back to the chair and threw up her hands. Teralyn was beginning to think that was Iris's favorite gesture. "Heavens, lass! Have a seat. About time someone taught you your stitching. Here, first you need to run the thread through the needle's eye . . ."

Teralyn felt she was all thumbs as Iris patiently showed her how to manipulate the needle and work it through the fabric in various types of stitches. Fromer excused himself to go outside to help Fen chop wood. Teralyn lost track of the time she spent sitting and stitching under Iris's critical gaze, the woman gently correcting her when she made a mistake and showing her how to tie knots and rethread.

As she stitched, the rhythm of the axe breaking wood provided a backdrop to her work. A warm fire radiated heat into the cluttered room as the evening settled around her like a contented cat. In no time at all, Teralyn fell into her own rhythm of poking the needle through the cloth and creating tiny stitches that formed lines and eventually filled in the scene inked on the fabric. She found the repetitive action of her wrist and the way the thread left color in its wake mesmerizing and relaxing. Minutes stretched into hours. The once-roaring fire in the hearth now crackled with glowing embers. Iris straightened from her hunched position and moaned. "Ah, lass, you've caught on quick-like. But the hour's late for an old woman such as myself. Pr'haps Fromer should take you back to the inn. I imagine Justyn will be comin' round for you at daybreak—to head back to the Heights."

Teralyn noticed a tone of disdain in her voice as she uttered the last word. She set down the stitching and noticed her back, too, was stiff from concentrating these many hours. As if on cue, she heard feet stomping on the front porch and the front door blew open, letting in a crisp blast of night air.

"Wood's chopped and stacked. And the moon is as full as she can be," Fen said while removing his wool cap. Fromer stood by the door while his father fell back onto the bench and unlaced his boots. Teralyn took in Fromer's shaggy hair and flushed face, sweat glistening on his forehead. Her heart quickened at the sight of him.

"Ready to head back to the inn?" he asked her.

She nodded and turned to Iris, who loaded up logs in the hearth, spurring the wood into a new blaze of fire and warmth. "Thank you, for teaching me. Where can I get these things—the needle and frame, and fabric like this . . ."

Iris stuffed the stitching into the bulging cloth sack and handed it to Teralyn. "Here—there's plenty of threads, extra needles, and a thimble. You keep this piece—you've done most of the work as it is. Will make a lovely pillow you can stuff with wool or goose down."

"Oh, I couldn't—"

Iris pressed the sack into Teralyn's arms. "Don't be silly, lass. Got plenty more around here. And it'd be good for you to practice. When you come back down, next visit, we'll get you on the loom—and show you how to spin."

"Oh, I'd love that! Thank you so much." She found herself engulfed in a hug, with large arms wrapped around her and squeezing the breath from her chest.

"Well, lass, you're like the daughter I wished I'd had! It pleases me to teach you."

Teralyn blushed and went to Fromer, who held her coat out to her. As she put it on and reached for her boots, Iris cleared her throat. Teralyn looked at Iris as she asked, "You say you've lived in the Heights all your life? Born and raised there?"

Teralyn wondered at her question. "Yes, my parents have lived there for over thirty years. They are researchers at the university. I've been down to the village only a handful of times in my life. But I plan to come down more often from now on."

"Ah . . . well, Fro will come and fetch you if you don't, no doubt!" Iris smiled, but Teralyn sensed some hesitancy. Why had she asked those questions? Fromer had told her the villagers didn't think well of those from the Heights, but Iris had shown her gracious hospitality, had not been all that offended by her ignorance of village ways. Yet, as Teralyn walked with Fromer out to the street under a bulging luminous moon, she knew there was something troubling Iris.

Maybe Fromer could explain why his mother had looked at her in such an odd manner as they left the cottage.

EIGHT

JUSTYN NEATLY folded his clothes and set them in his pack. He laid out his last set of clean trousers and a long-sleeved woolen shirt for his trip back home, almost longing for the biting cold of the Heights to cool off his mood. He couldn't wait to wash his dirty clothes, to get the smell of the festival—all the cooking aromas and dirt and grime—off his things. As well as the smells of his home—the sour stench of the wool bathwater and the stuffy, sickly-sweet pipe tobacco his father smoked. Whenever he visited the village and his parents, he felt he had to strip everything off and scrub clean, but something always lingered, some stain or contamination he could never remove. He had been trying for over ten years now to be rid of the village, but it was as if his very blood was tainted with its poison. He wondered how much longer he could tolerate it.

His mind drifted to Teralyn's face, but he swatted the vision of her away with bitter force. If he could rip her image from his mind, he would do so, regardless of the pain. He tightened the straps on his pack and paced the small bedroom. The room felt like a cage. If he hadn't promised Antius to return Teralyn safely home, he would leave that very moment. Here he was, in his childhood bedroom still littered with his early primers and picture books—his mother refused to throw out anything of his, no doubt wishing she could turn him back into the obedient, pliant little boy he had once been. He took in the lumpy mattress, the frilly eyelet curtains, the ratty braided rug and gritted his teeth. Fromer, on the other hand, was probably laughing with Teralyn in the sitting room of her inn. Sipping tea by the fire, leaning into her, caressing her hand, talking about meaningless, empty things—like music and goats. How he wished he could smash Fromer's face with his fist.

Justyn stopped pacing and threw open his bedroom door. He needed fresh air. Even though it was frowned upon to wander about after the moon began to set, he knew the only thing that would clear his head would be a walk—a very long walk without walls closing in on him. Away from his parents' smug disapproving stares, away from the villagers' dimwitted superstitions and criticisms.

He started down the hall but stopped when he heard his mother mention Teralyn's name in a hushed voice. He hung back out of sight and listened as she spoke to his father in a strange tone that riveted his attention.

"She says she's been in the Heights her whole life, Iris. So, there you have it." His father's voice sounded weary and resistant.

"But that hair! No one in Wentwater has that hair. You remember that baby-naming. How I told you the babe's predictions—a voice like a bird, and hair as white as the moon. And I've done some figuring—"

"—You're always figuring, Iris. Let it rest."

"—and that lass looks to be about the right age. T'was seventeen years since that witch showed her face—and nary a one's seen her since."

Justyn heard his father sigh. "So what, Iris? Good riddance and all that. Are you fixing to search out that marsh witch and ask her? You told me that day they burned down those poor folks' cottage—that they left the baby to burn alive."

Justyn peeked a bit around the corner and saw his parents lounging by the fire, staring into the flames. His mind jerked to that day—the day the women of the village, in their runaway panic, had burned down that home. He recalled how his own anger had smoldered as the snow fell about him. How on that day he vowed to find a way to leave his village—no matter how many years it would take. How he had stood there, watching the house ignite, picturing the crying baby in her cradle, fire licking at wood and hair and skin . . .

Justyn felt bile rise in his throat and his stomach lurched. How could anyone in their right mind commit such a heinous crime? Yet, his mother had taken him to school, acting for all the world as if it had been just another ordinary day in the village of Wentwater. Traditions had to be abided by, she'd told him with a sharp tone. Questioning set your feet on dangerous ground. Just put it out of your mind, she said, then pursed her lips and marched on. Justyn remembered looking behind him and noticing how the snow covered their footsteps, erasing where they had been. In the same way the villagers used tradition to cover their culpability. Yet, over the soft, white, pure layer of snow, a fallout of grimy black ash tainted the countryside. Even the heavens would not be silenced, a witness to their crime.

His mother's sharp tone grabbed his attention. "When they sifted through the chars, no body was found. Fen, they would've found something, don't you think? There're those that said the witch'd come back around and stole off with the babe. There had to be a reason she came to town that day."

"Well, you'd said it was to warn. That the babe would cause Wentwater's destruction. The undoing of the village and all that rot."

"But she saw it! Ursell saw it with her glass eye!"

Fen jumped to his feet. "For heaven's sake, Iris, listen to ya! Believing witch's tales and wicked predictions. Don't we have enough on our plates as it is with all the rules and traditions to follow? You have to heap on more with a curse an old witch uttered—"

"T'wasn't a curse—was a vision. She *saw* what was to come."

"The parents were banished and the babe done away with. End of story. No one saw the babe after that, did they? But you think this lass here tonight somehow is that babe? That although she was born and raised in the Heights, she's one and the same? What—did the babe crawl out of a burning cottage and make her way into some other woman's womb to be born? Get a grip on yer addled mind, woman!"

Iris huffed and stomped into the kitchen. She pursed her lips in thought, then said in a fierce whisper, "It's said Ursell predicted the Great Flood and no one listened to her. What if she's right in predicting the end of Wentwater—and somehow that babe survived. What if Fromer's lass isn't telling the truth? Have you considered that?"

"Iris," Fen said, heading toward the hallway. "You'll believe as you will. The Great Flood was three hundred years ago. If you think the marsh witch was alive back then, you're surely off your rocker. You've been listening to too many old widows' tales. And if her predictions do come true, then there's naught to be done for it, right? Worrying won't make it go away. Enough! I'm tired and off to bed. I'll hear no more of this foolish talk."

Justyn slipped back into his room and shut the door as his father tromped past him down the hallway. He shook his head at his mother's words. She was so entrenched in her ways, eager to believe any and every silly thing told to her. Teralyn did have unusual hair, but no doubt she inherited that color from someone in her family. Maybe one of her ancestors had come from the cities of the northern plains. His ignorant parents had probably never heard of those lands, but Justyn, through his studies, had read the translations of the tribal journals of the Akarak. Those northern people had pale skin and hair from spending much of their lives in caverns under the earth, seeking refuge from the glacial snows that fell most of the year. They inhabited a land where the sun shone only three months out of twelve, a faraway land of twilight and darkness. This was why knowledge was so invaluable! It dispelled unfounded superstitions and exposed falsehoods. With knowledge one could explain anything puzzling—given time.

Justyn fumed and stared at the steadily burning oil lamp that threw light into all corners of the room, illuminating details of things that would lie in darkness were it not for the lamp. What a perfect symbol of knowledge. Light that exposed and delineated truth. Maybe this would be a way to convince his mother that his course of life had value and importance. If he could but shatter her foolish beliefs, prove to her the predictions she feared were just the babblings of an addled old woman. Marsh witch! As if someone could really see the future with a glass eye!

Justyn's head churned with ideas. What if he could find this witch and expose her for the fraud she was? The villagers feared the marshes—thought they would be swallowed up by restless spirits if they ventured through them. What hogwash! And what if he could provide proof of Teralyn's birth and ancestry? Maybe her parents could enlighten him about Teralyn's heritage. As researchers, no doubt they could trace back their own family lineage over numerous generations. He could show all his findings to his mother and prove to her, once and for all, that knowledge was the most worthwhile pursuit in life.

And then maybe she'd stop belittling him.

Teralyn breathed a sigh of relief as she approached the front door to her home. Justyn's tiresome tirade about the villagers and their superstitious ways would now have to end—unless he planned to drag his argument over the threshold like some dog hanging tenaciously to an old bone. She smirked as she stopped at the stone archway framing the flagstone stoop. Justyn *was* a bit like a stubborn dog—tearing at pieces of her arguments and chewing them up, his voice almost a growl as he ranted and criticized her. What had she done to deserve such reproach? At first she thought he was jealous of her affections toward Fromer, but as they talked heatedly all the way up the cart road to the Heights, something else had seemed to be pestering him. Perhaps he was taking his guardianship a bit too seriously, for he clearly feared Antius would disapprove of her enthusiasm for the festival. As if she might pack her belongings and run off with the traveling minstrels—and then blame Justyn for her madness.

She turned and spoke in as polite a voice as she could rally. "Thank you, Justyn, for taking the time to escort me home. I'm sorry if I . . . caused you any aggravation." She pulled her coat collar up around her neck. Now that they'd stopped walking, the damp chill of the late afternoon made inroads down her neck and shoulders. Already she missed the humid, balmy clime of the low-lands. And her heart ached for Fromer—to look upon his joyful face and feel his arms around her. The cold temperature of the Heights and icy, constant wind only mirrored the stark emptiness she had felt in her soul ever since she'd said good-bye to the man she loved with all her heart.

"Teralyn, you don't aggravate me . . ." Justyn's words trailed and Teralyn studied his expression. Instead of the fury she had noted only moments before, he seemed pained. "Just . . . I don't see what you find attractive about that way of life. For someone who's lived with the privileges you've had—"

"And I don't spurn any of them. I *do* value my education and training. I know there is merit in acquiring wisdom and gaining understanding. But you of all people should know the precepts of discernment—the ability to process knowledge and use wisdom to weigh decisions, and to help form a view of the world that makes sense and guides one sensibly. Yes, I've heard this all my life. And it's that very training that's helped me see the need for more than a cursory education—"

"Cursory? Nowhere in the world can be found the wealth of knowledge that is taught in the Heights! Ours is no superficial, superfluous study. Men and women, like your parents, research for the greater good. Armed with knowledge like this, the world's problems can be solved. Knowledge gives you insight to study a problem from all angles, availing you the best course of action. It provides everything you need in life."

"Not everything." Teralyn sighed and set her pack down on the porch. The droning of the waterfalls enhanced the lassitude assailing her. Her parents wouldn't be home for two hours and a nap would be wonderful. Wrapping up in a thick down-filled comforter with a hot cup of tea in hand would be the perfect thing.

Although she knew she should be polite and invite Justyn in, she'd had enough of his company. Clearly, they weren't going to come to any agreement on this topic anytime soon. Justyn just could not see past his indoctrination to appreciate the value of a spontaneous and joyful approach to life. Maybe in some ways he was right—the villagers were steeped in traditions and rituals that seemed a waste of time and served no practical purpose. But it formed and defined their lives and who they were. And it provided order. What was the harm in that? If their punishments for straying were strict, they no doubt could be matched by the jurisprudence of the Heights. Punishment was meted out upon those who broke laws in her community just as was done in the village. A different sets of laws and repercussions, perhaps, but judgment all the same. Those who overstepped in the Heights were often banished and suffered penalties and disgrace. How was that any different from Wentwater?

"I would invite you in, but I'm awfully tired from our hike—"

He lifted a hand in protest. "I need to get back to my studies. I've been remiss this week and allowed distractions to divert my attentions. I'm guest lecturing a class at noon tomorrow and I haven't prepared. So . . . I'll be on my way then. Good-bye, Teralyn."

The word *good-bye* had hardly formed in her mouth when Justyn spun on his heel and marched off down the granite pathway toward the pass. She watched vacantly as he purposefully strode away, looking to the towering peaks and setting his face toward his dorm and the piles of books awaiting his perusal. She thought of his earlier words, when he had stopped in the road and turned her to face him. How he begged her to forget Fromer, to reject the lure of the village and the temptation of a reckless way of life. He had urged her to stay in the Heights and dismiss the week at the festival. His frantic tone had turned vicious, leaving her nodding her head in compliance, if only to calm him for the moment. Who did he think he was to demand such things? Just what was his problem?

Teralyn sighed as she opened her front door and let the warmth from the blazing fire in the hearth melt away her irritation. She had promised Fromer she would come down to the village at week's end. His tender smile and loving eyes came rushing into her thoughts, and her heartbeat quickened. She had every intention of keeping her word—and felt under no obligation to inform Justyn of her plans.

Justyn knocked on Antius's door with three loud raps. As much as the old man denied it, Justyn knew his hearing was not as sharp as it had once been. But instead of his mentor's raspy voice, a woman called from a back room.

"Coming, coming!"

The door opened to reveal a charwoman who dangled a grimy rag from one hand as she craned her neck to study his face. She'd apparently been cleaning the heavy stove; streaks of charcoal marred her cheeks. "You be one of his students, now?" she asked in a huff.

"I apologize for disturbing you, ma'am. Is Antius home?" Justyn recognized her; she cleaned many of the homes in the Heights, and he'd seen her mopping the hallways of his dormitory on occasion. He guessed she'd been working in the Heights since long before he'd been born. Her knuckles were knotted and bony, perhaps from all the years of scrubbing she'd done.

She pushed a stray gray strand of hair from her wrinkled face. "Nah, sir. Up in the lecture hall, putting a presentation together, he says. Would you be wantin' to leave him a note?"

"No, I'm headed that way; I'll find him. Thank you, ma'am . . ." Justyn turned to leave, then stopped. An idea formed in his mind. Before she closed the door, he added, "Excuse me . . . I, uh, have seen you around the Heights. If you don't mind my asking—how many years have you worked up here?"

The charwoman scrunched her eyebrows at the question, her look expressing inquisitiveness rather than suspicion. "Been going on these forty-odd years now, sir. Haven't missed a week. The Heights is practically my home. I see all the comin's and goin's—watch the students grow up and graduate, leave and start families. Nothing 'scapes my eye, sir." She lowered her voice and leaned in closer. "I see questions in your face. What you be wantin' to know?" Her look turned hungry, the way his mother's did when she was chewing over a juicy bit of gossip.

He swallowed his annoyance and self-reproach. He was collecting information, after all. Nothing indecorous about that. "Are you familiar with Rufus and Kileen—the researchers who live on second level?"

The woman nodded. "I be. Used to be their cleaning woman, back when they first got the babe. But, the woman's a bit particular, and after a time t'was her watching over me shoulder and such. Don't fancy that. Makes it hard to work with breath down your neck, if you get my meaning, sir."

Justyn's breath caught. "You said 'back when they first got the babe.' You mean when Kileen gave birth, no?"

"No, sir. Meant what I said. The woman never gave birth to that babe. Tried for years they did, a world of disappointment over it."

"Over what?"

"Not being able to bear. The good Lord never blessed them with children."

The woman pursed her lips together. Justyn waited for further explanation but none was forthcoming. He lowered his voice to match hers. "Then, where did they get the babe?"

Her eyes darted around and she closed the door, allowing only a crack wide enough to whisper through. "I've said too much. If you've a need to know more, ask Antius."

"Antius?" Justyn put his foot in the door as the woman attempted to shut him out. Now her eyes read fear. "Why Antius?"

"Well, he's the one brought them the babe, all them years back. Ask him—I can't be held for the telling."

"I understand. I won't mention our conversation. You can rest easy, good woman." Justyn extricated his imposing foot and stepped back.

A sigh of relief escaped her lips as she shut the door with a heavy click. Justyn stood on the stoop, his thoughts rolling one over another as his nerves tingled. His mother's words swirled in his head in a warning tone that sent a surge of unease through his gut. Justyn pondered the old teacher's affection for his young gardener. The kind of affection a father would bestow upon a daughter. Or, perhaps, a goddaughter.

Well then, Antius would know the truth about Teralyn. He would just have to seek out Antius and ask him about her. Somehow, he was certain his mentor held the key to this mystery—this strange young woman who had a puzzling connection to the lake.

Whether Antius would reveal what he knew was, however, another matter.

NINE

ALL WEEK LONG, music had lapped against Teralyn's mind. Lines of lyrics, threads of melodies—like small waves rushing up a shore, constant and relentless—vied for her attention. She had written more songs and poems in the last week than ever in recent years. She felt blessed that Fromer's passions had infused her, and her passion for him responded in kind. She strummed her harp, which lay across her lap, trying different fingerings and altering a note or two until she found the perfect chord.

"Tera, dear, I do love this scarf!"

Teralyn lifted her eyes from her harp as her mother breezed through the front door. Kileen unwrapped the burgundy scarf from her neck in the warmth of the house and set it on the hutch by the door.

"I'm so glad you like it. I wasn't sure if the color would suit you, but it does."

Kileen bent to plant a kiss somewhere in the vicinity of her daughter's cheek. Teralyn sat with her knees tucked under her on the living room divan, still in her nightgown. She hadn't bothered to dress—it being Sunday with an unappealing chill lingering into late morning. She planned on working in the greenhouse later— once she put the final chorus together for this song she was writing for Fromer.

"How is your songwriting going? Have you thought about scheduling a small performance—say, in Mercer Auditorium?"

"Oh, mother. This really isn't the kind of music anyone in the Heights would want to hear—"

"Don't be silly, Tera! You've a beautiful voice. Audiences love your pieces. I could talk to the administrator and have her put you on the schedule."

Teralyn set down her harp. "Mother, please. I-I don't want to perform. Not up here . . ."

"Then where?" She narrowed her eyes and studied her daughter. "You've been so withdrawn all week, not socializing at all. And that very nice boy who took you to the festival came by to talk with me and said—"

"Justyn? When?"

"Why, yesterday. He came to my office and we chatted. Teralyn, he's a wonderful boy—studious, ambitious . . . brilliant, really. And he seems awfully fond of you." Kileen waltzed into the dining room and began rearranging a huge bouquet of buttery daffodils that arched from a crystal vase on the polished table.

"He does?"

"So, I'm concerned. You need to get out of the house more—"

"I do get out."

"And not just to make your gardening rounds. You're of an age to marry. And Justyn's the perfect—"

"Mother!" Teralyn startled at the harshness of her own voice. Killen's hands dropped from the flowers. "I'm not interested in Justyn. He's too . . . stuffy and doesn't care for my music. The man I marry would need to love music the way I do, need to understand how important it is to me."

Kileen laughed and waved a hand in the air. "Tera, darling. I know you feel that way now. But those feelings will pass. You bury yourself in your music because you are shy and don't want to socialize. You use it as a curtain to hide behind. In time, that passion will fade, and more important things will consume you—things like a career, a husband, and having children. You can't expect suitors to line up at your door if you don't let them know you are interested."

Teralyn sighed. Before she could think of something to say in refutation, her mother whisked down the hall to her bedroom. Moments later, Kileen emerged with books in her arms. She took them to the hutch, where she slipped them into her large canvas shoulder bag.

"Where are you going?" Teralyn asked.

"Back to the library. I've come across an intriguing puzzle pertaining to the scrolls of *Shamma*. I think I told you about that lost city in the hills of Antolae. And Anthanus is meeting with me. He has some knowledge of the history of that region. If you need me, you'll find us upstairs in the history section. But don't wait up, dear. I'm sure to be home late. And your father is prepping the debate team. You can manage your own dinner, can't you?"

"Of course, Mother. Oh—I completely forgot! There's something I want to show you!"

Kileen waited by the door while Teralyn rushed to her room and brought back the bulging cloth sack Iris had given her. She ran up to her mother and pulled out the stitching she'd been working on.

"I've almost finished this first piece. It's taken many hours and my eyes get tired while making such small—"

Teralyn jerked as her mother grasped her wrist with a cold surge of anger in her eyes. "Where did you get this?" Kileen's tone was accusatory.

Teralyn stammered at her mother's sudden harshness. "Why . . . from a woman in the village. She's a weaver—the one who made your scarf."

"Why would she give this to you?"

"Well . . . she's Justyn's mother. I was invited over for Sunday dinner and she—"

Teralyn's words were slapped away as her mother grabbed the stitching and sack from her hands.

"I *knew* it was a mistake to let you go to the festival! But Antius insisted. Felt it would be good for you to study the music of the village, to broaden your horizons. Well, I plan to have some words with him!"

Teralyn stared in confusion as her mother stuffed the cloth sack into her canvas tote alongside the books.

"I don't want to *ever* see a needle or thread in your hands again—do you hear me?"

All Teralyn could do was nod as her mother turned on the heels of her sharp reprimand and marched into the cold, damp morning, slamming the door behind her.

"Where are you going in such a hurry?"

Teralyn lifted her head just in time to avoid colliding with Justyn—the last person she wanted to see. She took a quick look around the massive reading room at the students sprawled on couches with books on their laps or hunched over low tables with papers spread before them. Justyn's voice, hardly more than a whisper, seemed to reverberate off the walls. A few students raised their heads, but dropped them after a curious glance in her direction.

She allowed herself a brief look into Justyn's eyes and saw a fire burning behind his pupils. His simmering anger spilled out in his gaze. Before she could utter a word, he took her arm, his fingers hot to the touch even through the thickness of her sweater.

"Follow me. I need a word with you," he said, leading her through the room's double doors into the glass-covered atrium.

"Where are you taking me?"

Justyn huffed. "To a quiet place where we can talk without curious stares."

"But, I'm on my way to find Antius. I have no time—"

"And that's why you're carrying your coat and an overnight bag? What—you plan to camp at his office for a few days?"

Teralyn's face flamed with heat at his words. What in heaven was wrong with him? First her mother, now Justyn. Everyone was acting so strangely.

She resisted his pull on her sleeve. "Please, I have no time for this."

He yanked her to a corner behind a perfectly trimmed box-wood hedge, out of sight from others. In a low, harsh voice he said, "Don't try to fool me, Teralyn. I know you're going to the village. To see *him*. Don't you know how upset that will make your mother?"

"How do you know what my mother will think? And just what were you doing visiting her in her office? She told me you'd paid her a visit. What was that all about?"

"I warned you to leave Fromer and that world behind. You'll only cause your parents grief. And Antius too. Your life is *here*, in the Heights. Can't you get that through your thick head?"

"Even if it were true, it is not your place to tell me how to live my life. Who made you my protector and guardian? Just because Antius asked you to escort me to the festival, it doesn't mean you can now direct my every step. I'm nearly eighteen. I can make my own decisions!"

Teralyn searched his face but found nothing written there to explain his brash behavior. "You told my mother about Fromer, didn't you? And no doubt upset her." Her eyes widened as she recalled the way her mother spoke of Justyn, as if she carried a little secret. How she had gone on about him and marriage . . . as if she knew something . . .

Her jaw dropped in understanding. Justyn might do whatever it took to control her. To make sure she didn't return to Wentwater. He thought her actions would somehow jeopardize his standing in the university—although his reasoning was lost on her. Well, she'd had enough of his insufferable meddling.

She reached out to push Justyn away so she could go find Antius, but he grabbed hold of her outstretched arms, and, to her shock, pulled her into his chest and pressed his lips against hers. Strong, trembling arms enfolded her—arms she batted at and wriggled free from. Before he could seize her again, she slapped his cheek hard.

"How dare you?" Her breath came in spurts as she spit out more words. "Have you lost your mind, Justyn?"

A dazed look came over his features, and he faltered as he took a step back on the gravelly pathway. "I-I . . . Oh, Teralyn, I didn't mean to . . ."

He reached out to her, this time in a compunctious manner, but she ignored his arms and instead scowled in his face.

"You have some nerve. I don't know what game you are playing, but this has to stop." She turned and pointed back to the reading room. "There are a dozen smart, ambitious women in there who would no doubt love to be wooed by you. But I'm *not* one of them!"

"But, Teralyn, I love you . . ." The words seemed to come out of their own accord, as if Justyn regretted them the moment they tumbled from his mouth.

"Oh, please! You just can't stand to see Fromer in love. This has nothing to do with me. I'm just a conquest—something to parade around in victory. You will not be able to steal my heart or wrest my hand from his. And I resent you manipulating my mother—"

"Mother?" Justyn laughed, and the sound grated on Teralyn's ears. He leaned his reddened and sweaty face close to hers, mockery in his expression. "Kileen's not your mother."

Teralyn sucked in her breath. "What on earth are you talking about? Of course she's my mother."

Justyn stood there, inches from her, smug and condescending. "If you don't believe me, ask Antius. Perhaps he'll tell you the truth of your parentage." He grunted and pushed her off balance as he strode past her in a fury. "*If* he's brave enough."

Teralyn stood, agape, watching Justyn storm into the building and disappear in the throng of students. She looked down at her shaking hands and tried to calm her breath. Her lips hurt from where Justyn's rough kiss had bruised them. She adjusted her bag on her shoulder and smoothed out her sweater. She had to get away—away from Justyn's obsession and her mother's pestering. And no doubt, if she confided in Antius, he'd lecture her. As much as she loved the old teacher, she couldn't bear to hear his words of chastisement—or the supposed truth Justyn claimed he was concealing. She would seek him out later.

Right now, what she needed most was comfort. Comfort and love. Not obsessive love, not parental love, and not even the love of a mentor and friend. She needed love that came from a heart free of judgment and expectations. A love that would liberate and not imprison. She needed Fromer.

Justyn watched from behind the shelves of books, waiting for Teralyn to pass. As she hurried down the narrow hallway, he hung his head and pulled a hat low over his eyes, then fell in to step yards behind her. At first he thought she was heading to Antius's office, but then she turned toward the entrance doors and made her way to the oval.

A spattering of rain barraged him as he pulled his cloak tighter and dropped back a few steps so she wouldn't see him. His anger now smoldered like the dying embers in a hearth upon morning's arrival. Yet even embers in their last gasp could be painfully hot to the touch and leave a noticeable scar.

It was clear now that Teralyn was leaving the Heights and heading down to the village—to throw herself into Fromer's arms. And Justyn doubted that either Antius or her parents knew of her hasty departure. However, they would just have to wonder where she had gone without a word, for he had no time to inform them.

He had a marsh witch to visit.

• PART TWO •

"It is written in the Great Book that God, in the beginning, spoke, 'and it came to be so.' Allowing that God spoke the world into existence, it follows that the word precedes the desired result. However, it will always be noted in the ages to come that the pivotal historical moment in the history of Wentwater proved the converse to be true. Not only did the functional world vanish from existence due to the loss of a word, but now it can be said, for all intents and purposes, that 'in the *end* was the word.' . . . The ancient proverb that states 'my people are destroyed for lack of knowledge' is more literally translated from the *law'az* to read: 'for lack of a good word.' Hence, it is the *absence* of a word that wreaks destruction, as some words are critical to the survival and prosperity of society. And that is a sobering thought for any who carelessly cast aside words as of no account."

From Volume I of *The Annals of Wentwater*; Section III: "The Rituals and Superstitions of Wentwater Village"

*—Professor Antius, regent and historian
of the Antiquities Board*

TEN

WIND HOWLED and moaned like a starving wolf keening in the northern hinterlands. Antius stoked the fire, then sat back to listen. Over the years he'd found he could discern between the layers of wind ricocheting off the steep rock walls of the Heights. Sometimes the strands sang in strained four-part dissonance, but this night—one exceptionally dark and gloomy—the wind carried portent. Antius was not one to heed such sensibilities, yet there was no denying he had felt similarly the night the stranger had visited him with a bundle in her arms those many years ago. The villagers would call it prescience, and even some respected researchers in the Heights who touted the science of intuition might give credence to his feelings. But how could anyone make a determination on a topic that rested solely on emotion and a vague sensation of unrest? There was no logic in that.

Yet as he wrapped up in his thick blanket and propped his stockinged feet on the stool before the stove, dread rattled his old bones. Antimony perched on the high back of the stuffed chair, nuzzling close to Antius for warmth. The owl's restless pacing, back and forth across Antius's shoulders all evening, had set him even more on edge. Did Antimony sense something too?

Antius picked up the sock with the darning needle poked through it and perched his spectacles on his nose. Leaning close to his oil lamp, he pulled the needle through the wool while his mind wandered the dust-choked roads of the past. He liked the simple exercise of darning his own socks, although others thought it an odd thing for him to do. On nights like these, he sometimes allowed memories of Audra to swell in his heart until the pain burst it anew. But tonight he couldn't bear to revisit the years they had spent together—joy-filled years of quiet companionship and affection. With resolve, he bent down over his task and stitched closed the gaping hole in the heel. As he labored, he was struck by the symbolism of a futile attempt to close up a hole with such flimsy thread and on such an old sock that was ready for the trash heap. Perhaps it was time to discard memories that only pained him and were unmendable.

Antius stopped midstitch. He sifted through the sounds of wind and found another one emerging—bootsteps pounding granite. Before he realized the steps were heading toward his home, the door blew open and a hunched-over shape tripped and fell in a heap on his entry rug. Antimony hooted in fright and flew to the back room. At first Antius thought a bear had crashed through his doorway. The creature had leaf-ridden fur and emitted a feral woodsy stench that saturated his small sitting room and made Antius's eyes sting. Yet the groan was not only human but carried a familiar tone that sent a stab through his heart.

Antius stifled a gasp and rose from his armchair. He turned up the wick in the lamp, widening the circle of illumination, and carried it with caution, keeping a safe distance, torn between hope and dismay. But there was no mistaking his son in the mosaic of flickering light. Bedraggled, filthy, hair as wild as weeds, clothing torn and shredded—somewhere under it all was Ambel.

Antius rested a tentative hand on his son's shoulder and realized the poor boy was shaking uncontrollably and whimpering. How long had he been stumbling about in the biting wind? He set down the lamp and brought over his thick blanket. As he wrapped

Ambel up like a holiday package, he sought to make out his face, but Ambel kept it hidden under his bleeding hands.

"You're hurt! Whatever has happened to you, lad? Let me get you some hot tea and a warm, wet cloth to wash with."

"Father . . . please . . . something to eat . . ." Ambel's words rode on short bursts of breath.

"Of course!" Antius shook his head. Emotions rattled against one another—relief, fear, confusion, worry. What terrible misfortune had his son stumbled upon? He tamped down the anger that had so readily bared its teeth all these months. This was no time for outrage and lectures. Ambel needed tending and comfort. Antius's questions could wait.

He rushed to the pantry and brought out a loaf of bread, a brick of aged cheese, a sausage, and a flask of wine. Before he could set the provisions down on the rug, Ambel snatched at the cheese with one hand and the flask with the other. In silent horror, Antius watched his son devour the food as would a ravenous beast. Ambel gulped the wine in large noisy swallows; more of it dribbled down his unruly beard than made it into his mouth. While Ambel ate, Antius took the large kettle of heated water that sat on the edge of the woodstove and poured it into a basin, then dunked a towel into the steaming water and hauled it carefully to where Ambel sat licking his lips and fingers. Antius frowned in disgust. Had living in the wild all these months turned his son feral?

"Here, let me clean your hands. They are all cut up!" He reached to lift Ambel's chin, to wipe grime from his cheeks and forehead. It was then that Antius noted something odd about his son's eyes. Antius's voice dropped as if it were weighted down in his chest. Each word took effort to bring out of his throat. "Ambel . . . look at me."

Ambel turned his face in the direction of his father, but his vacant eyes looked past him, if they could even see at all. The pupils were covered with a cloudy gauze that kept Antius out. Somewhere trapped behind that barrier was his son, and Antius feared him lost beyond rescue.

"What . . . what happened to you, lad?" Antius's heart wrenched as he stared at Ambel's face. Not just his eyes but his entire visage seemed distant, as if his son had left his soul in some distant land to wander aimlessly. He finished cleaning Ambel's face, breathing in shallowly so as not to gag at the stench.

Ambel tipped his head in exhaustion. "It's a long story, Father. Days have merged into weeks. I know not what month it is—but I smelled spring in the lowlands."

"You have been gone nearly six months! And what of your companions—have they returned to the village . . . in the same predicament as you?"

Ambel groaned and dropped his head into his hands. Antius stroked his son's hair, smoothing the tangled mess as best as he could and hoping his gestures would find their way into Ambel's heart.

"I know not of their fate. We were parted ages ago—in an unnamed wood not far from the kingdom of Sherbourne." He lifted his head in a sudden burst of animation. "I saw her, Father!" He scrunched his face and anger filled his voice. "That king took my feather! And he plans to capture her and keep her for his own. He threw me into his dungeon!"

Antius pulled back. "What king? The king of Sherbourne?"

"But his daughter showed me kindness and released me. I escaped, depending upon the kindness of strangers to feed me and point me home." Ambel struggled to get to his feet. "I cannot stay. I must find her before the king does!"

"Find who? The king's daughter?"

"No! Haven't you been listening? The firebird! It is she who beckons me. I must be off—"

Antius grabbed his son's arm with force. "You fool—look at the state you are in! You barely made it home alive from this insane quest. And you are stricken with madness! I'll not allow you to wander after this apparition, this myth—"

"She is no myth or superstition, as you claim! I saw her. It was her brilliance that did this to me! She blinded me with her beauty. Now she is all I see, everywhere I turn; she even haunts my dreams. Cast aside your confounded logic and practicality and open your own eyes! There is magic in the world, and by denying it, you become the fool! I am tired of your lectures." Ambel fell back down in weariness and released a long, frustrated sigh. "Father, someday you will see how your own wisdom blinds you. When you deny the existence of what is magical, you deny a part of the world that wields power—power beyond what your books and learning can offer. And if you do not acknowledge that power, it will be your ruin! Just as in the days of the Great Flood. The villagers back then suffered the annihilation of their world due to their blatant disrespect for magic. You will see, one day, once more, how the wisdom of the wise perishes. Mark my words—you will see it!"

"Pah!" Antius replied. He pressed his lips together to prevent the outburst he feared would erupt.

Ambel lowered his voice to a whisper and crumpled on the rug. "I am sorry, Father. I am tired and distraught. I should get some sleep. We can discuss this in the morning."

Antius nodded, then realized Ambel couldn't see his gesture. "Let me draw you a hot bath and help you out of these clothes. You'll sleep much better once you've bathed."

As Antius led his son to the bathing room in the back of his house, he pondered Ambel's words. He, of all people in the Heights, knew there were inexplicable forces beyond what could be seen with the eyes. He had studied numerous tales in the annals of history of many lands. Tales replete with fantastic beasts and the recounting of miraculous events that defied reason. Axe heads floating on water. A rod turned into a snake. Oil in a jar that never ran out. A man who could walk on water and calm raging seas. Logic decried such things!

Had his son really seen a firebird—a creature of myth? There was no denying his son's strange blindness. How else could that be explained? And all Antius had to do was think back seventeen years to the creature who had appeared at his door. No, he dared not deny the magic in the world, nor any undisclosed power hidden from his understanding. That, he conceded, would not be wise. But it did not mean he would condone superstition—or outrageous obsession!

Antius turned on the tap in the tub that brought hot spring water in through pipes from the mountains' depths. Years ago, an expedition discovered heat vents deep in a cavern on the northern side of the Heights. Geologists and engineers developed a system of pipes to bring water from these thermal vents through the pass and into the homes of those living in the cliffs. An undeniably pleasurable benefit of the application of practical knowledge. Once more Antius was reminded of how essential wisdom was. How the pursuit of knowledge brought a higher quality of life. Answered the important questions in life. Provided the tools for problem solving and acquiring one's necessities.

As he filled the tub and helped Ambel out of his clothes, he kept his thoughts bottled up, not wanting to spur another argument. Antimony, cautious and unsure, gripped the edge of the tub with his talons and inched his way toward Ambel. Perhaps even the owl distrusted the change in his former companion. Antius left Ambel to soak and went back to tend his fire. Just as he stuffed another log into his stove, someone tromped up his steps and banged on the door. Another coming to call on this inhospitable night? Who would venture out this late in the dark to seek his counsel? A fresh rush of dread filled his heart. He approached the door with uncertainty and uncanny fear.

It took a moment for Antius to recognize the woman draped in a long cloak with a hood partly hiding her face. Before he could invite her in, Teralyn's mother pressed through the front door and into his home; her breathing indicated she had been running. Her unusual presence there confirmed his deepest fear. Something terrible must have happened. Had Teralyn gotten hurt? If so, why come here instead of to the healers?

"Kileen, how may I help you? Is Teralyn in trouble?"

Kileen removed her wet cloak and hung it on a hook by the door. "Antius, we need to talk."

She reached into a shoulder bag and pulled out what looked like a piece of linen cloth and held it out for his inspection.

Antius gestured her into the sitting room, but she stayed standing by the door, unmoving. He took the large square cloth from her hands and examined the neat stitching that depicted a pastoral setting. Why was she showing this to him? He had no interest in stitching.

She spoke in a hushed voice, looking around the room, no doubt making sure they were alone. "Teralyn gave this to me. She said she had made this. Someone in the village gave her a needle and thread and taught her how to stitch."

Antius felt the blood drain from his face. He had feared something like this would one day happen.

Kileen continued with a piercing gaze that unnerved Antius's heart. He had never seen her so agitated. "We did as you directed. Kept the house free from needles and thread, yarn, spindles. Antius, I never asked for an explanation—all these years. You made us promise unconditionally. And we kept that promise. Teralyn never asked, and we assumed she held no curiosity of such things. We made sure her years were full of activities and education—enough to occupy her mind and heart. And now this! All because you sent her down to the village!"

"Please, calm down, my dear."

"And Justyn—that student you sent to accompany her—tells me she's fallen in love with some fool villager!"

Antius shut his eyes tight as a world of cares pressed down on him. "Perhaps it is time to tell her the truth. She'll be eighteen soon enough."

"Fine," Kileen said, throwing up her hands and turning back toward the door. In a brisk motion, she pulled her cloak from its hook and threw it around her shoulders. "Tell her if you wish . . . if you can find her."

Before Antius could ask what she meant, Kileen stormed out the door. By the time he stepped out onto his porch, she had vanished into the cloud-soaked night. He stood for a moment listening to the sound of water pounding rock, no longer hearing a melodious strand of music pinging down the mountain. Instead, wind snarled and snapped at his ears, stirring up his fear even more. Teralyn had never run off before. What had happened at the festival? Was she in danger?

Antius ached with worry. First, his son. Now, Teralyn. The night's events validated his earlier feelings of dread. Perhaps they did defy all logic—these terrible presentiments of disaster. But he could no longer brush them under the rug as superstitious hogwash. The strange creature who had brought Teralyn to his doorstep those many years ago had told him this would occur, in a voice that rose up from deep water. *Mark my words, wise one. Try as you may, you will not be able to keep her hands from the spindle, nor her fingers from the thread. Innocent though she is, she will cause the unraveling of Wentwater. The people shall perish for lack of a word.*

Whatever had she meant—the people perishing for lack of a word? And how would this involve Teralyn? The strange woman's silky voice echoed in his mind—a calm, soothing tone unperturbed by her pronouncement of doom. Antius had thought it odd. Rather than exude pity or sorrow, she had seemed almost joyful—like a messenger bearing good news, and completely lacking in malice. Just as back then, the memory of her smiling face sent a shiver up his spine. But this time fear bubbled up in his heart, despite his attempt to quell it, reason it away. This time he knew that—casting logic and practicality aside—something terrible had been set in motion and he would be powerless to prevent it.

Justyn had lost sight of Teralyn. If he followed too closely, she would detect him, so he relegated himself to the shadows cast by the towering cliffs and hung back out of earshot. But he had little doubt as to where she was going—to his parents' cottage to find Fromer. Justyn let his anger propel him down the mountain. A waning full moon rose over his shoulder, lighting his way as he trekked steadily, sweat dripping down his neck and soaking the collar of his shirt.

As his boots pounded the rocky road, he searched his memory for snippets of conversation he'd overheard while growing up. His mother gossiping with her neighbors while hanging laundry on clotheslines. While shopping in the marketplace, pulling Justyn along on her errands. While leaning over the fence, surrounded by squawking hens, whispering loudly enough for him to hear. Always speaking in hushed tones, afraid something terrible would happen at the mention of her name.

Ursell. The marsh witch—the stuff of legends. Just as unbelievable as the legend of the *Tse'pha* that he had studied about—some ancient creature in the northern Wastes that had snakes for hair and spawned a monstrous sea serpent. If he hadn't seen Ursell for himself that fateful day, he would have brushed off his mother's words as mere fancy or exaggeration. But he'd not only seen the old ugly woman, she had turned and stopped when passing him. There he had stood—in a nearby yard, Fromer holding tightly to his hand. And when she swiveled her head and glared at him with that glass eye, a pain had stabbed his heart, making him choke.

He never mentioned the incident to his mother. For what would she make of it—this witch halting suddenly to face him? He dared not speculate. While she spoke in a grumbling voice that sounded like a creaking board, Ursell's face had lit up in recognition. "You!" she said. "You're the one." With a sneer and a cackle that made him tremble, she added, "I'll be waiting for you."

Over the years he had tried to squelch the memory of that morning, of the witch's words. But now they clanged in his head like a bell. Was she truly waiting for him? If so, why? Had she foreseen this day? He chastised his foolish thinking. No doubt her words had been tossed at him to scare him. She probably said that to all the children she encountered, to give them nightmares. He had learned from his mother's gossip that Ursell was thought to be hundreds of years old. How absurd! She purportedly lived in an abandoned castle engulfed in mud, in the western marshes two leagues outside the village. Tales recounted endless spells she had cast upon the village. Curses she had uttered through the centuries. Clearly, the villagers used her as a scapegoat—someone to blame every time crops failed or milk soured and their usual superstitious explanations failed. Word had it that she had even caused the Great Flood. Some fury unleashed in retaliation for being spurned or criticized or some such nonsense.

Justyn had never ventured into the marshes, nor had he known anyone who had. The villagers feared the place—and not just because of the witch. Specters were said to dwell there: restless spirits of the dead trapped among the reeds, eager to feed on anyone senseless enough to trespass into their territory. Another bit of superstitious nonsense! For that reason, there were no footpaths through the miles of mucky swamp. Infested with beetles and leeches and unnamed creeping things, swarming with biting gadflies—who would want to tromp through such miserable terrain anyway . . . let alone live there?

Justyn looked down the hill at the cluster of cottages in the distance. A few windows lit up by oil lamps gave a cheery glow to the sleepy village. Justyn pushed aside thoughts of a warm meal and a soft feather mattress and continued walking along the sheep trail that skirted the moors. Without meaning to, he pictured Teralyn standing on the stoop to his parents' home, knocking softly; Fromer answering in surprise, gathering her up and kissing her, stroking her hair the way Justyn had seen him do last week at the festival.

He clenched his teeth and picked up speed as the grasses and sedges thickened about his ankles. Soon, the trail petered out and spongy vegetation squished under his boots. He was glad he'd taken the time to scrounge some old knee-high mud boots in one of the gardening sheds near his dormitory. He had every intention of returning them once he found this witch and uncovered the truth.

If he had to, he would drag Ursell into the village and expose her for the fraud she was. The villagers needed to see the foolishness of their superstitious fear. If he could make them see that this witch was nothing more than a creepy old lady with a glass eye, then perhaps they'd listen to reason. Ursell was the key. Discredit her and their worldview unraveled. So much of their history was tightly stitched around this one insignificant woman. They were sewn up by rumors and fear such that they could barely breathe without worrying something catastrophic would happen. He grunted. The old woman at his naming ceremony had foretold he'd be a righter of wrongs. Well, he could think of nothing more wrong than the way the villagers were imprisoned by their beliefs.

He could be their deliverer—setting the prisoners free from the chains that bound them. How grateful they would be!

Clouds occluded the moonlight, leaving Justyn straining to see his way. Foul smells encircled him—rotting, putrefying vegetation. His legs ached from having to pull up one boot after the other from the viscous mud. Insects swarmed around his head, biting exposed patches of skin. He could feel tender welts swell on his cheeks and forehead. As he slogged through swaths of marsh, hour after hour, he stifled his uneasiness. Maybe he should have waited until morn to search for this witch. What if he got lost or mired? What if the witch didn't even live here? Was it worth wasting his time mucking about on such a quest? He thought of all the studying he needed to do. He had appointments this week with three professors, as well as a class to instruct and a paper due at week's end. Well, his mission was more important. His studies could wait. Surely he'd either find this witch and bring the whole matter to a quick conclusion or he'd wander around for a few hours and find nothing—but little worse for wear.

His thoughts returned to Teralyn and the cruel look she had given him after she slapped his cheek. He could almost feel the flesh sting where her palm had met with his skin. His indignation grew as the night dragged along. He pictured Fromer's laughing eyes as he played his fiddle onstage alongside Teralyn, who strummed her harp with a spark of joy he could not fathom. The more he dwelt on his brother and the affection he showered on Teralyn, the angrier he grew. Fury boiled like a hot cauldron of oil over a burning hearth.

By the time the first tinge of pastel dawn seeped into the cloudy sky, he felt ready to explode. He would find some way to wipe that happy smile off his brother's face. He was sick of that idiotic smile—a smile he'd had to live with all his years growing up. Well, he knew just what would break that simpleton's heart. If Teralyn refused to give Fromer up, Justyn would find some way to turn her against him. Discredit him somehow. Blame him for something that would turn the village against him. How hard would that be to do? Those mindless people would be quick to banish even Fromer if evidence pointed to some terrible misstep. All he had to do, then, was set Fromer up for a fall. But how?

So embroiled was he in his scheming, with his head cast downward to watch his footing, that he failed to notice the stone wall. He smacked his head against the hard surface and stumbled backward in fatigue and confusion.

He lifted his eyes and gazed up at the broad mud-encrusted wall that reached high into the sky with a glint of morning sun bouncing off it. Riotous vegetation draped down the wall's face, nearly burying the edifice before him. He could make out the outlines of hewn brick in areas where chunks of mud had cracked and fallen into the weeds. A roof of decaying shingles looked half collapsed from the ravages of rain upon the layer of sedge adorning the peaks in green icing. Leaf-choked gutters wrapped beneath the eaves, rotted and moss-encrusted. With one hand sliding along the wall, he sloshed through a pool of water and followed the stone until his hand met with splintery wood. He pushed matted hair from his face, then felt around the surface of the wood and found a ring of iron hanging in the center of the wooden slab. A door knocker?

Before he had a chance to ponder his situation, he heard a raspy voice call down from above him. He tipped his head back in a whorl of morning mist that seemed to part as the sound bellowed. There, high up in a pointy turret tower off to his right, a head stuck out an opening in the stone. In the dim light, Justyn could not make out the face, but even after all these years he recognized the scratchy low voice. It gave him a chill that penetrated deep into his already cold bones.

"Well, my pawky chap, I see you've found my abode. As I told you, young lad, I'd be waiting for you. Been waiting all these years . . ."

A tremble danced across Justyn's neck.

"So," she said with a cackle that carried loudly on the still morning air, "show yourself in."

ELEVEN

AT THE END of a long, dark hallway, an open door beckoned, and a faint light revealed the room beyond. Something rubbed up against Justyn's leg, and he jumped. Upon inspection, he realized it was only a cat—skinny, ugly, but no doubt harmless. He approached the door with hesitation, and two more cats sauntered out of the room before him and entangled themselves in his legs.

"Scat! Shoo!" he said in a hiss, unsure whether to enter or wait. The cats retreated for a moment, then gravitated back to his legs, sniffing the mud on his boots.

He heard footsteps—heavy, clomping steps that drew close. Justyn gulped and pushed down his fear. Surely he could hold his own against a small old woman. One crazy hermit who liked to rattle the villagers. Well, she would not be able to pull any of her tricks on him—he was too educated and smart for that. Now he would learn just who she was and what game she was playing. It wouldn't take long to uncover her methods and expose her.

As the woman hobbled over to him, she looked him over from head to foot. Justyn drew himself up tall so that he towered over her tiny frame. Yet when her glass eye rested on his face, his pulse quickened. Her gaze penetrated deep, and he had the uncomfortable sensation that she could see into his mind, riffle through his memories. He clamped down on his thoughts, but he felt her intruding in there, shuffling through images and snatches of conversation. Pinching spoken words with gnarly fingers, weighing them in her hands.

Justyn leaped back from her, but she held out her palms in invitation.

"Come in, my fine chap. Let's have a better look at you in the light." As Ursell studied him, he studied her. She looked no different from an ordinary villager, with her silvery hair bound in a scarf and wearing a simple smock, albeit faded and ratty. Of course, she had the glass eye, but her other eye looked cloudy and gray, just as any old hag's might appear.

He took in the small room he had entered. It resembled his parents' sitting room but without windows—and quite a bit more cluttered. A round table and two chairs sat in the center, and an old trunk abutted a rocking chair in one corner. A large spinning wheel took up most of another corner. Three oil lamps burned steadily, their wisps of smoke making the air stuffy and acrid. A large hearth inset into one brick wall sported a giant iron cauldron hanging from hooks. No fire was lit, leaving the room dank and clammy, although the smell of charred wood and ash lingered. Other rooms led off into darkness—a kitchen, bedroom, pantry, perhaps? Cats meandered through the room. One lay curled up on the rocker, another in front of the cold hearth. Every one of them watched him furtively through half-opened eyes. Their stares made him uneasy.

Justyn's attention was drawn to the walls, which were gray brick instead of wood, and barren of adornment. Shelves covered the walls from floor to ceiling, and crammed on every bit of shelf space were glass jars of various shapes and sizes. From where he stood, he could not make out the content of the jars, but each one glowed with a dull light—some pale green, some yellow, and a few deep shades of umber and mauve. Something flitted within each one, a lone firefly bumping against the glass. All the jars were sealed with golden lids. There must have been hundreds of them.

"Ah, admiring my collection, are we?" the witch said, her voice grating Justyn's ears. "It's taken me ages to gather so many. Each one special. I'll have one from you soon enough!"

The witch's laugh was worse than her speech. It sounded like nails scratching across a washboard.

"What do you mean? What do you keep in those jars?"

Ursell only laughed harder in response. "Here, come, sit. I see you have a *need*." She yanked a chair out from the table and tipped her head, waiting.

"A need?" Justyn fidgeted but remained where he was. He reminded himself he had nothing to fear. He was there to expose her. To show what a charlatan she was. He breathed out his tension. All right, he would go along with her ruse.

He sat where she indicated, then waited while she went to the trunk and opened it. When she returned to the table and sat in the chair opposite him, she placed a tarnished metal box the size of a toadstool in front of him.

"What's this?" he asked.

"The solution you seek."

"What solution? The solution to what?" Justyn pushed the box away and stood.

Ursell narrowed her thick brows until they joined in a livid line across her forehead. "Don't play games with me, young chap. Ursell sees exactly why you came. She sees your *need*."

Anger seared her eyes, and that gave him pause. Before he could back away, the witch jumped from her chair and grasped his wrist forcefully. "Ursell sees everyone's needs."

Justyn loosed a sigh and sank back down in the chair. "Okay, what's my need?" His stomach growled, reminding him how many hours it had been since he'd eaten anything. *Well, there's my need—breakfast!* He started to chuckle, but caught the witch's glass eye locked on to his face. A jolt of uneasiness erased his smile.

Without warning, an onslaught of images engulfed his mind, and along with them, a barrage of emotion. As he watched Fromer holding Teralyn, his rage and passion and jealousy flared, saturating the air around him and hovering visibly as an undulating dark cloud. The witch nodded, her eye pinning him in place, preventing him from the slightest movement. Memories spurted out like wine from a wineskin under too much pressure. Fromer stroking Teralyn's cheek; Fromer and Teralyn walking hand in hand; Teralyn scowling at Justyn, slapping his cheek. With each memory, his gut wrenched, and he fought the nausea rising in his throat. Sweat poured down the sides of his face, and his body trembled in rage, as if he could no longer contain the emotions within. Surely he would die; he was powerless to stop such fury from incinerating him.

Just as he started to slip off his chair to the floor, Ursell released his wrist. He slumped as a wave of relief washed over him, lessening the burning in his gut, although now the anger sat there, mordant, raw, volatile, with a pure sheen—the way silver looked after dross was burned from it.

"Ah," the witch said, circling him slowly as he sat there gazing vacantly at nothing. His mind felt stripped and barren. Nothing remained. A slate wiped clean.

"Now, there's a curious name. Fromer." She chewed her lip and continued to circle. "So much contained in that name. The essence of all that exists, the power to create and destroy. A fitting name for your brother."

Justyn tried to articulate words but his mouth wouldn't work. What nonsense was she spewing? The witch continued. "His name holds *form*—and *more*. All that is *former* and all that can be *reformed*. The very structure of all things lies in his grasp . . ."

The witch stopped her maddening circling and tipped her head at Justyn. "This should prove interesting . . ."

Justyn sat in silence as the witch pondered, her jaw working, as if rolling pebbles in her mouth.

In an abrupt motion that shook him from his strange stupor, she pushed the metal box toward him and leveled a crooked finger at it. "Open it."

His hand felt heavy as he lifted it from the table and clicked the latch on the box. He looked inside and saw only a small rectangle of strange cloth and a tiny spool of black thread with a slender needle tucked into it.

"Take it out," she ordered. Justyn, cringing at her abrasive voice, again did as he was told. The fabric felt odd, soft as water but hefty in his grip, like leather or thick wool. Yet the material was so thin it was nearly transparent. He held it up to the dim lamplight and it wavered and rippled. Justyn rubbed his eyes at the cloth's illusiveness.

"Now, you want control over Fromer," she said, her tone incisive. "You want to make him pay for the hurt he's caused. You want to discredit him, yes?"

"Yes," Justyn answered mindlessly. He couldn't take his eyes off the cloth.

"Then, all you need do is stitch his name on the cloth. Bind thread to fabric, his name trapped under your will. He will do all you bid and question nothing. The girl will be yours."

Justyn lifted his head and his heartbeat quickened. "Teralyn . . ."

The witch leaned in close, expelling hot, rancid breath into his face. "Yes. Yours. But for a price."

Desire and longing stirred in him, coupled with his smoldering anger. His every thought, every need, wrapped around the witch's words. Until this moment, he had only seen Teralyn as an attractive but irritating young woman. But now! He saw Teralyn's soft cheeks, her dark inviting eyes, her long graceful hands—hands that reached for his face and stroked him, her full red lips meeting his own. He sucked in a quavering breath and held it, afraid to move and shatter the longing that grew as wild as a bramble, entangling his heart in a morass of need. Somewhere deep in his mind, a niggling reminded him of his life back in the Heights. His goals and aspirations, his burden of responsibilities. That life seemed strangely faint and detached from him now. He was rowing a boat with the shoreline receding in the distance and growing dimmer each passing minute.

"I've . . . never stitched anything before," he said, fumbling with the needle and thread. "Can you not do this for me?"

"Ah, such a simple task. No, my young chap; for your brother to be bound to you, you must bind him yourself. And you cannot do this here."

Justyn stilled his hands. "Not here? Then where?"

Ursell wrung her hands in apparent delight. "Ah, in the place words originate. The place of power. Have you not read, my well-educated young chap, that in the beginning God spoke, and through his spoken word brought all of creation into existence? First comes the intent. Then follows the word. The word, having power, then turns intent into matter. All life hangs on a word. All things exist by the word of God. By means of the word spoken, worlds were formed. Think what would happen if a word were erased from existence. Why, the very thing it formed would *un*form. It would cease to be."

Justyn recited in his head from the ancient Great Book. *"All worlds were framed by the word of God so that the things which are seen were not made from things visible."* He looked at Ursell, bewildered. "How is it you know such ancient writings?"

Ursell cackled again. "Heavens, young chap. I wasn't born yesterday! Don't let my appearance fool you." She waggled her hand in the air and chuckled. "Now, you must journey to the place of origin, where all words are birthed, before they manifest in this world. And you must not tarry there."

"I . . . I don't understand . . ." Justyn thought hard, searching through the volumes of knowledge stored in his brain. What place did she mean? He'd never learned anything that described a place where words were formed.

As if reading his mind, Ursell leaned even closer, and with a smile that revealed a few gray rotted teeth said, "The stream of thought . . ."

"The what . . .?"

The room suddenly vanished. Justyn found himself hip-deep in water. A steadily flowing current wove around and between his legs, the way the witch's cats had done. He glanced around him in wonderment. He stood in a wide, flat stream, with high crumbling banks etched by rivulets of water dripping down their sides, still holding the cloth, needle, and thread. Although the water moved over half-submerged boulders and wrapped fingers around clumps of water reeds, a muted silence lay ominously heavy over him. He opened his mouth to speak, but nothing came out. Not even a whimper or the shush of his breath. Justyn knew he was not in his world, for nothing could suck away sound so completely. Had he lost his hearing? And where was the witch?

He looked up, but the sky had vanished, leaving only an imprecise shadow. The air around him had no weight or temperature and flowed as aimlessly as a dream. He looked down at his legs, wavering under the water, but he felt nothing. When he dipped his hand into the stream, he drew it out dry. Maybe he was asleep or under some spell. He tried to move his legs but they were locked in place. He heard a voice speak in his head. *The stream of thought, the place words originate.*

Justyn felt oddly calm. No longer hungry or thirsty, cold or warm, he lost track of time as the stream slipped along. Somehow he knew he was outside time, perhaps even outside existence. No doubt the witch had put him under a trance. He thought of texts he had read that spoke symbolically of the waters of life. He recalled the great prophet from the south who had prophesied of living waters that would flow from the heart and become a fountain of endless life. Citations and phrases flooded his mind, creating imagery that superimposed on the surface of the water around him. Water—so often used as a symbol to represent the very essence of life. That was what he was immersed in. Or so he thought.

His eye caught on a small eddy whirling close to the right bank. He leaned down and craned to see the bottom. Tiny silver fish darted about, spangling among the reeds. But as he looked closer, he saw they were not fish at all. They were odd shapes. Only after pondering long and hard did Justyn realize he was looking at letters—ancient letters from what some historians declared was the original language. The *law'az*, some texts called it. In his linguistics studies, he had only briefly covered the *law'az*. Practically nothing written in that language had survived to his day, but he knew the alphabet. His memory stored every written language he'd ever studied. But how odd! Letters in water?

He glanced back at the rivulets meandering down the banks. With closer scrutiny he saw that the drops dribbling into the stream were letters as well. Individual letters dropping into the stream one at a time, clinging to other letters. Now he saw words forming, swirling around him, joining, connecting, creating language, concept, thought, ideas, abstraction. Words sparked images, and the pictures flipped across his mind in rapid succession—disjointed flurries of color and form. They moved too quickly for him to identify them. The once-clear stream filled with metallic flashes, sparkling like a million stars, until the entire stream flowed as liquid silver. Words in some embryonic state, not yet brought into being. Not yet spoken, but ready to be birthed.

A great thirst came over him—but not for something to drink. Suddenly, he wanted to know each word in existence. To taste its meaning, to drink in the richness of its character and nuance. To absorb words into his very soul so that they lived and breathed through him. This pressing thirst grew to a frantic need.

He heard the voice in his head once more. *"Stitch the name. You have little time before you go mad."* The truth of those words bit him. The stream thickened; words congealed, their cohesion forming a webbing that enwrapped his legs even tighter. Some words floated to the surface, so light, they popped like fragile soap bubbles upon contact with the air. Other words sank from the heavy weight of their import, burying themselves in the mud around his feet. He gaped in the realization that every word had substance. How a burden of heavy words might weigh one down, tire one out. And how a right word spoken at a right moment might fill one with an unbearable lightness of being. *"Words are alive; cut them and they bleed."* Justyn recalled translating that phrase only recently in one of his assignments. Standing there, in the stream of thought, and seeing words wiggle with life made him wonder if that statement held truth.

Justyn threaded the needle, seeing in his mind's eye just how it should be done, though his head pounded mercilessly from the intrusion of so many concepts assailing him from the stream. He narrowed his eyes and forced himself to concentrate. Sweat stung his eyes. The thread was liquid between his fingers. With a steady hand, ignoring his raging thirst, he thrust the needle into the fabric and pulled the thread through. Soon, his hand moved rhythmically, without volition, as if the needle worked its own magic as he held it loosely in his hand.

Time slowed to a stop. The stream ceased to flow. Nothing in the world moved except Justyn's hand. The needle flashed, in and out, stitch after stitch, and Justyn concentrated on this one task, standing in silver, sweat trickling down his neck. It seemed to Justyn that all creation waited expectantly in silence for him to finish his handiwork. He could not even hear his labored breathing as he strained to complete the last few stitches. With a long exhale, he then tied off a knot at the back of the cloth.

He held his stitching up to see the finished product. *Fromer*. The six letters composing his brother's name looked plain and insignificant. Yet, somehow, he knew they contained all that his brother was—Fromer's hopes, dreams, and fears. All that he had been and all that he would be—past, present, and future. All contained within that one name.

Justyn grinned. He now knew he held more than a small piece of cloth. He held something he had ever longed for but imagined was forever out of his grasp. Power.

And with that realization, a laugh burst out, loud and abrasive, shattering the silver stream with a jarring vibration. The world around him dissolved in a fizz and explosion of sparks, ushering in a rush of familiar smells and sensations. The chill of the witch's sitting room, the ache of hunger in his stomach, the stale aroma of soot and caustic smoke all startled Justyn out of his timeless stupor. He blinked and found himself standing, no longer in the midst of a stream but on a tattered rug with a cat rubbing against his leg.

"Ah, my young chap, you're back," the witch said, patting a chair for him to sit in.

With shaky, stiff legs, Justyn walked for the first time in what felt like years. He sat and held out the cloth for the witch to see.

"A fine job; couldn't have done better myself," she said with another raucous, irritating laugh. "Now," she added, setting the cloth down on the table and putting her hands on her hips. "Let's discuss payment."

TWELVE

AS SOON AS his feet found dry enough ground, Justyn removed the mucky boots and hid them behind a large oak. He reached into his pack and pulled out his soft walking shoes, and his feet breathed a sigh of relief as he slipped them on. His legs ached from tromping through the soggy marshes for the last few hours. And his face and exposed wrists were covered in bug bites. He studied the moonless sky, searching out familiar constellations, wondering why the moon had yet to rise. He had no idea how much time had passed while he was at the witch's castle. What a strange structure to find half buried in a swamp! He had read about a king that ruled long before the Great Flood and wondered if that decaying and crumbling edifice had been his home. Justyn wondered if there were other buildings buried under mud—perhaps part of the original village of Wentwater?

As he headed toward the village under cover of darkness, the witch's words resounded in his mind. Just who was she, and why did she live in such an inhospitable place? Folklore wasn't his forte, but he imagined somewhere in all the tomes in the Heights' libraries there had to be some mention of this witch. He had never bothered to read about the Great Flood and the events leading to that catastrophe, although in grade school he had studied the standard requisite material detailing the history of his land. Yet no mention had ever been made as to how the flood occurred. And certainly nothing that involved a witch or a curse. Unless, of course, you listened to town gossip.

Now that he had encountered Ursell, there was no denying she had unusual powers. But he had little doubt his "vision" had been a result of some conjuring on her part. Tricks up her sleeves, no less. Some sort of hypnotic trance or power of suggestion she must have used on him. He chuckled and shucked off her warning. The payment she required of him was ridiculous and puzzling. First, he must collect seven red tail feathers from seven different roosters! What in the world did she need those for? And if he failed to return with those feathers in the next seven days, the spell he had woven would fail. As if stitching a name in a piece of cloth could really bind a person to the one stitching! She then told him that once he returned with the feathers, they'd "exchange a word or two." That would seal the deal. What in heaven did she mean by that?

Justyn had to admit he was curious. More than curious. Why not put her claim to the test? Hadn't that been the purpose of his visit—to discredit her? He had started this thing—he should see it through to the end. And it gave him the perfect opportunity to knock Fromer down a notch or two. Justyn knew just how superstitious the villagers were regarding their roosters and hens. So many stupid rituals revolved around those dumb birds! He would use this chance wisely—to advance his own agenda.

Justyn slowed as he drew near to the first cottages on the outskirts of Wentwater. He shook off his weariness and forced himself to concentrate. He hadn't had sleep in how long? At least he had eaten. Good thing he had stuffed his pack with food before setting out on this journey. Still, his stomach rumbled over his meager fare of nuts and fruit. Well, he would finish his task and at sunrise treat himself to a hearty breakfast. Fat hot sausages, fresh eggs, warm brown bread slathered with jam. His mouth watered as he hurried on his way. The sooner he finished this business, the better. And he would have plenty of time to make it back up to the Heights before anyone noticed he'd gone missing. It wasn't unusual for him to disappear for days on end, studying in some quiet, out-of-the-way place. No one would question his absence or ask of his whereabouts.

After a quick glance around, assured no one was watching, he quietly tiptoed into the nearest yard. With careful, slow movements, he unlatched a gate and made for a hen house. This late at night, the birds would be on their nests, sleepy and easy to calm. The rooster, however, might prove a different matter.

He lifted the catch and entered the small wooden house. A few hens cackled at his appearance but his shushing settled them right away. He cursed the darkness. Moonlight would help him see, but he dared not wait for moonrise to start his task. This could take him most of the night. He considered gathering all seven feathers from one rooster, but somehow he knew Ursell would spot his ruse. Better to follow her instructions exactly.

He listened to the sounds until he identified the rooster's throaty voice. It only required a few short steps and a hearty lunge to get the hefty bird contained in his arms. With a swift pull, he yanked out a tail feather while wrapping his free hand around the bird's beak. The rooster tried to screech and bite him, but Justyn had him pinned. He chuckled. All those years of helping his mother with her birds paid off.

Once he knew the rooster was pacified enough, he let him go. With a flurry of strong flaps, the bird fled to a dark corner, leaving Justyn with a slick tapered feather in his hand. Before exiting the coop, Justyn felt along the wooden floorboards with his fingers and gathered up a half dozen stray chicken feathers of various sizes. These he strewed around the dirt yard as he left in stealth under the cloak of night, laughing quietly. He could just imagine the horror these villagers would feel upon awakening to find such an ominous sign!

Six more times he repeated his steps in six more yards. He made sure to choose the cottages so they were spaced blocks apart, but leading specifically in one direction—to his parents' home. A splinter of moon lifted over rooftops as Justyn entered the last yard—his mother's closest neighbor's. After acquiring the seventh feather, he not only scattered chicken feathers in the neighbor's yard but along the road, outside his parents' gate, and—for a final victorious touch—on the steps leading to the front stoop of his own family home.

With a satisfied sigh, Justyn hurried off into the village and found an empty toolshed in which to catch some sleep. Exhaustion hit him like a brick to the head, and only moments after slumping to the floor with his back propped against the wall and his cloak draped over to keep him warm, he fell into a hard, dreamless slumber as Teralyn's haunting face smiled longingly at him.

Warm sun on Justyn's head shook him from his nap. Through squinting eyes, he looked out the shed door to a bright spring day. The heaviness and moisture in the air told him dawn had long passed. He stretched and stood on achy legs, cracking his neck and bending his back to force out the stiffness. His mouth felt thick and dry, and a stubble of beard covered his chin. One peek into his pack assured him he still had the seven feathers. With a grin, he hefted the pack onto his back and made his way down the cobbled road to the inn he had taken Teralyn to a week ago. Had it only been a week since the festival? It felt more like months. No matter. The deed was done and breakfast awaited! He knew he should find a creek or water pump and wash up, but his grumbling stomach urged him to postpone such considerations.

Besides, maybe in his grungy, disheveled state, he would be less recognizable in the village.

As he stood near the doorway waiting to be seated, he watched the villagers bustle about in the street. Peeking out from under his cloak hood, he couldn't help but overhear the agitation in the voices of women now alerted to the alarming signs disclosed by the morning's light. Hushed words, flurries of hands waving, heads waggling. Rumors thickened in the heavy air. No doubt the village was in a silent uproar as more and more villagers added their woeful tales of discovery.

Justyn snickered quietly as he watched the scene unfold before him. Voices were raised; arguments erupted. One woman with her hands on her hips faced down another right in the middle of the lane. Finger pointing led to verbal accusations. Two men came out their shop doors and had to pry the women apart, glancing up at the sky as if a lightning bolt might shoot down from the heavens in judgment upon them all.

"What's this commotion about?" Justyn asked an unfamiliar patron in all innocence. "Seems something terrible has happened."

The old woman, holding tightly to the arm of another, shook her head spasmodically. Fear danced in her eyes as her companion fluttered a handkerchief about her face in dismay. "Haven't you heard?" she said in a barely audible whisper. "Chicken feathers—all over town! In yards and on the streets."

Justyn frowned. "Why, perhaps someone's chicken has gotten out. Or maybe there's a wild one roaming the streets."

The woman's eyes widened in more alarm. "Heavens, don't even suggest such a thing! No, there's some evil at work here. Couldn't be just one hen responsible for leaving such a trail."

"A trail?" Justyn asked, prodding with his voice as he kept his face partially hidden. He looked up and saw the serving girl signal him over to an open table. "Did the trail lead anywhere?"

Justyn waited. The old woman nodded and grabbed her friend's arm tighter. "I shouldn't say. But . . . the signs were there . . . for all to see."

"Well," Justyn said with an encouraging smile, "no doubt the culprit will come to light. Someone's idea of a joke, I'm sure. Someone with no regard for the traditions and time-honored rituals. Perhaps it was the fella I saw late last night, as I came into town . . ."

The two women locked four hungry eyes on Justyn, barely moving or breathing in anticipation of his next words.

He bent down closer to their eager faces. "Why, I'd just left the Cygnet and made my way down Mulberry Lane. It was dark out, could barely see. But this young lad—oh, about twentyish, light hair falling about his shoulders—was sneaking around a yard, and he had some things in his hand that he was scattering about."

"Did you recognize the lad, sir?" one of the women asked, leaning in close.

"It was a bit hard to tell in the dark, but . . . yes." He lowered his voice even more, but spoke with careful enunciation. "There was no mistaking the young man. I believe his name is Fromer—Iris's son, the goat herder. Heard he's taken a fancy to a girl from the Heights. No doubt her influence is at the crux of the crime."

"A girl from the Heights!" the other woman said with a gasp. "No wonder . . ."

Her companion paled. "Ah, poor Iris. What trouble she's brought down upon her home!"

Justyn held up a hand as he caught the serving girl's impatient expression. He couldn't risk losing his table and having to wait for another. He was starving! "Let's not be too quick to come to conclusions, ladies. Time will reveal all, and as they say: a hasty act pays double later."

Justyn nodded good day to the two old biddies and made his way to his table in the back of the room. He thanked the serving girl for her patience and ordered a large plate of waffles with an extra portion of bogberries. As he poured tea from the teapot on his table, he stole a glance at the two women he'd left standing by the door. Already they had gathered a crowd and were whispering back and forth among themselves with anger and fear evident in their faces.

Justyn smiled as he spooned sugar into his cup and stirred. He took a deep whiff of the hot tea as the steam rose and warmed his cheeks. He let his hood fall over his forehead and kept his head down as more and more villagers assembled by the front door and occasionally looked his way. He realized at some point someone might recognize him, and that would not be wise. So he switched chairs so his back faced the door, then wolfed down his breakfast, barely taking the time to savor each bite, then left coin on the table and snuck out the back way.

Hours later, sweaty and achy, Justyn climbed the last big hill and arrived at the university oval just as a spattering of rain came down from the skies. Avoiding the stares of his fellow students, he kept his head tucked down as he hurried to his dorm and bolted the door behind him. A long, hot shower pounded the soreness from his weary muscles, and after dressing and shaving, he felt ready to return to his life as the studious postgraduate linguist. He rummaged through his pack and put dirty clothes in the hamper. The seven feathers he wrapped in a linen cloth and hid under the sweaters in his bottom dresser drawer. With a contented sigh, he picked up his satchel of books and headed out the front door.

As he buttoned up his coat on the steps to his dormitory, he heard someone call his name. He looked up to see Antius, of all people, hurrying toward him from the walkway.

"Justyn, where have you been? I've been looking for you for days!"

Justyn stopped buttoning and his jaw went slack. "Days . . . I don't understand . . ."

Antius studied Justyn with concern. "Is something the matter? Have you been sick? I had the resident advisor check your room, but he said you hadn't been seen in your dorm or your classes all week."

"All week . . .?" Justyn sucked in a breath as a shiver fingered his spine. Antius waited for an answer but all Justyn could do was shake his head.

"Perhaps I should take you to the infirmary—"

"Antius," Justyn said, his stomach roiling in nerves, "what day is it?"

Antius peered even harder at Justyn, as if trying to make sense of some madness he detected there. "Why, it's Friday, of course."

Justyn thought hard but his mind refused to cooperate. He had followed Teralyn down the hill . . . on Sunday. And that evening went into the marsh to find the witch. It should only be Monday afternoon . . .

He wobbled on his feet and his knees started to buckle. Antius grabbed an arm.

"You do look a bit wan, lad. I think a trip to the infirmary—"

"Where's Teralyn?" Justyn asked in a clipped tone. His mind spun, trying to gather up the week, wondering how he had lost so much time and what appointments he had missed. What would his instructors and peers think of his truancy?

"Teralyn? Why I expect she's off on her gardening rounds. Her mother had been a bit worried when she didn't show up on Sunday, but she apparently had gone down to the village . . . came back late Monday. I thought perhaps you had gone to look for her—"

"Uh, yes, I had. When I heard she went missing, I was worried . . ." But how could he explain being absent the rest of the week? "And . . . upon arriving at the village, I came down with a horrid case of food poisoning. Something I ate didn't agree with me, I suppose. I-I slept so much, I had no idea so many days had passed . . ."

Antius laid a comforting hand on Justyn's shoulder. "There, there, well, you seem to be back on your feet. We did miss you at the symposium. And I found another student to teach your class for you. No harm done. But, it'd be prudent to get some wholesome food in you, my boy. Perhaps you could join me for dinner . . ." Justyn looked into Antius's face and saw a blaze of consternation. "And, you've probably not heard the news, then."

"What news?" Justyn wasn't sure if he wanted any more surprises.

"Ambel—my son has returned." Antius's face turned sour. "And he's in bad shape. I'd . . . be grateful to have your company, to have you try to talk with him, if you've a mind to. He's always seemed to respect your opinions."

Justyn could tell from Antius's face that the old man still harbored ill feelings and apprehension toward his son. "I'd be honored to help you in any way I can, Antius. What time would you like me to come over?"

"Six would be fine. If you're not otherwise engaged."

Justyn thought of all the catching up he'd need to do—if he truly had missed a whole week of school. His paper would be late, but he hoped this food poisoning excuse would soften Professor Anthanus's heart and he'd allow an extension. His linguistics professor was a jovial enough man, but a stickler for promptness. "Six sounds fine. Now, I'd best search out Professor Anthanus and let him know I'm back."

Antius nodded, and Justyn rushed down the steps, heading toward the library, where his professor's office was located. His mind was a jumble of worries, and the loss of time distressed him greatly. Somehow that witch had kept him in a trance for nearly five days!

How had she managed such a thing? But, not to worry. He was smart; he would catch up and get his paper done in record time.

A smile inched up his face. Down in the village, trouble was brewing—trouble he had unleashed that would entangle Fromer. And since Teralyn was safely insulated up here in the Heights, away from the gossip, it meant that it would be a while before the news reached her. Justyn hoped that by then Fromer would be well discredited by his neighbors. He didn't allow himself to ponder the grief and heartache his mother and father would suffer, having Fromer blamed for such sacrilegious acts. But now was not the time for sentimentality or softness. It would take sacrifice and great cost to bring down the superstitious ways of an entire village—ways steeped in centuries of mindless tradition. Sometimes someone had to pay the price for the benefit of all. And he was only too glad to put Fromer on that altar. He couldn't wait to return to the village on Sunday and see what havoc had been wrought!

The steaming kettle's whistle drew Ursell's attention away from the small piece of cloth she held up to the lamplight. "Oh, hush up, I'm coming!" She touched the tiny stitches with her calloused finger, pondering the odd name stitched there. Even after close scrutiny with her eye, she could only see so far, and the vision was muddled at best. And that disturbed her. Never before had one simple word befuddled her so. *Fromer*. She'd never encountered a name like it, so full of implication and nuance—and mystery. The fate of Wentwater village hinged upon it, and yet . . .

The shrill whistle grated on her nerves until she couldn't bear it a moment longer. She flung the bit of stitching in the air and it landed on the lid of the trunk, beside the rocker. With hands pressed over her ears, she maneuvered through a mash of cats loitering in the narrow aisle leading from the sitting room to the tucked-away kitchen area, where the kettle blurted out steam in ferocious abandon atop hot coals in the cookstove. She mumbled in recitation as she prepared her afternoon tea, strings of words only she could hear and, had she any visitors, only she would understand. For these were just some of the many words she had collected over the ravages of time—words given in payment for some favor or other, some spell or enchantment one just had to have cast. She loved to roll them over her tongue, chew on them for good measure. They were hers, all hers.

Ursell smiled. But those words did cost them—every time. And each word, once paid and in her possession, ended up in a jar. And once contained, no longer existed in the world of humans. But did anyone care? Words dropped out of usage daily. Useless, archaic, obsolete words that no longer served society. Who would miss them? No one.

She felt a familiar tingling of power as she let her eyes light on her collection. Words at her disposal, to do with as she wished, which no one could take from her.

Ursell sipped her tea thoughtfully as she wended her way back through the parting sea of cats and plopped down contentedly on her rocker, which groaned under her intrusion. Her attention turned to the shelves of jars. Innumerable jars, each containing a forgotten word. Forgotten, yes, but not blotted from existence. For only the Maker of words could accomplish that, could *un*do what had transmuted from thought to substance.

She chortled, startling away a big tabby that had one paw already kneading her lap. Humans thought little about the *substance* of words. In fact, they carelessly tossed words around as if they were grains of sand, inconsequential, impotent. They spit them out indiscriminately. They were careless fools; fools every one of them. How readily they forfeited the slightest word, as if it didn't matter. Yet they could see, everywhere they looked, the devastation left in the wake of such carelessness—hurtful words thrown like daggers in anger, whispered words of deceit and betrayal bringing kingdoms and kings to ruin. A few carefully chosen words could reshape destiny and obliterate fate. However, among her collection of words, few wielded influence or power. They were words that amounted to nothing. Their absence in the world caused no disturbance at all.

But it was time for a disturbance. A big one. She thought back over the years to that fateful late spring day that lay mired under a season of relentless rain and flooding. The pain still stung fresh as it had all those years ago. She had thought the flood would destroy the village and with it wash away the bitterness and need for revenge. And if not that, she'd hoped perhaps the accumulation of years would suffocate the hurt, piled one atop another, burying the past. But the opposite had proved true. Instead of feeling mollified by the passage of time, her need had grown like a tenacious wild weed breaking through cracks in stone.

Yes, she had a need too, and she very well knew what it was— to see Wentwater undone, erased, forgotten from the minds and hearts of those who walked the world. She well knew a kingdom disappeared the moment it no longer existed in the memory of those who had lived there. Unlike words, Wentwater *could* be undone.

And she had given up hope. Until . . . the day she had seen the babe with her eye. The babe who had drawn her from the seclusion of her marshes and summoned her once more to that godforsaken village.

Yet how could she have resisted? The birth of the babe had set a string of events in motion, not unlike the force of floodwaters. And when a dam burst from such pressure, there was naught to be done for it, was there? She spoke of what she saw; she had given warning—fat lot of good that would do, though. She chuckled and rocked as she sipped, the rocker moving back and forth in a soothing rhythm. If only she could see how the pieces would come together. Ah, not come together; rather, fall apart. For that's what she had seen in her eye—the entire village coming apart at the seams. How? She had no idea. Only that the lass would be the cause. Teralyn.

Now—there was a name even more portentous than Teralyn's lover's. Delving into her name was to face contradiction and alarm. Ursell pinched her lips together. She would need to ponder long and hard to arrive at some clarity. For contained in the name *Teralyn* were both *early* and *late,* which failed to give Ursell any point in time for this downfall to occur. *Nary* and *any* a thing could happen, but it wouldn't *tarry,* because she only had one letter *R.* Would it be a failure or omission that destroyed the village, or perhaps one unexpected event that triggered it all? Ursell felt assured that through this lass she would *learn* all she needed, and that the repercussions of this one act would span over a *year,* or was it an *era?* And as hard as she might *try,* there would be no way to *alter* or *alert any* to the danger—not really. Any course of action could be *yea* or *nay.* As much as she might *yearn* to know, no *ray* of light would give *nearly* enough illumination to this strange puzzle. *Rant* all she liked, she would have to *lean* on assumptions and postulations, but she knew, in the end, there would be no *real* or *neat* answer to the question: Just how would this lass trigger the unraveling of Wentwater?

Ursell's eyes grew heavy as she rocked and mulled over all the many words formed in Teralyn's name. Just as she felt herself drift into a luxurious sleep, her large tomcat, Drake, leapt into her lap and nearly knocked the forgotten teacup from her loose grasp.

"Fool of a cat!" She slammed the cup down on the floor and pushed the tom off her lap, then blotted the spilled tea burning her arm. The cat jumped in irritation onto the trunk, and the small piece of stitching with the name *Fromer* on it slipped off the wooden surface to the floor unnoticed.

Had Ursell been a better housekeeper, she might have noticed the bit of cloth resting under the back of the rocker's left runner. But snatches of random fabric lay piled about the trunk and strewn across the floor, indicative of Ursell's lack of interest in tidying things, and hardly anyone would notice a little insignificant piece of stitching such as that. Yet its placement on the floor was hardly innocuous, for one tiny corner caught on the rough wooden edge of the chair, and as the witch rocked, the scrap of cloth was pulled ever so slowly underneath.

By the time the marsh witch's eyelids closed in heavy sleep, her chin tucked down in a relaxed manner, the knot at the end of the stitching—a knot Ursell in her forgetfulness had failed to examine as carefully as she had the rest of the stitching—snagged and came unknotted. And with each gentle rock, the runner tugged ever so slightly on the thin thread Justyn had stitched into the fabric of the world while he had stood in the stream of thought.

And the thread, slowly but surely, began to unravel.

THIRTEEN

TERALYN'S HEART pounded hard in her chest, berating her. But she had little choice. Justyn's enigmatic words would not leave her alone: *"Kileen's not your mother."* And what in the world did Antius have to do with all this? Surely, Justyn had been grasping at twigs, desperate to rattle her, concocting some fancy—the first thing to enter his mind. Just thinking of Justyn made her stomach churn. He had stolen more than a kiss from her, and she felt violated and confused. Why had he pursued her so, when she had never led him on, or given him any indication she took an interest in him? He claimed he wasn't jealous over her affections for Fromer, but how could Justyn's odd behavior be due to anything other than jealousy? Why did he begrudge Fromer's happiness—and her own, for that matter? He hardly knew her.

She clamped down on her wandering thoughts and focused on her task at hand. Although it was Saturday, her parents would be detained all morning with their research. The cleaning woman wasn't due to arrive for another hour. Teralyn wasn't quite sure what she was looking for; she knew only one place where a clue might be found to shed light on her mysterious parentage—if indeed there was any truth to Justyn's claim.

She steadied her shaking hand as she pulled open the small, narrow drawer on her mother's dresser and felt around behind handkerchiefs and evening gloves. Her fingers met with metal, and she grasped the bundle of small keys and pulled them out. She waited and listened to the muffled drumming of water on the cliffs, straining to hear if anyone approached her home. Releasing a pent-up sigh, she strode over to the elegantly scrolled trunk resting at the foot of the bed and knelt.

Her hand trembled as one key after another failed to fit into the tiny lock. Her mother had rarely scolded her throughout her childhood, and only once had Teralyn received a slap. The memory still stung after fifteen years. Kileen had walked into her bedroom to discover Teralyn draped in shawls and scarves, giggling in the tangle of cloth that she had pulled from the trunk in delight. Without explanation, her mother yanked the new playthings from Teralyn's chubby little hands and stuffed them back into the trunk. Using sharp, hurtful words, she told her daughter she must never, *ever*, open that trunk again. Those things were not for play. Teralyn recalled the hot tears that streamed down her cheeks and the burn of her hand after her mother had slapped her. Ever since that day, Teralyn kept her distance from the trunk, as if it contained evil spirits or some poisonous snake.

But now she had no choice. If there were secrets to uncover, they would be hidden in there. It beckoned to her. At the very least, she now had to satisfy her curiosity, and should it prove to hold nothing at all of value other than expensive clothing, what harm would be done?

She mollified herself with these excuses as she worked through the ring of keys. Finally, one slipped neatly into the tumbler and the catch clicked, releasing the tightly closed lid. With care, she opened the trunk and gazed at the contents, the colors and silky fabrics sparking memories of texture against her skin. A whiff of mentholated mothballs tickled her nose. As she emptied the trunk, she laid each scarf and shawl and doily and sweater in stacks so she would be sure to replace them all in perfect order, wondering all the while why such simple garments and lacework had elicited her mother's fervid response. Maybe she had exaggerated the experience in her child's mind. Perhaps Kileen had only been punishing her for disobedience. There seemed to be nothing in the trunk to warrant the ominous reproof Teralyn remembered from so many years ago.

She removed the last few items and added them to her stack and stared at the bottom of the emptied trunk. Nothing. Her spirits sank. What had she expected to find, anyway? Her anger at Justyn grew as she sat there, as the empty trunk questioned her. Why had he said such upsetting things to her? Kileen and Rufus were her parents. She had lived in the Heights her entire life. Surely if she had come from elsewhere, someone would have made a comment to her sometime. And wouldn't her parents have told her the truth? What would be the point in keeping something like that secret? That would smack of superstition, certainly not the kind of thing her parents, of all people, would stoop to! They embraced facts; their very lives were devoted to getting to the heart of a puzzle. So why would they perpetrate one?

With a frustrated snort, Teralyn picked up the first pile of clothing on the floor beside her and laid each piece atop the wooden slats that made up the bottom of the trunk. Yet, as she pressed and smoothed the neat mound of clothing, the bottom creaked under the slight pressure of her palms. She stopped, then pushed again, this time noticing quite clearly the way the wood gave under her touch. She once more emptied the trunk and ran a hand across the smooth wood and realized the bottom rested inches above the floor. A false bottom!

She leaned into the trunk's cavern and scrutinized the slats. A finger snagged on a slight edge of wood, and she wiggled it until the slat loosened. With a slight yank, the wood gave way, revealing a dark leather parchment case, thin and small, tied with a leather thong and resting on the true bottom of the trunk.

Her hands began to shake. Should she remove the case and replace all the clothing? How much time had passed while she'd sat there? Dare she take the time to look inside? She lifted her head and listened once more to the ceaseless droning of water. The thought of having to return to the trunk at a later date and go through more laborious stacking was enough to prompt her to untie the leather strap binding the case. There couldn't be much inside. And her curiosity was almost more than she could bear.

Without another moment of hesitation, Teralyn tackled the stiff knot of leather and flung open the covering to reveal only two objects. One slipped out into her lap—a thin gold chain with a small emblem dangling from it. Teralyn lifted it up to the light streaming through the bedroom window and studied the piece of arcane jewelry that was half the size of her thumb. A silver star with an inset gold star. And in the middle was a circular depression that clearly had once held something with those tiny prongs. A gemstone? A green-tinged crust, similar to the tiny barnacles that dotted the rocks under the falls, covered the metal. Fashioned in a simplistic design and not much to look at, the pendant led Teralyn to doubt it held any monetary value. Sentimental value, perhaps? If so, why sequester it in a locked trunk?

Teralyn's gaze dropped to the small folded piece of parch-ment—the only other item bound in the leather case. With a gentle grip, she unfolded the sheet, a wavering buttery sheaf that nearly melted under her touch. Scribbles of letters flowed across the page like ripples of wavelets on the surface of a pool, letters the color of lichen and moss. A scent rose from the parchment, algae and mud, which lingered about her face as she strained to make out words from faded imagery. Try as she might, she could derive no meaning from the string of words linked by flourishes of pale-green ink. But when she stopped trying to join them together and allowed her glance to touch each one alone, a visceral realization bit her with a sharp tooth. She dropped the parchment as if it were burning to the touch, and watched unblinking as her fingers dripped water onto the carpeting.

Images gathered like storm clouds in her mind, and she shook her head to drive them away. She sucked air as if fighting to stay above water, feeling cold liquid slip down her throat and into her lungs, stirring a panic, which she fought to force down. It took all the concentration she could muster to fold up the sheet and replace it within its casing. She unfurled her tight fist and found the chain with its trinket resting on her damp palm. This she stuffed into her billowing skirt's pocket while pushing away alarms of warning.

Willing her heart to calm, she slowed her breathing, stacked silk and linen and wool into neat layers, returned them to their resting places. Upon closing the trunk lid, she inserted the key that she held like a feather between thumb and forefinger, and turned the latch until she heard a defining click. In silence she returned the keys to their clandestine drawer and turned to look at a room that suddenly felt unfamiliar.

In a trance, she wandered lost from her parents' bedroom into the entry, past the drooping blooms of daffodils that seemed to avoid meeting her eye, and out the front door, where not even the remarkably warm morning could command her attention.

Antius could not take the slurping one second longer. He threw open the door and stormed down the steps, trowel in hand, wishing to attack more than just renegade buttercups, leaving Ambel hunched over a bowl of soup. But those pesky weeds would have to do, seeing that plunging any sharp object into his son's flesh wouldn't achieve the result he dearly wished for. Not even Justyn's even-handed and incisive arguments last night had swayed Ambel's foolish determination in the least. His son would not recognize reason if it slapped him in the face, impressing on Antius that Ambel's blindness was much more than a blight of his eyes.

Antius had spent the better part of the week with his nose buried in tomes, searching for tales of the firebird; searching for anything, farfetched or fabulous, that might enlighten him with a course of action. And a cure. Tales told of myriad creatures and plants that caused sudden blindness: exotic toads whose spittle contained a caustic substance, a strain of capricious vine with a veneer of poison on every leaf found in deep rainforests, even a type of dung beetle that could render a puddle of water acidic enough to burn away sight when splashed through in haste. Antius did not doubt Ambel had met with something in nature that had rendered him blind. But until he could suss out the source, the cure would not be forthcoming. The attending medics, rife with apology, could find nothing that hinted at a cause and eventually left him with a salve that Ambel refused to use. And Antius had found little on the firebird—only a brief fairy tale that imparted nothing of practical value.

He thought to send word to the princess of Sherbourne to see if she might shed light on the situation, since she had apparently freed Ambel from the king's wrath and dungeon. But it would take weeks for a response by courier, and when questioning his fellow academicians about the kingdom to the west, a place Antius knew little of, he discovered that the princess had recently disappeared and no one knew her whereabouts. And they warned him not to attempt contact with the king, as that might draw his atten-tion to their land, something his peers felt would invite trouble. Antius paid little heed to the politics and intrigue of the courts of neighboring lands; he left those concerns to the diplomats in the Heights. But it was evident in the gleam of his peers' eyes, and through vague innuendo, that the king of Sherbourne was not one to be bothered with something as inconsequential as a man stricken with sudden blindness.

Antius pursed his lips and studied his garden. For a brief moment, he lifted his chin to the sun streaming delicious heat and let it bake his careworn face. The cheery morning stood in contrast to his dark predicament. His heart weighed heavily, making him drop to his knees in warm loamy soil. He let his fingers work of their own volition, stabbing at the clumps of obstinate weeds that had seemingly sprung up overnight at the prompting of the sun in its surprise appearance.

And then there was the matter of Teralyn. If it was true that she had fallen for a man in the village, and that she'd taken up stitching . . . his stomach clenched at the thought, and at the reminder that he must speak with her, the sooner the better. She deserved to be told the truth; what she did with the telling would be her decision.

Antius glanced up from his growing pile of vanquished butter-cups. As if summoned by his thoughts, Teralyn came around the bend, dressed in a flowing skirt and breezy blouse, but her face, he noted, was fixed and stolid in contrast. She was evidently not there for a friendly social call, and he didn't doubt it had something to do with Kileen's reaction to the stitching Teralyn had presented her with.

He set down the trowel and removed his gloves. With a grunt, he stood, but left his arms by his sides, worried an attempt at embrace would be spurned. He sighed. Everyone seemed to be angry with him these days.

"Antius, I must have a word with you." Teralyn's statement was less accusatory than Kileen's had been, yet it was just as demanding. Antius's shoulders slumped. It would take more than one word to assuage his young gardener.

"Why don't we sit by the greenhouse?" he offered, gesturing her to lead the way. "We can speak undisturbed there."

Teralyn nodded, and they followed the path around the cottage in silence until they came to the small domed glass structure filled with greenery pressing to get out of its confines. The small wooden bench was unoccupied and sat under a weeping birch that filtered light in patchwork upon the ground.

"This is nice. Not too much sun. Don't you find this a glorious day?" He sat on one end and patted the other for her to sit upon, which she did a bit reluctantly. He noted an aura of disarray about her, something her neat appearance and carefully braided hair failed to conceal.

"Antius, I'm not here to discuss the weather."

"I know." He let his words linger between them until they evaporated. "Your mother told me about your young man in the village, and showed me your stitching."

"Is she?"

Antius looked at her. "Is she what?"

"Is Kileen my mother?"

"Oh." Antius blinked, trying to figure out what thread had led Teralyn to such a question.

"It's not a hard question, Antius. Yes or no?" She set her expression once more in stone.

While he worked at formulating an answer, Teralyn waved her hands in dismissal. "You don't have to answer; it's written all over your face." Before Antius could push more than air through his teeth, Teralyn burst into sobs. That was all it took for him to wrap his bony arms like wings around her and draw her close. He let her cry, feeling tears soak his shirt while he stroked her hair. The branches of the birch bowed in the slight breeze, as if they too were weeping in commiseration.

"Ah, my dear girl, it's a strange tale and hardly to be believed—if I didn't well know the truth of it."

Teralyn wiped her face with her sleeve and narrowed her eyes. "I want to hear all of it. No holding back. I'm tired of this mystery." She reached into her skirt pocket and drew out the gold chain and pendant. "You can start with this."

She dropped the chain into Antius's hand, but he didn't need to look long at it; he knew what it was. He looked off across the farther cliffs, where mist rose from the cascade of water like ghosts, and wondered anew why the woman from the lake had chosen him of all people in the land. She'd never said. "She gave that to me, not seventeen years ago, when she gave me an armful of child wrapped in water reeds. You were . . . maybe a year old, not walking, but had enough teeth to draw blood from my hand when she relinquished you."

Teralyn's eyes widened but she said nothing. He held up the chain and sunlight caught on its edge, sending darts of light piecemeal across Teralyn's face. "I don't know whose this was—hers . . . or perhaps your mother's . . ."

"She wasn't my mother?"

Antius shook his head, dropped the chain into his lap.

"Then, who was she? What was she doing with me? And why did she come to you? Did she live here in the Heights—" Questions tumbled out her mouth faster than Antius could catch them. They pelted around him like the hard hail that pounded in winter storms. The strange woman's face rose to the surface of his mind, her shape spun of mist and water spray. Her eyes had fixed on his, her silent determination wrapped like a garland about her head.

Antius spilled his tale of the night he'd heard the knock at his door, the way she handed over the babe, the portentous words she spoke that made no sense. He'd tried to refuse, but she wouldn't have it, leaving him slack-jawed with a fussing infant in his arms.

"I consulted with the other regents, who were as perplexed as I. Professor Arbulus was aware of an . . . incident . . . that had occurred months earlier in the village. A baby-naming ceremony gone awry. The sudden appearance of a hermit at the ceremony caused an uproar, leading to an unspeakable act of violence—or so the story went. The parents were banished from the village, and it was assumed the babe died in the fire set by the villagers, a fire meant to consume the cottage and everything within it—"

"A fire! But why?" Teralyn asked. "Why would they burn down a cottage and leave a child to die in flames? How could people be so cruel?"

Antius patted her hand. "Superstition. Fear. Apparently the marsh witch—that is how the villagers refer to this old woman— foretold that the babe would be responsible for destroying Wentwater. And that was enough to send them on a rampage."

"I don't understand. What does that have to do with me?"

"When they sifted through the charred remains of the cottage, no trace of the baby could be found. No bones, no body. Nothing."

"So, someone had rescued it."

"That's how it appears. Yet no one had heard a thing." Antius cleared his throat. "The woman who brought you to me the following year did not say as much, only that she could not continue to care for you and that you would need a home entrenched in water. That the falls in the Heights would nurture you somehow. Teralyn,"—Antius gathered her wandering attention—"this woman was not human, from what I could tell. Forgive me for my inability to convey her true nature, for she is nothing I have ever encountered—before or since. But she seemed to be a thing of the water, graceful and pale, as if her coloring had long ago washed away. She left wet footprints when she walked, and smelled of waterweeds and mud. We could only surmise that she came from the lake."

"Lake Wentwater?" A cloud of emotion drifted across Teralyn's face as if she were remembering something. Antius nodded. "And you think that perhaps I was that babe—the one in the fire." She scrunched in face in thought. "So, this . . . creature may have rescued me, and raised me as her own for a time. But where? Surely not in the village, for someone would have seen her."

"I cannot say. She did not tell me."

"So, Kileen and Rufus—they aren't my parents, then."

"No, but they love you and had longed for a child. This, I knew. I certainly was in no position to raise you. But they were. And they were overjoyed upon seeing you. Tera, they may not be your true parents, but they have loved you as their own. No less than any other parent would love a natural child. You see that, don't you?"

The cloud that hovered around her face darkened and gathered force. "But why did they keep it a secret all these years? They should have told me—"

"I made them promise not to. They have no idea where you came from. They don't know anything about the circumstances of your arrival."

Teralyn fell silent for a moment. "You mentioned earlier about a curse. How the woman said the babe would cause the unraveling of Wentwater. How did you put it? That the people will perish for lack of a word. Good heavens, what does that mean?"

"I don't know."

"And that you wouldn't be able to prevent me from stitching and spinning. What do you make of that?"

Antius felt as if he were swatting flies, the way her questions kept coming. "I don't know what to make of it, any of it. But those words prompted me to keep you as far from a needle or spinning wheel as humanly possible. As I so instructed your parents—which is why Kileen became distraught upon finding that piece of stitching you did."

Teralyn brushed snagged branches from her hair and stood. She faced him. "Honestly, Antius, do you, of all people, really believe that I could cause the downfall of an entire village just from making a pillowcase?"

"Of course not, my dear. I would have considered that strange woman's tale hogwash had I not seen her for myself. She spoke with . . . great confidence and foreknowledge."

"And since when do you believe in such things? You've often told me the predicting of the future was superstitious rot—to put it in your own succinct words."

Antius sighed equivocally. "I felt it might be best to err on the side of caution."

"Of superstition." Teralyn's tone chastised him.

He shrugged. "Perhaps."

Teralyn snorted and shook more questions from her head. "And the parents who were banished all those years ago—does anyone know where they went? Where do banished people go?"

"Away. Far away. Word had it they had originally come from Sherbourne. Perhaps they returned there." Antius had hoped his confession would lighten the burden in his heart, but he could see by Teralyn's guarded expression that it had driven a wedge between them. Would she ever trust him again? He let his eyes rest on the face forming in his mind's eye, seeing the small babe with the tumble of white hair and the irises of coal that had locked onto his once the woman had vanished into the falls.

"What?" Teralyn asked.

Antius cocked his head. "When I peeled away the water reeds that encased you, it took three towels to dry you off."

Teralyn stood there, unblinking, sadness swimming in her eyes. She seemed more lost and abandoned than on the day he first took her into his arms. "Here." He dropped the chain into her open hand.

She closed her fist, and with that gesture seemed to close off every possible ingress to her heart. "Maybe someone in the village will have answers for me."

As she turned to go, he laid a hand on her arm. "It may not be wise, Teralyn dear, or safe, to inquire in Wentwater. If the villagers think you are the one foretold to destroy the village—"

Tears splashed hot on his wrist. The storm cloud covering her face burst into a downpour. "All these years, I thought Kileen was my mother. And now . . . my real mother is somewhere, who knows where, mourning me, thinking I've been dead . . ."

"Tera—"

Before Antius could dislodge the lump in his throat, she pulled from his grasp and ran down the granite pathway, lost to him before she was even gone from his sight.

FOURTEEN

"G OOD GRACIOUS," Iris mumbled, throwing cupboard doors open while sweat streamed in rivulets down the sides of her face and neck. She tossed the lids off the barrels she had already checked a half-dozen times. "How can a half bushel of rutabagas just vanish into thin air?" After the shock of this morning's findings—five hen feathers on the front stoop!—her heart couldn't take any more surprises.

"What's that you're fussin' with in there, Iris?"

Fen! What was he doing home so early in the afternoon? "Uh, nothing. Just misplaced something is all—"

She heard a snort from the entry. "You're always misplacing things. What's it this time?"

She blew out a breath and threw her hands up. "The rutabagas. You didn't do something with them, did you?" she asked, coming around the corner. She was glad she'd been the first one outside this morning, checking the weather for signs before Fen stirred under the covers. The disturbing appearance of those feathers had sent her scrambling to gather and hide them before her neighbors caught sight of her.

"Rutabagas, right. Decided to make a few pairs of boots out of them. Start a new fashion trend."

· 158 ·

Iris scowled. Fen always made fun of her lapsing memory, but it wasn't a bit funny. "Well? What brings you home? Shouldn't you be at the shop?"

"Well, I was. But, odd thing. The drying racks I keep in the back of the shop, where I lay out the leather, are gone."

"Gone? Someone's taken them? Whatever for? And who would do such a thing?"

"Haven't a clue. Was having a bit of a chat with Farmer Denton out front. Next thing I know, the leather's all ajumble, strewn about the floor. So I came for some wood, to set up something makeshift until I can find them. Maybe a neighbor's borrowed them."

"Right out from under your nose?"

Fen shrugged. "The back door was unlocked. Always is during the day." Fen scrounged in a wooden bin by the front door and pulled out a hammer and box of nails. "I've got some timbers out back, with the saw. Say, did you put the rooster somewheres?"

Iris's heart hammered in her chest. "What do you mean? He should be in the yard."

"I've not see 'im." Fen pushed open the front door and headed down the steps, leaving Iris waving a hand at her flushed face. First the feathers, now the rooster? What in heaven's name was happening?

Iris followed Fen outside, but as he vanished behind the cottage, she spotted a group of her neighbors huddled down the street. One glance made her stomach twist. Surely they were staring at her, and in a most unfriendly way. Maybe she *had* been seen this morning, collecting the feathers. Oh, that was all she needed—to be the brunt of gossip! She strained hard, replaying her steps from last evening. She had counted all the hens as they sat on their eggs.

And the rooster—he had been in there too. Hadn't he? Could he have somehow gotten out and found a way through the fence?

Iris felt hot eyes burning on the back of her neck as she casually strolled the fence line, looking for holes or depressions. Maybe a fox or raccoon had dug under the wood slats. Her eyes darted furtively. No sign of the rooster. Had he gotten trapped somewhere?

And here was a strange sign! Iris tiptoed over to the large climbing rose bush that dangled over the back fence. Only yesterday the myriad buds had begun to open in bloom, but today—

"Fen!" she whispered as loudly as she could. Her husband turned from his wood pile with a long plank in his arms, exasperation in his face.

"What now?"

She swung her arms wildly to get him to drop his load and come to her side. "I don't have time for this, Iris. I need to get back—"

"Well, what do you make of this!" She glanced quickly around to see if anyone could spot her from the street, but she was too far back behind the cottage to be noticed. She kept her voice quiet. "The rosebuds. Look—every one of them gone. Not eaten or snipped off. Just . . . gone."

Fen pinched up his face. "Well, maybe it's still too early for buds—"

Iris blew out a frustrated breath. "No, Fen, you don't understand." She must be going crazy. She *had* seen buds bursting all over this bush only yesterday. White creamy buds. "They were here. Now they're gone."

Fen stood unmoving as he studied the bush. He shrugged and shook his head. The look on his face told Iris he thought her addled.

"They were! I'm not daft!" She followed after him as he hefted the two long planks on his shoulder and made for the front gate. "Something's wrong. I'm going to take a look at Nettie's roses!"

"Suit yerself," he said. The gate slapped closed behind him.

Iris turned and saw that the crowd at the end of the lane had grown. She recognized nearly all her neighbors, and they were not happy. Her gut wrenched and she hurried back into the house. Ducking out of sight, she reached to close the shutters covering the windows and forced her nerves to calm. Nettie's roses would have to wait. Something terrible was happening, and as much as she needed to make sense of this mystery, fear held her in a stranglehold. She slumped in the corner and kneaded her hands, straining to think of where she had misstepped.

The front door blew open and Iris let out a squawk of surprise.

"Fromer! You scared the living daylights out of me!" Iris clutched at her heart as it tried to burst through her heaving chest.

"Mum—what are you doing on the floor? And why is the room so dark?" Fromer rushed to her side and knelt. He took her trembling hands in his own. "Why, your hands are all clammy. Are you unwell?"

Iris forced herself to stand, but her knees could barely hold her weight. "Help me to the chair, over there."

Fromer guided her to the overstuffed chair, where she plunked down with a great sigh. Fromer, bless his heart, gazed at her with concern. "Now, don't fret, Fro. I had a bit of a spell, but I'm better."

"Well, a little sunlight and fresh air would help, I'm sure . . ." As Fromer left her side and threw open shutters, she clamped her mouth shut. She didn't want to worry him more than necessary.

"There's something odd going on, Mum. The villagers are out in the lanes. As I came through town, they were gathered in groups, talking to themselves. Glaring at me in a strange fashion. I don't know what to make of it."

Iris sat up straighter. "I noticed that too. Did you catch anything they said? Has something happened?"

Fromer shrugged. "I didn't stop to ask."

Iris thought for a moment and studied her son. "Aren't you back early? You finished for the day?"

Fromer frowned and pulled off his hat. "I suppose. I was going to trim the goats' hooves this afternoon, but I couldn't find my tray of rasps. I must have misplaced them. But no mind, I'll just—"

"You as well? Your dah was here just minutes ago. Said someone had taken his drying racks from the back room—right out from under his nose!"

"His what?"

"His racks. For drying leather."

"That's an odd thing for someone to take."

Iris wasn't sure she should say more, but she couldn't hold back. She drew Fromer close to her and spoke in a hushed voice. "And Fro—my barrel of rutabagas is empty. And the roses outside— why, they were budding only yesterday, and now the buds have all vanished."

Fromer's eyes widened. "There must be a thief in town."

"A thief that steals buds off bushes?"

Fromer blew breath through his teeth. "No wonder the village is in a fluster. I'll go out and see what I can learn. You still look a bit flushed, Mum. Stay here. I'll be back shortly. I'm sure there's a logical explanation for all this."

Logical? Nothing like this had ever happened in the village . . . odd things going missing. Iris watched Fromer leave the cottage, the door slapping closed behind him as he tromped down the porch steps. She rose from her chair and sneaked over to the window facing the street. A quick glance showed Fromer approaching a group of her neighbors huddled in front of Nettie's house. A terrible sense of guilt rolled over her. What, oh what, had she done? It had to be her fault. She must have miscounted the hens. Surely one of them had been left out last night. And the rooster too! With all those feathers lying around, no doubt a fox had made short work of them both, and that's why the feathers had been scattered all over the front stoop.

She glanced around the room as her panic rose. Had she forgotten to pull the hair from the brush and burn it? Did she leave wool overnight on the carding comb? Had Fen somehow walked into the house yesterday when she was restuffing the feather mattress? Oh, so many things could have happened right under her nose without her noticing.

She stood on wobbly legs and stumbled into the kitchen. As she poured a cup of water from the pitcher with a trembling hand, she heard a squeak of metal and a groan coming from the ceiling, the sound of nails pulling from wood, and heavy timbers settling. She tipped her head to look up at the iron pot rack, then took a hasty step backward, pressing against the counter as the dozen heavy pots and pans fell like boulders in a loud crash to the floor.

Iris gasped in terror as her cookware spun and wobbled to a stop around her feet, leaving a sharp ringing in her ears. The pot rack had vanished—right before her very eyes!

Teralyn slowed as she entered the village. Was it customary for the villagers to gather in the lanes like this at the end of the day? She thought they would be working; maybe today was a holiday she was unfamiliar with. Shopkeepers held brooms and dust cloths in their hands as they sidled up to farmers hemmed in by pigs and sheep. All were mingling in the thoroughfare, stern expressions on their faces. A few villagers noticed her arrival and leaned close to talk. One even pointed at her as she passed by. Teralyn smiled in friendly greeting, but all she received in return were scowls. How very odd. Was she wearing something that offended them? Or did she somehow stand out as a resident of the Heights, and that alone upset them?

In the sweltering warmth of the late afternoon, she kept up her pace. For the last three hours as she stormed down the mountain, brooding over her words with Antius and mulling over the mystery of her past, the sun had baked her like a loaf in an oven. Hot, tired, and grumpy, all she wanted was to check into a room at the Cygnet and wash up. But her need to see Fromer surpassed all other needs, and she made straight for his parents' cottage. He hadn't been with his herd; she'd found the goats grazing the hillocks attended by a young boy Fromer had appointed with the task. Unless he was off on some errand, she guessed he'd be home.

Raised voices drew her eyes from the road. A handful of irate villagers faced off at the corner, with finger pointing and shoving. She couldn't help but overhear as she kept her eyes locked on the ground before her feet and hurried past.

"You've been eyeing my ram for ages. No secret there."

"What? You're accusing me of taking the dumb beast? And where'd I put it—in my tub? Come check, if you've a mind."

"Well, no one else would be fool enough to steal him out of my pen. And did you take the rabbits as well?"

"Rabbits? What rabbits?"

"The ones in the cages, idiot!"

"Hey, get your hands off me!"

"Not until you 'fess up."

Teralyn heard a thump and more angry voices join in the fray. She turned the corner just as a fight broke out behind her. A woman ran toward her, shouting. She waved her hands wildly in the air.

"Has he gone this way?"

"Who?" Teralyn asked, dodging the flying arms.

"Arnold."

"Sorry, I don't know anyone named Arnold."

The woman gritted her teeth and stared Teralyn down. "Fool girl, he's not a fella—he's a rumphog. And a big one at that. You couldn't miss 'im if he came this way."

Teralyn backed up against a wall as more villagers barreled down the road. "I'm sorry. I've not seen him."

The woman shook her head in exasperation and continued her mad dash down the lane, calling out the hog's name.

Teralyn now began to run, dodging villagers as she headed for Fromer's cottage. The entire town was in an uproar. Every face reflected fear, anger, or bewilderment. Clearly, she had not chosen the best day to come see Fromer. She had no idea if this kind of panic was a regular occurrence in Wentwater or if the day's events were an anomaly. Nothing like this ever took place in the Heights.

She turned one more corner and stopped. There, in the evening twilight, stood Fromer. Soft light played in the hair that tickled his shoulders, but also cast a dark shadow on the ground before him. A chill raced over her skin as she slowed and took in the scene unfolding before her. Flanked by more than two dozen villagers, Fromer waved his arms above him as hands pawed at him. His face showed fear and confusion.

Teralyn ran up to the mob and yelled. "Stop! What are you doing? Give him room!"

"It's her! The girl from the Heights!" someone cried out. The crowd shifted their attention from Fromer to Teralyn, and the sea of bodies moved toward her. She caught Fromer's attention, and he tried to push through the crush to get to her. Arms enmeshed him in a net that prevented him from reaching her.

"It's her fault! She's brought bad luck upon us all."

Teralyn pushed back against the surging crowd, trying to see Fromer's face, but it was blocked from her view. "Me? What have I done?"

A gangly old woman raised her voice over the noise. "The lad's brought ruin to Wentwater by cavorting with this girl!"

Teralyn strained to see over the bobbing heads to where Fromer stood, held fast in the arms of two burly men. Voices cried out in a grating disharmony of sound, the antithesis of music. Sharp, jagged words sliced the air. More and more villagers arrived, layering their accusations and fear in a suffocating pile that Teralyn sought escape from. But the crowd engulfed her, urgent and forceful. Someone took her arm and held it in a viselike grip.

"Please, let me go. I've only just arrived in the village. Whatever the matter, surely—"

"Take her too. Summon the magistrate!" a man said.

"He'll get to the bottom of this," the old woman added. She drew close to Teralyn and spoke in a harsh tone, loud enough for the crowd to hear. "We don't know what you've done to cause such chaos, things disappearing from homes and yards. How did you manage? Cast some sort of spell? Use some of that arcane knowledge of the Heights to pull the wool over our eyes? Well, you'll not get away with it."

"This is madness! I know nothing of your troubles!"

Another man spoke over the din. "We can't do anything until the magistrate arrives. Best to confine them to home until then. We can't be out in the streets after dark."

A few villagers checked the sky and nodded. The old woman said, "Enough rituals have been broken for one day. Surely, more doom will await us if we linger. Take them to Iris's and post guards. Don't let anyone in or out of their house until the magistrate comes."

Arms swept Teralyn from her spot in the lane and moved her along; she didn't dare resist. Fromer was out of sight, but she felt relief knowing they would be confined together. She fumed. No wonder Antius and Justyn ranted about the villagers. Is this how they acted anytime something seemed out of kilter? If things were disappearing, then logic decreed they should look for a thief, or some other simple explanation for the untoward events. How could they so hastily jump to conclusions and place blame without researching the circumstances? As if someone from the Heights could *or would* wield magic over the village! How ignorant and foolish a notion!

She stumbled as the mob pushed her up the steps to the cottage. Fromer caught her and pulled her into his arms, and the villagers backed away. His arms, so warm and comforting, dispelled much of her agitation, and her shaking stopped. Teralyn read fear in the villagers' eyes as they slunk out the yard and hurried toward their homes in the dimming twilight. Three men remained, barricading the gate with their bodies, watching the lane—for the magistrate, Teralyn supposed. Whoever that was.

Fromer stroked Teralyn's hair with a tender touch. "Oh, Tera. Of all days for you to come to town. I'm so sorry."

She looked into his penetrating eyes and found something other than the distress she'd expected. Love simmered there, and her heart skipped in response. Whatever madness had possessed the inhabitants of Wentwater no longer held sway in her heart. In there, she only had room for Fromer, and he filled every corner of it. No doubt this trouble would pass, answers would be found, people would be mollified. Still, it unsettled her to think the villagers held such contempt for those in the Heights. The families there supported the livelihood of Fromer's neighbors. Did they really object to his relationship with her? And if they did, what would that mean for Fromer, and for his position in the community?

As if Fromer could read her thoughts, he said, "My sweet girl, don't pay any mind to those fools. In a few days, they'll have forgotten what got them all worked up. The smallest thing can bring them to hysterics."

"But what was that all about? I heard them claim I had cast a spell on them. That things were disappearing."

Fromer studied the men posted at the gate. One turned around with a sneer on his face. "Let's talk inside. I'm sure my mum must be distraught over this."

Fromer opened the door and ushered her inside. Teralyn noticed the room dimly lit with oil lamps, but the shutters were all closed. They removed their shoes, and Teralyn hung back while Fromer walked into the sitting room. "Mum, are you here? I'm home. And Teralyn's here with me."

Teralyn heard shuffling from the hallway, then a whisper. "Oh, Fro!" Iris hurried over and threw her arms around him. "I'm so afraid! I saw the crowd—and the men at the gate. Why are they here?"

Fromer rested a hand on Iris's shoulder and pulled back to look in her face. "Now, Mum. Everything will be just fine. The magistrate's on his way, and he'll clear—"

"The magistrate! Heavens!" Up went Iris's arms, waving the air as if swatting flies. "What have you done?"

Fromer shrugged. "Nothing, Mum. And Tera's not done anything either. She's just arrived, but for some reason the villagers think she has something to do with all that's vanishing from town."

"From town? So . . . it's not just—"

Teralyn watched Iris's face turn a pale shade as her jaw dropped. Iris lifted a shaky finger in Teralyn's direction. "It's . . . it *is* you . . ."

Fromer frowned and drew closer to Teralyn. "What are you talking about, Mum?"

Iris scowled and backed up two steps, her finger hanging in the air in accusation. "I was right! I knew it was you!" Iris let out a wail that startled Teralyn and made Fromer grab his mother's arms.

"Mum, what has gotten into you? You've got to get your wits about you. Let this all settle—"

Iris slapped away her son's hands and pressed against the wall. She narrowed her eyes at Teralyn. "You must leave. *Now!*"

"Mum, she can't. We're to wait for the magistrate. Please, tell me what you are carrying on about."

Iris spoke to Fromer, but kept her eyes locked on Teralyn. "The babe. The . . . the one in the fire all those years back. With hair as white as snow, eyes of coal. The witch foretold she would destroy the town. And now, look! It's coming true!"

"Oh, for heaven's sake! Just because a few rutabagas have gone missing?"

Fromer shut his mouth and cocked his head. Teralyn heard boots clomping up the steps, and then the door blew open.

"Iris!" Fen yelled. "Where are you, woman?"

"Here I am," she called out, her words fluttering.

Teralyn shook and Fromer wrapped her tighter in his arms. She had so much to tell him. And she had to tell him soon. Oh, what in heaven's name was happening? How had Iris come to understand in mere weeks what Teralyn never suspected in seventeen years? Antius had been wise to warn her. Clearly, the villagers remembered the words of the marsh witch, uttered so long ago. And no doubt they would be quick to turn her into a scapegoat for any and all troubles their village suffered if they discovered the truth. But how could she deny her past?

A shiver ran across the back of her neck. She thought of the woman from the lake who had left her in Antius's arms. She reached up to touch the pendant that now hung around her throat. What if that creature had spoken the truth? That Teralyn was destined somehow to bring Wentwater to ruin? But how? She had no magic, no powers! And she had no need or desire to see harm done to anyone. She was innocent! Nothing made sense.

Without meaning to, she sobbed in Fromer's arms. Streams of tears flooded her cheeks. Not even Fromer's embrace could keep out the chill that settled on her spirit.

Fromer pulled back. "You're . . . wet." He fingered the sleeve of her blouse.

Teralyn wiped her face with the back of her hand. "My tears . . ."

"No, you're *wet*."

Teralyn noted Fromer's puzzled look, then felt her clothes. Not only was her sleeve wet where she had wiped her tears but her entire blouse . . . and her skirt . . . and . . .

She reeled back from Fromer as her breath hitched in her throat. Fen, who had come alongside Iris, stood slack-jawed, mouth hanging open. Iris pressed a hand to her lips, wide-eyed. Teralyn clamped her own hand over her mouth as she backed into the sitting room, eyes riveted to the floor as her wet footprints followed her like an incriminating shadow.

FIFTEEN

JUSTYN HAD planned to wait until Sunday to head down to the village. He still had plenty of time to give the witch her payment—the seven rooster feathers. But he couldn't contain his excitement. Surely by now the village would be in chaos. And likely Fromer would have been hauled away into custody until the matter could be cleared up. But it wouldn't, would it? Justyn would make sure of that. The witch had supposedly given him power over Fromer. Justyn chortled. As if her enchantment could extend past the walls of her castle. All week Justyn had pondered his strange vision of the stream of thought. It had felt so real, yet he knew she had played tricks with his mind. Probably something in the smoke from the lamps, something toxic or hallucinogenic that had made him susceptible to suggestion for a time. Smoke and mirrors, no less.

However, in a fashion, she inadvertently *had* empowered him over Fromer—by requiring the feathers and giving Justyn the opportunity he needed to discredit his brother. Maybe that had been her scheme all along, only to claim he had wrought some magical binding by stitching Fromer's name into a piece of cloth. How stupid did she think he was?

He laughed as he skipped down the mountain, the village looming larger in the evening dusk as his boots tromped the dirt. Dust twirled in the scant light, and a heady scent of blooming shrubbery warmed by the day's sun cloyed the air. Ursell and her babble of mumbo-jumbo! And what in the world did she plan to do with rooster feathers? Concoct some potion to counteract warts? Use them to decorate one of the rooms in her moldering castle?

But just what did she keep in those jars? *"I'll have one from you soon enough!"* she had said in that raspy, irritating voice. Surely her voice was the reason the villagers had forced her out of town. No one could tolerate such an aural assault for long. Justyn mulled the possibilities. Those things in the jars seemed alive, but how could anything live in an airtight container? And the odd light they gave off—akin to phosphorus, but in such beautiful subdued colors. Perhaps some of the researchers in the Heights would know what they were. Maybe, he considered, he could steal one when he returned to pay the witch. Perhaps they were some type of firefly that haunted the marshes.

By the time he entered through the eastern gate, the lanes were dark and deserted. Even so, Justyn sensed fear behind every tightly closed curtain and shutter he passed. Not a soul looked out as he hurried by. His footfalls sounded loud in the stifling silence of the village, and when he climbed the front steps to his parents' cottage, he cringed at the way the creaking of the wood punctured the air. He pushed down on the latch, wondering if his parents had gone to bed with the chickens, but met with surprise when the door yanked open before him. His father stood, blocking the entryway, an iron fire poker raised in a threatening manner.

"Father!" Justyn faltered as he stepped back, nearly tripping and falling on the stoop. "What are you doing at the door with *that* in your hands?"

Fen let out a long breath and the lines in his face relaxed. "Ah, son. You scared me so. Wasn't expectin' you this early. Weren't you planning on Sunday?"

Justyn looked over his shoulder before slipping inside. Before he could reach around, Fen had already secured the door, then the old cross brace that barred anyone entering uninvited.

"Why are you putting the beam across the door?" Justyn asked while removing his coat. "Where's Mother?"

"Your mum is out of sorts. Lying down." Fen shook his head. Words failed him.

"What's happened? Where's Fromer?"

Fen sighed and slumped on the sofa. Justyn noted the chill in the room; the hearth was cold. His mother always kept a fire going this time of year. He stooped to pile on kindling.

"The magistrate's got him. Him and the girl."

Justyn jumped to his feet. "Wait—Teralyn was here . . . with Fromer? And the magistrate took them both?" When had Teralyn come down the mountain? He pursed his lips to keep from scowling. She would only complicate things, coming to Fromer's defense. And if the villagers turned on Teralyn instead of Fromer, why, that would send repercussions up to the Heights and . . .

"Where did he take them?" Justyn asked, rushing back to the entry and putting on his coat.

"To the Commons Hall, of course. But, Justyn, you can't go back out. It's night, and what with all the strange happenings, you'd best stay right here, in your own safe bed."

"No time," Justyn said, removing the wood beam barring the door.

"But, yer mum! She'll want to see you. And she'll have a fit—"

"Father, it can't be helped. I must assess the situation and right what's wrong." When he saw his father's stricken face, he smiled, knowing just what words would mollify his parents. "Remember, that's my destiny, my foretold position in this community—to be a leader, a fair and just voice for the people, to right wrongs. Mother will understand."

He swung open the door and turned back to his father, who had sunk even deeper into the sofa cushions, and said, "Make a fire for Mother and tell her not to fret. I surely won't be gone long."

Teralyn looked up when she heard the key jiggling in the lock. Despondency weighed down her head; it felt as heavy as an anvil as she tried to lift it. Her heart ached for Fromer, and she worried for his fate. The magistrate had hauled them both off in a huff, without explanation, only hinting that Fromer would pay for his actions. When the man tied Fromer's hands behind his back, Teralyn had gasped, but Fromer reassured her with his eyes. Even then, his every concern was for her. Not even her strangeness alienated him. She was a freak of nature—how could he love her? Yet, his soul was linked to hers, already too tightly woven to undo. No one had ever loved her so truly, without reserve or expectation. He loved her for who she was, not for what she could produce or accomplish or perform. She thought her heart would break from worry. And here she was, locked in a small dark room, sitting on a bench, powerless to help in any way.

The door swung open. In the glow cast by the oil lamp carried in by the guard, she recognized Justyn in the shadows and stiffened. What was he doing here? The smug smile he wore unnerved her. Had he something to do with why she was being held for questioning? She recalled his hurt look when she had slapped his face and spurned him. Was this his retaliation, then? The thought troubled her deeply, for she sensed Justyn capable of fomenting all manner of trouble in this village he loathed. What did he care if he incited an uproar? It would only serve to prove his point—that she should steer clear of Fromer and his "ways" and isolate herself in the Heights for the rest of her life. Married to him, of course.

Teralyn made no attempt to hide her annoyance. "Did you come here to gloat? Or have a fancy to rescue me from my predicament?"

Justyn's countenance fell, but she could see through his ruse. His eyes burned cold and emotionless. He waved the guard out of the small room, which contained only the bench, and came close to her. "I've come about your welfare. When I arrived in the village and heard you'd been accused of stealing, why, I had to come to your defense. I'm highly respected in the village, you know, and the magistrate listens to me."

Teralyn pressed her back against the wall and folded her arms across her chest. "I don't want or need your help. And if you're so keen on winning my admiration, then find a way to exonerate your brother. And what, pray tell, am I accused of stealing? A few chickens? A pot rack? Where would I stow them—under my skirt?"

Justyn smiled as if amused by her sense of humor. "The villagers don't think the way we do, Tera. I warned you, didn't I? When something goes amiss, they leap to conclusions, grasping at whatever explanation seems handiest and will fit into their worldview. You're the stranger in town. You've upset the balance. You waltz into the village, intent on stealing away one of their own, and things go missing. You've stolen a heart—why wouldn't you steal, say . . . a pot rack?" Justyn shrugged as if his line of thinking were entirely logical.

"That's absurd!"

"And, coincidentally, chicken feathers were found all over town yesterday morn. A trail of feathers leading to Fromer. Well, signs like that just can't be ignored, can they? Pointing to the guilty most pointedly, I'd say."

"No doubt you had something to do with that."

He leaned close to her face. "Me? I've been in the Heights all week. Classes, lecturing. Working on my next paper."

She scowled. His nearness set her on edge. She scooted over on the bench, but that only afforded him the opportunity to sit beside her, which he did.

"Then who is doing this? And why are things disappearing?" she asked.

"Why do you care?"

"Have you not seen your mother? She's panicky and in a fret that Fen can't calm." She had no intention of telling Justyn the real reason for Iris's near swoon—her own wet clothes and footprints. That would only make him more fixated on her. He already knew something about her true parentage; that much was sure. But what did he know, and how had he learned it? She thought back to her mother's comment last week. Justyn had visited her and they had spoken. Maybe she had told him then. Although, since Antius was Justyn's mentor, perhaps *he* had told Justyn all he knew about the strange woman from the lake who had brought her to his doorstep. Is that why Justyn was so besotted with her? Because she was an oddity, a mystery? Something to pick apart and study until he learned all he possibly could about her?

"Justyn, just go away. I'd rather rot here than listen to your patronizing."

"You need me, Teralyn. No one else will come to your aid."

His nearness made her claustrophobic. She stood and walked to the opposite wall. She fumbled for an acerbic response, but he was right—who would come to her aid? Her parents? Antius? How would they learn of her incarceration? And if they did, would it be too late? Antius's story rang in her head—the tale of the baby-naming ceremony. How they had chased the parents—her parents!—out of the village and set their cottage on fire. If they could so easily engage in such cruelty on a whim, what might they do to her—and Fromer? He knees weakened, and she slumped to the cold stone ground.

Justyn came and knelt by her side. He laid a hand on her shoulder, and she fought the urge to brush it away. "Listen," he said, "I don't want to see you hurt. Let me take you to the north gate, in secret. No one will know, and you can head back to the Heights. Stay up there until I return." His smile exuded warmth and assurance, but it belied the coldness that claimed his eyes. She sought to find something in those eyes, some sign of tenderness, but she could only decipher icy judgment. Yet what choice did she have? If she could get back to the Heights, she could enlist help from Antius and the other regents. Maybe, with all their books and knowledge, they could uncover the cause of these mysterious disappearances. They, of all people, had the resources to find an answer.

She nodded. "All right. But promise me, Justyn, that you will do everything you can to help Fromer. He is innocent."

"Oh, I know he is," Justyn answered, a little too readily. "Don't worry. I'll see to him. Now, come."

He offered his hand and she reluctantly took it. When he opened the door, he said, "Wait a moment," then left to speak with the guard.

Teralyn mulled over the night's affairs. Someone had to be responsible for things vanishing. She would point to Justyn as the perpetrator, but Iris had told how all the buds on her rosebush had been ready to bloom, and the next day every one of them went missing. Her pot rack had suddenly disappeared as if erased by an invisible hand, with the pots and pans clanging to the floor. No human could do such a thing. And although Fen wanted to blame Iris's overactive imagination, she had led them all into the kitchen, where the evidence could not be discounted. Before Fen had come home, he'd heard his neighbors arguing in the streets. Things were going missing now at alarming rates—and the list of missing items was extensive: eggs and mops, cooking oil and onions, rows of flowers, a feather mattress from a bedroom, even an entire wooden fence had just up and vanished.

Clearly, magic was behind this. Teralyn didn't know what to think about magic; she had been told all her life it didn't exist. That people used magic as a way of explaining the inexplicable, a lazy and ignorant catch-all for anything they didn't understand. Well, what else could be at the root of these occurrences? And now, having witnessed her own clothes become wet and her feet leave watery footprints, how could she scoff? Something strange was at work in Wentwater, some unknown power, whether deliberate or impersonal. And the only "person" she had heard of who might be wrapped in magic was the woman who had brought her to Antius seventeen years ago. Had she really come from the lake? Was that who Teralyn heard singing that morning of the festival, such mournful, compelling notes that had tugged at her heart and filled her with melancholy?

Suddenly, she had to know. Even if the woman of the lake wasn't responsible for the disturbance in the village, perhaps she would know its source. And how to stop it before harm came to Fromer. She would first take the matter to Antius, of course. But she had the feeling all his worldly wisdom and resources would fail to help.

Justyn returned. "Come," he said in a hush. "Follow me."

He reached once more to take her hand, but she kept her arms at her sides. In the lantern's light, she watched a flash of anger streak his face as he dropped his outstretched arm. He then spun around and strode down the dark corridor of the Commons Hall without another word. She sighed and followed. Her heart berated her for leaving Fromer behind. She strained to listen as she hurried in silence. Was Fromer there, behind one of those locked doors she passed?

She imagined his sweet melody playing, the tender pull of the bow eliciting soft, mournful notes from his fiddle—as if her heart could hear the music swelling in his own, yearning to merge with hers. But as she left the hall and ventured out into the starless night, the village disintegrating in the fog behind her, the fragile thread of music linking her to Fromer dwindled. And as she walked through the gate under Justyn's watchful eye, it finally snapped.

SIXTEEN

"AH, TERALYN, dear, do come in, come in!"

Teralyn nodded at stout old Arbulus, who gave his customary chortle upon opening the library doors while knotting his long beard in his fingers. She had never seen the fellow when he wasn't ebullient and boisterous and wondered if anything ever ruffled him.

"We're neck-high in research, and oh, what a fascinating hypothesis you've proposed, my dear."

Teralyn followed the grand sweep of his arm as he gestured her inside the cavernous, high-ceilinged room. His flowing robes swished as he walked toward the library table nearly buried in stacks of books, parchments, and papers. A smaller table nearby showed the remains of a hastily enjoyed afternoon tea, with cups and spoons littered among plates of crumbs. She recognized another of the regents—Anthanus—studying a parchment he held up to lamplight, which illuminated faint, washed-out lettering against a yellowed background.

Antius, sitting hunched over a hefty tome, raised his eyes and gazed at her over the top of his spectacles. Antimony, his owl, nestled close to Antius's ear. Teralyn came over and stroked the bird's head.

"Antius, your owl seems distressed."

Antius sighed with a forlorn look tainting his face. "It's Ambel. The fool boy's mind is so dislodged he doesn't even recognize his own pet. Upsets Antimony terribly." Antius shook off his mood with a brisk shake of his head. "But come, my dear. Sit beside me. We've spent these many hours trying to make sense of the strange occurrences down in Wentwater, but frankly, we haven't found anything of substance."

"Yet fascinating, nevertheless!" Arbulus chimed. "Why, evidence seems to be pointing to some sort of group mind-swaying. The mind is a powerful thing, you know, and with the rampant susceptibility to suggestion, as is such with those simple folk, no doubt all it took was one superstitious and frightened villager to claim an uncanny disappearance to set the whole village in a panic. Due to the heightened fear, which spread like an epidemic, their imaginations manifested—to them, of course; not in actuality—and, voila! Random items vanished into thin air!"

Teralyn narrowed her eyes. "You don't mean to say this is all a fancy of sorts, do you?" She turned to Antius. "I was there. I *saw* things vanish—"

Anthanus lowered the parchment he was studying and glared at her. His high-pitched voice came out in a grumpy squeak. "Such as? What did you *personally* see vanish? Hmm?"

Teralyn sifted through her memory, of the villagers rushing down the lane, of Iris pointing to the pots strewn about the kitchen floor. Of Fen claiming his racks had been stolen from his cobbler's shop. "I didn't actually *see* anything—"

"Aha!" Arbulus bellowed, the words followed by a deep belly laugh. "You see! This supports my theory. But it does little to prove the veracity of your wayward hypothesis."

"Wayward . . ."

"In a word—yes, my young girl. You've not the years nor the learning to understand. Why, I've spent a good portion of my life studying the intricate nuances of the mind's workings, my dear. The mind can conjure up the most amazing things under pressure. Don't discount the power of hysteria. Rulers from ages past wielded great power over the masses by inducing hysteria and fomenting lies—lies huge numbers of people believed, all because those around them believed. Almost a form of group hypnosis, if you care to call it that."

Teralyn grunted in frustration, and Antius laid a tender hand on her shoulder.

"Then, tell us, lass, what makes the most sense to you." Antius's tone softened her annoyance. Even if his fellow historians did not care to listen to her naïve, uneducated opinion, Antius would show her a measure of respect.

She drew in a breath, noticing she had all three regents' riveted attention. "At first I supposed someone had been stealing. Since the things missing seemed odd and unrelated, I thought whoever was pulling this prank meant to befuddle the villagers. Confuse and frighten them, turn them one against the other. But, as much as you may not want to hear this . . . I do feel magic must be at the root—"

In unison, Arbulus and Anthanus guffawed and held their heaving sides. Antius looked on with compassion as the other two regents doubled over with belly laughs, wiping their reddened faces as tears streaked down their cheeks. Teralyn felt her face flush.

When the outburst died down, Antius stood with a scowl. "My friends, your disrespectful attitude is uncalled for. Teralyn has spent much time recently down in the village. She has firsthand knowledge of the affairs you have only heard about. Just when was the last time either of you ventured down from the Heights?"

Arbulus patted his forehead, still tittering. He looked over at Teralyn. "My apologies, lass. Your ideas just leave me in stitches! My apologies." He turned to Antius. "Point and score, old boy. Empirical evidence trumps theory, and you're spot on. I've not visited the village in many decades. And I doubt my jovial companion over there"—he pointed to Anthanus, who was still wiping his face and sucking in great gasps of air to calm his mirth—"even remembers what Wentwater looks like, it's been so long for him." He wagged an encouraging finger at Teralyn. "Pray continue, lass. I'm all ears."

Teralyn could see the great restraint Arbulus used to keep from blurting out again. She spoke in a quiet, unassuming manner, but hoped what she planned to say would make them take this mystery more seriously. "The man I love has been taken into custody. He's been accused of causing this situation—and partly because of me. The villagers feel that somehow I am to blame, bringing chicanery from the Heights and upending their way of life. This does not bode well for the Heights. For if the villagers come to fear us, they may decide not to engage in business with those who live here. And then where would you, dear regents, get your clothing and cookware and fine foods, should such a thing come to pass?"

The smiles dropped from the regents' faces. Teralyn continued. "And I am worried Fromer will be hurt or, at very least, his reputation in the village will be marred. I can't allow that. So I am determined to get to the bottom of this." She stared at the great wall, covered in maps detailing all the known lands of the world. "I may not be all that educated, and I haven't traveled outside this realm as you men have. But I sense there is a pattern here, a pattern to the things disappearing." She stood and paced across the large wool rug that covered the wood-planked flooring. "The very first things to go were Fen's drying racks in his shop. Then Iris claimed the pot rack vanished, causing her pots to fall to the floor . . . and her barrel of rutabagas was empty. Then, the rosebuds. Not the bush, but just the buds. As I entered the village, someone claimed her rumphog had run off. And another accused a neighbor of stealing his rabbits—"

Antius came over to her and paced alongside her. "Rabbits . . . rutabagas . . . rumphogs . . . racks . . . roses . . ."

Arbulus jumped out of his chair. "All begin with the letter *R*."

Antius swung around and pointed at him. "Yes!" He then frowned. "But, what of it? Why in the world would items beginning with *R* disappear?" He looked to Teralyn, who frowned in thought.

"You regents well know the power of words. You immerse yourselves in them." She gestured to the many books piled on the table, then recalled what Antius had told her. The woman from the lake had said to him seventeen years ago: *"The people shall perish for lack of a word."*

"Words are symbols, and I sense there is power behind this disappearance, something to do with words. If you take a word away, wouldn't the thing it represents also cease to exist?"

Anthanus snorted. "You're speaking nonsense, lass. One can never take away a word, remove it from existence." He patted a stack of books. "Words are preserved forever—in books such as these. Words, thoughts, ideas, concepts—they remain eternal. There are unnamed things in the world—yet even they still have substance and exist, with no one to put a label on them. Conversely, there are innumerable words describing things that do not actually have form."

Arbulus held up a hand. "Yet I'm intrigued by what this lass has to say. Tell me, Teralyn. What else has gone missing?"

"Those items I recounted all disappeared on the first day I had arrived in the village. The next morning, I heard a farmer complain all his hens had stopped laying. And he wasn't the only one. Then by midday, a patch of mint, a mop. Some goats had stopped giving milk—all dried up overnight. Surely you cannot believe these things are all a result of a massive group hallucination. Did the goats and chickens also participate in this mental divergence?"

Anthanus was quick to jump in. "No doubt their livestock sensed their distress. Animals that are stressed will behave in such a manner. You, dear girl, are grasping at straws—trying to see patterns in letters to derive a meaning—just as the villagers look for patterns in cloud, wind, and chicken feed."

Teralyn turned to Anthanus. "How is that truly different from what you academicians do in the Heights? You look to your words for a pattern, for meaning. You may not read the signs from the heavens, but you interpret the signs from your mass of knowledge. Both cultures seek clues to explain their world. They read patterns; you read books."

Anthanus grunted loudly. "The two are nothing alike. Nothing! How can you compare the actions of a superstitious, irrational people to the educated?"

"Well," Teralyn said with all respect, "you haven't found an answer in any of your books yet, have you?"

Antius stroked the owl perched next to his neck as he continued to pace, his head down, studying the floor. "First the items with *R*. Then eggs. Eggs start with *E*. The other things—the milk and mint and mop—"

"The letter *M*," Arbulus blurted. "REM. What could that possibly mean?"

Antius stopped and came close to Teralyn. He spoke only to her, and engaged her eyes. "The village of Wentwater is indeed unraveling—one word at a time." He dropped his voice to a whisper and added, "Just as the woman from the lake had predicted."

Teralyn gulped. "But she said I would be the cause. How? Have I done something I am unaware of? I cannot make sense of this."

"Speak up, you two," Anthanus squeaked. "What are you discussing with such intensity?"

Antius kept his gaze on Teralyn and his voice intimate. "Nor can I. I think this calls for a visit to the village." He raised his head and cleared his throat. "Friends, I am going to Wentwater with Teralyn. I believe the situation is serious enough to warrant such a trip."

"But Antius," Teralyn said, "do you feel able? It's not an easy way down, and I don't believe we will be at all warmly received."

"Pah! I can hire a carriage to take us. As for the other, I am certain we have nothing to fear. As intriguing as your theory is, I believe what the villagers need is a strong voice of reason. Someone to calm their fears and put things in perspective. And once the hysteria has been assuaged, we can take a good, hard look at what is really happening." He gave his fellow regents a stern glance. "Knowledge is power, my friends. So, I will go acquire knowledge."

Arbulus and Anthanus laughed. "Well, visit the village, old fellow, if it pleases you," Arbulus said. "But I daresay you will find all the 'missing' items will have been neatly returned to their places upon your arrival. Someone must be behind this hoax—whether it follows a pattern of letters or no."

Antius held out his hand to Teralyn, who took it amid the steady chuckling of the other regents. "Come, lass. We should—"

Teralyn pulled back as Antius startled. He spun one way, then another. "Where is Antimony?"

Arbulus and Anthanus quieted. Their arms dropped to their sides as they looked around the room. "Did he fly off your shoulder?" Arbulus asked.

"No. He was right here, while we spoke." Antius knelt to the floor and peered under tables.

Teralyn joined his efforts. "I didn't see him. I thought he was nuzzled under your beard. And when he's in there, he's hard to spot."

Anthanus laughed. "Maybe, old fellow, he's still in there, entangled in that mass of hair."

Antius scowled and fingered through the thick beard. "He's *not* there, you fool. Help me find him!"

With great exaggerated sighs, the other two regents wandered the room, looking atop bookcases and behind chairs. Antius stood and threw up his hands.

"This makes no sense. He was just here, a moment ago. And all the windows are closed. Surely one of us would have seen him fly—"

Teralyn spun around as Arbulus gasped. With a shaky hand, he pointed at the wall.

"What now?" Anthanus said, his expression showing he was clearly fed up with all the drama.

"The maps. On the wall . . ."

Teralyn looked where he pointed. The walls were bare. A faint light outline of lint delineated where each map had been only seconds ago.

"Well, I never . . ." Anthanus said, his mouth agape.

Suddenly, something shifted underneath Teralyn's shoes. She fell against Antius, who grabbed her arm to steady them both. His gaze was pinned to the bare floor—a floor that only seconds before sported a huge woolen rug. Now the uncovered wooden floorboards stared back at them both, as if in mockery.

Teralyn sucked in a breath and caught Anthanus's bewildered expression. The doddering regent wrung his hands as sweat beaded on his forehead.

"Well, I never . . ." he repeated, for once unable to finish a sentence. It was apparent to Teralyn that whatever words he'd hoped would come out of his mouth—as with the owl, maps, and rugs—had vanished in a *whoosh*.

SEVENTEEN

JUSTYN AWOKE with a chill breeze wafting through his hair. He rubbed his eyes and saw above him a pale blue sky. With a start, he sat up and examined his surroundings.

"What on earth . . ." The walls of his parents' house were intact, but the entire roof—rafters and all—were gone. A shudder racked him from his head to the tips of his toes as he wrapped the blanket around him. Upon closer scrutiny, he realized other things were gone—including the soft feather mattress he had fallen asleep on only last night. He rubbed his aching back, which had no doubt been pressed against the hard wood planking for many hours.

The marsh witch! As much as he hated to admit it, she had to be the culprit. What other explanation could there be for such impossible occurrences? He rummaged his mind for another logical explanation but found none. No one could have removed the heavy roof while he slept. But how did she manage this? Could there truly be such magic in the world?

He frowned recalling the way Teralyn's boots had left wet footprints on the cobbles. Was everything and everyone in this village under enchantment?

He threw off the blanket and searched for his clothes. At least those were where he'd left them—in a pile on the floor. Drifting on the wind were voices, angry voices. Shouting, yelling, even screams. He pulled on his pants and shirt, laced up his boots, and ran down the hallway in search of his parents. When he reached the sitting room, he heard moaning. Before he could open the door to his parents' bedroom, his father slipped out to meet him.

With a sad shake of his head, he said, "Best you not disturb her, lad. She's in a bad way. All these goings-on have taxed her heart."

Justyn could see the fear and anguish in his father's eyes. No doubt they reflected what every villager felt at the moment—abject terror. Fen pointed numbly at the hearth.

"Last night . . . after you went to bed. I was—" He pinched his lips together, then blew out a hard breath. "I was tending the fire there. Just poking at the coals. And then . . . the hearth was empty. No wood, no fire, not even an ember left on stone. Right before my very eyes. Never seen such a thing, never, in all my days. . ."

Fen's gaze wandered, as if he searched for some clarity but could find none. Clarity, logic, sense—without a doubt, all those things had vanished overnight as well. Another loud, piercing moan drifted from the bedroom. Fen laid a shaky hand on his son's shoulder.

"I've got to attend to your mum. Be careful when you venture out. Some's not in their right minds."

Justyn nodded as he tried to think of something comforting to say. "I'll sort it out, Father. Trust me."

The door closed with a soft click. Justyn stood, deep in thought. If the witch were to blame, then what in heaven's name was she up to? Justyn had been given power over Fromer—or so she'd said. That didn't account for a missing roof, though, did it? He walked to the entryway and picked up his satchel. The rooster feathers were still in there. Had his visit somehow incited Ursell to turn her glass eye toward the village with hurtful intent? If so, why? All these years the witch had lived in seclusion in the marshes. What would prompt her to act now? And why make things disappear, unless her magic aimed to throw the village into chaos. Did this have anything to do with stitching Fromer's name in that piece of cloth?

Well, if he wanted to be the town's hero, then he'd have to confront the witch and uncover the truth. She was awaiting his payment anyway. But first, he needed to execute his more immediate plan—to make sure Fromer was blamed for this disaster. Ursell might be the source behind Wentwater's troubles, but no one would think to blame her. They'd seen no sign of her for seventeen years, and he had no intention of mentioning her name. No, it would be easy to cast suspicion on his brother. And if that witch truly did wield magic, and if her word was true, then he should have complete control over Fromer. And this was a power he planned not to squander. With Fromer blamed and out of the way, Teralyn would fall into his own arms instead of Fromer's.

He pictured Teralyn weeping as she pressed her head against his chest, her lithe body wrapped in his embrace. He could almost smell the sweet fragrance of her hair and skin, feel the silky smoothness of her cheek as he gently wiped the tears from her eyes. The witch had promised that once Fromer was out of the way, Teralyn would be his. Every inch of his body ached with the need to hold her, to have her be all his own.

He smiled as he flung open the door with a wash of excitement. For once he hoped he'd been wrong about magic and mystery—although all his years of intense research and study, all his lessons and books and classes, all his logic and reason battered against this one wish. Denouncing all he held true, he swept it aside with a brush of denial—every last vestige of his training and inculcation—to dwell on the promise of Teralyn trapped in his arms.

The young man driving the grocery cart pulled his pair of mules to a stop at the entrance to the eastern gate. Over the snuffling and pawing of the restless animals, Antius heard a din coming from inside the gate. He looked over at the driver sitting beside him, who merely shrugged, but Antius could tell the lad was agitated.

"This will do fine, young man. Grateful for the ride down the mountain." He offered a hand to Teralyn and helped her alight from the bench seat. He stood in silence beside her as the lad shook the reins and urged the recalcitrant beasts into the village. The mules had been compliant until they came over the rise and the village—bathed in clear morning light—came into focus. Perhaps, Antius thought with a grunt, they feared they would disappear along with the pot racks and rutabagas.

He meant to display a calm exterior to Teralyn; her face showed she mulled fears in the privacy of her own head that she dared not put into words. She needed his level head and years of wisdom to bring the situation handily under control. But how could he dissemble? The inexplicable disappearances in the library that had taken place before his eyes had left him flabbergasted.

He gritted his teeth, thinking of Ambel's smug expression when he'd told his son this morning he planned to go to the village. There Ambel had sat, drawing with broken pieces of golden chalk, seeing through other eyes that beheld a mythic bird, chalk smeared on his face and hands, his wrist moving in a flurry of passion, yet creating a rendition of beauty and elegance on the large sheet of paper lying on the floor between his splayed legs. Antius had stared agape at the drawing that seemed to tear through the fibers in an ache to fly off the page. Ambel had laughed and shaken his head. Laughed so hard, tears fell from his sightless eyes and dribbled on the firebird, making her feathers soften and glow even more. His son had never drawn a picture in his entire life, yet the very intricacies of the firebird spoke their own chastisement. Antius asked Ambel what he was laughing at, but the boy only shook his head harder, flinging tears like spatters of rain. When Ambel had recovered his voice from the deep well of his laughter, he said, "You are wasting your time. There is nothing you or anyone in the Heights can do to stop the unraveling of Wentwater."

How had his son—sequestered in Antius's small house—known of the troubles in the village? By losing his literal sight, had he gained some second sight, some strange gift of farsightedness? Antius's world had been upturned by things he could no longer deny. How could he call upon his powers of logic and wealth of knowledge when the rules had changed?

He let out a sigh loud enough to draw Teralyn's attention. She hesitated at the gate, listening. "What do you hear?" he asked. "These old ears are a bit stuffed with cotton."

Her lips formed a tight line. "Fighting. Yelling. Like the droning hum of a thousand bees, busy with trouble. Look, Antius, the town is in pieces." She pointed, her face incredulous. "The shops are missing walls and windows, all the roofs gone . . . I've never seen such a bizarre sight in my life. And . . ." She rubbed her arms through her long sleeves.

"What?" Antius came alongside her and stared at the piecemeal village. It resembled a half-finished painting. He strained to hear, but only detected a low rumble, as if the ground trembled from an earth shake. The lanes were empty, and large cracks formed welts in the earth, like sores. Was it even safe to walk through the village?

"The air feels parched. And the land." She looked at Antius. "Do you feel it? My skin is so thirsty it hurts. As if the village were perishing from want of water. Lack of rain, moisture. Yet it calls to mind the words the woman from the lake had spoken to you— 'The people shall perish for lack of a word.' Could the disappearing words cause a kind of famishment? Or dehydration?"

"Rain starts with the letter *R* too. Perhaps it hasn't rained in a while."

"Antius, it's only been a week since things started vanishing. This kind of parched condition would take months, if not years."

Words from the Great Book blared in his mind. *Man shall not live by bread alone, but by every word that proceeds from the mouth of God.* If food nourished the body, did words themselves nourish the soul? Could the villagers be experiencing both a literal and spiritual famine?

"And think!" Teralyn continued. "If the lack of one word could make a people perish, what then would be the result from the lack of many words? And are they all interconnected? Once you take away eggs, are chickens to follow?"

"I can't say." His old, crinkly skin always felt dry and taut. But then he recalled the comment made by the woman from the lake. How she said she'd brought Teralyn to the Heights because the babe needed to live immersed in water. That the falls and moisture there would nourish her. Perhaps Teralyn's skin was more sensitive than other people's. But why? That in itself was another mystery. If Teralyn had been born a villager, had the woman from the lake done something to her to change her? Just what magic was threading through this young lass's life?

Antius heaved a great sigh and stepped through the gate, with Teralyn following. If the woman had spoken truly, then Teralyn was somehow at the crux of the village disappearing. There had to be an answer to this puzzle! By all appearances, if something wasn't done, and very soon, there would be no village left. Ambel's words came back to haunt him. *You will see, Father, how the wisdom of the wise perishes.* The words bit into his skin, like nettles, making him shake all over.

He smoothed out his beard, keenly missing Antimony. As they walked down the deserted lane, he turned to Teralyn. "What do you think? Have all these things *gone* somewhere? Or are they utterly gone? And if they have gone someplace, then where? I've heard of magicians attempting to transmute objects, and there are those who conjecture that, under the right circumstances, one might be able to move objects through time. But those are just theories and fancies."

"Have you found anything recorded, from any land, that tells of odd disappearances? Any legends or fairy tales that might expose a pattern of sorts?"

He shook his head forlornly. "All the regents, and many of the professors in the Heights, have been queried. None can come up with any solid explanation. Clearly, what is befalling Wentwater is slowly drifting up the mountain. Although nothing else has disappeared other than what we witnessed in the library, how can the Heights be spared? How can we stop this madness?"

He knew his voice sounded desperate; Teralyn laid a consoling hand on his arm. "I am the key, Antius. Haven't you considered that those things vanished in the library because of my presence there?"

"Well, you weren't in the village when the rutabagas went missing, were you?"

Teralyn scrunched her face. "No, but I had been down for the festival, and perhaps my 'exposure' to the magic entrenched in Wentwater triggered this undoing."

"You give yourself too much credit—or blame."

Teralyn shook her head with determination. "I must be the cause. The woman from the lake said so. Don't you think we should try to find her first?"

"I sense she is not a creature one can just seek out. There are no superstitions or tales or songs about this woman fashioned of water. She has remained hidden all these years; what makes you think we can locate her? And if we do find her, that she would be able or willing to help us?" He recalled the woman's strange, peaceful smile as she had pronounced Wentwater's doom. "The downfall of this village may be her heart's desire. We have no information that tells us she is either friend or foe."

"But she saved me, didn't she? And she made sure I would be cared for. Isn't that enough for you?"

Antius didn't answer. "We don't have time, Tera dear. Maybe if—"

A loud outburst of shouting echoed down the lane. In the distance, Antius could see through the missing parts of cottages and shops to an explosive and roiling crowd gathered at the town center. Antius stopped and put a hand on Teralyn's wrist. "Wait. The crowd is out of control. And I fear it will not be safe for you, if they recognize you." He reflected on what Teralyn had told him. How Iris had been quick to name her as the cursed babe and told her she must leave the village. "Let's find a safe place to hide you, for the time being."

"And you think I'd let you just waltz into that fray alone? They'd trample you underfoot. Just another evil mischief-maker from the Heights. Oh, why did you choose to come down here? I can't bear the thought of seeing you roughed up."

Antius chuckled. "I don't think they'd try to tussle with me. They at least hold a deep respect for the aged. It's a strong foundation of their culture. Let me lead, and I'll try to talk some sense into them."

Teralyn searched his eyes. Her own were swimming with worry. "And say what? What could you possibly say that would calm them?"

Antius blew out a long breath and stared hard at the undulating crowd that seemed to grow before his very eyes. "I'm afraid, dear girl . . . I have no idea."

Justyn pushed his way through the sea of waggling arms and stepped up onto the large stone dais that stood five feet off the ground in the center of the town square. One long survey of the crowd showed nearly everyone from Wentwater was there. He used his honed oratory voice to boom out over the heads of the hundreds of villagers that pressed together.

"Fellow villagers. Friends. I know why these strange things have befallen the village. Listen to me." Heads swiveled his way, and the din lessened to a restless murmur—the way the wind in the Heights often sounded on a troubled night.

Many yelled back in complaint and demand. Others chastened their neighbors, telling them to hush and listen. Justyn held up his hand and straightened, presenting an authoritative stance, one he had practiced for years in front of mirrors when preparing to give a speech before a class or assembly. He knew the villagers would subconsciously respond to his air of authority. Directionless, frantic mobs always looked to a calm and confident leader. And Justyn would be that leader for them. They were ready to believe anything, any reason, if it meant the madness would stop and nothing more would disappear. He would make them promises—and then he would find that marsh witch and force her to reverse whatever enchantment she had beset on the town. He would then be vindicated and Fromer would be banished—at the very least. He didn't much care what fate awaited Fromer. He would leave his brother's fate in the hands of the villagers. The memory of the baby-naming fire flashed into his mind. Hot flames licking the roof, ashes choking the air. He smirked. Yes, let the villagers see to it that justice is served.

A strong man standing in front of the dais yelled. "Why should we listen to you? You abandoned the village to live in the Heights!"

Others threw their remarks into air:

"Who made you leader over us?"

"You can't just come down here thinking you have the answer to everything!"

"Go back up that mountain—it's your ignorant, disrespectful ways what's caused all this!"

Justyn kept his calm but raised his voice. "Friends, hear me out. Someone has broken time-honored traditions. Someone has blatantly overstepped, in order to bring ruin to Wentwater. These deliberate acts must be punished. Only then will things return to the way they were. Only then will peace once more reign."

"Who? Who!" The shouts echoed in the town square like the cries of owls piercing a quiet night.

"It all started with the feathers, did it not? Feathers scattered over town, in the lanes and yards, and on porches. You know that someone had to be responsible for such a travesty. And those feathers led to one specific house."

"Yer parents' house, young man!" a woman yelled back with a finger pointing in his face. "Would you so readily condemn yer family? Maybe this is yer doing—a grudge you've come to bear against yer poor mum and dah. Ye ungrateful child!"

Justyn narrowed his eyes and recognized the neighbor who had berated him at the festival. "My parents are not to blame. My poor mum is grieved by all this, and my greatest wish is to ease her troubled heart by bringing this curse to an end. But we cannot turn a blind eye to truth. There is a consequence for every action. If someone has blatantly broken the traditions, they must be punished. Or worse will follow."

"How can it get any worse?" a girl screamed. "Look around you—there's little left of Wentwater. We can't cook, can't eat. No pots, no food, no water. We're wasting away."

"Do something!" an old woman yelled. "If you know who's to blame, then tell us!"

"Yes, tell us!"

Justyn waited for tempers to boil. And when he felt the crowd was sufficiently agitated, he blurted out. "It's Fromer, my own brother! As much as it grieves me to say it, I must. For the sake of the village! I saw him with my own eyes as I came into town early last Sunday morning. Dawn had still an hour to wait, and as I neared my parents' cottage, I saw him! Sneaking through the village with feathers in his hands. Strewing them about, from one cottage to the next."

Amid the outcry, a man jumped onto the dais alongside Justyn. One of Fen's fellow shopkeepers, Justyn recognized.

"Fromer's a fine lad. Would never do what this fool brother of his says. I don't believe a word of it! Not one word! If anyone's the culprit, he'd be the fella!" He poked a finger at Justyn's chest. "Are you going to take the word of a wayward son against his loyal brother? He thinks we're fools, but we're not." The finger poked him hard three more times. "I don't know what game you're play-ing, lad, but you should hightail it out of the village before harm comes to you."

With a brusque push, the man forced Justyn from the dais and onto the dirt. Justyn smoothed out his clothes and climbed back up. He would not be so easily deterred from his mission. Now would be the ideal time to test the witch's words. She had prom-ised power over Fromer. That Justyn could make him do or say anything.

"Where is Fromer? Someone get him. I will prove what I say is true!" All he needed was a short confession of guilt, and the town would tear Fromer to pieces. Justyn stifled a smile and stood his ground. The shopkeeper waited, unmoving, with hands on his hips.

"Fine. Fetch the boy. As if that will prove anything."

"He's with his mum, tending to her," the neighbor woman said, spitting spite. "Doin' what any good son *should* be doin'."

Justyn drew in a deep breath and composed himself. He imagined standing at the lectern, about to give a speech by rote, an audience of skeptics eyeing him. Standing there, in front of the clamoring crowd, was little different. He would will Fromer to confess to his crime, and the crowd would rush the confessor out of town—the way they had done Teralyn's parents seventeen years ago. Justyn held no doubt any longer—Teralyn was the babe at the fateful baby-naming. But how she had survived the flames that still burned in his mind, he couldn't fathom. Obviously, someone had saved her—and had spirited her away to the Heights for her safety. The charwoman had told her Antius had been somehow involved, and Justyn had yet to find time or the courage to question his mentor about the incident.

The steady grumble of the crowd rose in volume as the masses parted and two strong men dragged Fromer up onto the dais. Jeers rang out amid protests. The crowd was divided, Justyn deduced, but they were desperate to blame. Perfect!

Justyn glared at Fromer, expecting to see hate and fury, but his brother's kindly look jarred him. He read not anger but sympathy in Fromer's face. How dare he gaze on him in such a patronizing manner!

Fromer's smug attitude was enough to prompt Justyn to speak without further hesitation. He faced the crowd and proceeded to detail his case against Fromer, not only recounting Fromer's heinous act of scattering feathers but revealing what had caused him to turn from loyal son and villager to traitor. It was that girl, Teralyn, from the Heights. She had wooed him and poisoned his thinking. So besotted was he by her striking beauty and soothing voice, he failed to see the bewitchment. Convinced the villagers were stupid and needed stirring up, Fromer set out to break down the time-honored rituals of Wentwater. And, with some sort of uncanny magic, his simple first missteps had opened the door to greater harm—the triggering of . . . *the curse*!

Justyn waited as a hush fell over the crowd. Whisperings broke out, which then carried in waves through the mob. Justyn could tell he'd only spoken aloud what had already been circulating Wentwater behind closed doors and with bated breath. As the din rose in turmoil, he yelled out. "You've seen her! You all remember what was foretold of the babe with 'hair white as snow and eyes dark as coal.' Don't you? And what had the marsh witch foretold? That the babe would cause the destruction of Wentwater. There can be no other explanation! Everything is coming true just as she foretold!"

"But she died in the fire!" women yelled. "She couldn't have survived!"

An old woman raised an arm. The crowd, recognizing the matriarch of the town, stopped shouting to let her speak. She stepped up onto the dais and raised her chin. The town magistrate accompanied her, and took a stance at her side.

"My fellow villagers, there is truth in this man's speech. Never before in the history of Wentwater has such destruction taken place—other than the Great Flood many centuries ago. For hundreds of years we have lived in peace and prosperity because we have held true to a way of life. We have kept to the rules and live honorably. And so it must be in this case. I, too, believe we are seeing the witch's words come to fruition, and the babe, now grown, has brought an end to our way of life—and it may perhaps mean the end of our very lives as well."

She turned to Justyn and furrowed her brows, with a severe look on her face. "But more than one individual in town has seen this young man, Justyn, speaking ill of his family. And witnessed his . . . interest in this girl from the Heights. Villagers have seen the two together, on walks by the lake and at the festival. It is apparent his accusations stem from jealousy and bitterness. Yes, the girl must be dealt with, for the sake of the town"—she turned to Fromer, who, Justyn noted, just stood there, eyes cast down, looking every bit guilty—"but guilt cannot be placed on this young man, whose only crime—as spelled out by his brother—was falling under the girl's spell, something over which he had no control. Fromer, therefore, cannot be held responsible in any way for the terrible things happening—"

"Wait!" Justyn cried out. The old woman's stern look returned as the mob murmured in reaction to Justyn's blatant disrespect of the matriarch. "Please forgive my outburst," he said, fumbling to cover his oversight with apology. "But why not let Fromer speak? I charge him to tell the truth, before this crowd. To make confession. Then you will see—if he is honorable enough—how he has meant for Wentwater to come to ruin. That he is in conspiracy with this girl from the Heights, and not just an enchanted victim!"

The woman drew herself up and gestured to Fromer. "Well, young man. What do you say to your brother's charges? Are they true?"

Justyn held his breath. His mind flooded with memories of standing in the stream of thought, of the silver sparkle of words as they flowed around him in that timeless place. As he stitched Fromer's name in the cloth with thread as slippery as water. How he knew at that moment he had trapped Fromer under his will.

As he stood on the dais next to Fromer, a heady feeling of empowerment surged through his veins, building in energy until he thought he would burst. He watched with eager anticipation as Fromer opened his mouth to speak. A heavy hush fell over the crowd while they waited expectantly. He fingered his ring—the ring he had earned for all his diligent years of study in the Heights. A ring that represented his worthiness and wisdom. His superiority and deservedness. The irony of this moment hit him. He had become the leader, the righter of wrongs, the voice of the people— just as the old biddy had foretold of him at his baby naming. Of course, Justyn had maneuvered affairs and taken advantage of those very predictions in order to stand where he was at that moment, but still . . . he couldn't deny her words had come true.

A smile inched up Justyn's face. He would relish this moment for all time. The moment when Fromer would incriminate himself and the town would chase him away. Far, far away, never to show his face in Wentwater again. Good riddance!

Justyn looked out over the crowd as Fromer prepared to speak. Excitement sparked his heart. There, coming through the parting mob, surrounded by a grumble of voices, was Teralyn. Ha! Just in time to witness Fromer's demise! But then, Justyn sucked in his breath and felt all the blood drain from his face as he recognized with horror the man who accompanied her—Antius! A tremor flitted over his skin as the aging professor caught sight of him upon the dais.

Before he could ponder the ramifications of Antius's presence there—in the heart of Wentwater and in the midst of such mayhem—a tingling struck his right hand. He looked at his fingers in time to watch his ring—his precious gold ring he'd earned by sweat and hard toil—vanish from off his hand.

EIGHTEEN

TERALYN STIFLED a gasp as she took in the scene before her. At the end of the lane, Fromer stood in front of the crowd on a raised platform, the sun lighting up his hair in brilliance, his face strangely serene. He caught her eye and smiled. He seemed altogether unflustered by the madness fomenting around him. Just what could he be thinking?

Her attention shifted to Justyn, who stood next to her beloved, stiff and scowling. The expression on his face told of a giddy power he felt, a power, no doubt, he wielded over the desperate, impressionable crowd. Justyn leaned down from the dais. She couldn't hear what he was saying to the magistrate over the shouting of the townspeople around her, some of whom seemed to suddenly recognize her. A loud and foreboding murmuring broke out around her, and heads swung in her direction, pinning her with baleful stares. Within seconds, arms clawed at her, pulling at her blouse, pinching her skin, slapping at her head. She screamed.

"Now then, that will be quite enough!" How Antius had managed to amplify his voice, Teralyn could not guess. But the loud rumble of his words rolled over the crowd, and the villagers backed away as one, giving her room to breathe. No doubt the old professor had mastered such a voice over his decades as instructor in the large assembly hall and auditoriums in the Heights.

Another wave of grumbling broke out, the sound cresting
and breaking like small waves over rocks. In the crush of bodies in the heat of the day, Teralyn sweltered, feeling sweat pour
down her neck and throat. She wiped her forehead with her
sleeve and tried to swallow past the dry lump in her throat. She
lifted her eyes to see Justyn's face as he spotted her and the professor in the crowd.

Although he presented a calm expression, Teralyn could tell the
unexpected arrival of his mentor greatly unnerved him. No doubt
Justyn was up to no good, and meant Fromer harm. A barely per-
ceptible strain of fear fell over his countenance. Maybe Antius's
presence there would change the outcome. Would the villagers
truly respect a regent from the Heights? She didn't see how—since
he had no answers for them, nor any suggestions on how to reverse
the blight afflicting the town.

"The lass is a witch!"

"Burn her!"

"She's cursed. And she'll be the downfall of the village!"

Teralyn hugged Antius closely as he strode to where Fromer
and Justyn stood. With his head held high, Antius batted at the
pressing bodies and grabbing arms. She could feel fury in his movement, a protective fury meant to keep her safe. He grumbled under
his breath, no doubt cursing the villagers as he practically mowed
them down with uncanny strength.

"I said—enough!" Antius climbed atop the platform with
Fromer's help. Teralyn clambered after him and threw her arms
around Fromer. He held her close and stroked her hair, his affection setting off another burst of jeers and shouts.

Antius took a good look at Justyn. In a low voice, he asked,
"Just what is going on here?"

Justyn gestured around them. "They're out of control and need
a strong, calm leader to take matters in hand."

"And you've appointed yourself to that position?" Teralyn heard the consternation in Antius's voice. He humphed. "You don't seem to be doing a very good job."

"They want a reason for the disappearances. Fromer here— my brother—is about to confess, and tell how he has caused this calamity."

Antius swiveled his head and looked at Fromer. "This is the lad Teralyn loves—your brother? And you accuse him of causing all this? Are you mad? This cannot be the work of man."

Justyn's eyes grew wide and his lips formed a sneer. Teralyn was stunned by his haughty response to his beloved mentor's comment. Justyn's words came out laced with cynicism. "Don't tell me, dear Antius, that you would attribute this wave of bizarre disappearances to magic? You—a regent from the Heights, a learned man of the highest order? If this town's unraveling is not the work of man, then of whom . . . or what?"

The mob's outcries lessened as villagers hushed their neighbors in an attempt to hear what the two men were saying. "Yes, tell us!" the magistrate ordered. "Wise one, tell us!"

The tangle of words wrapped around Teralyn like a sticky spider web—Anitus's words, Justyn's words, the words spat out by the crowd. Words encircled her, broken sentences, broken questions, ragged pieces of thought and speech shattered into fractured syllables and letters. A strange surge of energy, like a sudden breeze, riffled through the crowd. Someone spoke, but stopped midsentence. Another opened his mouth, but nothing came out.

Teralyn felt her head lighten and spin. Images wavered as Fromer's arms softened their hold on her. His arms felt light, weightless. She glanced over at his face, and it appeared luminescent, ethereal. The quality of light shifted in the air around her, caught in dancing dust motes. Shadows formed haphazardly on the ground under a noonday sun.

The broken words formed pictures in her mind, of radishes and eggs, and owls and maps, of fences and mattresses and roosters. Letters detached from their words and burned in her mind. First *R*, then *E*, then *M* . . . As in a strange alphabet soup, the letters bobbed before her eyes. She grasped her head with her hands, feeling it about to burst. In the blinding sunlight, the crowd wavered like a mirage in the heat as letters joined together. And as if reflected in the pool of her consciousness, she saw them in reverse, held up to water, showing her the obvious. REMORF . . . *Fromer* . . .

Fromer's name was at the crux of the trouble. This she now knew with certainty. But how, and what did it mean? His name was somehow stitched into the very fabric of the town, a town that was now unraveling. This made no sense! If the witch had foretold that she, Teralyn, would cause the downfall of Wentwater, how did Fromer figure in? Why his name and not hers?

Justyn's voice startled her. It sounded as if it came from the bottom of a deep, empty well. He fumbled for words that wouldn't piece together, and the crowd stared at him perplexed and frightened. She wasn't the only one hearing the breakdown of speech. One look told her that words were now vanishing from the minds and mouths of all. Thought lost cohesion; even Antius stood aghast, speechless. She could almost see the threads of thought snapping around her, leaving words dangling like overripened fruit about to fall and splat on the ground.

Yet even without words, an unspoken consensus formed, drawing the crowd close, their terror linking them in desperation. She feared for Antius, worried they would trample him as the hordes spilled onto the dais and rushed toward her and Fromer. Justyn quickly backed away, then fled through the tightening circle of bodies. Incoherent noises escaped from mouths, but the words had fled—no doubt to wherever the rutabagas and rugs had gone. Teralyn turned to look at Fromer and shrieked.

She tried to touch his face with her fingers, but her hand went clear through. His look of love never faltered as he gazed with longing deep into her eyes, his mouth open, urging speech to come. But Teralyn did not need to hear spoken what his heart made evident. His mouth formed the word *love* as a shadow fell across his cheek.

The crowd swarmed and pressed, but Teralyn could not take her eyes off Fromer. Shadow swallowed up the side of his face where the light was occluded, then spread like ink down his neck, over his chest and down his torso. He stood inches away and yet she could not find him; her arms flailed but sliced air. As his face succumbed to shadow, fat tears fell from her eyes to the ground, dampening the place Fromer had just stood, creating a puddle that refused to show her reflection.

NINETEEN

TERALYN SHOOK, more from fear than from cold, although the chill mud—now up to her knees—penetrated to her bones, making her bare feet throb in pain. The muck had claimed her shoes, and although she'd stuck her arm in and felt around, they weren't to be found. Upon retracting her arm, all she got for her efforts were hordes of beetles latching onto her skin. Those she scraped off with a shriek, hoping if she kept moving none would stick to her legs. She wrapped her arms around herself and trudged on. Where on earth was Justyn going? If she had known he planned to escape through such putrid, marshy terrain, she would have worn different clothes. But she'd had no time to prepare, or think.

In the mayhem at the center of town, while watching Antius try to speak to the magistrate, she had caught sight of Justyn from atop the dais. She could just make him out over the heads of the hysterical villagers—many of whom were running pell-mell like chickens without their heads. But Justyn seemed intent and focused—a man with a plan. And she needed to get away from those who meant to hurt her. So, ducking her head and pushing hard, she had weaseled out from the mob and run after him. She felt bad, abandoning Antius to deal with the crowd, but she couldn't risk losing sight of Justyn. Hopefully, Antius would find his way back to the Heights, where perhaps the disintegration of language had not yet afflicted the residents there. But would the regents be able to forestall the inevitable? Teralyn was doubtful.

Now, hours later and under the cover of darkness, she could no longer see him sloshing ahead of her. But she heard him, and let her ears follow the strident sounds he made through the muck, keeping her movements as silent as possible.

Oh, how she ached! Not just in her legs from slogging through the swamp, but in her heart. Fromer was gone! The thought that she may have lost him forever ate at her like an acid. Justyn *had* to know where he'd gone. She had seen it in his face—the cocky confidence, his visage concealing a secret. Yet Justyn had no magical powers. He'd spent his entire life devoted to learning and accumulating knowledge, denouncing the superstitious ways of Wentwater. Had something happened to change his views? She carried a fool's hope that he'd help her, yet she had no other recourse, no other lead. Whoever had cast the spell over the town might have the power to *un*cast it. *Oh, Fromer, where have you gone?*

Misery saturated every pore of her body, making her burdened and weak. She barely had any strength left to lift one numb foot after the other. Just when she thought she'd collapse in mud and let the swamp take her, all grew quiet. She strained to listen, hearing only the incessant whizzing of mosquitoes that buzzed her ears. With a tired wave, she brushed them from her face, then heard a new sound. A door opening on creaking hinges.

In the light of a quarter moon gleaming overhead, she made out a large structure, some sort of fortress, rising from mud. She tipped her head back and saw two turret towers pointing to the heavens, and the dark shapes of bats winging overhead. She rested her cheek against cool stone, hearing murmuring through the wall. What strange place was this? And who was Justyn meeting?

She inched her way along the rough wall, gangly vegetation slapping her face as she trudged in exhaustion, looking for a window that wasn't forthcoming. After an interminable amount of time, she came to the end of her strength. With a long sigh, she collapsed on a stone ledge skirting the wall, out of the muck, no longer caring that her clothes were caked, ripped, and clearly ruined. She could storm in after Justyn and take her chance with danger, or she could bide her time and wait until he came out. Neither choice appealed to her, but she had come this far—to the end of the marsh as well as the end of her hope. There was no place else to go.

"Ah, there's a good chap. Well done." Ursell studied the seven long rooster tail feathers, turning them in the light of an oil lamp and stroking them almost lovingly. "These will do nicely."

Justyn stood in the cold, damp sitting room, surrounded by the rows of jars, hemmed in by a dozen scrawny cats that wouldn't stop rubbing against his legs no matter how hard he batted at them. Dozens of lit tapers lined the table in the center of the room, casting flickering shadows upon the sealed glass jars that glowed with their tiny pinpricks of light and revealing deep-lined crevices in the marsh witch's face.

He put his hands on his hips. "I've done as you asked. And you promised I'd have power over Fromer. What did you do to him?"

The witch pulled her gaze from the feathers in her hand and craned her neck to meet Justyn's eyes. "Eh, what?"

"I stitched Fromer's name, just as you told me. And you promised Fromer would be under my will. And Teralyn would be mine. You didn't say you planned to tear the village apart by the seams, or that Fromer would vanish in front of the entire town—before he did my bidding!"

Ursell grabbed his shoulders with her bony fingers. Her glass eye locked on to him, and Justyn once more felt the uncomfortable sensation of the witch rummaging unbidden in his thoughts. He shivered with annoyance as she pulled back wide-eyed.

"Wentwater *is* unraveling—just as foretold! Heavens, what a bit of unexpected luck to have so much damage wrought so suddenly." She giggled in glee and rubbed her hands, making the joints in her finger bones creak and crack.

"So, this is your doing!"

"'Tis not—though I wouldn't mind taking the credit, dear chap. The lass was the one foretold to bring Wentwater to ruin."

"The lass? You mean Teralyn."

"None other."

Justyn shook his head in irritation. "And just how has she managed that? She's no witch—or is she?"

"Just an ordinary lass, but with power over *you*—that much is clear."

Justyn humphed. "You speak nonsense. Our agreement was I'd bring you the feathers in payment for control over Fromer. Now Fromer has vanished, and Teralyn is still out of my grasp. You have not fulfilled your end of the bargain. You're just what I thought—a charlatan and a fraud!"

Ursell narrowed her eyes and shot Justyn a predatory glare that drove like an icy spike into his heart. He sucked in a breath and tried to calm his fear. The formidable pain lessened but did not leave him. He drew in shallow breaths, willing the stabbing to ease. The witch drew close, forcing him to back up and trip over a cat, which landed him smack in the rocker in the corner. He sat with a thud on the hard seat and grasped the chair's arms.

Ursell poked a bent finger into his chest, and it felt like a knife penetrating his skin. "Take care with your words, young chap. They have consequences."

She spun around and paced the room, cats weaving in and out her legs in a macabre dance in the sputtering candlelight. "There's something I still can't see . . ." She strained to look past the walls of the castle, beyond the marsh, and off to farther lands. She clenched her fists and grumbled barely loud enough for Justyn to hear. "Drat! It must be out there, but the answer is tied up with that lass . . . somewhere . . ." The witch's severe look loosened into a grin. "Well then. Maybe my answer has just landed on my doorstep." She turned and flashed a toothless smile at Justyn. "Shall we go see?"

The witch strode from the room and out the front door. Justyn hurried after her, more befuddled than angry. *The witch is mad—just plain mad*, he repeated in his head as he stepped onto the front stone stoop. Darkness shrouded the marsh; the moon had set long ago. An eerie calm draped the night—even the insects waited in silence, as though listening, wondering. Justyn felt he was standing at the edge of a void, the night sucking away the world. A lone owl punctured the silence with a question that echoed the one ricocheting in his own head: "Who, who?"

Ursell stomped through the thick, miry vegetation in her stockinged feet, heading with deliberation around the corner of the castle. Not daring to venture out in such gloom, he waited for the witch's return, which surprised him by its expediency.

She had someone in her grasp, and was pulling the resisting captive by the collar of a shirt. His jaw dropped as he made out Teralyn's mud-streaked face and unkempt hair. The witch dragged her to the stoop, and he backed up to give them room, the space allowing for the incursion of inexhaustible questions.

"What are you doing here?" he asked, noting his heart pounded hard upon seeing her. He willed his breathing to slow, but it was a hard struggle.

"I should ask you the same. I followed you. Where is Fromer? What did you do with him!" She brushed matted hair from her cheeks, which Justyn noticed were flushed with rage.

Ursell stuck her arm between them. "Now, now, my two lovebirds. There's tea inside and a towel for your pretty little face . . ."

Justyn watched as the witch gently touched Teralyn's cheek, making her recoil. It was clear Teralyn held no fear of this woman, only disgust.

Teralyn huffed and followed the witch into the castle, storming by him and throwing him a mean look. Well, it was obvious the witch's spell was a hoax. Teralyn was hostile, distant. So much for her being under his influence, for his dream of Teralyn throwing herself into his arms. Yet, miles away, his village was under siege, disappearing in bits and pieces. What would come of his family, his home?

Although he badly wanted to stir up the villagers and break down their superstitious ways, he never wanted to witness the demise of Wentwater. And if the village disappeared altogether, that would spell disaster. The absence of Wentwater would mean the downfall of the Heights. There was no getting around that fact. Whatever the witch was up to had to be stopped and corrected or all would come to ruin! The witch had claimed Teralyn was the cause of the trouble. If so, then she had to be dealt with—forcefully, if need be. There was no denying Teralyn had some uncanny power—whether she herself would admit it or not. Regardless, the spell over Wentwater had to be stopped—whatever the cost.

He marched into the castle, stepping around the globs of mud the two women had tracked in. He threw aside his vision of Teralyn in his arms, wrenching the passion, frustration, and hurt from his heart the way one might skin hide from a beast. The bitter truth hit him—she would never be his. Even if Fromer failed to return from whatever hinterland he'd been whisked off to, Teralyn would never soften her heart toward Justyn, let alone love or marry him.

He gritted his teeth and sneered. Fine! If he couldn't have her, no one would. He wanted her gone—for good! Surely such an accomplishment was within the witch's purview. Why, Ursell could lock Teralyn in one of her crumbling towers.

The idea of Teralyn trapped in the castle, pacing the floor with nothing to do but stare out longingly over the putrid-smelling marshes, brought a smile to his face. Like a badger in a cage. Give her plenty of time to ponder her choices. Who knew—maybe in time she would rue her harsh treatment of him—and forget that fool brother of his! In time . . .

He entered the sitting room. Teralyn sat at the table, cleaning her face. The witch puttered in her little kitchen area, filling a kettle and gathering teacups. He cleared his throat. "Since Teralyn has fomented all this trouble in the village, I demand you lock her in a tower." Teralyn dropped the towel and gasped. The witch turned and pinned him with her glass eye.

"Ah . . . I see it, yes. A path unfolding. Hmm . . . curious . . ."

"What is?" Justyn asked as the witch returned with a tea service for three. She plopped into the chair next to Teralyn. "Sit, my dear chap. And drink your tea. I'll entertain your proposal."

Teralyn leaped from her chair. "I'll not be locked in a tower. Are you out of your mind? I do not answer to you—or him!"

"Sit!" the witch ordered with a sweep of her hand. Justyn shuddered at the command. It hung in the air and expanded into a wave of energy that pummeled his ears and made them ache. A glazed look came over Teralyn, and her face relaxed. She dropped back into her chair and stared impassively across the room, focusing on nothing.

"What did you do to her?" he asked the witch.

She shrugged. "Let's discuss your proposition."

"What's to discuss? If she's the source of the spell over the village, why not lock her up in your tower, where she can no longer influence anyone?"

"Young chap, don't try to pull the wool over my eyes! I know you care little for the fate of Wentwater. I know your heart! And don't forget! I see your need. Regardless—" She sipped her tea in a disturbingly ladylike manner, nodding to him to do the same. Teralyn sat unmoving, unblinking. "I'm willing to dicker. Are you willing to pay the price? It will cost you."

"I'll do anything you ask." He snorted. What would she want this time—six hairs from a rumphog's back? He walked around Teralyn as she stood frozen in place. He lifted his hand and made to touch her, then stopped when he saw how his fingers trembled. He dropped his arm to his side and turned to face Ursell. "Anything. Take my word for it."

Ursell clapped her hands and shrieked in joy. "Done! I'll have your word. And a hefty one it will be!"

Justyn paused. "What do you mean?"

"Your word—in exchange for Teralyn locked in the tower. And I get to choose. Oh, don't look so alarmed, young chap. It's a word you've no use for. You've never used it and never will. So, what's the fuss?"

Justyn grunted. The witch was spewing nonsense again. Well, if she wanted a word from him, what did he care? He had plenty. Volumes, in numerous languages. What was one word among thousands? And what good were words? You spoke them, or wrote them down. Created stories and documented history with them. How on earth could she take a word as payment? Well, what did it matter—as long as Teralyn ended up in a tower.

"How long will you keep her locked up?"

"Oh," the witch snickered, "long enough, I dare say. Deal?" She held out her hand for Justyn to shake.

"And what about Fromer? Is he gone for good?"

Ursell scrunched her face in thought. "Hard to say. I can't see that far . . . he is a shadow that crosses the face of the moon, that falls in gutters and spreads along alleyways. Always a shadow, nothing more . . ." Her voice trailed off wistfully, then she closed her mouth. The room grew thick with quiet.

Justyn ventured another question. "And what about Wentwater? Can you undo what's been done?"

His question broke her out of her melancholy reverie. "Heavens, chap, why would I want to do that?"

"Can you?" he demanded.

She waved a hand in the air. "It will just have to run its course—whatever it is."

"So you don't know the cause of the disappearances."

She gave him another toothless grin. "Haven't a clue, my dear chap. But, in time it will sort itself out somehow." Ursell lifted her teacup to her lips. "Bah, tea's cold." She stood and gestured to the teapot. "Want a fresh cuppa?"

Justyn shook his head and glanced at Teralyn. She hadn't moved, and he could barely tell she was breathing. The witch came to him and laid a hand on his chest. A strange chill sank through his shirt, through his skin, and into his ribs.

"Don't move," she said.

"What are you doing—?"

"Shhhh . . . now, tell me . . ." she said in a singsong voice. "What would you do if Fromer returned? What if the town blamed him for the mishaps and planned to hurt him?"

The answer came from a deep place in his chest, and as he drew it out, the chill penetrated deeper, like cold fingers reaching around obstacles, searching for a pathway. "I wouldn't care."

"You mean . . . you wouldn't come to his rescue?"

The fingers probed deeper, colder. "Not one bit."

"Even if they meant to kill him?"

Something clenched behind his ribs, as if she had punched him. Justyn worked hard to breathe as the tightening grew unbearable. "Good riddance, I say!"

"Ha, I've got it!" Ursell declared. She withdrew her hand from where it had pressed against him and raised it victoriously. Justyn saw she held nothing, but she stared at her hand as if she had caught something of value. The chill suddenly dispelled from his chest, leaving a tingle of an ache and the slight sensation that something was missing from his body.

"Easier than I thought. Normally one would find such a word lodged solidly in a heart, in a cherished and protected place, but this poor little thing was blocked, trapped outside with no way in. Just languishing forgotten and unused." She smiled with great contentment.

Justyn stared at her in confusion. What in the world was she going on about?

"Well, don't lollygag, dear chap. Be off now, on your way. Scat!"

Her abrupt remarks made him jump. "What about Teralyn—?"

"Never you mind. I've got it handily under control. To the tower she goes. And you, back to your life in the Heights, I gather." Her laugh made Justyn throw his hands over his ears. She pushed him out the front door, into the domain of night where the insects chirped and frogs croaked in a loud, raucous symphony.

As the door slammed behind him and he faced the miles of stinking swampland, he wondered what awaited him. Would Wentwater still be there? What would happen to his life, his future, so carefully planned out? He looked down at his bare finger, the one that hours earlier had displayed his beautiful graduation ring. Would that future vanish as easily? His heart sank with every step, berating him. All this had started when he had stitched Fromer's name. All he'd wanted was to see a look of love in Teralyn's eyes— had that been too much to ask for?

He stepped into the thick, cloying mud, sinking down to his ankles. His life felt just as mired. He recalled Antius's look of chastisement, his father's hopeless expression, his mother's mournful moaning. Then he remembered Fromer's peaceful countenance as he held Teralyn upon the dais, as he vanished from sight. And

Teralyn's heartbreaking cry as she reached for Fromer—arms, Justyn thought bitterly, that would never reach for *him.*

It was Teralyn's fault—all of it. She had made him do it. Now he understood how she was to blame for the unraveling of Wentwater. She'd given him no choice.

With that thought, Justyn lifted his chin and marched onward, toward the dawn of a new day—if there would be one awaiting him.

Ursell secured the tower door, then waved a hand in the air and muttered a long-unused phrase. As she hobbled down the stairs, she heard Teralyn's muffled cries and fists pounding the unmarked spot on the wall where the door had only moments before opened to her imprisonment—a door now shrouded in invisibility. Her lips creased into a smile and she hummed a little tune. When she arrived back in her sitting room, she reached for an empty jar—one of the many lined along a low shelf. With a grunt, she unscrewed the golden lid and stuck her nose into the jar and sniffed.

"A nice, clean home for you, my darling."

She made a fist and closed her eyes, envisioning the simple five-letter word she held in suspension over the stream of thought. Flashes of light, like darting fireflies, danced about her head, but she ignored all but one. That one glowed brighter than the others, with a more intense light, sparkling like a precious diamond with pure luminescence. The other lights paled in comparison.

Her heartbeat quickened as she reveled in the delight of ownership. Hers! This word was now hers. A word that kept humanity from sinking into the depths of depravity. A word that alone elevated man above beast. A word that brought God into the realm of humankind. Her mind reeled with the ramifications of this word missing from existence. Why, not only Wentwater would be affected but, no doubt at some point, the whole world! She would change the course of history—usher in a new era!

Even with her glass eye, she could not foresee the monumental impact of her simple act of capture. But monumental it would be! Even if the Keeper *had* survived the Great Flood, she would not be able to stem the flood of mayhem and destruction to come. The sacred sites established in the world would fall—powerless to keep evil at bay. All of them! The very thought sent a shiver of delight across her neck. She pictured them one by one, letting her glass eye roam from the putrid plain in Rumble to the icy cavern in Elysiel in the far north, from the disheveled remains at Sherbourne to the abandoned site at the house of the Moon. Tumbling to naught . . .

She snatched the bright and shiny word from the air and stuffed it in the jar she held in her other hand. The stream of thought dissipated around her, and her sitting room returned as she screwed the lid on tightly, the bright little firefly smacking again and again into the sides of the glass chamber it now found itself in. With a chortle, she cleared a space of prominence on her highest shelf and placed the jar with care in its allocated spot. She sat back at the table and sipped her cold tea, letting her thoughts mull over grandiose visions of the future.

All because a heartsick, jealous chap had stitched his brother's name on a piece of cloth. She shook her head, reminded of one of the proverbs in the ancient *Book of Kingly Sayings* from Sherbourne: "Do you see a man hasty in his words? There is more hope for a fool than for him." *Wasn't that the plain truth?*

Ursell jerked to standing. "Now, just where *did* I put that bit of stitching?" Her gaze scanned the room as she searched her memory for the last time she had seen it. The lad had handed it to her, and she had held it up to the light . . . the tea kettle had whistled, and then . . .

She rummaged through piles of fabric and bags of wool scattered about the room, tossing bits and pieces in the air. "It must be somewhere . . ." Curious cats sidled up to her, purring, pressing against her legs. The big orange tom meowed from the rocker.

"What? Do you see it?" She strained with her glass eye and made out Justyn walking over rolling fields toward Wentwater with the fiery eye of the sun blaring at him. She saw the village, barely holding on by a thread, only bits and pieces of wood and glass and fabric joining it together. The sight puzzled her. "How? How has this occurred? How has the lass managed it?"

She watched the big tom saunter back and forth behind the rocker. "What is it, my puss? What have you there?"

She crouched and examined the scraps of fabric on the floor. She picked them up one by one and flung them without regard, mumbling all the while. Then, her hand lit upon the piece she was searching for.

"Ha! Found you!" She narrowed her one normal eye and touched the cloth. Needle marks showed where the letters had been, revealing a faint outline of the word *Fromer*. A trail of silken thread led from the cloth to a splinter of wood under the rocker's leg, a tenuous umbilical cord keeping the village alive. Only a tiny stitch remained in the letter *F*.

"So that's what caused the affliction of the village. A simple loose thread. Imagine that!" She focused her glass eye once more on the village and grunted in joy, sounding much like a fat pig wallowing in a luxurious mud puddle. Without flinching, she deftly tugged on the bit of thread loosely connected to the cloth she held in her fist. As the poorly tied knot gave way and the thread came free in her hand, erasing the last vestige of the letter *F*, a shadow fell like a curtain over the village, miles away.

When the darkness lifted and the world returned to face the fresh spring morning, Ursell gasped.

She looked upon a primitive land, untouched, unmarred by human hands. Trees waved branches exploding with new leaves. A creek wended through fields rife with profusions of wildflowers. Off in the distance, the falls tumbled from the Heights in a roar into Lake Wentwater.

Ursell scanned the land, from sunrise to sunset, from meadow to the highest crag on the mountaintop, and a wonderful sensation of peace filled her heart. The quiet emptiness of the land showed not a soul anywhere about.

Wentwater village was no more.

• PART THREE •

"Those of us who hold knowledge in the highest regard ought to ponder well the puzzling events of recent history. As it has been painfully pointed out, the similarities of our methods of evaluation and conclusion—those of the learned in the Heights and the villagers steeped in ignorant tradition—are really not all that different. We, the educated, with our font of knowledge, could not string together words to arrive at the solution. In like manner—and truly, how does it differ?—the villagers strung words together in their fashion, using incantations and silly verbiage, and they, too, failed to stop the unraveling of the village. Both worlds—the academic and the ignorant—collided in failure.

"It pains me to admit the truth—that in this instance 'the wisdom of the wise perished.' Little did we know how literal that proverb would prove to be in the case of Wentwater. We do well—need I remind anyone?—to learn from history so we will not repeat our onerous mistakes."

From Volume III of *The Annals of Wentwater*, Section II: "The Unraveling of Wentwater in the Light of Historical Precedent"

—Professor Antius, regent and historian of the Antiquities Board

TWENTY

HOW MUCH time passed while Ursell rocked and gazed out contentedly over the unpopulated land, she had no idea. Apart from the cacophony of cat mewling twice a day, signaling her to feed her brood of felines that spent their days draped over various pieces of furniture, she paid little attention to the sun rising and setting or the stars wheeling in their constellations in the night sky. Such peace was a welcome diversion. No more would she be annoyed by the tedious, mundane comings and goings of the villagers, feckless souls plodding about in their daily doings, obstructing her vision of lands beyond, lands delightfully absent of people. The world was such a better place without them.

She reached for her tea as she rocked in her chair, finding only dregs of tea leaves clumped at the bottom of the cup. Her bones creaked in sympathy with the old rocker as she rose and plodded into the tiny kitchen in her slippers and nightdress. She hadn't bothered to dress or bathe for ages. Why should she? It was not like she was expecting company—ever. She laughed with gusto, and the sound sent cats skittering into corners and under the chairs and tables for cover. Only her big orange tom, too lazy to move, buried his head between two huge paws and waited for the reverberation to subside.

Ursell puttered around the kitchen, shaking jars and opening others to look inside, growing more frustrated by the minute.

"Drat! I thought I had another full batch of tea leaves." She couldn't think how she had drunk her entire stock of nettle tea, but—there was no denying it. Every container was empty.

She narrowed her gaze and looked through the castle walls, scanning hillsides and fields in search of a patch that would suffice, one requiring not too far a jaunt. Her stiff old legs could not manage the marshes as nimbly as they once did, and—she had to admit—she had gotten lazier as the seasons washed over her. But, she reminded herself as her gaze meandered the countryside, it might do her some good to get outdoors and take in a bit of fresh air. Good for the constitution, it was. No denying that.

"Ah!" She pursed her lips as her eyes widened. "A delightful patch of stinging nettle, why, filling the fields where the village once stood. How appropriate!" As she looked out at the spiky stalks of green growing thick and lush in what was once the town square, she reflected on the poetry of the image. A plant so painful and pokey, not unlike the thorns and thistles of the cursed ground outside the garden of Eden, rising from the ground in judgment—most fitting to overtake the ground where the village once stood. Yet a strange plant it was, the leaves of which were also soft and tender, and when steeped in hot water produced a sweet calming effect, as if in apology counteracting the pain with which their deceptive leaves pierced flesh and embedded tiny needles under the skin.

Visions of nettles filled her mind, mesmerizing her as they undulated in the breeze. Her glass eye locked onto the vast sprawling field of green and a strange realization brewed inside her and grew in strength, not unlike the steeping of tea. She saw bloodied hands, a worn spindle held in them, piles of nettles filling a room, bunches hanging from a ceiling, drying, their pungent aroma stagnant in the small space . . .

Ursell sucked in a breath. This vision overlapped with one that had visited her nearly eighteen years ago until the two merged, unfolding a scene that, up till now, she had only had scattered snatches of. Now the long-buried patches of memory pieced together into a coherent tapestry and made her suck in a breath.

She had entirely forgotten about the girl she had trapped in her tower! It was time to summon her, that lass, Teralyn. Ursell grunted, partly in irritation and partly out of curiosity. A path was forming that led in two directions. One toward the village, the other west, to the distant kingdom of Sherbourne.

Ursell narrowed her glass eye and skipped over hills and wended through forests until she met with the towering, crumbling walls of the ancient city rising up from the river valley. She punched through the wall of thick stone and searched through the throngs of people milling about in the marketplace, traversing the cobbled streets, prodding sheep, goats, and pigs down narrow rutted lanes. Sun sparkled in puddles as she felt herself pulled along a thread linking her hapless captive to another woman, joining one strand, one life, to one distant one, the strand fragile and oh so thin, but Ursell kept hold tightly until she came to its end—at a stall in the crowded street market along the Shambles of Sherbourne.

The aroma of rising dough wafted through her thoughts, and she heard the clatter of plates and cutlery. She widened her vision and saw skirts swishing over stone, hands palming silver coins that glinted in the light. Random strands of music carried on the crisp morning air—a fiddle and a fife—along with more explosions of smells—lilies, lilac, narcissus. Her eye took in a larger field of vision and saw bins of bundled flowers overflowing into the lane. Her mouth watered at the tantalizing scent of bubbling hot meat pies set on racks, fragrant potatoes steeped in herbs and wrapped in dough. Her stomach grumbled in the stirred-up memory of such tastes; her remaining teeth longing to bite down into one of the juicy pasties steaming on display.

Wrenching her eye from the delectable presentation of food, she slid behind the stall and studied the face of a woman busy wiping dry a washed wooden breadboard. The resemblance was unsurprising. Darker hair, yes, but the deep inky eyes, the same mouth. Ursell nodded in confirmation. Standing alongside the woman was another—a girl perhaps of ten or twelve years. Ursell could never guess ages. Numbers were outside her purview, held no appeal. They had no flavor or nuance; why bother numbering things?

The girl turned and spoke to the woman, and Ursell concluded this was a mother and child. *So . . . the lass also has a sister. A mother and a sister—or her lover. Which will she choose?* Hard to tell, and the thought of placing the choice before her charge sent her racing back the way she had come until she found herself standing motionless in her slippers and nightdress in the middle of her living room, the empty cup in her grip.

She ran a withered hand through her scratchy dry hair, realizing this wouldn't do, wouldn't do at all. At very least she could put on something clean, wash up a bit, run a comb through her tresses. This would prove an interesting occasion, no doubt. She could at least dignify it to some degree.

It was time to fetch the lass, Teralyn. Time to present her choices. For the life of her, Ursell really could not guess what the lass would choose. And the mystery of it tickled her. Either choice would cost her greatly. Once more the image of the nettles filled her mind's eye. That, and the bloodied hands. And then there was the broken heart.

Pain either way.

She rolled the name *Teralyn* in her mouth. *Yearn . . . learn . . . year . . . tear . . .* The lass had no idea what her name portended . . . but she would soon find out.

Ursell put down the cup and set her face toward the wash-room—a room she hadn't visited in quite some time. Surely she could find a towel and a bar of soap under the piles of unwashed laundry. Somewhere.

Teralyn glanced down at the large slab of gray stone that served as the floor in her circular room—her prison, she reminded herself. Her bare feet, dirty and callused, had made a slight track in the stone, a faint shadowed circle around the perimeter of the empty room.

Upon erasing the only door to the tower, the marsh witch had also erased all sense of time—as though the tower itself stood outside time. Without a window or even a tiny crack to reveal a sliver of the outside world, Teralyn had no idea when day or night came to call, no feeling for the sun's arc across the sky. The temperate, balmy room never grew cold or hot, never gave hint to the weather outside its walls. Her natural internal rhythms, thus disrupted, could not tell her when to sleep or remain awake. With nothing to occupy her hands other than to scratch pathetically at the unyielding walls for escape, she decided to occupy her mind. And that only led her to despair, to thoughts of Fromer, to the sad and fearful realization that his face and soft voice were fading more and more each day, so that she had to dig deep into her cache of memory to pick crumbs of him off the floor of her mind.

At first her interminable sentence inspired only anger, but after riding the waves of fury for so long, she tired, seeing it served no purpose other than to exhaust her. Her pleading with heaven seemed to fall on deaf ears; perhaps even heaven was blocked by the thick walls from hearing her cries. Yet, however long she lingered in this place, it was as though she had only just arrived. She never felt hunger or thirst or a need for a chamber pot. How odd was this! Yet, the evidence of time passage lay at her feet, in the worn impression caused by her endless, mindless circling. She could not deny that.

And what of the fate of Wentwater? Just what had Justyn done? How had he changed so—from ardent scholar and pedant to consorting with a witch! She could not make sense of his strange behavior. Had he stooped to magic to destroy a town that rejected him? Her heart sank at the thought, coupled with the niggling truth that it might have stemmed more from her rejection of him than anything else. And poor Antius! She couldn't bear to imagine the heartache he must now be feeling over Justyn—and over her.

She realized her hand was on her neck, touching the silver pendant, outlining the five-pointed star with her finger. A flash of light flitted across her eyes. She held her breath and dropped her hand. The light faded but a residue remained. Some sensation—the soft touch of cool water against skin, hair billowing against her wet shoulders, weightlessness. She froze and squeezed her eyes, hoping to force the memory from its hidden place, but saw nothing.

With trembling fingers, she once more outlined the silver star as it rested against her pulsing neck. She felt her heart beat through the skin of her throat, then felt another, separate heartbeat. This time she closed her eyes with resolve, pushing aside fear, letting the images stream in.

Water engulfed her just as it had before, as when she'd knelt in her parents' room and held the strange missive in her hands. But this time, the choking sensation lessened, then left altogether. She saw through blurred vision hues of green and gray, swaying shapes casting long shadows below her. Something held her in suspension, above and below, and she realized she was immersed in deep, dark water. The flash of light she had seen moments ago now reappeared as a flicker coming from the inky depths under her feet.

Her initial fear gave way to curiosity, then comfort, as two languid arms enfolded her, as she drifted down, down toward the light that grew brighter with each gentle surge of movement. In the muffled quiet of submersion, her eyes adjusted to her dim surroundings, and the flicker became the flame of a small candle. Fishes brushed against her, darted close then flicked away. The one who carried her slowed as they approached the singular light, then stopped. Teralyn felt the other's heartbeat against her back, felt a gentle sweep of hand brush through her undulating hair, a tender gesture that made her sleepy.

She floated, rocking with a nameless tide, enchanted by the candle that burned steadily in its holder. The small pale candle encrusted with tiny shells illuminated a circle around them. Lifting her head, she noticed other shapes in the water, shapes faintly lit as the candle's light snagged on edges and surfaces too dark and recessed to make sense of. From what she could tell, as she floated snuggly in those arms, she was encircled by giant slabs of stone, tall hewn monuments that stood and faced her, a ring of silent watchers. Her mind shifted to a memory of other walls, wooden ones, a roof overhead.

Then an acrid burning smell, and dark smoke thickening around her. Teralyn's throat closed up and she coughed, choking. She grabbed at her throat and realized she was screaming. The sound shattered her memories in pieces as the pendant burned into her neck.

Suddenly, the door that was no more reappeared in the wall before her—a tall wooden door that she had not seen in so long, she had almost forgotten it had once opened into her tower. Before she could utter a cry of surprise, the door blew open and the marsh witch strode in.

Teralyn gaped at the witch, who seemed a bit cleaner and tidier than she remembered. Even the witch's hair had been somewhat tamed and tossed up in a bun on the back of her head. What startled Teralyn even more than the unannounced arrival of her captor was the burst of bright light rushing into the room behind her. Sunlight streamed from the stairwell window and she couldn't wrest her eyes from the sight. A sun shone on the real world, her former world, the world she barely recalled. A sun that rose in the east and journeyed over her home in the Heights and the village of Wentwater each day without her.

"Are you ready, then, my dear lass?"

Teralyn found her voice. It gushed forth from her throat like rusty water from a long-abandoned spigot. "Ready for what?" All the ranting she'd planned to do upon first chance dissolved, so disarmed was she by the witch's question. The light streaked the floor like a splash of wet paint, and Teralyn's heart responded in a desperate yearning to be freed from this tower.

Ursell laughed. Teralyn threw her hands over her ears to blot out the sound.

The witch slapped Teralyn on the back, almost knocking her over. "Why, to see the fate of Wentwater!"

TWENTY-ONE

TERALYN THREW her hand across her eyes as she squinted in the bright sunlight. Brown-tinged grass tickled her ankles and a warm, fresh wind played with her hair. She drew in a deep breath and reveled in the glorious day rolling out like a carpet of wonder before her. How had the witch transported her here? Or was this a dream? In a glance, she recognized the knoll she stood upon—the place where she had first kissed Fromer after playing her lap harp. Her heart pounded in her throat and tears stung her eyes. The memory of that day overwhelmed her with its sweet pain, with the strains of music coming from her harp as Fromer sat and strummed, his gentle, clear voice whisking her spirit off over the fields. How long ago had they sat there, together? It seemed forever and a day.

Hot tears splattered her hands as she let the memory sear her heart as though it were a hot metal brand. If she could capture only one day, one moment, and preserve it forever, it would be this one.

"Well, a pretty sight, isn't it?"

Ursell's abrasive voice made Teralyn turn her head; she hadn't realized the witch was there, beside her.

"All those unsightly buildings and fences. Ha! And all those chickens and roosters. Such a ruckus they made. Gone, every one of them."

Teralyn lifted her eyes toward the horizon and searched for the outskirts of the village, once so easily seen from this hillock. "I don't understand . . ." She stared out at the rolling fields before her, endless fields of green, dotted with pink and white flowers. One good look told her months had gone by; they were well into summer, and fall was already making its appearance in the leaves of the stately birches, now splotched gold and crimson. She turned one way, then another, orienting herself. "They are gone! What did you do?"

"Heavens, lass. I didn't do a thing. T'was your undoing, remember?" The witch pointed her accusing finger at Teralyn.

"I did no such thing!"

"Ah, but you did. Maybe not directly. But your reappearance in the village set off a string of events. Perhaps beyond your control, yes, but spurred on by your beauty, no less." She came close to Teralyn, who backed up a step. "That poor chap. So taken by you, wanting you so badly, and well, you just wouldn't have him." She clucked her tongue. "Feeling so unloved. Shows what a lack of love will do to some chaps. Pushes them over the edge, it does. Isn't that just the way of the world?"

Justyn. "How is all this related to the disappearance of the village? And is it truly gone—all the people, everything?"

"Even the Heights."

Blinking back tears, Teralyn turned to face the mountains. Water gushed down the falls in a murmur sounding much like someone sobbing. A knife stabbed her heart. "The Heights are gone too?"

"All of it. Gone. Kaput. The fine university, your parents. Even that doddering old man you so love."

"Antius . . ."

Ursell flicked her hand in dismissal. "Yes, him as well."

Teralyn left the unspoken question of her heart poised in the air between them, but Ursell saw it with her glass eye.

"What you really want to know is if you'll see your beloved Fromer again. Isn't that right?"

Teralyn choked at the sound of his name. All she could do was nod as more tears slipped down her face.

Ursell began to walk around Teralyn, and as she walked, she stared out beyond the world, seeing things Teralyn could only imagine. Teralyn wept quietly as the memories—of the knoll, her playing her harp and singing, Fromer taking her hand, kissing her lips—saturated her until she felt herself drowning beyond the point of rescue. Hope fled, leaving her with despair and a wish to leave this world and join Fromer in whatever forsaken realm he must be wandering lonely, without her.

"There is a way . . ." the witch said, twirling a bit of her stringy hair around her finger, hair that the breeze had tugged loose from the clip. "It won't be easy. In fact, it is a long, painful road, with little hope of success—"

"If it will restore Fromer to me, then I will do it!"

Ursell stopped and spun to face Teralyn. "There is a risk! If you fail, all will be lost. One slip, and Fromer, his family, and the entire village—yes, and even your parents and those dwelling in the Heights—they'll be lost forever. Are you willing to take that chance?"

"And if I do nothing?"

Ursell smirked. "Well, then they will remain lost—seeing as you are the only poor soul left in the land that can save them."

Teralyn saw delight dance in the witch's one normal eye. She fumed. No doubt the witch was overjoyed at Teralyn's predicament. But, rather than discourage her, it gave her more determination to succeed. "Tell me, then. What must I do?"

Ursell held up a hand. "Now, don't be so hasty! There's another matter, another choice. Two paths heading in two different directions. You must choose. What matters more to you, I wonder . . .?"

Teralyn grew dizzy and wobbled on her feet. She steadied herself as though she were balancing on the back of a trotting horse. "What are you doing to me?"

The witch only grunted.

The world spun, blurring into smudges of pastel colors, and she heard a rumble and a low whistle, like wind pushing through a crack in a wall. Her body went numb and tingly, then the spinning slowed and her vision cleared. She held her head as her stomach churned in protest. Massive stone walls rose behind her. A cobbled street appeared underneath her feet. She found herself pressed in a crowd of shoppers and livestock, and a riot of competing smells assaulted her nose—meats cooking, breads baking, dust, waste, rotting garbage.

She was in a city; of this she was certain, although she had never seen one before. The only city she knew anything about was Sherbourne, the great city of the king, to the west. Someone bumped into her, but the contact was strange. Almost as if she were made of jelly. No one met her eyes; all looked past her—rather, through her. Where was she—and why?

She opened her mouth to speak but no sound came out. Instead, she heard the witch's voice in her head.

"Look. She is over there. The one selling pasties to the woman holding the reins of a horse." Teralyn searched for a horse, then found the woman the witch was directing her to find. A woman of middle age, with her long wheat-colored hair loosely tied in the back. Teralyn heard a chuckle in her mind. *"Why, that's the princess! Some disguise . . ."*

"What princess?" Teralyn thought. *"Why am I here?"*

"No matter," the voice said. Teralyn watched as the customer put some coins in the vendor's hand, then mounted her horse and rode off. The woman tending the stall leaned over to talk to a girl standing at her side, then opened her palm and showed the coins to her. Teralyn studied the woman's cheery face. Something seemed familiar about her. Had she seen this woman before?

"Look closer, lass . . ."

Teralyn wished she could push the irritating voice out of her head, but the witch's sticky words clung to her own thoughts. Teralyn disentangled herself and looked closer, and as if the very thought shifted into a command, Teralyn found herself only paces from the baker's face. An ache built in her stomach as a thought formed, a thought she fought against but that pounded hard on the door of her heart. Upon hearing the woman speak up close, Teralyn's face flushed with heat.

"Who is this woman? Tell me!" She looked at her hands opened before her and noticed they shook.

"Hmph, you know very well who. She's your mother. The one that left you behind seventeen years ago. Never came back to fetch you either—but then, I wouldn't hold that against her, now. She did watch from the far fields as her house burned to the ground. She'd lost all hope. But," —the witch chuckled— *"you can't blame her for getting on with her life, starting anew. Most would leave such a wretched life behind and never return, wouldn't you say?"*

As much as she wanted to believe the witch was creating a fantasy in her head, Teralyn knew in her heart of hearts the witch's words held truth.

"Oh, and that young girl, why, she must be your younger sister. Imagine that. You have a family living in the grand kingdom of Sherbourne. How overjoyed your mother will be to see you! Mourning for her lost babe all these years. Oh, the pain she's felt. Downright unbearable, must be. But, now . . . you can ease her pain.

Turn her mourning into rejoicing. Trade those ashes for beauty, you could say."

Teralyn's heart raced at the thought. Up till now she had feared dwelling on the hope that her mother was alive somewhere, missing her. The need to see her swelled like a wave threatening to sweep her away.

The witch broke into her reverie. *"You could leave. In fact, what is holding you back? There is nothing left here for you. You beloved is gone. Your home in the Heights—erased. Leave—and let the world you once knew vanish forever, as it will fully vanish once it fades from your mind and heart someday. Only memory—your memory—is keeping Wentwater alive. And once that memory is gone, well . . ."* Teralyn could almost sense the witch shrugging in finality. *"Out of sight, out of mind, as the saying goes."*

Teralyn's eyes lingered with longing on her mother and sister as they repositioned their baked goods on the display racks. She wrenched her aching heart from the marketplace and shut tight her eyes. In another whisk of dizziness, she swayed and threw her arms out for balance, and in moments felt the warm sun and light breeze once more tickle her shoulders. She opened her eyes and found herself back on the knoll, the fields stretching out in all directions as the sun inched toward the western horizon.

She turned to the witch, whose strange gaze told her she was seeing things no one else could ever see. Her voice returned. "You said I could save Fromer. What would I have to do?"

The witch cocked her head and narrowed her eyes. "See this field of nettle? You must spin it all into thread. And with that thread stitch the world back into existence." She folded her arms against her chest as if that explained everything.

"How on earth would I manage that?"

"Why, one word at a time, of course!" She chortled with a defiant air. "Although, I don't see how you could ever manage such a task. Why, it will take you seven long years to stitch every single word back into the fabric of existence. You—all by your lonely self, spinning, stitching. I just cringe thinking of the pain to your poor tender hands, pulling those stinging nettles through your fingers. And here's the thing—" The witch moved to stand directly in front of Teralyn, training her glass eye on her.

Teralyn gulped. "What else . . .?" The eye seemed to penetrate right through flesh and bone, boring into places deep in her body that awakened in a throbbing ache.

Ursell rocked her head from side to side and answered in a sing-song tone. "You may not utter a word—not a one! Not in song, not even in writing. For if you do, that word will disappear forever—*and* its manifestation in the world. Not until you have stitched every last word may you once again speak. And since your beloved was the first to go and the key to reforming all and more, his name shall be last, and his return last. The loss of his name meant the loss of Wentwater. Conversely, his return will return all back to the way it was."

Already Teralyn was near speechless; it would take little more to silence her for good. Seven years? "Why, Fromer may have forgotten me by then. I'll be older than he!"

The witch nodded thoughtfully. "That you will. But love knows no bounds, does it? Besides, to him, only a moment will have passed. A brief blight of sleep and then—life as it was. Would he be put off by a few stray wrinkles and two scarred hands? That's for you to find out. Don't you see?"

Teralyn tried, but the particulars escaped her. However, if no one were around to speak to for seven long years, she wouldn't care that she had to keep silent. And why would she feel at all inclined to sing? Her heart, already sensing the weight of the task, would defer to roaming the lonely halls of silence.

She tried to picture stitching each word, slowly, laboriously, using a needle, and thread made from nettle. Words tumbled into her head. There were so many! No wonder it would take seven years. And yet . . . the picture of her mother—her real mother—selling her wares in the marketplace bit at her heart, tearing off one small chunk at a time until Teralyn had to push away the voracious image.

Before she could regret her decision, she cried out, "I'll do it. I'll restore what has been lost, by stitching each word, as you instructed. But you must give me *your* word that all will return as you say."

The witch spat on her palm and stretched out her hand. "I give it. Shake."

Reluctantly, Teralyn shook the witch's gooey hand. As she caught the expression on Ursell's face, her hope sank like a stone thrown into the center of a lake. Clearly, Ursell believed she would fail, and no doubt that thought cheered her greatly. Teralyn rallied her determination, calling Fromer's sweet face to mind. Perhaps there would be time, years from now, to travel to Sherbourne, to find her mother. But for now, Fromer needed her. Antius needed her. She couldn't bear to think her world had vanished without a bang or even a whimper. She truly had no choice; she was Wentwater's only hope.

"How do I begin . . .?" she asked.

Ursell cocked her head and smiled. "Hmph, leave that to me."

The sky turned milky and swirled around her. Somewhere in the thick mist she heard the witch laugh, but she sounded leagues away. A chill wrapped her like a shawl, and she guessed it was more from trepidation than from the secret manipulations of the witch. In moments, the haze cleared, and before her stood a tiny cottage in the dead of night. More like one small wooden room as square as a box, big enough for perhaps six people to stand inside it in close proximity. A solitary window faced east, and she noted the peaked roof gave no evidence of a chimney.

A quick glance around told her the witch was gone. She opened the door to a spinning wheel situated in the center of the room, illuminated by an oil lamp hanging on a nail on the wall. A small wooden stool sat waiting before it. In the corners lay bolts of creamy fabric, piled liked logs one upon another to the ceiling. A woolen coat hung on a hook by the door, with two sturdy boots sitting below it. And resting on a small table next to the wheel were a small pair of scissors and a thin sliver of silver—a tiny needle with an eye so small Teralyn could barely see it. She may as well have been asked to spin straw into gold, so momentous was the task laid out before her.

She drew in a long breath and let it out in a tremble. A tear made its way halfway down her cheek before she even noticed. Quiet settled around her, as if the world held its breath in anticipation, as if the stars shimmered with curiosity at the challenge presented in the confines of the room.

With a swift turn, she spun on her heels, lifted her chin, and headed out into the dusky evening—toward the wavering, endless field of nettles draping the land before her.

TWENTY-TWO

TRIPPING OVER stones and roots, Teralyn hurried down the hill. Oh, if only she had a basin in which to keep water, then she wouldn't have to wear herself out this way. But there came a point, after hours of feeding the nettle leaves onto the bobbin, that she couldn't bear the burning a moment longer. Her hands screamed in pain, and only cold water could bring her relief. The tiny barbs of nettle embedded under her flesh were impossible to extract and felt like hundreds of beestings under the skin. The first few days she had screamed in pain, and her hands swelled twice their size. She'd tried to fashion gloves from fabric and thread, but they impeded her efforts to spin thread. At least she had the creek, and that was some consolation, although it was still a good ways from the cottage. Had she only been making thread a mere week? How would she ever endure such agony long enough to fill all the empty spools, to make enough thread to stitch back every single word in the world?

From the moment she'd begun gathering nettles, words washed across her mind, like shells tossed by waves onto a beach. She could picture them all, thousands of them, glimmering as they lay on sand under a hot summer sky. Each one crying out to her to be reborn. Days passed and the words clamored for attention, wanting to escape, to burst out of her head. But she quelled them, focusing intently on her work, on mastering the spindle and wheel, although she broke thread time and again. And if concentrating failed to chase the words away, she hummed melodies. Music comforted her now more than ever, serving as both solace and distraction as she experimented with lyrical lines of notes that pieced together in their own expressive language. Although she was unable to speak, each note and phrase articulated her pain and loss, and the rich sound of her voice filled the cabin as well as the long, lonely hours of night. At very least, it got her through each dark night until dawn seeped in through the window and awakened her with the reminder of being one day closer to seeing Fromer again.

As she fell to the dry grass along the bank and dunked her hands into the refreshing creek, she knew she had to find an easier way to carry out her task. She needed a bowl, something for water. She could fill her boots, but that would only cause them to mold and disintegrate—and she knew she would need those boots in the heavy winter snows. If she had a knife or some other sharp object, she could carve a bowl from wood. Her scissors were too delicate— only capable of cutting thin strands of thread.

She raised her eyes and looked around at the trees languishing in the summer's heat. A round shape in the crook of one tree caught her attention. When she drew closer to inspect it, she realized it was an abandoned wasp's nest. Would that work? With achy hands and numb fingers, she struggled with a sturdy broken branch to pry the mud nest from the tree trunk, careful not to break it.

She turned it thoughtfully in her hands. It was paper thin in spots, but very water resistant, she learned, as she dipped it in the creek and tested it. She could strengthen it by lining the interior with pieces of fabric—perhaps that would work. And surely there had to be something growing along the creek's edge, some plant she could use as a salve for her hands. She knew the villagers had been knowledgeable in plant lore. If only she had taken the time to learn more about the various healing plants as she gardened in the Heights. It had never occurred to her to be concerned about such aspects of plants. She gardened with shape, color, and bloom in mind. Well, she had years to experiment; why not start now? With no pot resistant to fire, she could not boil or heat anything. She would have to find something that only needed to be mashed and applied as a poultice.

As she explored along the bank, pulling up various plants and rubbing them, sniffing them, she was overcome with despair. Hard as she tried to be brave and resolute, she knew she was fooling herself. She would never last the winter, let alone seven years of solitude! Foraging for berries and edible roots made her more dizzy with hunger; what would she do when winter descended? She missed Fromer so much, her heart was bound to crack and break any moment.

With a throbbing hand, she wiped tears from her face. Off to the west, the sun hovered, shining brightly down on the kingdom of Sherbourne. Was her mother there, at her stall, selling her meat pies and pastries? Did she ever think about Teralyn, or had she forgotten the babe she left behind eighteen years ago? How could people in other lands still go about their daily business, talking, writing, using words even if those very words had vanished from Wentwater? What would happen if she left, went to Sherbourne, to a land overflowing with words, words as ordinary and abundant as apples and acorns?

Each morning as she woke, thoughts of fleeing plagued her. As she sat on her stool and kicked at the treadle with her foot, her hands hot and bleeding, she would wonder what her sister was like, if she too loved music and flowers. And as she lay down in the dark on the dirt floor, she would cry herself to sleep thinking of a land where there were down-filled mattresses, fresh baked bread warm from ovens, and comforting arms able to embrace her.

She stood and chastised herself. It would not serve her to dwell on such thoughts. Now was the time to decide. If she meant to go through with this insurmountable task, then she would have to harden her resolve, push those distractions of Sherbourne and Fromer from her mind and heart. Or, she could give up now. Why waste months, years, if she knew she would not see this through to the end? No, she would have to be decisive and focused if she wanted to see Fromer again.

Seven years, seven seasons. She would need to collect wood in the fall. Find a way to establish a small hearth in the room. Gather what she could for food to store through the winter. She *would* survive. Even though she knew little how to do so, she would trust heaven to help her. Surely blessings would come to one who toiled so hard, to one spurred by love and a sense of duty and honor, to one who would selflessly push aside her desire for comfort and happiness to save a land from oblivion.

She had not been taught much about the One who had brought all things into existence. But she knew from her scant years of observing beauty in the world that there had to be someone kind and benevolent, a source from which all good gifts in the world originated—gifts like music and song, love and tenderness. She could not believe, like so many did, that the heavens were silent and unconcerned—or full of harsh judgment. Somewhere deep in her heart, she heard another song, a melody that was an intrinsic part of her soul that sang out to another—to One who had put that song in her soul at the moment of her conception. A song uniquely her own, that rang out with life, with hope, with purpose. With an inherent sense of belonging.

Suddenly, Teralyn's ears filled with music. Wind swept through the trees, making branches dance and splatter sunlight across the hillside. Birdsong exploded in four-part harmony around her. Even the chirping insects in the grass at her feet joined in, adding syncopated rhythm to the emerging symphony. It was as if the whole natural world came alive in a riotous performance, cued and directed by an unseen hand, serenading her with music so ethereal, her heart lifted from its dark pit of despair and soared into the sky, beating hard like the wings of a dove seeking the radiance of the sun. She lifted her face to the warmth of the summer sun, let it drench her in amber light, as the music carried her far from her troubles and worries.

A smile rose on her face, which turned into laughter as peace soaked her from head to toe, a different kind of drenching than the one that left her clothes and feet trailing water. And then the peace settled, leaving the calm often seen after a storm, as floodwaters subsided, as the world righted itself. And in this place of calm, Teralyn picked up the wasp's nest and headed back to the cottage with a dance in her step.

Teralyn woke to the sound of snow sliding from the roof to the ground. She craned her neck to see out the window; in the dim morning light, a cold, cheerless sun inched above the horizon. She got up from her makeshift bed of fabric and matted dried grasses on the dirt floor and rubbed frost from the glass, looking out at the expanse of snow that buried the world in muted quiet. Although her head spun madly with all the words she had yet to stitch, the clamor remained confined there, between her ears. She was without a soul to speak with, without the yearning to sing—a yearning that had slipped away unnoticed years ago—and silence had become a constant companion, such that any sound now seemed loud and harsh.

In the milder seasons, when she could spin no longer and her hands ached beyond bearing, she took her mindless walks to the creek and soaked her swollen, bloodied fingers in the cold water. Her loneliness had been eased by the company of birds and other small woodland creatures. As they came to drink or grazed the meadows, they shared her silent vigil, and Teralyn felt a measure of comfort in that. Their appearance puzzled her at first. Why would rabbits and birds disappear from the village but not from the meadows? She had concluded that only the things intermeshed with village life had vanished. Fruit trees within the village gates were gone, but not the ones dotting the hills outside Wentwater. For that she was grateful, seeing that she would not starve before she finished stitching the world back.

At first she thought her heart would break from the solitude, from missing Fromer and the others she loved. But as the seasons ebbed and flowed, she merged with the rhythm of the natural world around her. She allowed the sun's course in the sky to define her waking and sleeping. Birdsong became her song, and she would hum their melodies as she gathered nettle in her skirt. As the cold winters impinged upon her, forcing her indoors, she drew those melodies from the wellspring of her heart to nourish her through the long, oppressive winters while she spun nettle into thread. She ached for the Heights—for the pounding of water, the soft spray that misted the air. Confined in her cottage, her skin grew taut and thirsty, and her soul itself felt parched. She spent as much time as possible at the nearby creek, soaking in the gentle current, immersing herself in water as the seasons allowed.

She could not count the endless hours she had spent at the wheel, feeding the barely moist nettle in through the spindle, watching it pull together into thin thread on the bobbin. The work had been not only painful but tedious, for it would be one thing just to produce thread at all. But to make a thread so thin as to fit through the eye of that needle! Too often her thread would break as she tried to narrow its width. The first weeks were the hardest, as her hands bled steadily, dying the thread deep red, and as she learned to coordinate the pressing of the treadle while she worked in the stringy plant matter. She would cry incessantly as the hours passed, as the large wheel circled endlessly and thread gathered on the bobbin. By the end of the day her hands would be raw flesh, so swollen she could not even run her fingers through her hair, the throbbing preventing her from sleeping.

But in time, those wounds grew calluses, and she often wondered as she sat silently behind the wheel if her heart were growing them as well. These many years of monotonous spinning had drained her spirit. Memories of Fromer and her life in the Heights would march across her mind, but she now stood afar off in the distance, detached, often with an empty, unfeeling heart, gazing at those memories as if a stranger to them.

Now the wheel sat untouched in the corner of the room. She had spun every last nettle plant she could find the previous summer, and the small room could hardly contain all the spools of thread lying in mounds that scraped the ceiling. She had felt such great relief upon switching tasks. As she threaded the needle and passed it in and out of the swatches of fabric, the swelling in her hands subsided—although after a time the interminable hours of stitching cramped her fingers just as painfully.

Now, with the world submerged deep in the throes of winter, she sighed in restlessness. She longed for this final seventh winter to pass quickly, for already hope was springing in her heart—a small seedling of hope that had slept all these years in dormant ground. Yet that hope was tempered with worry.

She turned from the window and looked at the piles of stitching, the hundreds of words lying about as if they had wandered off the pages of books and gotten stuck on flypaper. She'd thought that once she introduced word to cloth that things would start reappearing in the world, but that didn't seem to be the case. She had stitched every noun she could think of—from pots to potatoes—but each day as she ventured out, well into fall, she could find no evidence that what she had accomplished by all her years of hard labor produced any results whatsoever. And with the world buried in drifts of snow, there was no way to tell what, if anything, lay underneath.

Years ago, she would have to catch herself before she mumbled aloud without thinking. Now the frustration instantly voiced itself in physical expression—a frown, a grunt, even a scream. Had the witch tricked her? She'd thought this on more than one occasion. She hadn't seen Ursell since the day she had disappeared after conjuring this cottage. For all Teralyn knew, the witch could have fled the world and left her behind at this useless, futile task, laughing all the while at Teralyn's gullibility. But she had come this far; the seven years were almost up. It made no sense to give in to doubt or suspicion at this late time after committing to the job. She would just have to wade through the remaining months, stitch the words that barraged her mind—words that linked to some remnant of the life she once knew—and hope the witch's oath proved faithful.

Teralyn moved away from the window and sat at her stool. She picked up the piece of cloth she had left unfinished last night and reached down for a shriveled apple—one of the few left from her late fall gathering the previous year. She gazed at the mounds of fabric pieces filling the room as she ate her meager breakfast. Her threadbare skirt barely held together, and although she still had a few bolts of fabric left, the thought of stitching anything more than was necessary fatigued her. She had managed all these years in her one skirt and blouse; they would have to do until she finished her work. At that point, there might be a village once more situated in the valley below her, with shops and seamstresses and plenty of beautiful clothes to buy. On the other hand, if, when the seven years ended, all the words stitched failed to restore Wentwater, why would she need bother with new clothes? There would be no one to see them on her. Not Fromer, not family. Nobody. She dared not think what she would do then.

Her thoughts drifted to the lake. Was the strange creature that had brought her to Antius there—or had she vanished as well? Teralyn had often been tempted to walk as far as the shoreline, especially on warm spring mornings. But she feared what she would find there. Would the woman of the lake make an appearance? And if Teralyn could not use her voice and call her, how would she know to come? Besides, Teralyn worried she'd be tempted to speak, aware that the need to converse would be irresistible. And if she spoke, all her hard efforts would be lost. So all these years, she'd kept her distance, wondering.

As they regularly did, the four walls of her small cottage began to close in on her. Before the strangling sensation of claustrophobia overtook her, she laid down her stitching and pulled on her boots. She threw open the door to a blast of frigid air, then shut it behind her. If only she could shut out her exhausting task, give up as she so often longed to do.

In the cold silence that seemed to press down on her shoulders, she tromped down the hill and climbed the far ridge, struggling as she waded through deep drifts, ignoring the frost penetrating her bones. Branches on distant trees hung heavy from the weight of snow; they seemed to sag in shared misery with her heart. A snowshoe rabbit in gleaming white fur hopped across the field before her, but aside from that one small creature, the world lay buried in silence.

Frosty steam blew from her mouth as she crested the hill, feeling weak and undernourished. For a brief moment, she indulged in the memory of that breakfast she had eaten with Justyn all those years back at the festival—steaming waffles with whipped cream and bogberries. Her mouth watered at the memory. Her frustration and despair blossomed wildly at the thought of real food, and more words came to mind—words of delicious fruits and baked goods she had yet to stitch. She realized she had held off stitching those words for good reason. They only made her ravenous.

Finally, at the top of the hill, panting and out of breath, she lifted her eyes to a winter wonderland. The expansive view was breathtaking in its scope, with snow blanketing the entire world spread out before her. Yet something in the distance caught her eye. She had gazed out at this view hundreds of times over the years, hopeful, wishing, disappointed. For this was the view that had encompassed the village of Wentwater, where she had once upon a time looked down at cottages and shops and lanes—and the north gate she had wandered through that day to find Fromer with his herd of goats. And because she was so familiar with this view she had studied for hours in great detail, her eye quickly caught on the small out-of-place object sticking out of the snow.

She strained to see in the hazy winter light, and her heart skipped a beat. She held her breath and her jaw dropped as she shielded her eyes for a better look. She had no doubt what she was seeing—a triangular shape poking through the snow.

The roof of a cottage.

Ursell grumbled as she squished through the marsh, leaving her horde of cats caterwauling on the castle's front stoop. Like the fury of lava breaking through hard layers of rock, seeking release, her grumbling grew in her gut, spewing upward out of her mouth in anger. She never thought Teralyn would last this long. Why, by the end of last summer, Ursell was certain the lass would give up and leave for good. The long, hard, lonely years had surely taken their toll on the poor girl, she'd thought. With her keen, observant eye, Ursell could tell Teralyn was ready to pack it up and give it up.

Ursell stomped harder as she trudged through the thick muck. She fumed thinking how Teralyn's face had lit up upon seeing that rooftop, her raised spirits catching the attention of Ursell's glass eye. That was all it had taken. Now, with spring melting the snow and more of the village materializing in the valley, the lass worked with a doubled fervor, infused with hope and excitement, wandering across the moor daily to inspect the changes as she continued her stitching.

Well, there was no way Ursell could have known Teralyn would be so stalwart and faithful. It was beyond prediction—or foreseeing. Thus was the contradiction of her name—*nary or any* consequence could result. And Ursell had underestimated the strength of human love. Now her lovely life of peace and quiet would soon be disturbed by the return of the villagers and their silly superstitious ways. The thought was almost more than Ursell could bear. But she was no fool; she had a contingency plan set aside all along. Not one she wanted to do, not at all. But what choice did she now have? It was either this or spend the rest of her life watching the village get on just fine—all her hard-won effort to stamp out Wentwater for naught. And she had to act now—before the people reappeared in one big explosion. The lass was close to finishing; it was near time. The last thing Ursell wanted was to run into anyone from the village as she made her way to the lake.

In her glass eye, Lake Wentwater loomed large and mysterious. Although she could see to the far ends of the world in all directions, she had never been able to penetrate below the surface of the lake to see to its depths. And that greatly disturbed her. Some magic was at work, something ancient and powerful, and she did not want to accept the truth that stared back at her instead of her own reflection when she peered into the water. Her pulse quickened as her feet met with firmer, dryer ground, as she left marshland behind her and trampled the tall spring grass beneath her mud-caked toes.

She dared not believe that creature still existed! Surely she had died in the Great Flood, swept away in the ravages of water that had engulfed the land from east to west. Not in three hundred years had Ursell seen any indication that the Keeper of that rock pile lived. When the floodwaters had subsided, she had searched the land high and low for her and found not a single clue indicating she had survived. But who or what else could hold sway over the waters of the lake? Could it be those ugly slabs of rock held a power of their own, concealing themselves in obscurity from curious eyes? They did originate from an otherworldly source; there was no telling what true properties they held. Ursell had sensed their enchantment back when they towered in the center of the former village, in the bowl of the valley that was now the deepest part of the lake. But more likely—and what Ursell dreaded most— was that the Keeper knew a way to conceal herself, to wrap herself in water and vanish from sight.

That would take some doing, it would. For Ursell could see things buried and secreted away deep in the bowels of the earth, deep in the heart of mountains, through dense, impenetrable rock. She could trace the wending veins of gold and silver for leagues, the countless gems only known by burrowing beetles and sightless earthworms, treasures many humans would fight entire kingdoms to claim. Why, with her glass eye, on a clear night she could even see to the closest stars, study their churning fires as if sitting on their very hearth.

So the lake was more than an enigma. It filled her with a sense of dread that grew as she neared the shore. She had thought hard to find another way to bring down the village for all time. If a flood couldn't destroy Wentwater, nor an unraveling spell, then what could? It would have to be something even more powerful than the forces of nature and the forces of magic combined. And there existed only one thing more powerful than those two forces.

Words. How well she knew that truth! For nature and magic to exist, they relied on words. Everything came into existence through words. First the word in the mind of God, then the spoken word. The three most potent words in the universe were "Let there be . . ." A word could destroy a kingdom where a thousand armed men storming a wall could not. A simple word could annihilate a love that had endured great trials and pain. Just one word could cut sharper than any two-edged sword, if it were the right word.

And clutched in Ursell's hand was the very thing that would accomplish her desire, once and for all—the jar containing the word she had drawn from Justyn's heart. Now with the village returning, the jar was not safe. The lass was not the only one who knew about the castle in the marsh. She could not trust Justyn, not at all. Once he returned to find Teralyn back in the arms of his brother, he would come calling at the castle. Not that she couldn't handle one foolish human. But it was too risky, leaving that particular jar lying about. No, the safest place for that word would be the one place on earth where no one—not even she herself—could fetch it. The one place hidden from view of all—the bottom of the lake.

As much as she hated to part with her treasure, it would not serve her purpose if it somehow landed in the wrong hands. As adept as she was in her dark arts, she knew there were others in the world with greater magic, no doubt able to undo her spell and find a way to open the lid to the jar. No mere human could. Only by speaking the word contained in the jar could the lid be released or the jar shattered. Yet once a word was trapped inside, it disappeared from existence. So it was an impossible task, a paradox. None of the villagers would know this word, and because it now ceased to exist, all manifestation of the word would also cease. And this was her trump card, what would bring the downfall of Wentwater thoroughly and permanently. For, without this word, human society could do naught but fall to ruin. Quickly or slowly, it mattered not. Only that it was inevitable. And once the jar rested deep in silt at the bottom of the dark lake, Ursell could sit in her rocker and drink her tea with contentment, watching the slow performance of Wentwater's final act until the curtain fell. And what a performance that would be!

Upon cresting the last rise, she caught sight of the lake. The sun, now peeking over the eastern crags of the Heights, streaked the water with golden rays. Ursell forced down rising trepidation as she strained to see through the glassy film of the water, but it was only a mirror to the cottony clouds that passed slowly overhead. She marched resolutely down the hill, squashing wildflowers as she hurried. Sweat tickled her neck and her palms grew clammy. She felt oddly conspicuous, as if she were being watched. She chuckled to ease her discomfort. Silly, there was no one about. Teralyn was stitching in her cottage far across the lake and up over the hills. The only creatures around were the moles and gophers she could see under the ground, traversing their dark tunnels, nursing their young in burrows stuffed with tufts of dry autumn grass. A few birds winged in the air on the early morning breeze; worms wiggled underfoot. She was letting her overactive imagination get the best of her, she was.

She inched down to the edge of the water and peered in. Nothing. She laughed again and shook her head. Enough with this foolishness! She held out the jar and studied it. The little golden light flitted in the glass, banging again and again in an effort to get out.

"Sorry, little one. But you'll remain in this jar forever—so get used to it!"

She lifted her arm, ready to throw with all her strength, then stopped. What was that she heard? Singing? She quieted even her heartbeat and listened, but nothing other than the wind pricked her ears. Before she could hesitate again, she pulled her arm back and with a great grunt heaved the jar far in toward the center of the lake.

She rubbed her hands together, then wiped sweat from her brow. "There. Done." She looked to the spot where the jar had penetrated the surface, then gasped. She could now see the jar sinking in a slow spiral down, down through the water, as if it had punctured the concealing spell sealing the water's surface and allowed her a way in. With her glass eye, she followed the jar, riveted by the sight of it, and holding tightly to it for fear she would lose this connection. She very much wanted to see to the bottom of the lake; this she had yearned for for centuries. And now her greatest wish was coming true.

She dropped to her knees on the bank and watched as the jar fell through darker, colder water. She could smell fish and algae and rotting matter in this part of the lake, but could see nothing but the jar and its tiny sparkle of light. But wait! A second light. Ursell rubbed her eye, but both lights remained. One in the jar and the other—it was hard to tell just what it was. At first it looked like another light traveled beside the jar. But upon closer scrutiny, she realized the second light came from far below, a flickering light that seemed to be coming from . . . a candle!

No! It cannot be! Ursell struggled to pull back her gaze and return to shore, to safe, dry land. But once her eye caught on the flame, she was trapped. *The flame of truth!* That meant her greatest fear was true. The Keeper lived! Only the Keeper could keep the flame of truth lit. It was beyond belief. Despite her efforts to wrench away her gaze, she could not move. She was locked in place and could only wait. Anger roiled but could not quell her terror, for she sensed the Keeper drawing near, although she could not see her.

The brilliance of the fire grew, and as it did Ursell became aware of imposing shapes around the Keeper. The stone circle stood in silent vigil around her and the flame of truth, which sat on a pedestal in the center of the circle. The *Sha'har Sha'mayim.* The Gates of Heaven. One of the seven sites established in the world of man-kind, to keep evil at bay. One quick glance told her all the stones were still erect; even their capstones remained in place. The Great Flood had not toppled them over, as she had hoped. How was that possible? The force of water that great should have knocked them over like a row of dominoes. Perhaps she had underestimated heaven's power. No doubt she had.

She gulped and tried harder to pull away. If only she could close her eye! For the first time in her life, she didn't want to see anymore, but she had no choice. Another vision came into sight, and her heart sank heavier than any stone that had ever fallen into Lake Wentwater. Before her stood her castle, caked in mud, the sun beating down on its turrets. She watched in horror as bubbles erupted in the muck all along the edges of her home. Mud rose until it reached the front stoop, then curled up over the stone, frightening her waiting cats into the foyer. A groan followed—the groan from the weight of the hewn walls starting to sink.

This was no prophetic vision—she was witnessing what was transpiring now, as she knelt along the bank of the lake. Her jars! Her cats! They would all be engulfed in mud unless she hurried back as fast as she could manage. She had no time to fume.

Suddenly, she was looking again at the surface of the lake from the shore, barricaded from piercing through its mirrored surface that only reflected an impersonal sky. The Keeper had released her—but had also sealed her fate. Ursell would now have to leave her castle, this land, leave it all far behind. She would never find peace within a hundred leagues of this cursed place as long as the Keeper lived at the bottom of the lake!

Drat! So be it. She could only hope that the spell on the jar held. She doubted the Keeper had magic enough to counter it. What good would it do to worry? This was out of her hands now.

She hurried up the hill, panting hard but pressing herself to greater speed, wishing she had spent more time exercising and keeping up her stamina all these years. She feared she would arrive back at the marsh only to find the castle under tons of mud. Her dear cats! She doubted very much they could tread mud until she arrived to rescue them. She gazed ahead and watched her home slip further, then quickened her pace, hoping her heart would not explode from the strain.

Her grumbling returned with a vengeance. All the way home, she cursed the Keeper. Upon arriving, it took all her remaining strength to pull open the door against the oozing onslaught of mud seeking entry. With a loud *thwup*, the door gave way and mud disgorged her into the hallway. As she slogged through mud up to her knees and waded into her sitting room, she kept up her grumbling. Even after she had gathered up all her jars in a huge burlap sack and rushed out, back through the muck, heading west, in the opposite direction of Lake Wentwater, she kept up her litany of complaint. With her cats meowing in protest as they tried to pussyfoot after her, stepping in the depressions made by her footsteps and trying futilely to fling mud from their paws, she never ceased her grumbling. But now, there was no one to hear her complaints. She had left Wentwater behind. Well, why should she care, anyway? All the nettle she needed for her tea was gone. There'd be plenty of it in the west, over the range of mountains between here and Sherbourne. Plenty to fill her few empty jars and keep her warm and contented for another eon of time.

TWENTY-THREE

TERALYN FELT strangely like a trespasser as she pushed open the gate leading to the steps of Fromer's cottage. Wandering through the empty village no longer unnerved her. Instead, now on her forays into the town, she paid attention to what was missing, looking for words she had yet to stitch.

But there weren't many more left. Despite her weariness from the months of tedious, painstaking work, pushing that tiny needle through fabric, stitching words with barely discernable stitches, her spirit soared. The witch had never said the words had to be large. She realized after the first few dozen that she was wasting time and energy by stitching words of a readable size. Now, one would have to look closely to see that the blur of red thread actually spelled anything.

She knew she must be getting close to finishing. Already this week, the livestock had returned, almost as if they had all been created on one day. Even though it had taken her weeks to finish the list of creatures, none had appeared until a few days ago, and their scampering in hordes about town startled her when she entered through the north gate. Chickens filled the lanes, followed by stray sheep nibbling at the grass poking up through the cobbles in the street. Dogs, horses, pigs all wandered about, seeming quite content and carefree. Why they hadn't returned to their various pens and yards, Teralyn had no idea. Regardless, their sudden return to the village cheered her heart.

She pushed aside a big rooster as she climbed the steps to the front stoop of the cottage. *No doubt the villagers will be beside themselves with agitation when they see all the chickens loose, their feathers scattered about the town.* The reestablishment of so many remembered things set her heart pounding, but she reminded herself to take care. How easy it would be for her to say "shoo" to a bird in her path. Even that one word would once more unravel the town before her eyes. She made sure to never stay long, or relax enough to drop her guard. Having not spoken in seven years, though, dispelled the habit of any sudden vocalization. Up until now, she had let her joy manifest in humming. But when she had awakened this morning, an idea had struck her, and she'd hurried to town.

She entered the cottage and made for Fromer's room. Her pulse quickened as she spotted his fiddle case on the floor next to the bed. *Soon,* she consoled herself. *He'll be in my arms soon.* She walked past the bed and found what she was looking for—her lap harp. She had brought it to town that fateful day, not knowing that chaos and panic would greet her. Before she and Fromer were carted off with the magistrate, she had left her instrument in his room.

Oh, how she missed her harp. With loving care, she extracted it from its case, then ran her hand across the strings. It was still in tune! As she fingered chords, she found her skill hampered by the thick calluses on her fingers. It was like using sausages to press down on the fret board. But even so, the music that came from her harp as she sat on the floor was a balm to her soul. She let the resonating sound coat over the years of pain and sorrow. Each note spoke to her in its own language, wordless yet pregnant with meaning. How music could do that always amazed her—speaking to her spirit so fluently outside any human language. Her harp seemed alive, spilling out emotion, telling her how much it missed their communion.

Hours passed, with Teralyn reacquainting herself with her old friend. She found great comfort that eventually nullified the ever-present ache that had been in her heart for seven years. For this she was grateful.

By the time she walked outside, the sun was hovering on the western horizon. She swung her harp case over her shoulder and headed out of town, back to her cottage to do more stitching. She could tell she'd even put on a little weight; her rib bones no longer stuck out. It was hard to resist indulging in all the cheeses and meats and pastries on display in the store windows. She figured they would spoil if no one ate them soon. Still, she was mindful to only take a little bit of this and that from the various shops, so as to not deplete any one supply. Who knew when the villagers would reappear, and these staples meant their livelihood.

By the time she reached her cottage, the dark canopy above her was twinkling with stars. She felt filled—with music, with hope, with anticipation. It was almost as though she herself had been stitched newly back into the world, for she felt invigorated and whole for the first time in seven long years.

Spring warmed to summer, and the air thickened with sapphire dragonflies and golden honey bees. With her needle pinched between her fingers, Teralyn pulled the fine thread through the piece of fabric as she sat on her stool next to the window, letting the balmy summer morning invigorate her. The world stirred with promise, for at this moment she had only one more word to stitch. When that was done, she would be ready for the final touch— Fromer's name. She looked over to the corner where she had laid out the soft cotton gown the deep-green color of the lake. Beside the dress sat a pair of matching slippers. She had tried on dozens of dresses yesterday, wondering which one would be the most stunning, yet unassuming. She wanted Fromer to feast his eyes upon her. She had taken coins from her harp case and left them in the shops to pay for these purchases. She didn't want to chance wearing the dress around town and being labeled a thief.

The witch had been adamant. Fromer's name would be the last word and he would be the last to return to the village. Why?—she had not been told, other than that he was the key somehow to all that had happened. *"The loss of his name meant the loss of Wentwater. His return will return all back to the way it was."* She pushed everything from her mind but her task at hand, careful to keep her stitches neat and tight, then tied a tiny knot when finished. She let the scrap of cloth drop to the ground as her ears pricked.

After so many seasons of solitude, her ears were finely tuned to the slightest sound carried on the air. She could barely contain her joy, for she had not heard these sounds in all the years she had sat at work in this small room. There was no mistaking them. These were the sounds of people going about their daily activities. She could make out laughter—and singing! She jumped up from her stool and ran to the top of the hill, laughing as she ran. Such a joyous sight to behold! Even from this far away, she spotted villagers on the streets, talking, chasing after pigs, gathering chickens. She put her hand across her mouth to keep from shouting with joy. The villagers were back! That meant Fromer was there as well—or did it? She had yet to stitch his name. As much as she longed to run as fast as her legs could carry her to Fromer's house, she restrained herself. It wouldn't take long to stitch his name. Perhaps an hour. And the sooner she did so, they sooner she would be in his arms!

Spurred on by that hope, Teralyn took one long, last joyous look out over the village, then hurried back to her small square room situated on the knoll, eager—for once—to pick up needle and thread and continue stitching.

Huddled in her blankets, Iris kept moaning. Fen fussed over her, offering her tea and biscuits, but nothing could ease the consuming fear that had swallowed every bit of her sanity. She had lain awake all night, bundled against the night's cold, certain the stars themselves were glaring down in judgment upon her. She spent hours mulling over her every misstep that had caused this terrible situation, but there were so many! Was there one terrible thing she had done—or was this curse the accumulation of all her errors? And if her forgetfulness had brought on such ruin—was there any hope? Would Wentwater come apart at the seams, never to be repaired?

The thought of having to leave her village and begin life elsewhere caused another loud moan to erupt from her mouth as she thrashed under her covers. She hid her face with her pillow, no longer able to face the blue sky above her where her roof once existed.

"Iris, folks are gathering in the square. We should go—see what the magistrate says. Who knows—maybe by now they'll have sorted it out. Couldn't hurt to check now, could it?"

"Oh, Fen, it's no use, can't you see? I've gone and done something terrible, I have. And I try; I try so hard to follow all the rituals and traditions. But it's to no avail. For ten things I do right, there's ten others I mess up."

Fen stroked her hair, no doubt hoping to calm her. She could tell from his tone that he grew weary of her complaining. But she just couldn't help herself!

"What the—"

Iris stopped moaning and listened. What was Fen going on about now? Something else that disappeared? She rubbed her arm across her forehead, wiping the perspiration. Suddenly, the room seemed stifling hot. From under her mountain of blankets, she asked, "What is it, Fen? Now what's wrong?" She regretted her question; she didn't want to hear the answer.

But his tone changed, became joyful and lighthearted. She almost dared to peek out from her covers. "Look, Iris! The roof's back in place, back where it belongs." She heard him get up from the edge of the bed where he'd been sitting. "And the rug! Why, it looks as though the spell's been broken."

Iris threw the pillow off her face and looked up. The roof was surely overhead. She leaned over the side of the bed. The rug *was* back. Fen wasn't making this up!

"Oh, bless the heavens! Oh my word, oh my!" She squirmed out from the blankets and stuffed her feet into her slippers. Fen moved out of her way as she barreled out the bedroom and into the sitting room. One glance out the window revealed the missing rooster perched on the fence. Why, everything was back as it was—the hearth, the pot rack in the kitchen—everything.

She sucked in a breath and willed her heart to stop pounding so hard. There was still one more thing, though, she needed to check. Then she'd rest easy. Then she'd know the heavens had forgiven her for all her careless mistakes.

Fen followed behind as she rushed into the storage room. With a trembling hand, she lifted the lid to the large wooden barrel situated by the back door. A great sigh of relief poured out of her as her eyes gleamed in joy.

The barrel was filled to the brim with rutabagas. Fat, purple roots that gave off a pungent, earthy aroma. She leaned her face over the rutabagas and breathed in their scent as though it were the fragrance of the heavens. She couldn't recall a more wonderful smell in all the world.

Justyn shuddered as if someone had just breathed on the back of his neck. He spun around and shielded his eyes, scanning back across the meadows to the distant marshes. For some reason, he couldn't make out the towers of the castle. He thought he could see

them from here. Was that witch up to something? He could swear
she was watching him with her glass eye. It made him uneasy to
know she could see all his doings from afar. Suddenly, the air felt
much hotter than moments ago. He took a few more steps, then
stopped, puzzled. He didn't recall the grass being this tall—or this
brown—when he had come this way hours earlier. Well, he hadn't
been paying much attention to his surroundings while hurrying to
the witch's castle.

He thought of Teralyn trapped in the tower and that brought
a smile to his face. One meddling person out of the way. Served
her right. Fromer gone, now Teralyn. Justyn could enter the village unhindered, in full control. However, just what would he find
upon returning?

He felt a tingling on his left hand. He held it up, and to his
great surprise, his ring materialized on his finger! His eyes widened as the ramifications of this reappearance sank in. If his ring
had reformed, no doubt other things were returning to Wentwater.
Perhaps the entire village had been restored. Had this happened all
because the witch locked Teralyn in the tower? Well, whatever the
source, this was his golden opportunity! He would walk into the
village, take credit for the restoration, and the townspeople would
be filled with gratitude. He would tell them he had confronted the
marsh witch (and he could just picture their gasps of horror) and
demanded she reverse her wicked spell. He would relate how he
had threatened her and forced her to bend to his will, and how she
had to lock Teralyn in the tower to restore the village. He would
be a hero, and they would respect his wisdom, eager to listen to his
list of needed changes!

He began running across the meadow until he found the sheep
trail that led to the village. Off in the distance, water poured down
from the Heights, the falls glistening in the sun. He almost passed
the trail; the shrubs alongside it had grown massive and unruly,

nearly burying it. Odd. When he had taken the path earlier in the day, those shrubs hadn't been there. Or so he thought. He looked down the hill to the creek wending through the lowlands. All the cottonwoods seemed taller, much taller.

He shook his head and continued on, pushing through the thick vegetation that now blocked his way. But when he came to the top of the next hill he stopped. His heart pounded so hard it hurt his chest. What was this?

Never in a million years could he mistake the form standing on the rise ahead of him. Although her back faced him, and she wore a strange ragged smock with her hair a mess, he had no doubt he was seeing Teralyn. And her hair was long, down to her waist. Even despite her disheveled appearance, she radiated the elegant beauty that had captivated him only weeks ago. What odd enchantment was this? How had she gotten out of the tower—and arrived here in such a shape? Was he dreaming or back under the witch's spell? Everything felt askew and wrong—the weather, the hillside, even Teralyn. Almost as if time had sped past him, leaving him behind somehow.

And when Teralyn turned abruptly and ran back up a far hill, his jaw dropped. Even from this distance, he could tell her face had aged. She seemed years older, and her features were careworn and drawn, the way someone might look after weeks without sleep. But her smile attested to her joy. The kind of joy that could light up one's face, a joy that came from the deepest place in one's heart.

And there could only be one reason for Teralyn to smile in such a fashion—Fromer!

Justyn squelched the longing growing in his gut, the longing to touch her face, kiss her lips. He followed her until she disappeared over the next hill. When he reached the top, another strange sight met his eyes. A small cottage standing in the middle of nowhere. Surely that structure had not been there before now. He'd trekked across these hills countless times and had no recollection of a cottage. Yet this one had clearly seen many seasons. The sagging roof and the overgrown weeds wending up the walls attested to its long history. And odder still, Teralyn threw the door open and went inside, as though she lived there! What in heaven's name was she doing in such a place?

He thought about his plan to gather the villagers and tell them of his heroism. He could already hear the cheers and cries of praise and relief as they listened eagerly to his every word. The moment he had schemed for was at hand. Well, his plan would have to wait yet a little while.

First, he needed answers. He had to know how Teralyn had gotten here, and what she was up to. And he had to know if she'd seen Fromer, if he was back. None of all that had transpired made a lick of sense. If the village had reappeared and Teralyn was no longer locked in the tower, he could not even think what would happen next. For all he knew Fromer could be taking the credit for saving the day.

Justyn scowled and marched toward the door to the dilapidated cottage. He would give Teralyn one chance to explain. And if her answers weren't forthcoming or seemed at all dissembling, then . . . he would make her rue the day she'd met him.

TWENTY-FOUR

HUNCHED OVER in concentration, Teralyn didn't even
realize the door had opened until she heard it bang hard
against the wall. She spun around and nearly fell off her
stool. Justyn! She clamped her hand over her mouth and clenched
her teeth. She must not say a word—not when she was so close.
She only had three more letters to stitch in the cloth and she would
be done. She could then speak all she liked. But how could she
make Justyn understand?

She stood and pleaded with her eyes. *Leave, please. You must
leave.* She shooed him toward the door with her hands, but he
grabbed her wrists.

"Teralyn, what in heaven's name are you doing here? I just left
the castle and the witch said she would lock you in the tower. And
here you are in this cottage—acting as if you lived here! How can
this be?" He studied her face. "And you look older, much older.
Speak to me; tell me what's happening!"

All she could do was shake her head and point to her throat.
She pulled back, trying to get away from his grip, but he held on.

Justyn narrowed his eyes. "Don't play games with me, Teralyn.
And what is all this?" He let go of her wrists and gestured to the
stacks and stacks of cloth pieces filling the small space, burying
the spinning wheel and the last few piles of cloth. "What have you
been doing in here—and why?" He picked up a random bit of

cloth and brought one close to his face. "Why, this is a word." He looked at another piece. "These are *all* words. I don't understand. Tell me! Are you creating some more magic to bewitch the town? I want answers!"

Teralyn shook her head again, which clearly angered Justyn more. He grabbed her shoulders and shook them. Then his anger dissipated as quickly as it had formed. He was so close to her, she could feel his breath on her neck. The room began to grow unbearably hot.

He stroked her hair and looked deeply into her eyes. "Teralyn, oh, Tera. You have to talk me, tell me what you are doing. For, you see, if you don't . . ." He grabbed a swath of her hair and he pulled it, forcing her face even closer to his. Their lips were nearly touching, and Teralyn felt him tremble. She yearned to tell him to stop, to let go. What could she do to make him stop?

His hot breath brushed her cheek as his lips traveled toward her ear. A shiver ran from her head to her toes. He whispered slowly, enunciating each word. "If you refuse to tell me what you are up to in here, I will have to tell the village the truth. That you are . . . a witch!"

He pushed her away in disgust and gave her a sour smile that exuded every ounce of meanness a person could possibly contain. "I gave you the chance—to choose me over Fromer. Renounce him now—and I'll see to it the village hails you as its savior, by my side. I will tell them how you helped restore things. Marry me, Teralyn. Together we can rule over Wentwater, influence the village to give up their superstitious ways, and spur them on to educate themselves, never to commit such terrible travesties as . . . those inflicted upon your own mother. To think, they burned down your house and banished your parents. Don't you want to see those old ways gone for good? With you by my side, no one will ever suffer such persecution and humiliation again."

Justyn waited for her to speak, but Teralyn only stood, unblinking, silent. He was possessed, infused with madness. Under that marsh witch's spell—no doubt. There could be no other explanation for his behavior. The moment hung heavy with Justyn's judgment and anger. She feared making any slight gesture, worried any movement at all would set him off even more.

He exhaled loudly. "Fine, then. Have it your way. You'll regret this."

With those final words saturating the air between them, Justyn scanned the small room. His eyes lighted on the small piece of cloth resting on her stool, with a needle stuck in it. And beside the cloth sat an almost empty spool of thread, blood-stained red.

Disgust and anger welled in his face. He scooped up the spool and stuffed it in his pocket. Teralyn clawed at him and screamed in a wordless howl, but he pushed her to the floor and stomped out the door, slamming it behind him. She tried to get to her feet but her head pounded where it had smacked the hard floor. That spool! It was her last bit of thread, and what she needed to finish Fromer's name!

She inched over to the window, in pain, and saw Justyn striding on the wave of his fury down the hill. Teralyn moaned and tried to calm her shaking hands. She didn't dare think what Justyn had planned and what it would mean for her and Fromer. A terrible foreboding gripped her and she feared for Fromer's life. She had to hurry and finish stitching his name, for then she could rush to the village and find him. But without any nettle thread, how could she finish? She had to do something!

She looked over at the emerald dress, lying there neatly pressed and sparkling. It embodied all her hopes and dreams, which presently seemed to be unraveling. Well, if figuratively, then why not literally? With a heavy heart, she carefully cut the knot to the thread that had been used to stitch the hem. Then, as hot tears splashed her hands, she carefully pulled out the thread until she had a long enough piece. Perhaps this last little bit of cotton thread wouldn't matter. Most of Fromer's name was composed of nettle—wouldn't that do? She prayed with fervor it would, and then with trepidation and fear gripping her heart sat on the stool, picked up the piece of cloth, and started in on the letter *M*.

Teralyn's feet ached almost as much as her heart. Already the sky was darkening; the first early stars sprinkled the sky with tiny pin-pricks of light—light that gave neither illumination nor warmth. She willed herself not to panic. Over the last few hours, she had searched everywhere. Her words, unused for so long, had come out at first in a froglike croak. Villagers stared at her, puzzled, trying to make sense of her vocalizations. Odd that every word that she could picture perfectly in her head, knowing them intimately from stitching them into cloth, took such effort to form with her lips and push out her throat. By the time she had hurried down every lane in the village, inquired of nearly everyone she encountered, she was terribly spent. Her throat was raw, clogged with unspoken questions. Not even Iris or Fen had seen Fromer, but they hardly acted alarmed when she arrived at their cottage and asked his whereabouts.

"Surely he's off with his goats," Fen had said. "Have you checked the moors? If you wait here, he'll no doubt show up in time for dinner." Iris only eyed her suspiciously, but no wonder. Seven years had made its mark on Teralyn. Seven years of hard, tedious work, living in that tiny room, focused on her task. She made a point of hiding her hands, for she knew they would elicit questions. However, Fromer's mother busied herself in the kitchen, peeling rutabagas, and didn't press for answers. No doubt Iris still suspected Teralyn had somehow caused the unraveling of the vil-lage. Would any of the villagers ever trust her?

She politely excused herself and ran off toward the hills. Thankfully, she had not bumped into Justyn the entire day, although that caused her to wonder just what he was up to. What if he had found Fromer and done something to him? Justyn's heartless expression and bitter words plagued her. She would not put any manner of cruelty past him. Oh, she just had to find Fromer!

Upon leaving the village, she hoisted her dress so that the unraveled hem wouldn't drag in the dirt of the uneven goat trail. She had tried to keep the beautiful gown clean, but now it was beset with wrinkles and streaks of dirt, and no doubt smelled of her perspiration. Her hair that earlier had been brushed perfectly in place, tied with a ribbon in back, fell in disarray over her shoulders. She could no longer hold back the outpouring of tears. Seven long years she had waited for this day! To see Fromer's eyes light up upon finding her; to fall into his embrace; to feel his warm, strong arms encircle her, comfort her, erase all the pain and heartache. Maybe Fen was right—that she'd find Fromer with his goats on some far hill. But no one at all had seen him. Wouldn't someone have, at some point during the day? The village and its surrounding lands were not all that vast. And given Justyn's state of mind . . .

She hastened her step and called Fromer's name over and over, but it came out in ragged pieces from her hoarse throat. By the time she had circled twice around the lowlands where Fromer usually grazed his goats, night sucked away the last glimmer of light, casting a pall across the expanse as far flung as her hopelessness. The moonless canopy weighed heavily above her. Teralyn dropped to the ground in exhaustion and despair. She knew she needed to be patient and hopeful. Justyn couldn't have vanished from the world again. He may have returned to the Heights. Or to the witch, to seek her magic once more. Would Ursell retaliate in anger, seeing that Teralyn had succeeded in her task? The very thought sent a pain to her gut.

She strained to see in the dark, but her vision was limited. Perhaps Fromer had searched for her earlier and assumed she had gone home. He could be in the Heights this very moment, visiting her parents. The thought eased her sadness, although she just couldn't see Fromer leaving for the Heights without informing Iris or Fen. An idea came to her, but she squelched it in fear. She wouldn't dare return to that castle and ask the witch to find Fromer with her glass eye. Although . . . she might seek out the woman of the lake. Maybe it was time, finally, to try to make contact. But who knew whether she was still there, after all these many years? Antius could have been wrong. Maybe the woman hadn't come from the lake at all. A creature as fluid as water might never remain long in any one place, or form.

Teralyn wiped away her tears and sat on the grass, numb, weary. Yards away, the little creek murmured condolences as water skipped over rocks. How often this quiet place had soothed her heart. And sitting here now, far from the village, she almost felt as though the world was still gone. She should be overjoyed that she had succeeded in restoring Wentwater. She had endured a difficult, long trial and seen it through to the end. A part of her longed to hurry back up to her home in the falls, to see her parents and throw her arms around them. Oh, how she missed them! Yet for seven years the image of the woman in the marketplace in Sherbourne had taken root in her soul. Her real mother, who did not know Teralyn was alive, called to her. It did not make her love Kileen and Rufus any less, for truly they had raised her all these years with love and affection. But there was no denying this need to restore yet one last thing in the world—the lost relationship between mother and daughter. She would at some point have to journey west and find her.

But not until she found Fromer and determined he was safe.

She sank into the silence of the night, her ears still keenly tuned to the slightest sounds. Nothing was astir. Only the melody of the creek sang to her, and she let its song soothe her like a balm. She thought nothing of the hours as they drifted by, for time had changed for her over the years. No longer marked by schedules and appointments and daily chores, no longer fractured into pieces that could be compartmentalized. Time now flowed like a stream of thought, seamless and unremarkable.

She must have slipped into a sound sleep, for she suddenly jolted upright. Although her senses seemed heightened, nothing appeared out of kilter. Yet she felt eyes upon her, as if she was being watched. She got to her feet and brushed off her dress, then searched the darkness for movement. The warm night air hung moist and balmy, draping like a shawl across her shoulders. Even so, a chill tingled the back of her neck, making her wrap her arms around her chest. After a time, when nothing stirred, she started back up the trail toward the cottage. But she had only taken a few steps when a light shimmered before her, nebulous and ethereal, in human shape.

She blinked as the unformed light gathered in definition and outline. More curious than frightened, she drew closer as a face coalesced in the dark, illumination coming from within the one appearing before her. Was this a ghost? She had heard of such things in stories, and those stories had scared her as a child. But after all she had seen and experienced of magic in recent years, she no longer felt trepidation when faced with the extraordinary.

Perhaps Ursell was up to her tricks again. Or was this something Justyn had conjured to scare her? She humphed and reached out a hand to touch the manifestation, to see if it had substance, but stopped in shock when the shape spoke.

"Teralyn . . ."

Fromer's voice, although barely a whisper, fell heavy with love upon her ears.

Overjoyed, Teralyn reached out, but she fell through him. "Fromer! Is this truly you?"

She regained her footing and pulled back to search his face, drinking in the features she had almost forgotten. He nodded. "I don't understand. What's happened to you? Why aren't you whole? I stitched your name—you should be restored."

His form flickered like a candle in a breeze. "I do not know, my love. The last I remember, I was standing on the dais in the town square, next to you. Then . . . I found myself in this state, floating over the village, at the whim of the wind. I could see everyone below, but couldn't alight anywhere. But after a time, I managed to move to the place where I set my attention. I could hear all the voices of the villagers, and sifted through every one; finally, yours called me here."

"Oh, Fromer! How I've missed you. All these long years."

He lifted his hand and let it hover an inch from her cheek. His face shimmered with adoration. "I have seen all you have done— the stretch of years as you spun and stitched. And somehow I've seen your choice—that you could have left Wentwater behind, left me behind. But you chose to stay. And for this I love you more than words can say."

"But you can't remain like this, like a ghost! Oh, I've failed! Surely the thread I used in place of the nettle is the cause. The witch was adamant that I'd have to use the nettle thread to stitch everything back—including you! I can't spin more thread; all the nettle's gone from the land. And Justyn took my last spool. Who knows what he's done with it. Fromer, I'll have to go back to the witch."

Fromer held up a wavering hand. "My love, I've drifted over the marshes. The castle is gone—and so is the witch. I've seen no sign of her anywhere."

Teralyn's heart sank deeper than ever. "Then there's no hope! Unless we can find Justyn, and the spool of thread. Can you search for him, lead me to him?"

"I will. But, Teralyn. What if it's too late? You've completed the stitching. Can you undo my name and restitch it properly? What if that doesn't work?"

She couldn't help it. Her tears returned full force, gushing down her face. Her dress became drenched, and her hair sagged with water that spilled to the ground and pooled around her feet. Fromer stared, puzzled.

"This happened to you before—while we were at my house. What does it mean?"

Teralyn grabbed hold of her skirt and squeezed water from it. "I believe it has something to do with the lake."

"Lake Wentwater? Why?"

"A strange creature, whom Antius calls the woman of the lake, brought me to him as a babe. Antius believes she cared for me for a short time. I have odd visions of being underwater. I think they may be memories."

Fromer grew silent, then spoke again. "At one point I drifted over the lake, and I noticed a tiny spark of light coming from its depths. It was the oddest thing. And then I thought I heard singing. But I was at the mercy of the wind, and was whisked away before I could see more."

"Do you think it's possible this woman may live there—underwater? Fromer, now that you can determine where you go, can you not venture into the lake's depths and find her? She may know how to help us, help restore you back to your true form. What other recourse do we have?"

"I'll go. But, Tera, you must come as well. However, you look exhausted, and it would be better if you were rested and not stumbling about in the dark of night. Go back to your cottage and change into dry clothes. And get some sleep. I'll meet you there in the morning, at the shoreline."

Teralyn lifted her arm, and Fromer placed his hand to meet hers between worlds. Only a fraction of an inch separated them, yet the distance was uncrossable. Fromer's smile, though, held love enough to travel to the farthest star. It comforted Teralyn's broken heart as if he had reached through the fortified vault of time and space and gathered her in his arms. His words followed where his smile led.

"I love you, Teralyn. Do not lose hope. We will get to the bottom of this puzzle. I won't let anything keep us apart—even if I have to spend decades as a ghost, wandering the entire world for an answer. Do not lose heart."

Teralyn's throat choked up too much to answer. As she nodded in reply, his shape quivered and a breeze kicked up. She watched the blur of light fade until the meadow returned to darkness, but like that eternal flicker of light Fromer had spotted deep below the lake's surface, a tiny spark of light had now been lit in her heart that a flood of waters could not easily extinguish.

A spark of hope.

TWENTY-FIVE

AN ACHE started up in Justyn's gut as he looked up and saw his mother heading his way, tugging on his father's sleeve in the bright early morning light. The look on her face was hard to read, but regardless of whether she was angry or afraid, Justyn knew he'd get an earful, as her loud voice announced her arrival down the lane.

He wove through the crowd that had gathered around him in the town square, aiming for the raised dais. If he hoped to rally the villagers to his side, he needed to squelch whatever concerns his mother was bringing to him. He had little doubt of what she intended to say.

"What's this I've heard, Justyn?" Iris spread out her arms, ready to mow down anyone in her path. With a huff, she stopped in front of her son, her eyes narrowing in judgment. Villagers grumbled and stepped back, poised to listen. "You're taking the credit for putting the village back together? Why, it's been said that only hours before you blamed Fromer—your very own brother—for the horrible curse that befell us all. What in heaven's name are you going on about? And just where *is* Fromer? No one's seen him since he vanished before the eyes of all the town! Did you have something to do with that?"

Justyn sucked in a breath and his mother sucked in hers, readying herself to dump another pile of accusations on his head. His father took advantage of the moment to add his opinion.

"Your mum's in a fit, looking everywhere for Fro. If you know where he is, better tell us, lad. And just how in the world did you manage to lift the curse, if in truth you did?" With those words, loud shouts rose from the crowd. Justyn could see that even with the village restored, tempers were still on edge. Without understanding why their town had unraveled, no doubt they feared it would happen again without a moment's notice.

Justyn gestured with his arms in an attempt to quiet everyone down as he climbed up onto the platform. "If you'll give me a minute, I'll explain everything. It's exactly as I stated the last time I stood here." He waited until he had their rapt attention. More people came down the lanes, their faces curious and concerned. He thought back to how he'd planned to break down the traditions and rituals by exposing their foolishness. How he meant to expose the witch's chicanery and show the people of Wentwater that none of their superstitions held power. That all they believed was a lie. But now! Everything Ursell had predicated *had* come true. Teralyn *had* caused the unraveling of the town, just as she had predicted. And it all started when Justyn tossed the feathers about town in an attempt to discredit Fromer. In some odd, convoluted way, breaking the time-honored traditions had wreaked destruction. He would never be able to change the way they viewed the world. They would never come to appreciate the need for wisdom and knowledge. No, he knew now it would be foolish to try to sway the villagers to his way of thinking.

But he could still accomplish his other goal.

He had hoped ridding the town of Fromer would turn Teralyn's heart toward him, but it was not possible. Teralyn would never relinquish her love for his idiot brother—wherever he was. No doubt Fromer would soon make a grand appearance in the town, and Teralyn would run to him and loyally stand at his side.

A strange, persistent ache grew in his chest, one that had germinated after he had stitched Fromer's name that day, and it never fully subsided, even when he lay in bed at night, seeking sleep. It niggled at him like an insatiable hunger—and every time he thought of Teralyn, it pained him afresh. He could just picture the look of love burning like hot embers in her eyes as she gazed at Fromer. The pain grew unbearable.

There was still time to prevent that most undesirable reunion. *If I can't have her, neither will he!*

Justyn raised his hand and his voice. "Don't dismiss the wisdom of the town matriarch. She was correct when she said Fromer was not to blame for his bewitchment by the girl from the Heights. She—Teralyn—was the babe foretold to bring destruction to the town. It was she who put not only my brother under her spell, but me as well. I sorrowfully admit it—I was smitten by her too, and her magic caused me to spurn my own brother, and set me at odds against him! Her intent all along has been to bring this town to ruin—and this she almost did! If I hadn't acted prudently and confronted the marsh witch—"

With those words, an outcry reverberated through the throng of listeners. Shouts and screams filled the air, but Justyn hushed them all. Iris waved her hands in Justyn's face.

"The witch! In the forbidden marshes!" Iris gasped. "How could you even think of seeking her out?"

"There was no other way. If I hadn't slogged a path through the marsh and demanded the witch undo the curse, why, none of us would be here today! The village would have vanished forever. You saw what was taking place, and how nothing could be done to stop Wentwater from disappearing one piece at a time. Is this not true?"

Justyn waited as the crowd, settling into an agreeing murmur, swayed to his way of thinking. Now was the time to move them to act. He reached into the satchel slung across his shoulder and pulled out a handful of cloth.

"The witch knew a way to reverse the spell and restore the village. I forced her to use her powers, although it was a great contest of wills. But in the end, she gave in. She is only an old harmless hag, forgetful and bitter, and she is not the one who cursed the village. She only foresaw in her glass eye what would unfold across the years, and that is why she came to the baby-naming ceremony that day—to reveal what she saw. That and no more.

"Do you see these?" he yelled, waving the blood-stained pieces of stitching in the air. "These are words Teralyn stitched into cloth, using thread she spun from nettle, tainted with her own blood."

At the mention of blood, the villagers as one turned ghastly pale and shrieked. Justyn chuckled inside. He could only imagine what superstitions surrounded the use of human blood. He thought about the small spool of thread hidden in his satchel. Teralyn had thrown a fit when he grabbed that—obviously she needed that spool. Well, she wasn't going to get it.

Justyn continued. "This is witchcraft—pure and simple! And she has not finished with her plans! Why, even as I stand here, she is sitting in a cottage just north of the village, stitching spells into fabric—like these. What she has up her sleeve, we can only guess. But now that the village has been restored, do you think it likely she will stop? Before she can do more damage, we must do something! The cottage is filled to the roof with these things. And she will not utter a word to explain her actions."

Iris grabbed hold of Justyn's arm. "That's what the witch said! That she saw the lass spinning and stitching, bringing Wentwater to ruin!" Women in the crowd nodded, some tongue-tied with the memory of that fateful day of the fire.

Justyn continued. "I say we burn the cottage and everything in it, to prevent another curse from plaguing our village. What will she do next—cause rot to crumble our homes and taint our food?

Poison our water? With such power as she's shown, who knows what terrible events could follow? We must act quickly; we must act now!"

"But where's Fromer?" Fen asked, his voice full of worry. "What if the lass has him under her power? What can we do?"

Justyn looked into his parents' distraught faces, then lifted his eyes to take in the fear and agitation of the crowd. "I do not know. Only that we must hurry! Every moment's delay increases the chance of doom!"

He jumped off the platform and headed down the lane with the crowd following at his heels. As they passed through the village, others joined the stream of bodies heading toward the north gate, so that by the time Justyn had reached the last shop in the lane, he could not see an end to the sea of people trailing him. He pictured the small cottage in flames, recalling the one burning seventeen years ago as the flurries of snow swirled around his head. And just as the residents of that cottage had been chased away, never to be seen again, so too would Teralyn be banished from Wentwater. Whether she would return to the Heights and hide the rest of her days, he did not know. But of one thing he was certain—she would never spend another moment in Fromer's embrace, nor show her face in the village again. He would make sure of that.

But where *was* his fool brother, anyway? Hiding? It wasn't like Fromer to set their mother's heart worrying—Fromer, the dutiful, obedient son. And he was not one to hide in fear. No, something had happened to him, of this he was sure. But what?

Just as he reached the open doors to the gate, a young sheep-herder rushed toward him, galloping down the hillock out of breath.

"I saw him! Fromer!" The lad's face was drained of color. Justyn read fear in his eyes.

Justyn halted. Iris, nearly collapsing from the exertion of running through the village, slumped heavily against his shoulder, gathering breath as Justyn helped support her.

"Where is he? Where's my son? Is he all right?" Iris reached out and yanked on the boy's sleeve. The rest of the crowd kicked up dust as they stopped abruptly behind Justyn.

The lad looked from one to another, fumbling for words. "I was out on the moors, with my herd. And I spotted a cottage, one I'd never seen before. When I approached, a woman came hurrying out—with long white hair and a shawl wrapped around her shoulders . . ."

"Teralyn," Justyn muttered as the crowd gasped.

"And Fromer was with her?" Fen added, coming to Iris's side and linking his arm through hers.

The lad's eyes darted from Fen to Iris to Justyn. "As she passed me by, with nary a word, I saw something . . . floating in the air alongside her . . ."

Justyn took hold of the lad's sleeve and pulled him closer when he stopped talking and shook his head.

"You must tell us—what did you see!" Justyn demanded.

" 'Twas a ghost! It had to be. I saw his face—it was Fromer . . . but he was—"

"Look!" a woman in the crowd screamed. Justyn spun around to locate her—a young mother clutching a babe in her arms and pointing off toward the hills. Justyn looked where she pointed as screams rose from the mob and not a few women fainted and fell to the ground. Chaos erupted, with some villagers running back toward the center of town in fear and others cowering where they stood, as if their feet were glued in place. Iris pinched Justyn's arm so hard he squealed in pain.

"Wha-what's that? Drifting over the hill?" Iris's voice shuddered in terror.

Justyn didn't know how to answer her, for he had never seen such a sight in his life. Was this another of the witch's illusions? Something she sent to terrify the villagers? If so, she was succeeding.

He stared as the nebulous shape drifted toward them—and there was no denying that the form and appearance resembled Fromer. Justyn scowled. This had to be something Ursell conjured up. If so, what had she done with Fromer—locked him in her tower instead of Teralyn? Would this madness never end?

Amid the hysteria of the mob, Justyn raised his head, searching for signs of Teralyn. She had to be somewhere close by. If he could find and grab her, he would make her talk—he would! And if she remained silent, why, that would only support his claim of her witchery. He would not need to do anything to encourage the villagers to run her out of town.

Justyn yelled over the din. "Listen, friends. This is just some trick of the witch Teralyn, something she fabricated to create hysteria. Calm down and let's find the girl. Then we'll have our answers."

"Fromer!" Iris cried out. "Fromer, where are you?" Iris still clung heavily to Justyn's sleeve. He tried with care to pry her fingers off, but her grip was like an iron vise.

To the horror of all, the formless shape hovered before them a few feet over the ground, and now attained detail—such that there was no longer any doubt in anyone's mind that this was Fromer. Sweat trickled down Justyn's neck. He pulled at his collar and wiped his forehead. "This is just a trick! Do not be frightened!"

He waved a hand at the apparition. "Go! Begone. You are an illusion, nothing more. Leave this place!"

Justyn's mouth snapped shut as the apparition spoke. Iris shook so hard, still clutching onto Justyn, that she rattled his teeth.

"Mum . . ." Fromer spoke in a voice made of wind that lilted on the air and drifted through the fear-stricken, speechless crowd. "It is I. Something's wrong, and I am not yet able to return, not fully. But don't fear, Mum . . ."

Iris screeched and leapt backward when the ghost of Fromer reached out a comforting hand as if to stroke her hair. "Teralyn will find a way to bring me back. She believes the woman of the lake will have an answer. She's headed there now."

"Bu-but what has she done to you! You're . . . a ghost! And who is the woman of the lake? Fro—you're making no sense!"

But Fromer did not answer her. His shape wavered and became a diaphanous cloud that flitted across the moors, then rose high into the air and sped overhead—in the direction of the lake. Justyn followed with his eyes and a smile rose to his face.

"To the lake! That's where we'll find the girl. You've seen what she's done to Fromer. We must stop her, or the village will be haunted forever by the specter of my brother! And who will be her next victim? You?" He pointed at an old woman with fear engulfing her features, then turned to the gruff farmer who had chastised him earlier—who now didn't look quite as smug. "Or you? Maybe she'll turn us all into ghosts. What then?"

Justyn tried to move as the crowd stampeded past him, spurred on in a frantic panic, but he was left behind in a froth of whirling dirt and debris stirred up by hundreds of boots clomping like a runaway herd of rumphogs. He looked down, wondering at the heavy load weighing on his feet and preventing him from running. There his mother lay, where she had fallen in a swoon—a huge lump entangled in his legs, with her hands tightly clenched around his ankles. He shook his legs, then reached down in an attempt to extricate her pinching fingers from his flesh, but she was as a boulder in his path.

He glanced up upon hearing someone clear his throat. There stood his father, waving the dust from his face as it settled about them. Fen said not a word but just gave an apologetic look and shrugged.

"Wait, lad." Antius tapped the shoulder of the young driver of the delivery cart. "What's that afar?"

The lad yanked on the reins and stopped the two mules, pushed his hat back from his eyes. He craned his neck, then turned to Antius. "Not sure, sir. Looks like a crowd running down the trail to the lake. In a hurry, too, from what I can tell."

Antius looked up the mountain to the Heights swallowed by clouds. Even now, he found himself still shaking over the recent occurrences. One minute the village had been tattered in bits and pieces, and the next moment everything was back in order. Except Teralyn had disappeared—along with Justyn. He had spent the entire day yesterday searching up and down every lane, inquiring at every door, finally hearing word from a shopkeeper that she had seen them both headed west right after the debacle in the town square, although not together. Rather than try to pursue his gardener and his prized pupil, Antius had thrown up his hands at the whole incident, exhausted and trembling. He gave his aching and hot feet a break in the closest tavern and drank two cups of tea (accompanied by a few digestive biscuits), but that had failed to calm his fluttering stomach. After a fitful, disturbed sleep in a local inn, he awoke with a pounding headache. He'd had enough of the village. Even though he hadn't been down to the lowlands in years, this strained visit was more than his old heart could manage. It was time to go home and trust that Teralyn and Justyn would return, safe and sound. He had students awaiting him; he could dawdle no longer.

The mules snuffed and pawed the ground. Antius swung his attention back to the lake far off in the distance. A low rumble of voices carried to his ears, but he couldn't make out a word.

"What are they going on about, lad?"

The driver shrugged. "Can't say, sir. But they all seem to be in a frantic haste. I've been making my rounds since daybreak, but only to the outlying farms, so I've not been in the village all day. Can't think what could have them riled up like this."

Antius grunted. "Probably another upset over some ritual being broken." He shook his head and watched the blur of motion in the distance, then looked back at the Heights smothered in swollen dark clouds. "Well, it's best I be on my way home. These old bones have had more excitement than they bargained for. And it looks like we're heading into a squall. Appreciate the lift, young man." He gestured for the driver to continue. "May as well tackle the mountain."

"Yes sir." With a cluck of his tongue, the driver got the mules moving. Antius sighed as he looked out at the distant lake, a serene mirror reflecting a few stray passing clouds, calm, undisturbed.

If only his heart could be as calm.

TWENTY-SIX

AS THE HOT summer wind tugged her hair, Teralyn waded through tall stubbled grass that crackled and broke underfoot as she made for the lake. Streaking through rents in the overhead clouds, shafts of sunlight painted the surface of the water with a shimmering patina that rippled under the persistent breeze. The waters churned as if agitated from below, from creatures roused in the deep. The sight disturbed her, although she couldn't say why.

She slowed as she neared the water's edge, scanning the skies for Fromer, but he was nowhere to be seen. The sprawling fields spreading away from the lake lay quiet, baking in the heat, as if all life had once more vanished under some enchantment.

Murky water prevented her from seeing more than a few feet below the surface; whatever secrets the lake held would not be easily disclosed. She now knew her idea to find this water creature was a desperate hope. No one had ever seen this "woman of the lake" save Antius—and that was seventeen years ago. And even he admitted he did not know from whence she came. How foolish to believe some creature formed of water actually lived and breathed in such a dark and inhospitable place. Even if Antius's speculation were true, how would one summon her? And would she come upon being called?

As if the accumulation of her seven long years of toil crashed down upon her shoulders, Teralyn buckled under grief and despair and dropped to her knees. Disappointment rattled her heart as she thought of Fromer. His nearness had produced a bittersweet pain. Oh, how much better it would have been to not see him at all than to sense him so near, near enough to touch him and hear his sweet voice, and yet be separated by noncontiguous worlds. Would she be tormented forever by this thin veil, this invisible barrier keeping him at finger's length from her life and heart?

As she wept into her hands while kneeling at the lip of the lake, her tears dropped onto the water; like tiny pebbles, they sent ripples outward, broadcasting her pain across the surface, only to peter out unheeded. A noise tickled her ears and she jumped to her feet, hoping to see Fromer. But what met her eyes set her heart pounding in fear.

It appeared as if the entire village of Wentwater was running toward her. With agitated arms waggling, they cut a swath through the field, their fury preceding them on a wave of cries and shouts that nearly toppled her into the water. She took a few steps away from the lake's edge and steeled herself for their approach. As they crested the last rise, someone pushed to the forefront of the mob, and Teralyn felt the heat of anger surge up her neck and color her face.

Justyn!

What had driven him to such obsession? He had to be under some spell, pressing him toward madness. She thought back to his brooding during the festival, his lurking in shadows while watching her and Fromer play music onstage under the lantern lights. But even then, as well as when she had been at his parents' cottage for dinner, he'd only seemed sullen and worried. Then something had changed, something . . . and it all started at the time the village began unraveling. Teralyn did not doubt the marsh witch was responsible. What had prompted Justyn to seek that horrible creature out? Had he made some dark bargain with her, and now—this was the consequence?

She turned to face Justyn as he ran down the hill and stopped in front of her. She had seen with her own eyes the way he and the witch had met in conspiracy. And his jealousy and resentment toward Fromer, refusing to allow his brother a chance at love.

She could no longer hold back her rage. "You should be ashamed of what you've done, Justyn!"

He caught his breath as the crowd spread out and encircled them. Teralyn sensed the volatility of emotions roiling around her, as substantial as a blast of wind. He narrowed his eyes at her—any vestige of tenderness had long ago shriveled up under the heat of the fury so plainly evident on his face.

"Me—ashamed? Enlighten me. What have I done but combat your spell and restore the village? I have risked life and limb, even battled the marsh witch, to counteract your efforts to destroy Wentwater—"

"*My* efforts! Why in heaven's name would I want Wentwater destroyed? You are the one who berated the villagers' ways, who spoke with disdain of the superstitions and rituals that you felt imprisoned them in ignorance."

Teralyn turned to the crowd and pleaded with her voice. "I came to your village to attend the music festival. I played on your stages and ate your food and bought your wares. I fell in love with one of your own, and was welcomed in his parents' home. Why— tell me—why would I intend harm?"

"Only you could answer that, Teralyn. But you cannot fool anyone anymore." Justyn gestured to the mob, who pressed near, drinking in every word. "Everyone in Wentwater knows the prophecy. That the babe had been foretold to destroy the village—and you nearly succeeded! If I hadn't intervened, you would have had your wish—a land barren and abandoned for all time."

"You are mad! It should be obvious to all that you arranged for this to take place—just so you could take the credit for restoring the village." She turned to face the crowd again.

"I saw him at the marsh witch's castle—and he was conversing and drinking tea with her!"

Justyn laughed raucously. Teralyn looked into the faces bearing down on her and they were disbelieving. "Can't you see what he is up to?"

A burly man pointed at her. "We'll not listen to your talk any longer—witch!"

Others raised voices in outcry. "Witch! Witch!"

Teralyn starting shaking. "I'm not a witch! I'm just a girl from the Heights. I mean no harm. You must believe me!"

"We've seen your stitching!" an old woman said. "Just as fore-told! Stitching spells to bring Wentwater to ruin!"

"No, I did that to bring the village back proper. I spent seven long years stitching every word back into the fabric of life so that the village could return."

"Seven years?" the burly man challenged. "We're not stupid rumphogs. 'Twas only a few days ago that the village started disap-pearing." Others grumbled in agreement.

"Look around you! Haven't you noticed how everything is overgrown? How the trees have gained in height and breadth?"

"It's a trick—an illusion. Another of your spells!" someone called out.

Teralyn's heart pounded hard, making her ears ring. The crowd pressed closer.

"And what have you done to my brother?" Justyn demanded. "Have you turned him into a ghost to haunt us, to scare the villag-ers out of their wits?"

"Why would I do that? I love Fromer! It's your fault—you took my last spool of thread, the thread I needed to bring Fromer back! Give it to me!"

Justyn announced to the crowd: "See! She admits to using witchery."

"No, you don't understand!" Teralyn cried out, but her words were drowned in the overflowing cauldron of fear and terror that manifested in the shouts of the mob. Soon, it seemed everyone was chanting, their voices rising in pitch and desperation with each shout. There would be no reasoning with them anymore.

"Witch! Witch! Witch!"

Justyn raised his voice over the din. "If you're not a witch—prove it! The ancients threw their witches into water, to see if they would float."

Teralyn gasped as the very suggestion sent the villagers wild with intention.

"Drown her! Drown her—before she can cast more spells!"

Teralyn's head spun as arms grabbed her and bodies pushed. The crowd closed in so tightly, she could barely breathe. Surely, they didn't mean to toss her into the lake—she couldn't swim! *Fromer!* She called out in her heart, despairing over his absence. *Where are you? Help me!*

Before she could utter another word of protest, she felt herself being lifted by uncountable arms. Hands wrapped across her face and she struggled to breathe. Suffocating heat made her vision falter and the sky turn black. She struggled against the surge carrying her—no doubt to the lake's edge. But she couldn't see a thing as her own panic began to flood her heart, drowning her in a fear as consuming as water. The cries and shouts melded into one ugly voice, incoherent and intractable. Her efforts to free herself failed; she was sorely outnumbered.

With a powerful sway, the arms holding her swung her first in one direction, then the other—releasing her into the air where first the unfettered surprise of freedom greeted her, and then the shock of chill water as she splashed down in an eruption of spray and the lake sucked her in, summoning her into a cold, dark world that watched in silence as she sank, choking, to her demise.

Time muddied and swirled around her as she sank, as she struggled interminably against her prison of water—which strangely loosened its bars as her desperate need for air fled and calm soothed her bursting lungs. In one moment she had gone from the panic of drowning to an ease of familiarity, as if she had reentered some warm womb that had once nurtured and fed her, reassuring her she was safe and protected, just as the walls of a mother's womb dispelled fear. In such a place, darkness was welcome; confinement in water provided a buffer against the sharp, jagged elements of life. It was not a harbinger of death but of life.

Released from her panic, Teralyn marveled at the sensations tickling her senses. No longer needing to suck in air, she wondered at her clarified vision. Never had she looked through water as though protective lenses covered her eyes. Absent was the distortion, the bending of light, the skewed distances normally seen while gazing through water. Teralyn saw through the murky green the way she would look upon land under an unobstructed summer sky. She felt neither cold nor wet—nor much of anything, for that matter, other than the niggling awareness that she had been there before—in the depths of the lake, in such comfort and security. It was reminiscent of the remembrance of a dream, the way she sometimes felt upon falling asleep and being jarred with a memory of a former night's wanderings, the way tendrils of dreams lingered in the back of her mind only to be summoned forth once more.

She allowed her body to sink of its own accord as the life she left behind, above the surface, disappeared from both sight and mind. The quality of silence, so profoundly different from the outside world, engendered a heightened ability to hear, and soon silence gave way to a chorus of sounds coming from every direction. She heard fish nibbling on grasses growing out of the silt below her. She heard small rocks shifting along the sloped bottom of the lake as crawfish scuttled across the riprap laid decades ago to contain the water in times of flood. She heard the slow swish of tails moving back and forth, denizens of the deep that swam in measured patrol searching for food through the layers of thermocline. How she identified these sounds and their sources, she had no idea, but she knew them as truly as she knew her own name.

And then she heard a sound that widened her eyes and set her heart racing.

Singing.

Of all the beautiful, sublime voices she had ever heard, on stage or even in nature, none—not even Fromer's with its timbre of love and adoration—stung her with such poignancy as this voice. Not just familiar, this voice resonated with every fiber of her being, making each heartstring vibrate in rich communion, filling her with longing so painful she wanted to cry out.

But there was no need to, for out of the shadows a figure emerged, barely discernable, its shape undefined but wrapped in song. As it approached Teralyn, water shifted, and before her appeared a face that broke through the hard casing of her memory, startling her. How had she forgotten? This face, long ago imprinted on her heart and mind, triggered a tumble of memories.

Teralyn gasped as the memories filled her vision, memories of warm arms and soothing lullabies and rocking, rocking in the gentle surge of water. Pictures flitted through her mind as she gazed in awe at the woman blending with the water, who, Teralyn realized, was telling her a story—the story of her rescue. For deep in the heart of the lake, those many years ago, this woman had been disturbed in spirit. Something untoward tickled the surface of the lake, a strange substance—snow mingled with ash. Upon emerging from the lake, the caustic smoke stung her sensitive eyes. But what stung worse was a babe's cry of distress, a sound her even more sensitive ears discerned amid the cackle of hungry flames. In moments, Teralyn's rescuer had arrived at the burning cottage, forged through fire that spat and hissed at her watery intrusion, billowing smoke in great plumes that clung to her like a garment. She scooped up the howling babe, enfolding her in wet arms, and carried her to the lake, to her home.

Now, those same arms enveloped her, wavering in the sway of water, rekindling not the burning fire of her former life but the buried love that Teralyn never knew dwelt in her heart. An unspeakable name attached itself to the woman's form, a name that glowed with tenderness. Teralyn's heart overflowed with aching and understanding.

As the woman stroked Teralyn's undulating hair, she spoke without speaking.

"My sweet girl. I knew one day you would return to me. That you would hear me calling you."

"But I didn't. The villagers threw me into the lake!"

Words floated near Teralyn's head. She could not see nor hear them, but she sensed them caressing her ears.

"I saw you that day. Kneeling on the shore. Listening."

Teralyn understood. She had been called. "I heard your singing."

"Yes. Only you could. I sang your song."

The questions that had burned inside Teralyn now seemed unimportant, as if water had doused their insistent flames. A part of her wanted to linger in the depths forever, in this safe, uncomplicated world, but another piece of her heart cried out for Fromer. She looked into the woman's eyes and saw compassion.

"Come." The woman gestured with her head and turned toward the depths. Teralyn followed as they wandered through ever-darkening shades of green until a faint light appeared below them. The light grew to a brilliant tiny flame that illuminated the bottom of the lake. When they stopped next to the pedestal upon which the candle burned, and touched lightly on the bottom, silt kicked up in cloudy puffs, then settled over her feet. Surrounding them were a dozen or more giant slabs of stone, encrusted with shells and algae, with fish darting around the sides and tops of the rock, eying them curiously. She had seen this place in her vision in the castle tower.

"What is this place?" Teralyn asked. "It seems ancient and beautiful."

The woman rested a hand on one of the towering rocks. "In the ancient language, they are called the *sha'har sha'mayim*—seven sacred sites that were placed in the world.

"Heaven established them to keep evil from entering the hearts of men. But the enemy saw to it they were either destroyed or desecrated. Most of the sites have been abandoned or have fallen to ruin. Thus, evil has gained a stronghold in the hearts of men."

"Who is the enemy—do you mean the marsh witch?"

The woman's laughter caused the water to ripple. "She is only one small pawn. And she will not cause Wentwater trouble any longer. She has fled the land, and I daresay shall not return ever again."

"But I must find her! She is the only one who knows what has befallen Fromer. And who might know how to return him to the land of the living."

From the strange hidden folds of her sea garment, the woman produced a glass jar. A tiny amber light flitted inside. Teralyn gasped.

"One of the witch's jars! She has dozens of them in her castle, lined on her shelves. Just what is this?"

The woman held the jar in the space between them alongside Teralyn's question, and Teralyn beheld the same amber glow in the woman's eyes. "A word she has captured—or stolen."

"What is this word, contained in this jar? And how did you come by it?"

"The witch threw this in the lake only days ago. No doubt it is a very important word and the one I believe is responsible for all the turmoil in the village."

"I don't understand."

"When a word is taken from existence, all it symbolizes and all its ramifications disappear as well. You may have stitched every word back into existence, but you did not stitch this one, for it had already been stolen. Yet, for some reason, the fabric of human society must be so tied up with this word that it cannot endure without it. This is Ursell's wish—it has always been her intent to see the village destroyed. She tried to sweep it away with the Great Flood. And she tried to unravel it through her magic. But you thwarted her by your determination and great sacrifice, by stitching the world back into existence."

"Yet Fromer is a ghost! I stitched back his name—shouldn't he be whole again?"

The woman grew thoughtful as she stared at the flickering light inside the jar. "It appears he can't become whole unless his name has been stitched back properly. You will have to either find that spool of nettle thread or gather nettle and spin more. But this jar represents something much more urgent and dangerous."

"Wh-what do you mean?"

The woman wrested her gaze from the jar and met Teralyn's eyes. "If this word does not return to humanity, not just Fromer but all in the kingdom will be lost. This word is the key. You must break the jar and release it, but I am unsure how it must be done."

"Can I not just smash it on the ground? The jar is made of glass. It should break."

The woman shook her head and green hair caressed her face. "The only way to break such a bewitched jar is to speak the word it contains. Only the word itself can shatter the glass."

"But, then, it is an impossible task! Without knowing what word the jar contains, without the word even existing anywhere in the world, it cannot be spoken—and the jar cannot be shattered. And Fromer will never again rest in my arms!"

As Teralyn cried great tears that merged with the water surrounding her, she felt the woman's arms embrace her. Teralyn buried her head in the woman's neck and wept as a song drenched her in commiseration. How much time passed as she emptied her heart of pain, she could not tell. But gradually the aching subsided and a balm of comfort coated her. She pulled back and looked in the eyes of this strange creature who felt more a mother to her than Kileen ever had.

"Do not lose hope, Teralyn. The mysteries of heaven are often beyond our grasp, as even the world is one unfathomable paradox. Evil can never truly triumph over good, as hard as it may try. Look to heaven—and your heart—for the answer. For the heart is the one fortress the enemy cannot storm, if it remains true." She rested a hand on Teralyn's shoulder. "And I know yours is the truest of hearts, my sweet one."

The woman of the lake took Teralyn by the hand and led her over to the pedestal, a carved and delicate structure that stood nearly as tall as she. "This is the flame of truth, and e'er it burns brightly. Nothing in this world can put it out. Keep this flame burning in your thoughts and in your heart. Truth is a powerful weapon, sharper than any double-edged sword. Wield it carefully, yet confidently."

Teralyn nodded, but she was not sure just what this woman meant.

"And I have a parting gift for you."

Those words brought sorrow to her heart, for as they were spoken, Teralyn knew without doubt she would never again see the wondrous creature who had rescued her not once, but twice.

The woman reached again into the folds of her translucent robes and withdrew a ridged shell that fit in her palm. To Teralyn's surprise, when the woman tapped on the shell, the lid rose and opened to a fleshy pink bed upon which a small round pearl rested.

"This is the pearl of great value—the pearl of wisdom. Your wise men and women in the Heights take pride in their accumulation of wisdom, and many are wise indeed. Yet none have such a gem. The wisdom of this pearl cannot be found in any books or scrolls. It cannot be bought for any price—its value is beyond imagining." She gently lifted the pearl from its house of shell and reached her other hand out. "Your necklace."

Teralyn felt at her throat and found the clasp to the silver chain around her neck. She unlatched it and handed it to the woman, who placed the pearl in the center of the star pendant. It fit as if it had been designed for this very pearl. She then placed the necklace around Teralyn's throat and fastened it with a soft click.

"There are those who would sell everything they own to acquire this treasure. But this pearl is a gift given to a heart receptive to it. Let it serve you throughout your life, and guide you into all truth."

Teralyn fumbled for words. "Thank you. I am grateful."

The woman then handed her the jar. "Take it to the village and trust heaven to make a way. Do not give in to despair, but rejoice with the truth. Whatever the cost."

Teralyn took one long last look around her as the woman of the lake, her rescuer, comforter, and guardian, led her upward through the reeds and kelp. Soon, the shimmer of sunlight began to filter through the layers of water above her until the surface shone like glass, reflecting both the hidden world beneath and the natural world above. Teralyn pushed her head through a bed of clouds, and as her face met with the warm, dry air, she sucked in a breath long in coming. One quick look around her told her that not only had the villagers left but the woman also had vanished, never to be seen again. Teralyn's heart sank like a stone dropped into the lake, for she did feel that, when she surfaced, a part of her heart had broken off and fallen to the depths to remain forever behind.

TWENTY-SEVEN

JUSTYN SAT on the front steps of his parents' house, shaded from the midday sun by the eaves overhead. He could hear his mother's moans as she lay upon her bed, lamenting over Fromer. For the life of him, he could not understand what had befallen his brother. Had he really turned into a ghost? He smirked at the gullibility of the foolish villagers—they had fallen for his tale of Teralyn the witch casting a spell over Fromer. And they hadn't hesitated to do his bidding.

The ache in his heart started up with a vengeance, but he squelched it. Teralyn was drowned. The image of her struggling and gasping for air sent a pain through his gut. Well, good riddance! Her face—her agonizingly beautiful face—would haunt him no more. No more sleepless nights with her soft voice plaguing him. No more having to watch her moon over Fromer, love burning like the sun in her eyes. No more having to stand so unbearably close to her, smelling the fragrance of her hair and skin, unable to touch her.

He needed to return to his life in the Heights, but first, he had to go back across the marshes to the castle. The witch had to be responsible for Fromer's strange disappearance—and the conjured specter that had been seen on the moors, sent no doubt to spur the villagers once more into a fit of hysteria. What was Ursell doing? Hadn't she been paid with a word—some word she'd taken from him? She had promised he would have power over Fromer, and she had broken that promise. And now his mother was inconsolable. If Fromer did not return soon, his parents, as well as the rest of Wentwater, would no doubt turn on him. For now, with Teralyn dead, they were mollified. But should that ghost return . . .

Justyn leapt to his feet. Every minute he delayed jeopardized his reputation as the savior of Wentwater. He slipped into the house to gather his things and repack his pack. Hopefully, a few veiled threats would get Ursell to stop her shenanigans and return Fromer to the village. He knew what would sway her to his will. Those jars. Undoubtedly, they were her most precious possessions—whatever they contained.

Justyn searched the back storage room until he found a heavy metal pry bar. He hefted it in his hand, weighing not just the iron but the image of smashing her neat rows of glass jars as she looked on in horror. He listened for a moment as his parents spoke in hushed tones from the bedroom. When he returned with Fromer, how they would rejoice and thank him. The village would again sing his praises for removing not just Teralyn but the cursed ghost terrorizing the village.

Justyn laughed aloud. Poor Fromer! How his heart would break when he learned what happened to his beloved. Maybe, overtaken by grief, he might join Teralyn in those watery depths. Wouldn't that be the icing on the cake?

Justyn slung his pack across his back and opened the front door, about to slip out, when he heard another uproar in the lane outside the cottage. *What now?* A tremor shook his chest. What if that concocted vision of Fromer had returned? Just what he needed. How would he slip past the villagers if they congregated in the streets? Before he could think what to do, his parents came rushing out of their bedroom.

His mother fanned herself with a fluttery hand. "Oh, Fen! Now what's the commotion? I don't think I can take another fright. Go see what's got the neighbors riled up this time."

Justyn's father looked him over. "And where are you off to, lad? Back to the Heights? Not even an ounce of concern over your missing brother?"

Justyn laid a hand on his agitated father's shoulder. "Of course I'm concerned over Fromer. But Teralyn is gone. Which means she can no longer bewitch him. Surely Fromer will return soon. And I'm off to look for him."

Iris let out an exasperated sigh. "Please, Justyn. Find your brother. Bring him home to us. I don't think my heart can bear any more grief."

Justyn forced the corners of his mouth to form a smile that he hoped would convince his parents of his concern. "Stop fretting, Mother. I will—"

Screams of fear filled the air, rattling the windows of the cottage. Iris screeched and fell to the rug as Fen threw open the door. Justyn came alongside his father, and his jaw dropped. Words fled his gaping mouth as if running for their lives.

It couldn't be! This had to be another of the marsh witch's enchantments! Anger boiled to overflowing. This was the last thing he needed—an apparition of Teralyn marching down the center lane of the village!

Justyn walked down the steps to the gate with his father lagging behind him. He could sense fear in the air around him—thick as the mosquitoes that swarmed the marshes. The sun overhead shone a radiant light upon Teralyn as she strode toward him; the villagers trembled as they watched from behind shrubs and peeked around the corners of buildings. Justyn narrowed his eyes and studied her form. She seemed real enough. But he, as well as most of the inhabitants of Wentwater, had watched her sink into the lake's depths. And they had waited on the shore for nearly an hour, with no trace of Teralyn resurfacing. There was no way she could have swum to some other shore and climbed from the lake unseen. She had to have drowned! No one could survive that much time under-water—no one!

Teralyn stopped a few feet from the gate. Justyn studied her, aware his hands trembled. He clasped them behind his back as he stood, resolute, his brain spinning with confusion. The sight of her so close unnerved him. She seemed even more beautiful than ever—as if some inner glow radiated outward through every pore of her skin. And a strange aura of peace and confidence blanketed her. She was no longer afraid, no longer angry. Her composure agonized him as much as her proximity.

The world seemed to stop spinning and hold its breath as villagers dared gather closer, silently, gripped with unspeakable terror. They no longer cried "witch," although no doubt the accusation was foremost on their minds. For how else could Teralyn have survived all that time underwater? When she opened her mouth to speak, she shattered the spell she had woven.

"I'll have a word with you, Justyn." She turned to face the villagers and more screams erupted from the crowd. "Come close and hear the truth."

Only now did he notice Teralyn carried something in her hand. His eyes widened and heat rushed to his cheeks. She held one of the witch's jars! Where had that come from? And what did she plan to do with it? Did she know what the jar contained? Had the witch given it to her?

Questions festered in his head. He looked down the lane and did not like what he saw. The villagers were enthralled with Teralyn, hanging on to her words, filled with intense curiosity. For Teralyn spoke with calmness and authority.

She held up the jar for all to see. "This is what Justyn gave the witch—the price he paid for power. Power over his brother, Fromer. And power over me."

As the sun's light hit the jar, the tiny spark inside flitted and banged against the glass. One of the villagers yelled out in a shaky voice. "Wh-what is it? What's inside the jar?"

The crowd grew oddly quiet. Justyn grunted. Why were they listening to her? It was obvious they were all terrified by her. He would have to rally their support once more. He interrupted Teralyn just as she began to speak.

"Don't listen to her! Don't you understand? She has proved herself a witch. You watched with your own eyes as she sank to the bottom of the lake. Only a witch could survive such a trial. And now, she will spin words and ensnare us all. We must destroy her!"

"How?" a man yelled back from the middle of the lane. "If neither fire nor water can kill her, then what can stop her?"

His words set off an explosion of panic. Justyn waved his arms to calm the crowd. "Listen! This girl is only human. Whatever magic has protected her can be undone."

"Nothing you have done or said has worked!" a woman in the crowd yelled. "And your brother is still missing."

Someone behind him called out. "Let her speak!"

Justyn felt a hand push him aside. He turned his head and saw his mother reaching for the gate latch. He stepped aside and let her pass.

Iris marched down the lane, her chin held high. She stopped in front of Teralyn and shouted for all to hear.

"Lass, if you know the truth about Fromer, where he be, then tell us. Tell us the truth."

"Yes, we want the truth!" villagers cried out.

Justyn watched Teralyn's hand lift to her neck and touch something at her throat. She surveyed the crowd; most stood at a safe distance, but Justyn saw they strained to hear her words. She looked at his mother, her eyes filled with compassion.

"I fell in love with Fromer at the festival. You were witness to this. For reason of jealousy—or madness—Justyn could not bear to see us so happy. He went to the marsh witch and bargained. He wanted power over Fromer, and in return, he was to pay her with seven rooster tail feathers. Those he gathered one night while the village slept, and to stir up trouble, he scattered chicken feathers across town."

Gasps erupted at the telling, but Teralyn pressed on. Justyn felt his face heat up even more. He clenched his fists and gritted his teeth. He would have rushed at her and stopped up her mouth, but all eyes were upon her. She would be heard. At the lake, they wouldn't listen to her; they shut their ears and buried her pleading cries. But now! What had changed? She radiated some strange light. Another spell? Was this Ursell's doing as well? If he didn't shut her up, she would convince the town he was at fault—for everything!

"I followed Justyn that day—right after Fromer vanished into air. He returned to the witch to pay her her due. But he wanted more. He demanded the witch put me in her tower, and for doing so, she demanded a stiffer payment." She held up the jar. Sunlight glinted off the glass, breaking piecemeal into rainbows that splattered faces with color.

"This is the word the witch took from Justyn's heart."

"What word," his mother asked, "and what does this have to do with Fromer?"

"Yes, tell us!" another shouted.

"Tell us!"

Teralyn looked to her left, her chin lifted to the sky. A smile inched up her face as she lowered the jar.

"I will let him tell you." She pointed as a gray shape congealed a few feet from where she stood.

"Who?" Iris asked in a shaky voice, clutching her chest.

Teralyn turned and laid her hand on Iris's wrist, then patted it. "Your son. Fromer," she said.

Teralyn stepped back as Fromer appeared before her, morphing into a form that seemed substantial but for the fact that his feet hovered a foot above ground and shafts of sunlight streaked through his bones, mottling his skin with a radiant hue. Despite his ethereal, angelic nature, those gathered around Teralyn melted in terror at the sight. Villagers moaned and shook, some covering their eyes with their hands, others wrapping trembling arms around their bodies. She could only imagine how this manifestation must rattle those of a superstitious nature. What could be more frightening than seeing one of their own with one foot in the material world and the other in shadow? There would be no ritual or ceremony to ward off such a fearsome fate.

As Justyn came toward them, the matriarch of the village ran in haste down the lane and pushed through the terrified mob. She stopped a few feet in front of Fromer and waved her arms wildly.

"Do not let it speak!" she yelled, covering her ears with her hands. "It will bewitch us all!"

Teralyn reached out to try to calm the woman, but was answered with the smack of a hand across her cheek. "Please," Teralyn pleaded, moving to a safe distance from the woman's swinging arms. "Heed Fromer's words. We need your help, everyone's help. Perhaps together we can find—"

Justyn strode up to Teralyn, bringing his face up close. He pushed words through his clenched teeth as he spoke to her. "I don't know who or what you are. No one could have survived that long underwater. You are some aberration, an abomination. The villagers have every right to fear you—and banish both you and your ghostly lover from Wentwater."

The matriarch waved her arms in the air. "Yes!" She looked at Teralyn with anger searing her face. "Leave, now! Let us live in peace. Stop tormenting us!"

Teralyn met the old woman's eyes with steeled determination. "Allow us at least to speak our minds. And after that, if the village is in agreement that we should depart, we will leave—Fromer and I—and never return to Wentwater."

The matriarch scanned the faces in the restless crowd, then nodded. "We will hear what you have to say. But be quick about it."

"Thank you," Teralyn answered, knowing how much courage it took for the villagers to acquiesce. How their world had been upended these last weeks! After such an upheaval, would they be able to return to their traditional ways ever again?

When the grumbling and nervous mutterings grew quiet, Fromer rose a few feet above the crowd, hovering like a leaf that ruffled in the breeze.

"We don't know what word is in that jar. But unless it is released, Wentwater will tumble to ruin," he said, his voice strained and thin, stretched across two worlds. "And although the woman of the lake does not know what word has been taken, she assured Teralyn that without it—without its existence in the world of humankind—the village will surely unravel again. With no hope for restoration. . ."

The matriarch spoke again. "Then open the jar and let the word out!"

"It cannot be opened, nor the jar broken . . ."

One of the shopkeepers, still holding a broom in one hand, grabbed the jar from Teralyn's grasp. "Let's see about that!" He threw the jar to the cobbles with all his might. The jar lightly bounced a few feet, then came to rest undamaged next to Iris, who stared at it quizzically.

Iris stomped her feet and put her hands on her hips. "How could you, Justyn? How could you do business with the marsh witch? Look what you've done to us—to the whole village! To Fromer!"

Angry words started flying again. Teralyn jumped back as Iris grabbed Justyn's shirt collar and shook him.

"It was the only way! I had to bargain with her to save the village."

Fromer raised his voice over the rising swell of shouts. "That's not true. You went to the witch to find a way to control me—in order to win Teralyn's heart. You couldn't bear to see us in love, to see me happy." Teralyn heard a strange anguish in Fromer's voice, a pain that wriggled out of his heart and laced his words. "Why, Justyn?" he asked, looking down into his brother's eyes. "Why couldn't you have been happy for me?"

Justyn snorted. The grumbling crowd pressed closer. Justyn pushed a man who pressed up against him. "Hey, back off!"

"It's your fault, lad. Everythin' was just fine 'afore you came back to the village. 'Afore you went to the witch and started spreading feathers—"

"And lies!" another man yelled. More shouts poured into the air like liquid wrath.

"All yer fancy talk about saving the day!" one of his mother's gossipy neighbors chimed in. "And you went to that witch to break up those two lovers. Jealousy—that's what prompted you. Not some heroic mindedness." She spat in disgust at Justyn's feet.

Another raised her voice above the din. "Well, if the jar can't be broken or opened, how can the word be set free?"

Fromer sighed. "The word trapped within must be used in order to open the jar."

"Well, that makes no sense!" Iris shouted back. "If the blasted word's gone missing, how can you use it?"

"It's a trick!" someone else yelled.

Teralyn felt her own ire rise. She stared at Justyn and felt nothing but contempt for him. She felt it like a plague gone rampant—this fury of judgment coming from within and without. And she could almost smell the bloodlust for condemnation. The crowd wanted to punish someone, and, to her surprise, so did she. She searched her feelings and felt nothing but the desire for justice.

All eyes riveted on the one who had brought them to the brink of ruin. Justyn's expression shifted. No longer did he seem propelled by arrogance and confidence. Now, fear marred his features as the crowd replaced their angry words with physical blows. Justyn covered his head with his arms as the villagers of Wentwater struck him with their fists and threw rocks at him.

"Kill him! He deserves to die!"

"He must be punished for his evil deeds!"

"Make him pay for his crimes! He's destroyed our way of life!"

Swept up in the fury of those around her, Teralyn knelt and felt along the ground for a rock. She could not contain the urge consuming her, the urge to lash out and hurt Justyn. Justice must be served. Suddenly, she understood. The old laws of an eye for an eye and a tooth for a tooth reflected the greatest wisdom of the ages. In her mind, she knew his punishment was due. The villagers were right—he deserved to die! There was no way around it.

She groped through the kicked-up dirt and found a hefty rock. This would do! When she rose to her feet, she saw Justyn cowering, bent over, barely visible under the sun-tinged dust stirred up by the villagers, who pounded him with blows and threw stones and sticks at him.

Teralyn took aim and let her fury propel the rock toward Justyn. Not even his pained look at seeing her smile affected her, or inspired pity. She felt a keen sense of satisfaction in watching Justyn die before her eyes. Yes, satisfaction indeed.

"I'm sorry!" he managed to whisper out of his bleeding mouth. "Please . . ."

"Too late for that!" Iris cried out, beating Justyn over the head with a bulging sack.

"Sorry won't fix anything!" the man with the broom added, whacking Justyn on the back with it in fury.

"Wait!"

Fromer's cry carried tremendous power, rattling heads and forcing all to stop and look up. Teralyn shaded her eyes as Fromer hovered above Justyn.

"Wait for what?" she asked. She wondered at the strange look on Fromer's face. Almost as if she was staring into the eyes of a stranger. She couldn't make sense of his expression. He looked pained. Why? How could that be? Didn't he see this was the only way to handle Justyn's traitorous acts?

Fromer's nebulous hand hung in the air as if he yearned to stroke Teralyn's hair, the way someone might try to soothe a frightened animal. But rather than making her feel calmed, Fromer's attempt only riled her more.

"Go away, Fromer. You're interfering with justice!" The crowd around her exploded in angry agreement, forcing Teralyn to yell to be heard. "You of all people should want to see Justyn die. He's treated you with contempt! He must pay!"

Teralyn scoffed as Fromer lowered to the ground, placing himself in front of his brother—as if he could somehow deflect the sticks and stones hurling at Justyn.

"Out of the way, lad," someone yelled as more rocks were hurled. One large missile nicked Justyn's face and he cried out.

"Please, everyone—stop!" Fromer yelled.

"I said, get out of the way, lad. There's nothing you can do to stop us. Your brother will get what he deserves!"

More rocks fell upon Justyn. Teralyn noticed how he cowered and shook against the wood fence, bent over and hiding shamefully behind Fromer, which offered him no protection other than a distraction. Villagers reviled him, shouting names.

"Coward! Fool! Traitor! Trickster!"

A group close to Teralyn started chanting for Justyn to die. Without thinking, she joined in with their mindless repetitious demands, swept up in the mob's one intent—to get past Fromer and see him pay.

Why was Fromer defending him? He just stood there, tall and unwavering, as the sticks and stones flew through him relentlessly.

This was all wrong. Something was very wrong. But she just couldn't make sense of it. She only knew in her heart a great unsettling discomfort, and a feeling that something of importance had drained from her heart, leaving her with a gaping hole. Something was missing inside her, something vital, and its absence sickened her.

"Fromer," she yelled, "why are you standing there protecting Justyn?"

The volley of rocks trailed off. Villagers, breathless and poised to continue their rampage, stopped and listened.

Fromer spoke with simple conviction. "Can't you see Justyn feels remorse over what he did?" He leaned over and encouraged Justyn to his feet. Teralyn looked at Justyn as he stumbled aright—at his bruised and bleeding face, at his eyes filled with pain—and felt nothing but contempt. She looked down at her hand gripping the jar. Her knuckles were white. She loosened her grasp and watched the tiny light flitter madly inside the glass, as if trying with all its might to burst out.

Justyn cleared his throat and shook dirt from his hair. "I am sorry, truly sorry. I never meant for anyone to get hurt, for any of this to happen . . ."

Before the mob could burst out in another outcry, Fromer shook his head, puzzled. He searched Teralyn's eyes, confused. "What is wrong with you, Teralyn?" He raised his voice and scanned the crowd. "What is wrong with *all* of you! Before you stands a man full of regret. Do you not have any compassion in your bones?" He waited, tipped his head. Sun beat down on them all, sharing in their harsh judgment. Silence fell, thick as mud.

"Justyn," he said. "Even if no one here can muster any tender feelings for you, I forgive you. I know you lashed out at me because of your deep unhappiness with your life. Because you have never fit in to our village or ways of life. Never felt understood or truly loved . . ."

Teralyn gaped at Justyn's tears, which poured down his filthy face, streaking his cheeks with brown wet tracks. Fromer continued.

"Even though you meant to do harm, I know you only wanted good for the village. You have worked so hard these many years to better yourself, to be a force for good in this world. To excel, to be a teacher, to encourage others." He sighed, and Justyn appeared to wither under Fromer's loving gaze. "You have a true heart, Justyn. I know this. And I have always loved you and always will."

Fromer turned back to the crowd. "Let him go. Let Justyn return to his life in the Heights. He will not bother you ever again. And I . . ." Fromer turned to Teralyn. She thought her heart would break at seeing the distant expression lacing his eyes. ". . . will leave Wentwater. Go far away, so you will not fear being haunted ever again. Whatever has been done to me, I will learn to live with it. I will find a place of solitude where I can exist and not inspire fear. I ask only that you let my brother leave in peace."

Murmuring rumbled through the crowd. Teralyn felt a strange, hot stirring in her chest, as if her heart burned. And then heat travelled up from her hand—the hand that held the jar. She lifted it to the light and saw the glass shimmering with illumination.

Both Fromer and Justyn riveted their gazes on the jar, and a hush spread outward, like a rustling wind. The air thickened and congealed. "Something is happening—" Justyn started to say, but was interrupted when Teralyn yelled in surprise.

The jar exploded in her hand, and shards of glass smacked her face and arms. She ducked and covered her eyes with her fingers, dropping what was left of the jar to the ground. Upon wiping away the tingling specks of glass from her face, she felt an overwhelming sense of despair. Tears pooled in her eyes and her heart felt stricken, as if someone had stabbed her with a knife. She glanced around and saw the villagers suffering from similar distress. What on earth was happening?

A flash of light caught her eye. She turned back and looked over at Justyn, who sat slumped on the dirt, crying in great sobs. Fromer knelt alongside him. Dancing on the dust motes in the air, the vibrant prick of light that had escaped the jar neared Justyn's head and hovered for a brief moment. Fingers pointed as the villagers stared wordlessly at the strange light that seemed to capture the essence of the sun.

Then, the tiny flame rested on Justyn's chest. Justyn pulled back and stared at it, wiping his face and sucking in a breath. Without a sound, the light burrowed into him and disappeared. Justyn let out a small noise, then choked back a cry. A strange expression came over him, and it appeared to Teralyn the light had not only gone somewhere deep inside Justyn but had altered the flush of his skin, bringing color back to his cheeks and a spark to his eyes, like rekindling a candle that had long ago been snuffed out.

Justyn looked up and met Teralyn's gaze. His pain had been replaced with something else. She read relief and peace in his visage. As if some very great burden had been lifted. And she, too, felt as if a huge boulder had been lifted from her heart. The weight of judgment had nearly suffocated her, and its absence was as refreshing as a summer rain shower clearing the oppressive heat from the air. But what had transpired? What caused the jar to break? The woman of the lake said only the word trapped inside could break the jar. Well, whatever word it was, it had been released. Released not only into Justyn's heart but into the hearts of all in the village. One look at the villagers made that truth apparent.

Iris stumbled past her and fell down next to Justyn. "Oh my, oh my! Justyn, my poor lad." Iris grabbed Justyn's head and cradled it tightly to her ample chest. Justyn did not resist, but laid his hand on her hair and stroked her tenderly. Teralyn could not hear his words; he spoke quietly and listened as his mother crooned over him. He seemed thoroughly spent.

Teralyn marveled at Justyn's changed demeanor. It was not a look of defeat or of having given in. His countenance had softened; something hard and resistant had broken, like a dam with a crack finally breaking apart and allowing a flood of water to cover the land. And that's just how it seemed to her—as if some great flood had washed over him, washed away his hurt and jealousy and frustration, leaving him with a cleansed landscape, absent of the painful briars and brambles that had entangled his heart. His eyes, no longer complicated and burdened, lifted to meet hers. Teralyn smiled at him in response.

Fromer, who had been hovering and watching his mother rock Justyn in her arms, moved aside as Fen came running up to Justyn and embraced him. He floated over to Teralyn and gestured for her to follow him. They stopped before Justyn, who reached into his satchel with a shaky hand and pulled out the small spool of red thread. His eyes were full of apology, and Teralyn's heart ached, appalled as she was at her own cruel actions moments earlier.

With a nod of thanks, she closed her fist around the spool, and with Fromer following on the wind, hurried back to her cottage and the small piece of cloth sitting on her stool.

Teralyn laid down the re-stitched fabric and drew in a breath as Fromer reached tentatively for her. His arms—now solid and every bit as warm and strong as she remembered from those many long years ago—gathered her up and squeezed her tightly. Tears pent up for seven years streamed down her face, soaking her shirt, but no longer drenching her from head to toe. Joy now saturated her entirely, making her heart sing a jubilant song of gratitude. The years of worry and weariness dropped from her, making her feel light on her feet.

Fromer swung her around, and they laughed and spun in each other's arms as they skipped down to the knoll where she had first spoken to him. There they stopped and looked back over the village rooftops. The creek that had so often comforted her sang to her in its soft rippling voice.

She caught her breath, and Fromer brushed her hair from her face to drink her in with his eyes.

"Fromer, what happened back there? Some madness had overtaken me—all of us. Except you. You weren't touched by it. And how did the jar break, and what word was trapped inside?"

Fromer stroked her hair and shook his head. "I'm not sure. Maybe because I was barred from the world, the word in that jar hadn't been taken from my heart. All I kept thinking as I watched everyone I loved turn on my brother with vicious intent was that judgment, judgment alone, would never truly bring justice and resolution. Judgment has its place in the world, but it is not the most important thing. There is something greater than judgment. And even if no one else believed that, I knew it to be true in my heart. And I had to stand by that truth, no matter the cost. Even if it meant losing you—the most precious thing in my life."

Teralyn felt her heart jump at his words. "But, what was it, Fro? What is greater than judgment?"

"I'm not sure what to call it. I only know that all I could feel in my heart was my love for Justyn. And that overrode all the pain, hurt, and anger wanting to well up. Somehow the force of those feelings must have affected the jar and caused it to break. I didn't speak a word to shatter it."

"No, but actions speak louder than words, don't they? And by your actions you showed a compassion none of us felt. Maybe that was the word trapped inside."

Fromer shrugged. Teralyn studied his face, more radiant than ever before, as the midday sun streaked his wheat-straw hair with gold. The sight of him, and his closeness, made her heart beat fast. Finally, he was hers, completely and forever.

"Kiss me," she said, a smile spreading across her face.

Gladly, he did.

TWENTY-EIGHT

ANTIUS LOOKED up from his desk as a knock sounded at his front door.

"I'll get it, Father." Ambel came from the kitchen with a mug of tea in his hand. "It must be Teralyn—here to make sure we haven't forgotten what day it is."

"Pah, as if I could forget!" Antius chuckled and gave his neatly shaved and impeccably dressed son a long perusal. What a refreshing change—to see Ambel back in his full senses, his vision restored, and his spirits lifted out of that morass he'd been mired in. Even now, weeks later, Antius still had no clue as to what had stripped his son of the madness consuming him. He thought back to the day he had left Wentwater village. A strange day it had been, the world suddenly overgrown and wild, as if time had sped up without his noticing. He had arrived back in the Heights, leaving the chaos of the restored village behind him wondering where Justyn and Teralyn had run off to that morning—only to find Ambel similarly restored. His son had flung open the door, his eyes bright and clear, his laughter ringing in the air—a sound that brought him unspeakable joy.

"Father, you're back!" he had said, grabbing him and pulling him into a strong embrace.

"Wh-what's happened? How have you been freed from that madness? How is it you can now see?"

Ambel narrowed his eyes and chuckled. "Magic, Father! No thanks to the herbs and salves and those sour remedies from the infirmary. The queen of Sherbourne was under an enchantment—turned into that firebird, she was! And when the evil binding was broken, those bound to her were released. Even me, this far from Sherbourne—imagine that!"

"What are you talking about? How could you know these things—things taking place in a kingdom thousands of leagues away?"

Ambel pulled Antius into the house and shut the door behind him. "I just know, Father. Here, I've made supper—your favorite summer squash stew. Come sit, eat. You must be hungry."

Antius watched, stunned, as his son bustled about, setting the table for two, piling food on plates and pouring wine into two glasses. Antius sat as Ambel pushed his glass toward him across the table.

"A toast, Father." Ambel lifted his glass. Sunlight glinted off the amber liquid that shone as warm as the sunny feeling Antius felt in his heart. He had so often prayed for this moment but never believed it would come. His mind spun.

"What are we toasting?" he asked.

"Why, magic, of course! I told you—do not discount the magic in the world. All the wisdom of the world is no match for magic. And I can see your brain churning, trying to understand this miracle. Well, some things just cannot be explained away by logic and the accumulation of knowledge."

Antius sighed, remembering and cherishing that precious moment while Ambel opened the door and let in the fall breeze. Teralyn rushed in along with it, and Antius stood to greet her. She was dressed in a billowing gown of deep-green crepe, with her hair entwined in pearls. He'd never seen her so beautiful—or so happy.

She threw her arms around him, then pulled back and scrutinized his garb. "Why, Antius—I don't think I've ever seen you dressed in such fancy attire!"

Antius felt his cheeks flush. "The occasion merits it. Not only are we celebrating your eighteenth birthday but your betrothal as well. I can't imagine a more deserving occasion for dressing up."

Teralyn laughed. "Nor can I." She turned and studied Ambel. "And you, Ambel—so handsome. No doubt some young lass in the village will take a fancy for you!"

Antius groaned. "Please. I've only just had him returned to me. Don't go marrying him off so soon."

"Don't worry, Father. I have something more important to attend to than attracting some young woman's attention."

Antius's heart sped up. "Now what?" He tried to keep the agitation out of his voice. But Ambel's sparking eyes told him he had another harebrained idea. "Please don't tell me you're off to chase down some other mythical beast . . ."

Ambel looked at Teralyn and raised his eyebrows. "You tell him."

Teralyn took Antius's arm. "After the wedding, Ambel is going to accompany Fromer and me to Sherbourne."

Antius nodded, a bit confused. "So you can find your true mother." He looked at his son. "But why are you going with them?"

Ambel laughed and threw back his head. "I must meet this queen of Sherbourne! I have heard she is just as beautiful as the firebird. And after all those months of seeing her in my mind's eye as that irresistible creature . . . well, I just have to see her for myself. Even if it's from a distance."

"Hmm . . . perhaps she'll want to hear your story," Antius offered. "And maybe it will lay all your wonderings to rest."

Ambel laughed. "At least for a time! But there will always be some other mystery in the world to investigate, no doubt."

"Pah!" Antius said. He worried at the still-obsessive tone in his son's voice. Was Ambel just exchanging one obsession for another? He hoped not.

Teralyn laughed, then intertwined her arms in theirs. "Are we ready then? My parents are waiting at the oval with the carriage."

As Antius let himself be escorted out the door and into the glorious fall day, he thought about the strange occurrences that had transpired over recent months. Already, he had begun a treatise on the bizarre unraveling of Wentwater. His research was leading him in unexpected directions, opening his eyes to not just the validation of magic in the world but also to a deeper understanding of the heretofore unforeseen dangers of depending too exclusively on wisdom and knowledge to solve all the problems in the world. Wisdom was what had blinded him and the other regents from seeing and accepting truth, and this was a sobering realization. While forming his arguments and gathering supporting materials over the last few days, he'd come to see the necessity of acquiring something not readily found in the academicians living and teaching in the Heights—humility.

It was true—he not only had to admit it to himself, but those who read this treatise would be forced to confront the fact that there were some pitfalls in relying solely on acquired knowledge and wisdom. Sometimes knowledge puffed up so much that it blinded the mind and heart to the truth. He knew that many reading his treatise would hold him in disdain for his brash and self-deprecating observations, but what of it? Let those with ears to hear, hear. He knew one thing for certain—if he and his peers were to learn from history, as they were all so sworn to do, there was one clear lesson to glean from the unraveling of Wentwater: that one cannot discount the magic in the world.

Along with his treatise he would present a proposal—and he had to prepare himself for the outcry of opposition it would garner. But it was time. He would put forth the idea of opening a fifth school of study in the Heights, to go with Wisdom, Knowledge, Understanding, and Discernment. The School of Magic. And he would recommend Justyn's appointment as new regent to oversee the development of the curriculum of the new school. It would be a radical departure from decades of tradition, but Ambel's words kept rattling in his head. *"If you discount the magic in the world, Father, you will see how the wisdom of the wise perishes."* He now knew his son's words were painfully true. If they kept to their present course, the Heights would one day be shrouded in ignorance and denial, with those living high up in these clouds unaware of their blind and arrogant foolishness. And that, undoubtedly, would lead to *their* eventual undoing.

"There they are!" Teralyn called out, pointing through the crowd of students to a coach drawn by two finely groomed horses. Antius watched as Kileen and Rufus alit from the carriage and embraced Teralyn, the daughter Antius had brought to them eighteen years ago. It seemed only yesterday . . . Antius stood back as Teralyn chatted animatedly with them, and as Ambel swung his bags up onto the back, atop the other packages and baggage loaded to take down to the village.

Kileen broke away from the preparations and came alongside Antius.

"Isn't she a beautiful sight, Antius? I'm so happy for her." She took his arm and led him toward the carriage. "I suppose we worried over nothing. She seems so happy—and Fromer is just perfect for her."

Antius frowned. "But won't you be sad—with her living down in the village?"

Kileen waved her hand, dismissing his words. "I just want her to be happy. That's all I've ever really wanted for her, Antius. And down there she can play her music to her heart's delight."

He patted her arm. "You've been a wonderful mother to her. She loves you dearly and will never forget you."

A tear escaped down Kileen's cheek and she wiped it away. Her voice came out in a whisper. "I hope not . . ."

"Once she finds what she's seeking in Sherbourne, she'll be back. Her life is here. Fromer is here. She won't vanish from your life."

All Kileen could do was nod.

Antius thought about the woman of the lake—a third mother to Teralyn. Would she make an appearance at the wedding? He considered all the strange things Teralyn had told him—what happened when she'd been thrown into the water, and the memories and images the woman of the lake had shown her. Teralyn had told him of the strange circle of stone slabs the woman had called the sacred site, submerged at the bottom of the lake. Supposedly one of seven places heaven had established in the world to keep evil from taking over the hearts of men. It was hardly to be believed. But his curiosity had been aroused; now he would have to dig in to the fables and legends found in the ancient texts and see if he could find any reference to them. Strange that he had never encountered any such tale in all his years of research.

But he knew better now than to scoff. Perhaps even a year ago he would have brushed aside her account out of hand as some hallucination or daydream. But not now. And hopefully, never again would he be so quick to dismiss things that smacked of magic.

"Come, Antius," Teralyn said, holding the carriage door open for him. "We've a celebration to attend!"

Antius gave her a kiss on the cheek and stepped up into the carriage. He looked back at the massive school buildings wet with the mist gently drifting off the falls flanking them. Already, he could smell winter on the air, a crispness that bit at his face, reminding him how short the summer had been. He thought about the flowers in his small garden, already withering and dropping petals. And his now-towering maples with most of their leaves blown off and littering the ground around his home. Like his life, the seasons had skipped by too quickly.

Last week Teralyn had told him a fabulous tale of how she had spent seven long years alone in a cottage, stitching a vanished world back into existence, word by word. That would explain why his maples had grown so tall overnight and why Teralyn appeared so much older than he remembered. He'd thought it was just his old eyes playing tricks on him. He almost started in on what else might have caused such inexplicable occurrences, shaking his head in denial and planning on telling Teralyn she was delusional. But he caught himself and nodded, listening in awe, recalling the day in the library when his owl, among other things, had inexplicably vanished right before his eyes. There *were* things in the world that could not be explained by anything other than magic. And for once the idea had not made him scoff in disagreement. Instead, he felt like a young boy again, full of wonder at the world, eager to uncover its secrets—if they would be forthcoming.

For the first time in a very long while Antius felt a stirring of excitement. There were wondrous things out there to be discovered. He just had to open his eyes—and his heart—to see them.

Teralyn slipped into the carriage and sat beside him. Her parents boarded and took the bench across from them. The driver jiggled the reins and the horses began plodding down the lane, toward the long road down to the village of Wentwater. There, awaiting them, would be music and dancing and gaiety such as he had not seen in a very long time. For the first time in—well, he could not even recall any time—both the residents of the village and those of the Heights would celebrate together in union and harmony. Oh, they might still disagree on many points of how to live and when to plant and what rituals or traditions should be observed, but after the fiasco of Wentwater's unraveling, he dared hope that the two disparate groups would interact with more compassion and acceptance of each other. After all, neither those in the Heights nor those down in the village below had been able to unravel the mystery of why Wentwater had almost vanished forever. And perhaps they never would.

Antius studied Teralyn's joyous expression as she looked out the window and watched eagerly for the village to come into view—where her beloved would be waiting for her.

A smile rose on his face. So, he had to admit, despite all his industrious efforts and research, he might never uncover the answer, never know just how everything fell apart. And for the first time in his life, he didn't mind his lack of wisdom and knowledge and understanding and discernment. He had found something even greater in his trusting that all was as it should be.

Faith.

TWENTY-NINE

AMID THE flurry of all their family and friends congratulating the newly wedded couple, Teralyn strained to see above heads to find the one person she really needed to speak with before she and Fromer headed with Ambel to Sherbourne. Sherbourne! Called the Crown of the East. Well, for them it would mean a fortnight's travel west, but as anxious as she was to meet the mother she had only seen in her dreams, her heart tugged at her, laden with a deep affection she had acquired for the villagers of Wentwater. And as much as Justyn decried any attachment to his home, Teralyn knew from the expression on his face as his father patted him brusquely on the back that he belonged to the village as much as to the Heights.

She met Fromer's eyes as he laughed with some of his neighbors—three old women that couldn't stop patting his neatly coiffed hair. She smiled and tipped her head, letting him know she'd be back—as if she could stay away from him for long! He nodded and broke out in more laughter at something said, and as more fingers poked his ribs in joviality. It seemed everyone from Wentwater had come to join in the celebration. The glorious fall evening brought with it a warm breeze that ruffled the colorful banners and ribbons adorning the trees in the central park. And there were at least a few dozen residents of the Heights—even old

Arbulus and Anthanus hadn't been able to resist a jaunt down the mountain to witness such a historic event. Teralyn giggled. No doubt volumes would be written of this landmark day—although she doubted she would read any of it. *"Books and books,"* she remembered saying to Antius. What had she added? *"You can spend so much time buried in books and accumulating your precious knowledge that you forget to live life."* She, along with everyone else, enjoyed a good book, but nothing could take the place of a good *life*. And that was what she planned to enjoy with Fromer—for many years to come.

As she wended through the crowd, nodding and smiling at the exuberant guests, she delighted in seeing the villagers finally happy and at ease. Life had returned to normal in Wentwater, a little worse for wear, perhaps, but no permanent damage done. And maybe, as Justyn had hoped, their eyes had been opened to new ideas, new ways of looking at the world.

Behind the milling crowd, three musicians climbed up onto the stage—the very stage where Teralyn had first laid eyes on Fromer and heard him play his fiddle with such joyous abandon. She waved at Fromer's friends, already feeling the thrill of joining them shortly. She would only need to change out of her gown, throw on some comfortable clothes, and tune her harp. Just the sight of the players taking their places and positioning their instruments set off cheers in the crowd. This would be a night of music and dancing few would forget. She would sing and play, with Fromer at her side fiddling to his heart's content, long into the night. Her heart raced in anticipation.

When she came alongside Justyn, he turned and smiled. Even now, Teralyn marveled at the change in him. She cringed recalling how she had wished him dead. Guilt coursed through her as she looked down at her hand and pictured the rock she had gripped and flung at him. The horrible memory of rocks and fists pounding him as he curled up behind Fromer still haunted her some nights.

But Justyn didn't hold any bitterness toward any of them. When Fromer had shown him kindness and Justyn broke under its freeing power, it seemed all his pain and hurt disintegrated, crumbled to dust that the wind blew away to far-off lands. Even now, as he took her hand, his face carried none of the desperation or intensity she'd always seen there before.

"Teralyn, I haven't had the chance to tell you how beautiful you look. I am really, truly, happy for you. And for Fromer."

"Thank you, Justyn. And I'm so happy for you—you've made regent! And you already have a posting in the school. You must be so proud."

He shook his head and let out a long breath. "More grateful than proud. And if you saw the pile of books and scrolls on my desk—well, it will take months to go through and catalog all the material to create courses and their corresponding syllabuses—" He caught himself. "Don't misunderstand; I don't mean to complain. It's all just a bit overwhelming."

Teralyn laid a hand on his arm, noting his beautiful graduation ring on his finger. "I'm sure you will be up to the task. You've earned it. And your students will enjoy hearing your tales—especially of the unraveling of Wentwater."

He threw his head back and laughed. "I think I'll skip that subject. Let them research it on their own—and come to their own conclusions. Antius has been grilling me for days on what transpired—for that treatise of his. And I end up with more questions than answers, to be sure." He narrowed his eyes and smiled. "I bet you could answer some of my questions—like, what really happened when you sank in the lake? And how did you show up in that cottage after I left you in the witch's tower? Did you really spend seven years alone—"

Teralyn pinched her lips together, then said, "Well, if you treat me to another breakfast of waffles and bogberries, I might just tell you everything."

"Agreed. After you return from your trip with that pesky brother of mine. *If* he'll spare you for a few hours. But you have to tell me the truth—from start to finish."

"Which no doubt will end up in some published paper of yours."

Justyn's face flared red. "Well, yes, but that's not the only reason I want to hear your story."

Teralyn chuckled at his flustering.

"Are you teasing my brother again?"

Teralyn spun around and Fromer wrapped his arms around her. "Of course not!" she answered.

"Well, it looks like it. You've made his face go as red as a rutabaga."

Justyn shook his head. "It can't be helped. Your *wife* has a way with words."

Fromer laughed and tugged on her gown. "That she does. And it's time those words were put to music. Come, Tera, we're requested on stage. The guests are growing restless for a jig."

Teralyn leaned over and kissed Justyn on the cheek, making his face burn a deeper red. She looked at him directly and sensed him squirm just a little under her gaze. "I'll be holding you to your promise."

"What promise?" he asked, puzzled, as Fromer pulled her away from him and across the room into a bevy of chatter.

"Bogberries!" she mouthed.

His eyes widened in understanding. He nodded and mouthed something back, but she couldn't see him any longer. Her husband had taken her arm and swung her around. Under the soft moonlight, beneath an explosion of stars, Fromer leaned in and kissed her—a deep, loving, warm kiss. Teralyn felt a shiver tickle her neck as another unraveling began in her heart. This one, though, she welcomed with every breath in her body. Fromer could tug at her heartstrings as much as he liked, for she knew they would never break—only resonate in harmony with his, creating a song that would forever entwine them.

He pulled back and touched her throat. "I never did ask you—where did you get this odd necklace? It seems ancient."

"It belonged to the woman of the lake. She had given it to Antius all those years back—when she brought me to him. But this pearl—she put that in the center when I encountered her in the depths. She said it was a pearl of great wisdom. That it would guide me in life so I would make wise decisions."

Fromer's eyebrows rose and he stroked her hair. "Really? How do you know it works?"

Teralyn laughed and caressed his cheek. "Silly! I married you didn't I? And no doubt. . . that's the wisest thing I've ever done."

Fromer pulled her into his embrace once more and she melted in his arms. Every word in her head—every known word in the world—vanished in a flash, disappearing from existence, but it didn't cause her distress. Much to the contrary.

All that remained was Fromer. And his kiss.

And that was fine with her.

"Oh dear, oh dear . . ." Iris turned first one way, then the other. She took a quick peek out the window at the faint light smudging the sky. It was nearly dawn. She clutched her chest in relief as she watched the rooster strut and take his position atop the fence. But still—where'd that blasted box go?

Familiar tinges of fear caused perspiration to erupt on her forehead. Even in the chilly house, with the last embers on the hearth long extinguished, Iris felt a flush of heat. Surely she had placed the box right there, on the sideboard, before they went to bed. The thought of things going missing again set her heart racing. It couldn't be happening all over again, could it? Had she forgotten to shake out the rugs before laying them back down? Or maybe she failed to polish the silver on the last full moon. Oh if only—

"Iris!"

Fen's voice rattled her so that her knees nearly gave out from under her. "Fen—you scared me!"

He held out his arms. In his hands was the box she'd been searching for. "Is this what's got you in a fret?"

"Where was it?" She was afraid to ask. She hoped she hadn't left it in some ridiculous place.

"Under the bed clothes. You must have accidently buried it when getting dressed."

Rather than sounding chastising, his slight chuckle exuded warmth. "One of these days, Iris, you'll give yourself heart failure with all your fussing. A missing box is not the end of the world."

She took the brightly beribboned package from his hands. The rooster in the yard announced the arrival of dawn with a throaty cry. "Well then, let's be off. I want to be sure to give Fro's bride her gift before they leave. And give them a proper sending off."

"I doubt they're even up yet. 'Twas a long night, with all the music and festivities."

"Even so, I don't want to miss them."

"What's in there?" he asked, pointing at her package.

"Oh, just some threads and needles. Some lovely lace and patterns. Seeing how much she loves to stitch and all, I thought she'd enjoy passing the time busying her hands while they journeyed."

Fen nodded. "You might suggest she sketch some scenes of the countryside. Maybe give you some new ideas for yer pillows and such."

Iris clapped her hands. "Why, that's clever of you. Hadn't thought of that. I'll be sure to ask. Surely there's more to the land than hills and sheep." She paused a moment in thought. "Fen?"

"Hmmm?" he said, working on lighting his pipe. "What?"

"Do you ever get a hankering to visit other lands? See the great city of Sherbourne?"

He grunted. "Why should I? Got ever'thing we need here. Fertile lands, crops, fruit trees, clean water. No sense longing fer something far away when you have all you need at home."

Iris sighed. "S'pose you're right. But what about the Heights? You think maybe sometime we should take a trip up there, visit Justyn? See that big fancy school of his?"

Fen scratched his head. "S'pose we should. He'd like that."

"He would."

"Well, come along then." Fen opened the front door and cold air blew in. Iris grabbed her coat and fed her arms through the sleeves. She stepped out onto the porch as Fen went to the hen house and let the chickens out. He took the wooden scooper and scattered feed across the dirt. The hens pecked and cackled as they vied for the best angle to gobble up the most food.

"Hmm . . ." Fen said with knitted brows, kneeling and studying the pattern of the feed. Iris's heart sped up and sweat broke out on her forehead again.

"What? What's it say? Something bad? Please don't say it portends a bad day for traveling. What with Fro and his bride heading—"

Fen straightened and laughed. "Read into it whatever you like, Iris. All it says to me is there's a brood of hungry chickens wanting to eat their breakfast."

Iris scrunched her face and smacked Fen playfully with her hand. "Fine, make fun all you like. You scoff too much and it'll catch up with you. Disaster will strike. Mark my words."

Fen laughed and opened the gate. He gestured with his hand to allow Iris go first. "Whatever you say, love."

Iris grunted and headed down the lane toward the Cygnet Inn, where Fromer and Teralyn had spent the night. She turned her head and caught a quick glimpse of Fen, then buried her chin in her chest and chuckled silently. Joke all he liked—she'd caught him studying the clouds overhead to see how to plan his day.

AFTERWORD

"... This prophet of renown, perhaps quoted more than any in history and draped in conflicting theories as to his true origin and nature, shines a direct light on the heart of the matter. With unprecedented authority, he challenged the leaders of his day—those who prided themselves on their scrupulous adherence to law and propriety—by admonishing them with these words: 'Go, and learn what this means: *I desire mercy, not sacrifice.*'"

"As with any teetering culture, when the inhabitants of Wentwater placed more value on blindly following their traditions than on the bestowing of mercy, they risked their downfall. No longer can one ignore the words penned in the Great Book: 'Mercy triumphs over judgment.' Those in the prophet's land paid the hard price when they spurned this truth. They tossed mercy aside and suffered the destruction of their nation and culture. One might ask, Would the village of Wentwater make the same tragic mistake, and what factors should be examined by historians in order to formulate a theory on how a people might be swayed in one direction or another?"

"May we learn this difficult lesson, the great pearl of wisdom that cannot be bought at any price—except at the cost of our future and perhaps even our wits—that words hold power, sometimes uncanny power, and that by not only our actions but by our words will we be judged righteous or be condemned."

From Volume V of *The Annals of Wentwater*, "Conclusion: Learning from the Wisdom of the Ages"

—Professor Antius, regent and historian of the Antiquities Board

THE END

A DISCUSSION OF
THE UNRAVELING OF
WENTWATER

T HE GATES OF HEAVEN collection of fairy tales draws from Scripture, as well as traditional fairy tales, to help expose readers to intriguing concepts in the Bible. What fascinated me as I explored the themes for this book was delving into the power and handling of words. *The Unraveling of Wentwater* is a celebration of words and language. And as I came up with a plot, I kept returning to verses in the Bible that showed how God wielded words to create the universe. He spoke, and all things came into existence. "Worlds were framed by the word of God, so that things which are seen were not made of things which do appear" (KJV). Is there anything more profound than that statement?

Along with words themselves came the pitfall of acquiring words in order to boast. Another verse kept niggling at me: "I will make the wisdom of the wise perish." I wondered about a culture that extolled wisdom and the acquiring of knowledge as paramount—to the discredit of any other pursuit. In contrast, I conjured up a village the complete opposite—steeped in superstition and ignorant of established knowledge. Yet they had their own brand of "wisdom." I then wondered what could happen that would befuddle both cultures—a mystery that neither the wisdom of the wise nor the superstitions and folk knowledge of Wentwater could solve. We live in a time when gaining knowledge and putting scientific reasoning on the altar to worship is prevalent. There are tremendous benefits to acquiring wisdom, but without godly wisdom, all the knowledge of the world will fail us.

I was also intrigued by the juxtaposition of mercy and judgment. Victor Hugo's famous novel *Les Misérables* invaded my thoughts often as I developed this story, Justyn reminding me of the character of Inspector Javert and his obsession with justice. Without a shred of mercy in his heart, Javert could not bear Jean Valjean's mercy toward him and so ended his life. His action is symbolic to me as a reflection upon society, and so the survival of Wentwater—even of humanity—hinged upon the need for mercy in my fairy tale.

On a lighter side, I drew from the famous fairy tale "Sleeping Beauty" to come up with the inciting incident—the baby-naming ceremony that gets invaded by the marsh witch. In "Sleeping Beauty" the evil fairy curses the babe, saying she will prick her finger on a spindle of a spinning wheel before her eighteenth birthday and die. I loved the idea of taking words involving stitching, thread, needles, spinning, weaving, and using common phrases and expressions throughout the book in a lyrical and metaphoric way. There are dozens of places where expressions like "thread of thought," "hanging by a thread," "unraveling a mystery," "leave me in stitches," and others are "woven" into the "tapestry" of the story. I also play on the word *word*. We have so many sayings: Mark my word, give your word, upon my word, words escape me, it's written across your face. Once you realize this play is going on, you will no doubt see many more instances of expressions using the word *word*. Yet, I also wanted to emphasize how powerful words are, and that if they are not handled carefully, they can cause harm. The marsh witch warns against the careless use of words when she scolds, "Be careful with words. They have consequences."

Here, then are some questions for consideration, for personal or group study, for schools and book club discussion groups. In a word . . .

1) The Bible speaks of the wisdom of this world being foolishness with God (see 1 Corinthians 1:18–25). Certainly, not all worldy wisdom is foolish. Just what do you think Paul is talking about in this passage? Although he is specifically dealing with the good news about Christ, how could this principle apply in other general ways in considering fads and trends of society that contrast to principles of godly living? (See James 3:13–18.)

2) James chapter 3 also goes into a lot of detail about the power of the tongue: i.e., what damage our words can cause, and how we need to be careful about what we say. The marsh witch felt humans threw words about carelessly and warned "they have consequences." Jesus said in Matthew 12:36–37: "I tell you, on the day of judgment you will have to give an account for every careless word you utter, for by your words you will be justified, and by your words you will be condemned." Read the verses before it and explain what is the source of our words. Does that give you an idea of how we might be able to bring forth words that are justifying rather than condemning?

3) Introducing each part of the book are excerpts from Antius's treatise about the unraveling of Wentwater. Through his musings on what happened, he has learned some important lessons

about wisdom, mercy, and humility. What are some of his observations and warnings? What is the great pearl of wisdom he claims we all must learn?

4) James 2:13 says "mercy triumphs over judgment." The witch claimed that human society would fall to ruin without mercy, and we saw how Fromer showed mercy to Justyn, even though Justyn deserved judgment. Just how and in what ways does mercy triumph over judgment? Why is it crucial we show mercy to others? (See Matthew 5:7, and revisit James 2:13.)

5) Antius has trouble believing there is magic in the world. His son Ambel tells him he should be careful not to discount or dismiss inexplicable things. Antius, in the end, realizes some things have to be taken in faith. He ponders accounts he'd read about miraculous things that had taken place, but has trouble believing their veracity: an axe head floating on water, oil that never ran out, a rod that turned into a snake, a man who walked on water. Which biblical accounts is Antius referring to?

Scriptures and Quotations[1]

1 Corinthians 1:19: "I will make the wisdom of the wise perish" (author paraphrase).

Hebrews 1:3: "[He] sustains all things by his powerful word."

Hebrews 11:3: "By faith we understand that the worlds were framed by the word of God, so that the things which are seen were not made of things which are visible" (NKJV).

Proverbs 1:2–6: "For learning about wisdom and instruction, for understanding words of insight, for gaining instruction in wise dealing, righteousness, justice, and equity; to teach shrewdness to the simple, knowledge and prudence to the young—Let the wise also hear and gain in learning, and the discerning acquire skill, to understand . . . the words of the wise and their riddles."

Proverbs 3:13–14, 16–17: "Happy are those who find wisdom, and those who get understanding, for her income is better than silver and her revenue better than gold . . . Long life is in her right hand; in her left hand are riches and honor. Her ways are ways of pleasantness, and all her paths are peace."

---

1. Taken from The New Revised Standard Version of the Bible unless noted otherwise.

Proverbs 27:22: "Crush a fool in a mortar with a pestle along with crushed grain, but the folly will not be driven out."

Proverbs 29:20: "Do you see a man hasty in his words? There is more hope for a fool than for him" (NKJV).

Hosea 4:6: "My people are destroyed for lack of knowledge."

Matthew 9:13: "Go and learn what this means, 'I desire mercy, not sacrifice.' "

Matthew 12:36–37: "But I say to you that for every idle word men may speak, they will give account of it in the day of judgment. For by your words you will be justified, and by your words you will be condemned" (NKJV).

James 2:13: "For judgment will be without mercy to anyone who has shown no mercy; mercy triumphs over judgment."

OTHER QUOTATIONS:

"A man thinks that by mouthing hard words he understands hard things." —Herman Melville

"When ideas fail, words come in very handy." —Goethe

"Words are alive; cut them and they bleed." —Ralph Waldo Emerson

"Where words fail, music speaks." —H. C. Anderson

"A wise man hears one word and understands two." —Anonymous Proverb